THE PHARAOH CONTRACT

RAY ALDRIDGE

BANTAM BOOKS

NEW YORK • TORONTO • LONDON • SYDNEY • AUCKLAND

THE PHARAOH CONTRACT

A BANTAM SPECTRA BOOK / SEPTEMBER 1991

ISBN 0-553-29118-1

Published simultaneously in the United States and Canada

PRINTED IN THE UNITED STATES OF AMERICA

RAD   0 9 8 7 6 5 4 3 2 1

SLAVE MARKET

The bar was dark but for the bluish glow of the holotank in the corner. A dozen or so humans gathered there, intent on the flickering images.

Auliss led him to a table and signaled a barmech. It was soon apparent that she was a regular at The Little Friend.

On the holotank the hot sunlight of Pharaoh glared on a dry wash, where three children, two girls and a boy, were playing some elaborate game. They seemed to be twelve or thirteen, just at the threshold of puberty. The tank's viewpoint shifted among the players, occasionally zooming in for a close-up of the boy.

"It's the boy," Auliss whispered. "He's the one."

What was she talking about? He started to ask her, but the holotank switched modes. The scene of the playing children shrank down into the lower third of the tank, and a chubby smiling man, dressed as a Pharaohan, appeared in the top.

"Hello, hello," he said. "Key your bids now."

"Science fiction with the color and imagination of fantasy . . . A memorable quest through exotic worlds of strange humans and semi-humans."
—*Jack Williamson*

Ask your bookseller for these
BANTAM SPECTRA titles you may have missed:

To my mother,
MURIEL RICE ALDRIDGE,
*who has always been so
surprisingly unsurprised by my successes.*

Shackles bloom on chain-linked vines,
   Iron roses.
From the gloom, the scrape of shovels . . .
   Who gardens here?

—scratched into a broken wall in
the ruins of a slave pen on Sook.

CHAPTER 1

I N THE dim red light of the Beaster Level, pleasure seekers pressed against Ruiz Aw, a sea of wild eyes, wet mouths, sweat-slick bodies. He moved cautiously through the clamor and stink. Confusion protected him. In this grinding jostle, who would notice Ruiz Aw, who would report him to his employers?

The thought of discovery sent a shudder through him, raised goose bumps on his skin. The Art League's inquisitors would ask, "Ruiz Aw, tell us. Just what were you doing on Dilvermoon? What mischief brought you to the hold of Nacker the Teach, notorious bootleg minddiver?" And, "Ruiz Aw, how did you happen to be there so soon after receiving your net? Tell us, Ruiz Aw." Ruiz could conceive of no explanation that would satisfy those grim personages.

He imagined he could feel the death net behind his eyes, tangled around his mind, squeezing.

They can't be everywhere, Ruiz told himself. And: *It's too late to back out.* The thought echoed: *Too late, too late, too late.*

But no one pointed, no one shouted his name. The tightness in his shoulders eased slightly as he approached the freekill sectors. Once in that concealing dimness, away from the robot monitors that crawled the ceilings of the tourist areas, he would feel safer. There, where blood might legally be spilled, he could cope.

He paused at the radiant point of a half-dozen corridors, where a large domed hall provided space for the herds to congregate.

In the half-light of the overhead glowstrips, the hall seethed. Beasters walked, staggered, crawled, swaggered, hopped. Every near-variant of humanity was represented. Everywhere pointed ears quivered, teeth glinted, fur grew luxuriantly in gardens of human flesh. Gleaming selenium scarabs—the personaskeins, the devices that filled each beaster's brain with the chosen beast—clung to the base of each skull. No other adornment was permitted on the Level, no garment that might conceal a weapon.

Ruiz watched the passing faces with sidelong glances, concealing his curiosity, fascinated by the animal lusts and fears and rages that twisted the human features. His own personaskein, set at legal minimum, showed him the shadow-shapes that lived within the beasters, ghostly color-less outlines that swirled about the human shapes. That tall, rawboned old man with the carefully coifed mane of white hair, for example: What had moved him to abandon his executive desk for the uncertainties of the Beaster Level, to play the noble stag? And what of that well-kept young woman? She was skillfully painted with fashionable body toners, she wore her thick orange hair in a love knot, and her sharp little fingernails were buffed into crimson perfection. She wore the persona of a great serpent; she stood waiting in the shadows and in her eyes was a slow careful hunger.

Nearing the far side of the open space, Ruiz observed a pack of wolfheads lounging against the bulkhead, a dozen men and women with wide yellow eyes, facial hair in griz-zled tufts, and furry bodies as hard and narrow as slats.

As Ruiz approached, the pack leader stepped forward, eyes glowing with interest.

Ruiz suppressed annoyance. The wolfhead smiled, revealing long canines and a thick red tongue.

Ruiz masked his face with indifference, though his gait stiffened almost imperceptibly. He passed under the biolume sign that flashed PANGALAC LAW ENDS HERE into the darker corridor beyond. Ruiz felt movement behind him as the pack gathered.

LEROE CALLED THE brethren together, making the snuffling sound of inquiry.

"Meat goes into the killing grounds," he said, and growled, a soft sound, full of pleasant anticipation.

"Dangerous?" asked Camilla, his mate, second in the pack. "It moved with great confidence; it smelled of much purpose and little fear."

Leroe snarled, and Camilla edged back, wary of his strength. "Perhaps the meat is too stupid to be afraid," Leroe said. "It is only one, soft with humanity. Can we fail to feed?"

All around him the pack expressed agreement. Red tongues licked black lips; eager whines echoed in the corridor.

Leroe fell silent for a long moment, reviewing his impressions of the meat. His man-mind was not so deeply submerged under the personaskein that he forgot Camilla's intelligence, greater than his own. So he considered further, as carefully as hunger and bloodlust allowed.

The meat was a tall man, heavy shouldered, coppery skinned, with short black hair. Muscle flowed smoothly on that rangy frame. The meat had ignored Leroe as he passed, but Leroe thought he had detected a glint of challenge in the meat's hard eyes.

And the tall man's skein was set very low, so that he projected only a suggestion of inhumanity, some sort of predatory creature. But he lacked the *face,* the face that all beasters wore, a gelmask twitching and shuddering in a storm of animal impulses.

Leroe decided. The meat might struggle, the meat might flee, but the pack was strong and swift, and the meat was only one man, unaugmented in ferocity. How dangerous could he be?

"We hunt." Leroe pulled his lips back into an eager happy snarl, and the pack howled with delight.

Leroe turned and loped into the dimness, following the scent. Behind him the pack scampered.

RUIZ HEARD THE pack, faint in the distance, and he accelerated into a striding run. The wolfheads would never catch him, but he worried that they might attract other predators. So he ran, keeping to the darkest side of the corridors, wasting just a little of his breath on curses for Nacker. The minddiver lived deep in the freekill sector of the Beaster Level, where none but the most fanatic of beasters and a few suicidal or fatally ignorant tourists might be encountered. But at least the hold was far from prying eyes, and so, for the most part, Ruiz was satisfied with its location—except when he was forced to run like a deer to his destination, when he would much prefer to stroll in easy comfort.

At the end of one long dim hallway, Ruiz paused for a moment, to hear a quick patter of feet. Shadows flickered behind him. Startled by the pack's speed, Ruiz picked up his own pace, lengthening his stride and pumping great gusts of air through his lungs. The pursuit dropped back, and Ruiz smiled.

Soon, he thought, soon he would arrive at the minddiver's bulkhead—with plenty of time to go through the lengthy identification procedures that Nacker required.

At that moment, a throat-torn corpse flopped from a lightless niche directly into Ruiz's path. Ruiz's reflexes carried him soaring over the sudden obstacle. All might still have been well except for the blood that formed a slick just where Ruiz's foot touched down. And even then, Ruiz might have gone down with minimal damage, had the tigerheart not come bounding forth after her kill, slamming into Ruiz before she noticed his presence.

Ruiz sprawled, flailing, his left leg twisting under him at an awkward angle. He felt the reinforced cartilage of his knee tear; an instant later the pain seared through him.

Ruiz rolled away, expecting to feel the tigerheart's claws. But when he sprang up, he saw that she was intent on retrieving her meal. Her bloody teeth were locked in the nape of the corpse, and she growled deep in her throat, dragging her kill back into the darkness. She watched Ruiz with glittering eyes, her pale hair tangled about her broad flat face. The blood sheeting down the knotty contours of her body was black in the dim light.

Ruiz glided back, ignoring his injured knee. The tigerheart disappeared into her lair and the wet ripping sounds of feeding began. He whirled and ran on, afraid he would hear the sound of the wolfheads at his heels. His gait was no longer his normal skilled drive; now Ruiz ran with a hitch. A knife stabbed through his knee each time his left foot hit the steel deck of the corridor. The pain was bearable for now, but the injury limited his speed. He dared not push beyond a certain point; to do so might cause the total collapse of the joint. The breath no longer pumped effortlessly in Ruiz's chest, and now his heart thundered and sweat streamed down his straining body. The scent of fear boiled from him. That rich odor would spur the pack on, he thought.

It wasn't long before he heard the scrabble of clawed feet. With rolling eyes, he searched the empty corridors for waymarks. How much farther could it be to the minddiver's hold? There! That splash of purple biolume, a graffito in the style of the Longhead Crocs. And there! That twisted post of black iron at the three-way juncture—he remembered that clearly from his last visit.

Ruiz pounded on, heartened. It could be no more than three hundred meters to Nacker's bulkhead.

He began to believe that the situation would not deteriorate further. Once in the minddiver's hold, Ruiz could avail himself of the best reconstructive equipment, and his strength could be restored in hours. Ruiz's face tightened in a grin of exertion and optimism.

Then the pack swooped from a side passage a moment behind Ruiz, breaking into a spontaneous chorus of high-pitched yowls. It came to Ruiz, as he strained to pull away

from the eager claws, that the pack had used a shortcut.
And why not? Much prey probably came this way.

Before he reached the rotunda that housed Nacker's in-
gress, Ruiz managed to gain a few paces on the pack. Still,
he would have no time for the entry procedures, would have
to fight, would have to find a good spot to get his back
against a wall before his knee gave out completely. As the
injury worsened and exhaustion made it harder to keep his
attention focused, it became more difficult to control the
pain. Now each step was a hot spike driven the length of his
leg. Almost as distracting as the pain was the grating, slipping sensation in his knee as the cartilage slowly crumbled.

Ruiz burst into the rotunda, which was lit by ceiling
strips of glaring blue lume. Ruiz noticed dark patches here
and there on the floor, and little piles of gnawed bone. A
dozen open corridors led away, but one former corridor,
sealed with a blast door, led to the minddiver's hold. Ruiz
fled across the littered steel floor of the rotunda toward it,
knees lifting high and breath sobbing in his lungs.

Behind him the pack broke out of the passage and sent up
joyous cries.

In the face of this more immediate danger, Ruiz had forgotten his fears of League observation. Accordingly, as he
approached the blast door, he bellowed, "It's Ruiz Aw! Tell
Nacker! It's Ruiz Aw! Let me in!"

Not unexpectedly, there was no immediate response. As
he reached the door, he limped to a stop and whirled to face
the pack.

They didn't pounce instantly; instead they spread out in a
semicircle around him as he crouched with his back to
Nacker's doors.

The pack was evenly divided between men and women.
Where the fur thinned enough to expose skin, no fat diffused
the striations of flat wiry muscle. Reinforced fingernails
were shaped into knives, and fangs grew to the maximum
permitted length. The leader danced back and forth, making
little mock rushes, smiling, his yellow eyes gleaming with
good humor and anticipation. When he spoke, his voice
bubbled from deep in his throat. "You run well, meat," he
said. "Still, your run is over."

Ruiz spent no breath on replying. If they wasted enough time taunting him, he would regain his wind and Nacker might open up.

But the pack leader was eager. He sprang at Ruiz, claws outstretched, and at almost the same instant three others leaped in.

Ruiz stiffened his hands into blades and struck the leader, crunching his fingertips into the wolfhead's flat nose, splashing bone splinters upward into the brain. The wolfhead's flying body stiffened in spasm, and the yellow eyes went dull. With a slam of his left hand, Ruiz guided the corpse to his right, where it smashed two of the other wolfheads aside into the bulkhead.

That left one attacker on the other side. He managed to twist away slightly from her first slash, and her claws scored a triple line across his shoulder instead of laying open his throat, as she had intended. But Ruiz couldn't avoid her teeth, and she bit into the heavy muscle on the right side of his chest. She brought her knees up, preparing to push away with the mouthful of Ruiz's flesh that she had captured, and her weight threatened to overbalance Ruiz. For a moment he was sure he would fall beneath the pack.

But he got his good knee under him and pushed back against the wall. In the same movement he slammed both hands to her head, over her pointed ears, and was rewarded by the lovely pop of cracking bone. She shuddered and dropped away.

The undamaged wolfheads were scrambling to regain their feet, and Ruiz sidled a few steps along the wall. "Come," Ruiz said in low tones, as ferocious as he could make them. "Come." He bared his own teeth, which, though not as impressive as the wolfheads' fangs, were still strong and white.

The wolves hesitated for a moment, unsure. Two of their most dangerous packmates had been destroyed, so quickly. But they were only imitation wolves. The personaskeins that moved them were crude simulations, all bloodlust and bravado; they lacked the native caution of real wolves. Ruiz watched the eyes kindle with renewed rage.

The wolfheads moved closer. One female bent over the

corpse of the leader, stroking the tangled fur of his face. "Leroe, Leroe," she said in a small whimpering voice. She closed the staring eyes and licked her bloody hand.

She turned her eyes on Ruiz. He managed a scornful laugh. Her face congested with rage, and she sprang at him. The rest of the pack was unprepared to follow instantly, so Ruiz was able to kill her with a blow to the throat. She writhed on the steel, expiring. "Nacker," Ruiz called, watching the pack gather its courage again. "Nacker! I've got a death net, Nacker. Let me in before the League hears all about you."

Abruptly the blast door levered in, and Ruiz tumbled into the security lock, landing on his back.

Before the pack could decide to follow him in, two of Nacker's huge Dirm bondguards stepped into the opening, brandishing nerve lashes. The wolfheads retreated, snarling, and the door closed.

When Ruiz got to his feet, he saw Nacker sitting in his prosthetic floater, under a dome of clear crystal. The minddiver looked like a freak preserved in a bell jar, some unlikely hybrid of sea slug and human. In fact, Nacker was just a man with no muscle tone, or hair, or healthy straight bone. Ruiz had learned that there was no medical necessity for Nacker's condition. Nacker suffered from phobias that included almost all natural functions; therefore, the minddiver avoided as much as possible all such things as eating, excreting, sweating, breathing.

A net of cranial studs wreathed Nacker's head. Through these he communicated with the universe and did his work.

The synthesized voice with which he greeted Ruiz was always different from visit to visit. Now it was high and clear, an elf's voice. "Ruiz Aw. You arrive in an undignified manner." Nacker's vaguely formed face was motionless as he spoke, and his eyes were unfocused.

Ruiz took resentful inventory of his hurts. Blood dripped down his chest from the lacerations there, and his knee was swollen to the size of a small pumpkin. "If you lived in a more civilized district, I'd have arrived in better style. And why did you take so long to open up?" Ruiz touched the back of his neck, deactivating the personaskein.

"If I lived where the League could easily reach me, they'd burn me out, as you well know, Ruiz. They think I'm almost as good as the Gencha. We know better, eh? And as to my tardiness, why, I moved as quickly as I could in safety. I'd never deliberately expose you to danger. Or at least danger you couldn't handle. Anyway, it was most entertaining, watching you at your work." A sweet laugh rang out.

Nacker's motives were impossible to fathom, Ruiz thought. Nacker was rumored to be a vastly wealthy being, so it wasn't just the money Ruiz paid that impelled Nacker to help him. The minddiver seemed to like Ruiz, but what of that? Or perhaps the minddiver hated the Art League and enjoyed tweaking the League's nose. In any case, it was fortunate that Nacker was willing to perform his indispensable services for Ruiz. Six times before, Ruiz had visited the minddiver, and six times the work had been satisfactory. Nacker was reputed to be trustworthy; Ruiz's extensive investigations had uncovered no instance in which Nacker had betrayed a client to the League.

"And so," Nacker continued, "you carry the death net? You wish the standard arrangement? Good. Kaum will conduct you to the infirmary, and after, we'll begin." Nacker's throne floated silently out of the lock.

CHAPTER 2

Nacker's infirmary was complete and comfortable. The patient had a wide choice of diversions: sensiedreams, holodrama, a small euphorium, surrogames of all varieties. Ruiz Aw was in no mood to be diverted, however, so he sat and glared at the inoffensive Kaum as the Dirm bondguard clamped a therapeutic coupling around the damaged knee. The coupling's diagnostic slate immediately lit with red-tagged assessments.

Kaum's moonstone eyes grew large, and the purple membranes of his ears stiffened with surprise, as he tapped at the slate. "Whooo, Ruiz, you was running on fumes, there." The Dirm eased the coupling into a more comfortable position with exaggerated care.

"Uh-huh," answered Ruiz in a poisonous monotone. Ruiz was still irritated with Nacker, and by extension all that belonged to Nacker. There was no reason but Nacker's whim for the additional injuries Ruiz had suffered in Nacker's dooryard.

Ruiz needed Nacker, unfortunately. Without Nacker, he would never have taken the job on Pharaoh. He sighed.

Kaum daubed Ruiz's wounds with replicant gel, and covered them with stim pads. "That should do it, Ruiz." The Dirm bondguard's normally placid eyes showed hurt when he straightened up. "Give it two hours, or three. You'll be feeling better."

Ruiz felt a twinge of guilt; Kaum was a good-natured being. His reptiloid race—if not terribly quick-witted—was loyal and strong and uninclined to gratuitous violence, which was why they were always in demand as low-level muscle. Ruiz managed a wry smile. "Thanks, Kaum. I feel a little better already." He patted the Dirm's massive arm.

Kaum seemed happier for Ruiz's feeble pleasantry, and he smiled in the manner of his kind, flaring the nostrils at the top of his skull. "Don't mention it, Ruiz. Always happy to do for a cutie like you." Kaum tweaked Ruiz's cheek gently with fingers like scaly sausages and lumbered away.

Ruiz repressed a shudder. "Hey, Kaum," he called. "When's Nacker going to be ready?" He couldn't afford an extended stay in Nacker's hold; the League would soon notice his absence.

Kaum paused at the door. "As soon as you're out of pain. He's considerate, in his way."

Ruiz lay back against the couch. "I guess so."

NOT A MUSCLE in Ruiz's body was capable of movement. Silent impellers inserted into strategic vessels oxygenated and circulated his blood. No sound or light or any other sensation reached him; the only active neural tissue in his body was in his brain. It was a particularly helpless feeling. Ruiz concentrated on armoring himself down into a hard dense kernel of personality.

Inside his head, Ruiz heard the synthetic voice of Nacker. It growled up from subsonic rumbles, and then squalled into the upper range, as Nacker experimented, seeking perfect resonance. "Testing. One and a-two and a-three and a-four—who does Ruiz Aw adore?"

Ruiz would have ground his teeth, had that been possible.

Nacker chuckled. "So, Ruiz," he said, "you're anxious?

Very well, already I sense the death net. A particularly powerful one. Are you sure your employers have told you everything you should know about this assignment?"

"Meaning what?" The thought lifted away from Ruiz, flew up into blackness, where Nacker intercepted it.

"The League appears to be extraordinarily concerned that their interest not be revealed and that they get *something*, some bit of information, however small, when the net collapses and sends its data home. You're going to die and transmit at the first drop of the shoe. . . . The death scenarios are remarkably all-encompassing, far more extensive than would be warranted by a simple game of poacher catching. I would guess, my friend, that you are a silver bullet. Aimed at some hidden monster."

Ruiz was silent. Here was an unpleasant discovery, indeed. "What can you do?"

"As always, Ruiz, quite a lot. I say without modesty that no one else could help you significantly; the League's done a very thorough job. Can it be that they suspect your loyalty, at last?" Ruiz heard a synthetic chuckle, an insectile scraping at the unprotected surface of his mind. "No, no, of course not, you're their best, true? It was unkind of me to bring up uncertainty at such a vulnerable moment." Nacker became businesslike. "So. The death net, like all Gencha work, cannot be completely subverted. I can blunt the urgency of the compulsion—give you, perhaps, time to change the parameters of the situation enough to gain a respite. But you'll still die, if you can't wiggle free from the trigger situation in time. Or I can to some extent degrade the death net's operant synapses so that if the net is triggered you may only become extremely ill, rather than irrevocably dead. In that case, the net will send no data home, and also you will experience substantial personality decay, should you survive. Please choose." Nacker's last statement was made in formal tones.

Ruiz considered. The decision Nacker required pivoted on a philosophical point: Was anything worse than death? Some would answer no, without hesitation. But he suspected that not many of these absolutists worked for ruthless corporate entities like the Art League or had Ruiz's wide experience of life on the League's client worlds. Ruiz could without effort imagine countless scenarios in which he would prefer death. On the other hand, it was Ruiz's love of his own life that had brought him down here to Nacker, through the dangers of Beaster Level, and the deadlier dangers that would confront him should the League ever get a whiff of his presence here.

Still . . . if he ever found himself helpless in the hands of his enemies, the Ruiz Aw that might recover from an aborted death net would no longer be Ruiz Aw, but a stranger. He had known victims of botched minddiving. They navigated the unsteady currents of their constricted lives carefully, slack-faced and dim-eyed, objects of pity and revulsion. He would prefer a definite death to such an uncertain approximation of life.

"Slow the trigger ramp of the set as much as you can, but leave the synapses alone."

"As you say. I'll have to cohere some touchstone memories until I get my bearings." Nacker's voice took on a strong tinge of disapproval. "You will insist on autodiving, against all professional advice. Paranoia, paranoia, Ruiz. Each time I swim you, the geometries are new. You have so many areas locked down or self-circuited. It's a wonder even the Gench can get a net to stick."

"It never seems to have any trouble. And it doesn't talk as much, either."

"Go away, now," Nacker said, and Ruiz poured down into his deepest, safest place.

NACKER PAUSED FOR a moment before transferring in, to look through his own sensors at Ruiz's motionless body. Ruiz lay on the immo-bed, encased in an amber block of shockgel, his head sprouting a thick crop of silver wires. The scars of Ruiz's encounter with the wolfheads were fading quickly; if the dive took any length of time, the scars would be invisible before Nacker returned to his bell jar and his own moribund body. In the gel, Ruiz's dark skin had an almost metallic smoothness and density, as if it would turn a knife, as if it could be polished into a man-shaped mirror.

Nacker examined Ruiz's hands where they floated in the gel, curled into half-fists. Nacker marveled at the hands. To think that such dangerous objects could be so beautiful; the strong fingers tapering, the knuckles curving into perfect scimitars of bone, the whole knitted with wiry muscle and sheathed in lustrous skin.

A moment passed in this pleasurable contemplation. Then Nacker dropped his probe in, delicately, delicately, cleaving Ruiz's holomnemonic sea, a needle falling point first into the abyss. He sank deeper and deeper, sliding effortlessly around the middepth reefs of Ruiz's protective self-circuits. He danced nimbly away from the massive, sensitive cables of the Gencha death net, a structure anchored in the abyssal trenches. With equal agility he avoided the fine skein of League mission-imperative that fogged the depths like the tendrils of some great demanding jellyfish.

At last Nacker settled to the floor of Ruiz's mind and came to rest in the slurry of decayed memories, the dead diatoms of experience that rained down continuously from above. Here he lay quiescent for a long time, extending his perceptions upward, mapping the artifacts of Ruiz's personality as they wheeled overhead in the slow currents.

When he was satisfied, he detached a bubble of stimulation from his own substance. It rose, twinkling, until it shattered on the stony underside of one of Ruiz's early memories, a massive thing, so heavily encrusted with protective substance that it was probably no longer accessible to Ruiz.

RUIZ WAS FIVE years old, helping his demi-father in the barn. It was Ruiz's special task to gather the warm nodules of orms flesh from the nests when the orms crowded out into their runs for their breakfast. It was a good task, one of Ruiz's favorites. The freshly budded nodules squirmed in his hands as he collected them into the brood bucket, their tiny palps searching his palms for the feeding pores his human skin lacked, and the sensation was a pleasant harmless tickle. The weight of the brood bucket when he was done was another reward—each nodule represented a small but measurable amount of credit toward his family's independence. And though in his young mind the concept of independence was a fuzzy one, he knew beyond doubt that independence was a Good, and that the converse quality, bondtotient, was a Bad. This he had learned from the long faces and hushed voices around the dinner table whenever the latter word was spoken. Of late the faces had grown longer and the voices less hushed, a situation that worried Ruiz when he thought of it.

It didn't seem to help that Ruiz brought in as many nodules as ever. And no matter how much he exhorted the orms, they refused to bud more than their usual number of nodules. They stared at him with their dull, multifaceted eyes, uncomprehending, while Ruiz tried earnestly to explain how important it was that they do better. Sometimes, if the voices around the table had been very loud, Ruiz ended up crying at the orms, frustrated and tempted to throw pebbles at them, to punish them for their stupidity.

But not today. Today he was happy. He was carrying the brood bucket across the compound toward the wombshed when a glittering contraption came rushing into the enclosure and settled to the ground with a puff of blown dust. Ruiz was so startled that he dropped the bucket, spilling several nodules out onto the dirt. Immediately he set the bucket upright and began retrieving the precious lumps. By the time he'd picked them all up, the hovercar's doors had, with a pneumatic hiss, lifted open. Out stepped the overseer, a thin snake of a man with a long braided beard and tattoed eyebrows. The overseer's name was Bob Piyule, a name that brought almost as much tension to the family conferences as the mention of bondtotient.

From the meltstone commonhouse came most of the older family members. Ruiz was curious and wanted very much to stay and listen, but the nodules were his responsibility, and if they were not soon taken to the wombshed they would die. So he carried them inside and distributed them as quickly as he could among the empty conveyors.

When he was finished Ruiz rushed back out into the yard. But when he saw that all the family elders were gathered, gazing at Ruiz with varying degrees of sadness, he stopped in his tracks, afraid. The other children watched wide-eyed from the darkness of the cottage windows. He became more fearful when all the elders looked away, except for his bloodmother Lasa, who stood with tears running down her ordinarily serene face.

Ruiz sensed impending tragedy. He ran to Lasa on stubby legs, tears trembling in his own eyes. She lifted him, hugging him so that he could barely breathe. But she said nothing, nor did anyone else.

"What's it? What's the matter?" Ruiz asked in a voice that squeaked with fear.

The overseer had a nasal, prim voice. "You're making far too much fuss over the child; you'll frighten him needlessly," said Bob Piyule, taking hold of Ruiz's shoulder. "Don't be afraid, Ruiz. You go to a greater family than this huddle of dirt scratchers. You go to the Lord's School. If you are diligent, one day you'll wear fine clothing and serve the Lord."

Ruiz clung more tightly to Lasa. Bob Piyule pulled at him, to no avail. "Come, Lasa," the overseer said, "is this dignified?"

Ruiz's demi-father Relito spoke. "What's dignified about child stealing, Piyule?" Relito's voice, ordinarily harsh, sounded now as if he spoke through a throat full of stones.

Bob Piyule released Ruiz and whirled to face Relito. "Child stealing, is it? Can Lord Balliste steal what is already his? A less generous master would sunder your family and redistribute the members to more efficient production units, as I have many times advised him to do. Instead, he is merciful."

"Yes, merciful." Relito laughed bitterly.

Bob Piyule's narrow face flushed, and his eyes took on a dangerous glitter. "Enough," he said. He took Ruiz by the arm and roughly tore him away from Lasa, who fell to her knees, looking as if something inside her had broken.

HERE THE MEMORY tattered and streamed away into darkness. Nacker still lay quietly in the ooze at the bottom of Ruiz's mind. *A farm boy, a common slave,* Nacker marveled. *Who would ever have guessed*? This incongruity amused Nacker anew each time he entered Ruiz's mind.

It was a long time before another touchstone memory drifted into position to be stimulated, long enough for Nacker to grow anxious, worried that one of the subtle guard filaments of the League mission-imperative might brush against him and trigger the death net before he could escape. Or that he'd be attacked by one of the great predatorial neuronic patterns, cleverly birthed by Ruiz to protect his mnemonic ocean from clumsy invasion. But nothing touched him, and eventually Nacker released a second stimulating locus. It detonated against another memory: Ruiz grown almost to manhood.

RUIZ WORE THE fine clothes that the late Bob Piyule had promised him so many years before, and he crouched at the right hand of Lord Balliste. But nothing else was as it should have been. The front of Ruiz's brocade coat was stiff with drying blood, the blood of the Lord's last bondguard. A sonic knife burbled in Ruiz's hand, transmitting its hungry shimmy to his flesh.

They were hiding in a short passage off Lord Balliste's audience room. Lord Balliste fondled a gem-encrusted punchgun, shifting it from one hand to the other. The Lord was grown old and weak in both body and mind; his liverish lips trembled, and the breath wheezed in his shriveled chest. The Lord kept up a cackling mutter as they waited. "When they get here, when they get here, then we'll see, eh Ruiz, then . . . I want an ice, a nice fresh lime will do. . . . Why are you dressed in red?"

The Lord nattered on, but Ruiz ignored him. He strained his ears, listening for the next sounds, now that the heaviest explosions had ceased. The free-lance emancipators were finished below, and any moment they would arrive to complete their contract with the former slaves of Lord Balliste.

Lord Balliste was whispering in more urgent tones. "Why, Ruiz, can you tell me? I treated them well, I observed the proprieties. How is it they turn and feed on me now?"

Ruiz didn't answer. He had heard the scrape of cautious boots in the audience room. "Hush, now, Lord. Perhaps they will not find us back in here, if we are very quiet."

"Yes, yes, you're right, young Ruiz, you're the only one who kept faith." Lord Balliste clamped his mouth shut, mercifully.

There was a long interlude of silence; then the tapestry that covered the passage twitched. After a moment, one of the emancipators lifted the tapestry slowly aside with the muzzle of a half-stocked splinter gun. He was a large graceful man in scuffed carbon armor, and he followed the muzzle of his weapon with the smoothness of a weasel flowing into a rat hole. Ruiz held perfectly still, hoping that he and the Lord were adequately hidden behind the jumble of dusty chairs stacked in the back of the dim passage.

The man was as still as a statue for six heartbeats; then he turned to go, and Ruiz prepared to release the breath he'd been holding.

At that moment Lord Balliste chose to rise and fire a burst from his ceremonial punchgun. The burst smashed the leg of the emancipator. The impact whirled the man about, and he lost his grip on his weapon. He slid down the wall.

The Lord laughed and pointed the punchgun with a flourish.

Ruiz made his decision.

He stood up and slipped the sonic knife into the Lord's long skull, just in front of the ear. The punchgun clattered to the floor. Ruiz tugged up, and the knife snarled out of the top of the Lord's head, spraying liquefied brains, a fine mist that haloed the Lord for a moment before the body folded over.

In the next instant, two more emancipators rolled under the tapestry, ready to fire. "Wait!" the injured man said sharply, and they did, a restraint that Ruiz found remarkable, under the circumstances. But both weapons and two cold pairs of eyes were trained on him, as Ruiz switched off his knife and laid it carefully aside. He crossed his empty hands over his head and stood still.

The injured man looked down at his shredded leg, then

back at Ruiz. "You'll need a new job," he said. "If we can stop the bleeding, maybe I'll have one for you."

NACKER FELT A ghost shiver go through his probe-self. Each time Ruiz Aw had come to him, Nacker had touched this memory, and each time Nacker found it disturbing. There was nothing wrong with the decision Ruiz had made; it was the only one that had offered him any chance of life. No, Ruiz could not be faulted on either ethical or practical grounds for his betrayal of the slave-Lord. It was rather the speed with which Ruiz had switched allegiance that chilled. Nacker understood, not for the first time, that Ruiz might react with as much swift lethality should he and Nacker ever find themselves at cross purposes.

Nacker supposed it was from the emancipators that Ruiz had acquired the tools of his trade: intimidation, torture, murder. Evidently the emancipators had been good teachers, but Nacker was sure that Ruiz had been an especially apt pupil. Nacker remembered the economical grace with which Ruiz had destroyed the wolfheads, the odd light in Ruiz's eyes.

These thoughts disturbed Nacker's concentration, so he put them from him. He waited again, until a whole cluster of touchstone memories drew into range. Nacker energized them in rapid order, no longer aware of content, but only chronology.

The last memory Nacker touched was a small thing, flickering among the deepest currents, swift and elusive. It appeared to Nacker that Ruiz had left the memory unprotected, as if Ruiz hoped for its demise. But the memory was too strong, too active, too crucial to the man that Ruiz had become. Nacker's curiosity was aroused.

RUIZ WAITED TO die. His thoughts were sluggish and poorly formed; he was sinking into the unresponsive clay of his failing body. So the blaze of Line's sun no longer burned him as fiercely as it had three days before, when the Lineans had strapped him to the needle tree. The pain was no longer urgent, as the tree's thorns slowly quested deeper and deeper into his body. Occasionally a thorn would penetrate some sensitive organ, and Ruiz would thrash briefly until his small strength was exhausted, but he had stopped screaming.

The part of him that still lived traveled among memories.

. . . Ruiz, arriving on Line in a nighttime drop. He fell from the skies in the company of two hundred other emancipators, all of them full of confidence and righteous anger. He remembered that younger self with as much amazement as scorn. He could hardly imagine how he could have seen the universe in such simple terms: Slavery was evil. Eradicate it.

. . . The horrendous callousness of the Lineans, devolved alien cetaceans who bred humans in small isolated communities for various specialized markets. The alien breeders committed unspeakable acts against any of their slaves who by word or deed or omission supported the rebellion. Images flickered through Ruiz's darkening mind: hideous death, torture; all the colors of horror, red of blood, black of burned meat, the pale clotted flesh of corpses. How much was his fault, the fault of his unforgivable naïveté? Ruiz tried to shake his head, but the thorns held him fast.

. . . The despair Ruiz had felt when, after months of bitter fighting in which thousands of innocents had perished, he had discovered that his company of emancipators had been hired by the Art League, the vast multisystem conglomerate that for several millennia had controlled the majority of legitimate slavery in the pangalac worlds. He had gone to his commanding officer, full of betrayed rage. "Why?" he had asked.

"Because it's better. It's not perfect, but it's better. The Lineans are monsters. The League is a business." His commander's face shifted in remembrance, until Ruiz could see only a steel mask, an inhuman shape, devoid of expression. "It's better, Ruiz."

. . . The clean fury that had impelled Ruiz to recruit from among his fellow emancipators a group to oppose both the Lineans and the Art League.

. . . His futile campaign, unsupported by the slaves, successful only in prolonging the agony on Line. It had ended in another treachery, one that had brought him to this slow sacrifice on the needle tree.

The last trace of the memory, one that seemed only carelessly etched into the artifact that carried it, was of the League agents who had taken Ruiz alive from the tree. There was no tinge of gratitude in the memory—only a stony acceptance.

WITH THE GEOMETRIES firmly established, Nacker extended his sensorium along the floor of Ruiz's mind, spreading out through the concealing ooze of dead memory. Nacker came to surround the roots of the death net where they struck deep into Ruiz's cerebral bedrock. No direct attack on the net was possible; any such efforts would be detected instantly, triggering the net. But indirectly there was much that could be done. A thin slippery film of passionate energy, drawn from Ruiz's libidinous reserves—the essence of love-of-life—could be injected under the anchorage system of the death net. If the net was triggered, the cables would slip harmlessly for precious moments before they tore loose. The only drawback to this approach was that it would leave Ruiz, his brain buttered with sexual energy, somewhat vulnerable to romantic impulses. But nothing was ever gained without loss. Nacker found this an amusing—and personally satisfying—solution to Ruiz's problem.

And besides, Nacker thought, *no other solution would work as well.*

He had chosen no easy technique. Each anchorage point had to be approached with exquisite caution. The actual insertion of the lubricant required a delicacy that only a half-dozen non-Gencha minddivers in all the pangalac worlds could have managed.

At last he was done.

But before he withdrew, Nacker treated himself to a recent memory, of Ruiz in his hideaway.

Nacker watched comfortably from behind Ruiz's eyes as Ruiz went out onto his terrace, built at the edge of a great rift. Scattered about at the edges of the terrace were deep planters, in which bloomed flowers from a hundred worlds. Outside, nothing but raw rock; inside, the sweet smell of blossoms.

Ruiz filled a long-spouted watering can from a tap and began to water the beds, slowly and methodically. The fierce blue sun was moderated into a warm caressing light by the same boundary field that retained the terrace's atmosphere. The only sound came from the bees that buzzed among the flowers, moving to and fro between the beds and the hive that stood in a shaded corner of the terrace.

Nacker sank more deeply into the memory, seeking Ruiz's thoughts as he went about his task, but Ruiz seemed empty of thought, empty of emotion, existing only in the moment, and Nacker wondered how such a thing was possible.

Each time Ruiz came to him, Nacker found such a memory and marveled at it. So strange, that Ruiz Aw—feared enforcer for the Art League, a man who killed with a directness and detachment that was surely pathological—should spend his uncontracted time on an empty lifeless world tending flowers, all alone.

A very odd man. Nacker withdrew into himself and remembered a conversation he had once had with Ruiz, on one of the enforcer's first visits to his hold.

"You're a former slave yourself," Nacker had said then, full of wry amusement. "How can you work as a slave catcher for the League?"

"There are worse masters. The League treats its property as well as is practical."

"Do you feel no qualms of conscience?"

Ruiz had looked at him with neutral eyes. "Should I?"

"Well . . . perhaps. Some would."

Ruiz made no comment for a long moment, then spoke in a patient voice. "Have you ever heard of Silverdollar, the ice world? It's somewhat beyond the pangalac frontier, spinward. A mining planet."

"No," Nacker said.

"They have what amounts to a sapient fish there; it lives under the ice for most of the year, emerging into open water only during the equatorial thaws. Well, it's not really a fish; it's warm-blooded. But it has gills, so I call it a fish. Perhaps the fish aren't really sapient, since they have no technology at all, but they have a language of their own, and they'll tell you strange fish myths that you can almost understand. They absorb new languages with extraordinary ease. It's not just an idiot savant ability; the fish are in high demand as translators of poetry and novels and other verbal works of art. They seem to have the ability to transcend the species barrier, to translate the intent and the specific emotional coloration of a work. No one understands how this is possible, not even the fish. Their existence has spawned several competing new schools of neurolinguistics, but no one really has any idea how they do it."

"They must be very valuable."

"Oh, yes. For years, the only supply came from hunters who ventured under the ice, a dangerous business because of the other predators of Silverdollar. Clones raised off Silverdollar were nonverbal, useless as translators; some unknown factor in their native environment triggers the development of the facility. The price of one of these fish was consequently very high, until entrepreneurs came to Silverdollar and built a hatchery. They enclosed a suitable area of under-ice ocean with a force field and burned open a thread of open water. The fish, thinking that the thaw had come early, congregated along the thread, where they were easily scooped up, cloned into multitudes, and released into the safety of the field. It worked well and the entrepreneurs became wealthy."

Nacker could not find the relevance of Ruiz's story. "And what does this have to do with your work?"

"The fish are slaves; would you agree?"

"Yes. . . ."

Ruiz had turned away, so that Nacker could not see his face. "The hatchery is heavily fortified, protected by both planetside and orbital weapons. The security forces are Dilvermooners, numerous and well trained. No frontal assault would succeed, unless the attackers were willing to burn a hole out of the ocean—which would defeat the purpose of the exercise."

Ruiz stopped, as though his story was finished. Nacker finally grew impatient. "And so?"

"And so." Ruiz sighed. "What if you were willing to take a job at the hatchery? What if, some dark night, you were to creep forth with a dip net and a bucket? Which approach would yield the greater number of liberations?"

Ruiz fell silent.

Nacker thought about the story. After many minutes of silence, he said, "So, Ruiz. Have you gotten any use from your dip net yet?"

But Ruiz had lost interest in the conversation and wouldn't answer.

NACKER DREW HIMSELF back into a probe of minimum caliber and began the touchy business of rising back to the surface of Ruiz's mind.

RUIZ HEARD THE last of the liquefied shockgel draining away, slurping down the immo-bed's drains. He opened his eyes. Nacker sat at his side, unmoving, as always.

"Ah, you're with us again," Nacker said. The synthetic voice was an exhausted whisper, for effect. Nacker could as easily have reverted to his elf voice, or any of the other vocalizer styles the minddiver favored.

Ruiz ran his fingers through his wet hair, raking off the silver halo of probe wires. "Yes . . . what success?"

"Enough, my friend. Though, as always, I remind you of my motto: I do good work; still, don't get caught."

CHAPTER 3

RUIZ AW hurried back through the Beaster Level without incident, driven by the Art League mission-imperative that filled his mind. When he emerged into the civilized corridors of Dilvermoon, he took a tubecar to the launch complex where he kept his starboat.

The *Vigia* was a small boat, somewhat battered on the outside, but well maintained mechanically and luxurious within. Ruiz boarded her with a sense of homecoming, and when her hatch closed behind him, he felt safe for the first time in days.

The mission-imperative accepted his boarding as an acceptable movement toward completion of the mission he had contracted to perform, and so its compulsion relented. Ruiz felt the easing of the compulsion as a pleasurable languor, and he resolved to enjoy the sensation while it lasted. Ruiz took a snifter of good brandy into the lounge, where he sprawled comfortably in his favorite chair. He breathed a long sigh, releasing tension. He took a warming sip, then set the snifter aside and closed his eyes. He thought about Nacker's analysis of the mission—that the Art League was willing to spend him to get even a bit of information on the poachers who were working Pharaoh. Why? True, Pharaoh was a lucrative world, but the League owned a thousand as profitable. What was it about that particular world that made it so special? Or was it something else?

Ruiz reviewed his visit to the League factor who had hired him this time. The factor was an old woman with the long face and delicate bones of a Cygnan, named Alldiusen Miktyas.

"Come in, come in," she had said, bowing and rubbing her wrists in the Cygnan manner. "Always a delight, Citizen Aw. So happy you are available."

Ruiz nodded carefully, and chose a chair well back from Miktyas's desk.

"Smoke? Powder? Wet?" Miktyas indicated the bar that ran across the back of her office, beneath a large holostill of the Meadows of Morrow.

Ruiz shook his head. "No, thank you. You offer a contract?"

Miktyas smiled widely, revealing small blue teeth. "Indeed, and I'm pleased to see that you have lost none of your refreshing directness. So, to business! We suffer from illegal harvesters, in a prime lowtech world we own in the centerward fringe of the Manichaean region. You know of Pharaoh?"

Ruiz rubbed his chin and thought. "A desert Hardworld? Some sort of performers? Conjurors?"

Miktyas clapped her hands together, making a small flaccid sound. "Truly, you're well informed. Yes! We would send you there, to gather information, and if possible, terminate the illegal harvesting, though our contract would be fulfilled if you can identify and locate the criminals, to be dealt with by the Legal Arm of our beloved employer. But there's a healthy bonus for termination, as always." The factor winked and laughed, her horsey face quivering with forced jollity.

Ruiz felt a bit ill, as he always did when accepting employment with the Art League. But he maintained an expression of polite interest. "What information is available?"

The factor shut off her laugh in midchortle. A gravely

earnest expression descended over her features, as though a shade had been drawn down. "Well. Very little. This is why we are prepared to raise your usual rate." The factor swiveled a screen so that Ruiz could see, touched it with skinny fingers. A swarm of amber characters flowed across it, listing the payment schedule for a hundred contingencies. Ruiz leaned forward, looked carefully at the screen. He was somewhat taken aback by the hugeness of the compensation, and a blip of suspicion crossed the horizon of his mind.

"Many of your contingencies deal with posthumous compensation," he said, in a neutral voice.

The factor sighed heavily. "Such is the nature of your work, Citizen Aw. Not so?"

"It's so," Ruiz agreed.

"Should the worst occur, your heirs will be well cared for."

Ruiz saw no reason to mention that he had no heirs. "Am I the first to study the problem? No? Then what information have your operatives gathered?"

"As I said, very little. The poachers seem to have an efficient counterintelligence organization; our people disappeared without useful trace. Naturally, you're not to discount the possibility that they've infiltrated Pharaoh Upstation, or the League infrastructure on Pharaoh."

"Naturally," Ruiz said dryly. He considered at some length, until Miktyas squirmed impatiently.

"And so," Miktyas said. "Your opinion?"

Ruiz leaned back. "Is there no information at all? What help *can* you provide?"

"We have excellent backgrounding, language learning, cartographic conditioning—the usual. We can provide you with dossiers on the illegally harvested troupes, but this information is limited. The poachers make very clean snatches. We have an extensive network of League observers in place on Pharaoh, who will assist you in any way you desire. Your budget is essentially unlimited. We're very disturbed by this problem; we want swift and decisive action."

Ruiz considered. "What will you require of me?"

The factor rubbed her wrists, making a dry reptilian

sound. "Enhanced degree of mission-imperative, of course. A terminal contingency net—our finest Gencha work."

Ruiz felt a lurch in his stomach, though he'd expected the death net. No one would pay that much without a guarantee of *some* return on their investment.

"Is that absolutely necessary? The death net?"

The factor's face curdled with disapproval. "Must you so refer to it? The TCN is only and merely a contingency mechanism. We hope, of course, that you return in perfect health, but yours is a risky trade, and if you meet with disaster, we want to know why. We'll be much likelier to avenge your murder, with the net transmitting the circumstances of your demise. Don't you want that?"

Ruiz sighed. "Oh, sure. Sure. When?"

Miktyas leaned forward, her eyes alight with urgency. "Now. Today. We have the Gench practitioner waiting in the lab; it's ready to do the installation. What do you say?"

Ruiz sat silent for a long time, considering, looking inside his heart.

Finally he said, "Why not?"

MIKTYAS CONDUCTED RUIZ down a dozen levels, deep into the League medical section.

The laboratory was dimly lit by red glowstrips, in deference to the nocturnal being who worked there. The Gench took no notice of their approach. It sat motionless, except for its three tiny eyespots, which appeared to circulate over its skull in random patterns. In actuality, the hairlike sensors on the creature's scalp were simply activating and deactivating in sequences that gave the illusion of movement.

Ruiz's gorge rose. In the humid air of the laboratory, the rotting earthworm stink of the Gench was stifling. Tufts of frizzy umber fiber sprouted from its baggy, three-legged body. The tufts clenched into hard little buttons, and then relaxed, as the factor stood before the alien.

"Your customer, good Gench," Miktyas said, patting Ruiz's arm. "You have the specifications?"

The Gench shifted on its stool, and its eyespots collected into a clump at the front of its skull. A vertical neck slit drooped open, and it spoke in a whispery voice. "Of course."

"Fine, fine," Miktyas said, rubbing her wrists. "We should begin, then."

The Gench shrugged, a motion that ran clockwise around its body, and rose to its footpads. "As you wish." It nodded at a human-contoured chair, and Ruiz seated himself and leaned back.

The Gench made no preparations, used nothing like the elaborate technology Nacker used later to hobble the Gench's work. It simply stood in front of Ruiz and extruded a glistening white filament from one of its mouths. The filament stretched out, until it was as thin as a hair; then it touched Ruiz at the right temple and sank through his skin. "I remember you again," it said, and then Ruiz's world turned black.

He woke, as always, sooner than expected, but he kept his eyes closed and so he heard the last words that passed between the factor and the Gench practitioner.

"The work went well?" Miktyas asked anxiously.

The Gench sighed. "Well enough. This one's mindsea is always difficult to swim in. He protects himself well, almost like one of the Real Race."

Miktyas sniggered. "The Real Race. . . ."

"You should be merry, if you can. We Gencha were making ourselves into gods when humans were bits of slime floating in the sea. Do you think all are like *me*, a trained animal in your menagerie? Elsewhere, the Gencha still Become." Nothing in the whispery voice betrayed anger, or any other emotion, but something touched Ruiz with chilly fingers.

"Never mind that. The net is anchored, the mission-imperative implanted?"

"Yes. Your rat will run its maze, and when it dies, you will learn what it has learned. This one will project a strong signal, at least," the Gench said.

Ruiz allowed his eyes to flutter open. The factor rushed to help him sit up. "Citizen Aw! How do you feel?"

Ruiz passed a shaky hand over his face and glanced at the Gench. It had seated itself on its stool again, and its eyespots flickered over the far side of its head, only occasionally sliding into brief view. "Well enough," Ruiz had answered.

RUIZ NOW SET the brandy aside and rose to his feet. The walls of the lounge were a soft cool white, as were the furnishings. The only spot of bright color glowed from a niche set into the far wall. Ruiz went toward the niche, stopped before it. Each day, the *Vigia* placed in the lounge niche a different thing of beauty from Ruiz's large collection; this day it was a spirit mask from Line, its humanoid features carved from a single blue moonstone, then inlaid with swirling bands of red jelly opal.

The boat chose at random, but somehow these choices had come to have superstitious meaning for Ruiz, as though the selection were an omen. He looked down at the mask and shuddered. The moonstone mask had come to him through stupidity and misplaced trust, a souvenir of betrayal. He kept it not only for its beauty, but also to remind him of the dangers of trust.

In the course of his bloody years on that harsh world, Ruiz had fallen in love, been delivered to his enemies by his beloved, and finally learned the cynicism that now served him for a conscience.

He found himself wishing that he could withdraw from the Pharaoh contract, but at the thought, the mission-imperative stirred in his mind, pushing the wish away. He could almost feel the death net in the depths of his mind, deep-rooted, a hair-trigger cancer, waiting to kill him. "Too late," he said to the moonstone mask. It seemed to look back at him, laughing, its empty eyeholes full of formless certainty.

He turned away, no longer capable of relaxation.

"Time to go," he said to the *Vigia*.

AN HOUR LATER, Dilvermoon was a fading silver glimmer in the rear screens, and Ruiz began to study. During the three-week passage to Pharaoh, Ruiz Aw took the datasoak every eight hours, filling his memory with Pharaoh—language, customs, religion, the million details he would need to slide unnoticed through that world. In recovery he slept a great deal, but when he was awake he occupied himself by studying the charts of Pharaoh's one habitable plateau, rising high above the boiling desert that covered the remainder of Pharaoh's surface. In the center of the plateau, long ago, the spore ship had landed its cargo of embryos, a monumental misjudgment, with so many sweet fertile worlds to choose from. But the colony had taken hold and now flourished, within peculiar constraints.

The charts glowed in the holotank, clean lines in primary colors, but Ruiz saw the images of the datasoak, superimposed on the charts. The sterile clay of the arid plateau, streaked with a million dead shades of brown and black. The scattered oases, green-purple, each centered in its lacy spread of catchment basins and collection canals, like monstrously complex spider webs.

In the murky steams below the plateau, monstrous creatures lived. Occasionally one would climb up and ravage the countryside until it expired from the rarefied atmosphere and relative cold. Eventually the Pharaohans had incorporated these monsters into their religion, as demons—and built a wall around the edge of their world to keep them out.

The Pharaohans had slowly and painfully solved the problem of the infrequent rains and limited their population growth by a ruthless program of priestly culling. Gradually their lives had grown sedentary and secure enough to permit a flowering of craft. The Pharaohans excelled at the lapidary arts, made marvelous glasses, and porcelain of great vigor and dignity. Some of these were valuable enough to warrant export. From the venom of indigenous reptiles, the Pharaohans distilled potent hallucinogens, which were in limited demand on the pangalac market—appealing to wealthy consumers who enjoyed the cachet of primitive experiences.

Their technology typified the odd mixture to be found on long-owned Hardworlds—those planets on which humanity had only an uncertain grasp on existence. Their metallurgy was relatively sophisticated. They built steam cars of good quality, but their periodic attempts to build railroads were always thwarted by League agents, to prevent them from establishing a basis for wide-scale industrial development.

But as on all worlds, the most valuable trade on Pharaoh was in people. The conjurors of Pharaoh brought enormous prices on the pangalac worlds. These performers had created a high art with their outrageous sleights—their great plays were passionate theater enhanced by feats of illusion. Legerdemain was the factor that knit together all aspects of Pharaohan life.

Conjuring constituted the only practical means of movement upward through the rigid caste system. A famous conjuror, who for some reason was not harvested by the League, had an excellent chance of ennoblement. And were he to be harvested, his fellow Pharaohans would celebrate his disappearance as a transfiguration and envy him his new status as a demigod in the Land of Reward. The Art League encouraged the development of the art in other ways. Exceptional performances were rewarded by rainstorms—produced by invisible League technology, but ostensibly the accolade of the gods. Those nomarchies rich in conjurors were therefore rich in all things.

At one point Ruiz watched a flatscreen promotional production, distributed by the Art League to potential buyers of Pharaohan conjurors.

The opening shot displayed the League's logo, a stylized androgynous human silhouette in red on a black ground, wearing silver chains made up of linked five-pointed stars. The League anthem swelled up, a stirring orchestration featuring a large chorus.

"Welcome, Citizens," said an assured voice, riding over the music. "This presentation is brought to you by the Art League, an autonomous nonaligned corporation, chartered on Dilvermoon and licensed on all pangalac worlds. The Art League—the foremost supplier of sapient merchandise in the galaxy for over three thousand standard years. The Art League—the foremost practitioner of the greatest art, the art of shaping sapience into usefulness." The anthem crescendoed and concluded on a dramatic ringing note.

The logo faded, to be replaced by a shot of Pharaoh,

hanging in space. The point of view zoomed in, dropped violently toward Pharaoh's surface. "This is Pharaoh," said the voice. "One of the League's most interesting and unusual client worlds. Today we take you to witness one of the great religious plays called Expiations."

Ruiz advanced the recording past the local color segment, until he reached the beginning of the performance. He listened as the voice explained that the plays served both religious and judicial purposes, in that the gods were entertained and criminals were executed in the course of the entertainment. In the major performances, the criminal was called a phoenix and was encouraged to participate willingly in the play by the hope that a sufficiently magnificent performance would lead to a resurrection after the play's conclusion—a hope encouraged by the League's technicians, who sometimes resuscitated and released the victim.

He advanced it again. The screen showed an Expiation in progress, the conjurors acting out their parts with the extravagant, larger-than-life gestures characteristic of precinematic theater. They performed with a hot-eyed intensity that Ruiz found disturbing, and he moved the recording forward again, stopping it at a point where the point of view had moved within the stage, revealing the activities of those who labored in the sweaty darkness, managing the apparatus that made the illusions possible. Here was a different sort of intensity—but still painful to watch, Ruiz thought. None of these folk understood that they strove only to make themselves and their fellow Pharaohans attractive to the League's customers. The Pharaohans had forgotten their pangalac origins, except for a few vague and discredited legends concerning people from the stars. For all they knew, the universe ended at the edge of their plateau, with only the demons below and the gods above to fear.

He switched off the screen.

THE MOST DEMANDING, yet most pleasant moments of the passage to Pharaoh were those Ruiz spent practicing small feats of sleight of hand. These skills would be necessary when he walked Pharaoh's dusty roads in his chosen disguise as a snake oil peddler, one of a caste of itinerant drug peddlers who customarily performed such minor tricks in the course of hawking their wares. Pangalac technology could rcplacc skill in most instances, but there were still elementary principles of misdirection and showmanship to be absorbed.

Ruiz found an odd sense of accomplishment in mastering his few tricks, and what time he found between recovery and the next bout of datasoak, he spent polishing his skills, until he could perform his repertoire without fumbling.

CHAPTER 4

W HEN the *Vigia* reached orbit above Pharaoh, Ruiz's head ached with the new knowledge it contained. He approached the Art League's orbital platform with an emotion close to relief. Here would be people, several thousand of them: League employees, consultants, contractors, transshipping travelers. The possibilities for distraction seemed promising.

From below, the platform was a less intense darkness against the blackness of space, showing no lights that some upstart genius on Pharaoh might observe. A crude telescope was well within the technical abilities of the culture below, and although such a development would be suppressed by the League infrastructure whenever it seemed to verge upon realization, the League took no chances.

Ruiz guided the *Vigia* carefully into her assigned slot, and when the last clashing sounds of the lock-on faded away, he unhooked his acceleration webbing and sighed.

"To work," he muttered.

He dressed in a black zipsuit—suitable garb for an enforcer—then debarked. In the lock area, a young woman waited for him. She was small and very slightly plump, with short, curly, blond hair and an apparently genuine smile.

"Citizen Aw?" she asked, stepping forward.

"Yes."

"Welcome to Pharaoh Upstation," she said, beaming. "I'm Auliss Moncipor. I'm to conduct you to Factor Prinfilic's office. Will you follow me?"

"Gladly," he answered, with somewhat more amiability than the situation called for. Auliss Moncipor appeared a pleasant and guileless person, for a League employee, but Ruiz wondered why he was even thinking such things. He walked behind her as she led the way through one of the access tubes that tied the platform's modules together. He found himself admiring the flex of her buttocks through the thin material of the League-issue overalls she wore. *What's the matter with me?* he wondered. Why was he feeling such a flush of heat at the proximity of a rather pretty, but otherwise unremarkable young woman? He shook his head violently, hoping to clear it. It *had* been a long, lonely trip from Dilvermoon, but ordinarily he postponed his romantic impulses to a time and place where his profession and reputation were unknown—as a matter of principle and of elementary safety.

They arrived at the factor's office, which was guarded by a small killmech. The sight of the assassin device restored Ruiz's sense of proportion, to some extent, and he was able to raise his gaze to the young woman's face as she turned.

"I'll announce you, Citizen Aw. A moment, please." She went in, and more than a minute passed. When she returned, she took Ruiz's arm and guided him through the door. He was briefly but acutely aware of the warmth of her hand.

The factor was an ancient Dilvermoon herman, tall and thin, with disproportionately heavy breasts. It had the distinctively elongated and sexually ambiguous features of its kind, framed by an elaborately coiffed mane of white hair. A blue caste-mark flowered on its wrinkled cheek, identifying it as a member of a prominent clan. It extended a hand in greeting. "Ruiz Aw," it said. "So happy to meet you. I'm Prinfilic; your servant." Ruiz reluctantly touched its somewhat clammy hand and then sat down unasked. Auliss left through a side door, smiling over her shoulder.

Ruiz forced himself to alertness. The hermen of Dilvermoon were among his least favorite self-created lifeforms; their amoral cleverness was legendary. He wondered that a herman had ascended to such a responsible position in the League, which was as paranoid about its employees' loyalties as any other far-flung conglomerate.

Prinfilic folded its well-kept hands and leaned back. A look of covert disdain flickered through its eyes. Like hermen in general, it apparently had a highly developed sense of its effect on unmodified humans. But it smiled easily.

"You're a welcome presence here, Ruiz Aw. The losses have gone far past acceptable levels in the last year or so. But you arrived here much more quickly than I had expected."

Ruiz ascended to a slightly higher plateau of alertness. Was there a detectable level of guile in the herman's voice? Was the herman in some way involved with the poachers on Pharaoh? Ruiz reminded himself to be especially wary as long as he remained aboard the platform.

"League Central did not inform you?" he asked.

"Yes, yes, but . . . the message arrived in a message drone, not six hours ago. Apparently you were contracted immediately following the decision to open this new line of inquiry, and you left without delay."

Ruiz said nothing. He allowed the silence to congeal, until the herman finally cleared its throat and spoke again. "Well. Your authorization is of impressive scope; the League must have great confidence in you. For the duration of your stay here, you will be the factor. How may I facilitate your investigations, Ruiz Aw?"

"I don't know, as yet. When I do, I'll tell you." Ruiz glanced about the factor's office. It was elegantly decorated, if a bit fussy. The walls were covered in some fine-grained silvery leather, seamed with vertical stripes of wine-colored velour. At exactly spaced intervals, in pools of white light, Pharaohan effigies hung at eye level. Ruiz rose and went over to the nearest. It was, he decided, a dustbear's snarling face, carved from what seemed to be the top of a human skull, stained with rusty pigment, and surrounded by a ruff of black feathers. A red thong held a swag of finger bones and little silver bells. Ruiz touched it and it made a strange, dry, shivery sound.

"A wonderful piece, eh?" Prinfilic spoke at his shoulder, and Ruiz restrained an impulse to jump. "I collect beautiful things from dirtside; it makes my time here pass more entertainingly. And it might make my retirement a bit more comfortable, or so I hope. What do you think; is it valuable?"

Ruiz moved away; the closeness of the factor made him uneasy. "I'm no judge," he said.

"Ah. Well, how long will you be with us?"

"Not long. I'd like to service the boat. Then I'll get right to work."

Prinfilic looked genuinely disappointed. "Ah, no! Surely you'll spend a day or two with us. At least. Why not have a last taste of pangalac life, before you go down to the dirt-grubbers?"

Ruiz looked at Prinfilic curiously. "Why do you say *last*? I plan to return soon."

Its cheeks colored, a bizarre effect on a face so old and rapacious. "I meant, of course, the last time for as long as your mission requires you to be dirtside. Please accept my apologies if any offense was conveyed."

"Sure," Ruiz said.

Another silence ensued, and Ruiz imagined that he felt the weight of the factor's disapproval. He ignored it and moved about the office, staring at the effigies that decorated the walls. Here was a daybat, its fierce raptor's head carved from polished russet granite, with rubies set like beads of blood along the muzzle's serrated edges. There was an arroyo lizard, with eyes of blue sapphire and teeth of amber. An obsidian Helldog wailed from a disk of gold and silver filigree.

Ruiz absorbed from these artifacts a sense of vigorous life, undiminished by civilization's constraints. He grew uncomfortable, for reasons he could not name, and so he finally stopped looking at them.

When he turned, Auliss Moncipor had returned. He felt again that odd heat, and a mild sense of embarrassment. She apparently received a portion of the involuntary message he was sending, and she seemed at least somewhat receptive, with a glisten to her eyes and a slight smile on her pretty mouth. The factor directed a keen glance at Ruiz, then another at Auliss.

"Go with Citizen Aw, Auliss. See to it he has all he needs," Prinfilic said. It smiled, too, though its smile wasn't as attractive as the one Auliss wore. "And please, Ruiz, reconsider. Surely you can spare a day or two. Or at least, a night? Eh?"

AULISS LED RUIZ through the passageways of the platform, but now she moved at his side, occasionally touching him with a soft hip, and directing him with a hand at his elbow.

"You'll want to see to your boat first, I'm sure," she said. "We'll go to Maintenance Sector. You have your vouchers?"

He patted his pocket.

"Good. I should have known you'd be prepared." She cast an artlessly flirtatious look at him.

"Yes. Always prepared."

"And after your boat is ready? What then?"

"I'd planned to leave. Can you suggest a better plan?"

She laughed. "Yes."

RUIZ INSTRUCTED A phlegmatic technician in his requirements. He patted the armored flank of the *Vigia,* a gesture of foolish sentimentality.

Finally he authorized access to the noncritical areas of the boat.

Auliss led him quickly back to her quarters, which were in a small module at the far end of a lengthy spar.

When they entered, he recognized the decor as appropriate to the home of a Pharaohan noble of modest pedigree. In the center of the green-tiled entrance court, a small fountain splashed lazily in the light artificial gravity. Incense drifted in the moist air, a scent of sweet-flowered desert shrubs.

"Come in," Auliss said, tugging him inside. "What do you think?"

"Pleasant," he said, glancing about.

"Well, we're probably unduly influenced by the dirtsiders. After all, it's our main entertainment, watching them at their odd little lives." She seemed faintly apologetic, as though Ruiz had caught her in an admission of provinciality.

"No, no, it's a fascinating culture," Ruiz said. "And a lucky coincidence that you've arranged your rooms so authentically. I can begin my acclimation before I leave the platform." But he thought, as he said this, that he was unlikely to visit any noble homes.

But Auliss seemed pleased by his diplomacy. "Good! I like to be helpful." She stroked his arm and pressed lightly against him.

She seemed to transmit a carnal current to his body, another intense shiver of lust. He grew alarmed. He couldn't understand the source of these abrupt passions. It was as though his mind had become a stranger's, for the moment. He wondered if this disturbing condition was related to Nacker's handiwork.

"But first," she said, "a meal and some Pharaohan wine. Have you had any yet?" She seemed innocently enthusiastic, as though her question had no other meaning than the obvious one.

"No," he answered. "Though I'd like to try a little."

She colored, and he saw that she understood him well enough.

A curtain at the far end of the entryway lifted aside, and a very young Pharaohan woman stepped through, to stand with downcast eyes and folded hands.

Auliss glanced toward her. "Oh, this is Meraclain, my bondservant. She's an excellent cook. While we eat, if you like, she can entertain us with some traditional songs of the desert. Her voice is quite passable."

Ruiz's throat was suddenly dry. Auliss was attractive, but Meraclain was beautiful—the difference between a gaudy artificial gem, and a cabochon of black opal. Meraclain had long, thick, black hair, brushed back from an oval high-cheekboned face. Her skin had the look of ivory velvet, her eyelashes were long, and her dark mouth curved to perfection. She wore a gauzy robe that concealed nothing of her body, which was elegantly spare, as handsome as her face.

"Mistress? You'll be wanting dinner for two?" When she spoke, the illusion of grace suffered somewhat. Her voice seemed rather nasal and whiny, and Ruiz made a note not to encourage her to sing. *Perhaps she dances,* he thought, and recovered some of his equilibrium. This evidence that he worked for slavers had cooled a bit of his ardor, but not enough to make him leave. *Perhaps,* he thought, *Auliss is no worse than I,* though this rationale did not comfort him entirely.

Auliss conveyed him into an inner atrium, where they dined under an armorglass bubble that revealed a disc of starry space.

The meal was tasty. Though Auliss told him that the seasonings were adjusted for pangalac tastes, Ruiz was still pleased by this evidence that his sojourn on Pharaoh might not be a culinary trial.

When they were done, Auliss went away for a few minutes, then reappeared in what seemed to be a pangalac adaptation of Pharaohan seraglio wear, a wispy aquamarine scarf that wrapped around one thigh, cinched her waist and then veiled her small breasts with a mist of color, to finish with a turn around her shoulder. Her skin was very smooth. She soon pointed out that the knot at her shoulder would succumb to a single tug, which he confirmed.

She made love with more enthusiasm than skill. Ruiz found this charming and disarming.

After a period in which they lay together, looking up through the bubble at the stars and sipping a sweet Pharaohan wine, she asked, "Shall I call Meraclain? I trained her myself, but she has a natural aptitude. I think it's a cultural thing."

Ruiz was momentarily tempted; but then he felt a flicker of weary distaste. And perhaps Auliss might take any interest in her bondservant for disappointment in her unassisted performance. "Another time, perhaps."

Auliss smiled, and Ruiz perceived that he had made the correct decision. "Perhaps. A shame you're not already wearing your Pharaohan disguise; we would ask her to critique its authenticity. How will you go? You could easily play the part of a noble, with your height and features."

"Alas! No such appealing role for me. I'll learn more and travel faster as a snake oil peddler than as a muckety, though my bed won't be as soft." Ruiz touched Auliss's breasts delicately and lay his head against them. She laughed and pulled him down into the cushions for a more measured exchange of pleasure.

An hour later, he had become restless, which Auliss sensed and seemed not to take personally. Perhaps she had kept company with other League agents whose mission-imperative allowed them little relaxation. After a while, she suggested that they dress and go up to the crew recreation area.

"Why not?" he said.

As they left, he glanced at Meraclain the bondservant. She returned his look boldly.

THE CREW AREA began with a broad corridor in the main module of the station. The station employed thousands of humans and a number of other beings, and at first glance it seemed to Ruiz that there was a different bar for each of these, marked by a string of glowing holosigns that disappeared around the curve of the hull.

Auliss tugged him toward one of these, called The Little Friend.

Inside, the bar was dark but for the bluish glow of a holotank in one corner. The tables clustered around the tank, and a dozen or so humans gathered there, intent on the flickering images.

"Come," Auliss said. "Let's see what we can see." She led him to a table, signaled a barmech, exchanged greetings with several of the others. It was soon apparent that she was a regular at The Little Friend.

The barmech provided them with drinks, a pale smoky brandy that Auliss recommended. Ruiz looked at the holotank, curious to see what Auliss found so entertaining.

The hot sunlight of Pharaoh glared on a dry wash, where three children, two girls and a boy, were playing some elaborate game. They seemed to be twelve or thirteen, just at the threshold of puberty.

The children stood a few meters apart from one another, in a roughly triangular pattern. At the feet of each was a pile of stones. The game seemed to involve guessing, bluffing, and physical agility. The children would engage in a vigorous dialogue, laughing and making faces, then at some unseen signal extend their hands, which would contain a varying number of stones. A shout would go up, and the children would dart for each other's bases. Occasionally a collision occurred, which was cause for more laughter. The tank's viewpoint shifted among the players, occasionally zooming in for a close-up of the boy, who had clean regular features, strong white teeth, and heavy-lashed sloe-shaped eyes.

All in all, an engaging scene, Ruiz thought, though, glancing at his fellow patrons, he wondered at the intense attention with which they watched the children.

"It's the boy," Auliss whispered. "He's the one."

What was she talking about? He started to ask her for a clarification, but the holotank switched modes. The scene of the playing children shrank down into the lower third of the tank, and a chubby smiling man, dressed as a Pharaohan, appeared in the top.

"Hello, hello," he said. "Key your bids now."

Ruiz felt his face grow stiff.

Auliss smiled eagerly at him. "I wish I could afford him, but he'll go too high for me. I had to scrimp for a sixmonth before I could get Meraclain. And she's getting a little old; she must be sixteen or seventeen by now. I'll have to start saving again." She seemed to sense his disapproval, though he struggled to keep it from showing on his face. "Oh, it's perfectly legal, Ruiz. The League allots its surface agents a personal quota, as long as they don't draw it from the traditional conjuror families, or any specially tagged specimens.

Only the conjurors can be profitably exported outsystem, after all. It's only fair compensation for the hardships of our life here, don't you think? And it makes our tour here on the platform so much more civilized."

Ruiz nodded, a bit jerkily. "I suppose." His flesh crawled a bit where she clutched his arm. All around them the other patrons were entering bids on the keypads set into the top of the table, in a murmur of excited anticipation.

A moment later, a spotlight flashed on, to pick out a heavy-jowled sweating man, whose companions whooped and thumped him on the back. "Oh, he won the boy cheap," said Auliss, looking quite vexed. But then she seemed to recover her good humor. "Well, perhaps I'll do as well next time. I can hope."

"Umm," Ruiz said, noncommittally. "Is it expensive to keep two bondservants?"

She ducked her head, a bit embarrassed. "Well, yes, actually—what with paying the life-support fees and the luxury penalties. But if I can't sell Meraclain to someone with different tastes, I'll have her mindwiped and released back into her natural environment. I'm not the sort that would space an unwanted helot, after all."

"I'm glad to hear it," Ruiz said dryly. He felt an overpowering desire to leave—to see the last of Auliss Moncipor. "Ah . . . it occurs to me that my instructions to the technician were insufficient . . . would you excuse me briefly?"

She nodded, and patted his arm absentmindedly, her attention already fixed on the holotank, which now displayed a scene of what Ruiz guessed to be a Pharaohan schoolyard. Scores of raggedly dressed children played on the hard-packed clay. The holocam swooped in to examine a small girl with delicate features and large violet eyes, who was speaking seriously to a crude doll.

Ruiz lurched forth from The Little Friend, stomach sour. He went directly down to the bay in which the *Vigia* rested, intent on leaving the platform as soon as possible.

He walked out onto the bay's wide steel floor, to see a figure in technician's overalls slide furtively from the *Vigia*'s dorsal drive tube. Instinctively, Ruiz hid behind a column of service plumbing, and observed.

The technician was a small slender man, who glanced about quickly and then drew a levitor pallet from the tube, upon which some rather large delicate object had been carried, judging from the loose straps and contoured blocks with which the pallet was equipped.

Ruiz's carefully nurtured paranoia flared up brightly. He followed the technician, gliding from covert to covert, as the man left the bay. The man stopped at a storeroom and guided the pallet inside. Ruiz stepped into the storeroom, making no sound. The technician, intent on stowing the pallet in a wall rack, did not notice him.

Ruiz kicked shut the door and seized the technician's arm. Pivoting, he slammed the technician into the wall, face first, hard enough to stun, but not hard enough to kill. The man bounced off the wall and fell on his back, face bloody. Ruiz knelt on his chest, patted him for weapons, found none.

"What did you do?" Ruiz asked, gently.

The man looked up through a red mask and tried to smile. He pushed bits of shattered teeth from his mouth. "Sir?"

"What did you do to my boat?"

"Maintenance, of course."

Ruiz took hold of the man's nose, which seemed broken, and gave it a vigorous twist. The man opened his mouth to shriek and Ruiz clamped his hand on the man's windpipe. Just before the man's eyes rolled up into his head, Ruiz released his grip. "No noise."

The man nodded, no longer smiling.

"We'll try again. What did you do to my boat? Don't dissemble; when I'm finished with you, I'll crawl up the tube and look, so you might as well tell me. While you're at it, tell me who ordered you to do whatever you did."

"Well, since you put it that way," the man said, and died.

Ruiz remained atop the corpse for a moment, watching the eyes glaze. Odd, he thought. Surely he hadn't banged the fellow into the wall *that* hard. A death net? But where would a conspirator find a Gench to do the work, here in this undeveloped system?

Ruiz took the technician's tool belt and trotted back into

the bay. At the vent, he discovered a tiny discolored pinhole where the technician had burned through the *Vigia*'s skin, disabling the sensor cable that serviced the tube. The *Vigia* would have been unable to report the invasion of her innards. He shinnied up the dorsal tube and found, emplaced into an injector nacelle, a rather large block of monocrystal explosive, enough to reduce the *Vigia* to a cloud of drifting molecules. He examined it with great care, found no booby traps or any evidence that it could be remotely detonated. Apparently the saboteur was relying on Ruiz to fire the tube on entry into Pharaoh's atmosphere, which was a simple and foolproof plan. It would have succeeded nicely but for the attack of distaste Ruiz had suffered in The Little Friend.

Ruiz detached the block and shinnied down the tube. He carried the block into the storeroom and set it next to the corpse, then hotfooted it back to the *Vigia,* which he entered and buttoned up for departure.

He had an uneasy moment when he signaled the bay to evacuate and open a takeoff slot. Would the bay respond?

A field flashed down the bay, squeezing the exterior air into the far end; Ruiz felt the field's passage as a tug at his viscera. The outer clamshell cracked open, and the stars blazed through.

Ruiz sat back. "Take us out," he told the *Vigia,* and she answered with a sweet harmonious tone, the sound of her engines. The boat swooped through the opening clamshell into free space, and Ruiz felt a sudden lightening of his spirit.

He accelerated around the curve of the world, crossed the terminator into the sunlight, and slowed for descent.

CHAPTER 5

RUIZ dropped into the murky steams of the uninhabitable lowlands, a hundred kilometers from the edge of the great plateau on which the Pharaohan culture had survived. The Pharaohans called the lands beneath the mists Hell, and Ruiz could see why. The temperature in the depths was just under the boiling point of water, the atmosphere was unbreathable, and the animals that lived in Hell were tough, dangerous, and as hideous as the most vividly imagined demons.

He guided the *Vigia* through the corrosive mists, until he hovered five hundred meters below the lip of the plateau, safe from the eyes of the Pharaohan priesthood, which maintained observatories along the top of the escarpment.

Then he considered the recent events. An attempt had been made to expunge him before he could begin his mission. The poachers therefore conspired with persons on the League's orbital platform. But who? The factor? The Dilvermooner was Ruiz's first and obvious choice; but the obvious choice wasn't always the right one. In an organization as far-flung as the League, interunit chicanery was an unfortunate constant. There could have been a half-dozen factions vying for advantage on the platform, which—like any other strategic outpost—boiled with intrigue. It might have been a one-man operation—just the tech, instructed to watch for League agents and then to take a run at arranging a fatal accident. Or . . . he suddenly wished he had not been so frank with Auliss Moncipor. Or it might indeed have been the factor, in which case Ruiz was still in considerable danger.

He devoted some thought to the matter, while the *Vigia* hovered in the steamy dark; then he issued orders and the boat began to move. As the *Vigia* passed around the perimeter of the plateau, she dropped radio repeaters at irregular intervals. The repeaters took up stations in the clouds.

Four hours later the *Vigia* had completed her circuit of the plateau. Ruiz touched the vidscreen, entered the factor's personal code. The signal flashed around the repeater string, beamed upward when it reached a randomly selected point, then jumped to another. Prinfilic answered immediately. "Hello? Ruiz Aw? Is that you?" The factor looked slightly rumpled, as though the hours since Ruiz's departure had been unpleasantly eventful.

Ruiz allowed the vid to transmit his image. "Yes, Ruiz Aw here."

"Where's *here*? I can't seem to get a fix on your position."

"Well. Just a precaution. Did you find the dead assassin?"

Prinfilic's eyes wavered slightly. "Yes," it said. "Assassin, you say?"

"Didn't you find the block of crystal?"

Prinfilic's odd smooth face went a shade paler. "Crystal? What crystal?"

Ruiz watched the herman closely. Either Prinfilic was a superb actor—not inconceivable—or the factor was not entirely in control of the situation on the platform.

"The crystal that I picked out of *Vigia*'s ass and left by the body. It was gone?"

Prinfilic drew a deep breath, and a muscle jumped in its jaw. "It was gone."

Ruiz smiled. "Then you have a problem, too, I'd guess.

At any rate, I'm forced to adopt a policy of compartmentalization. Apparently elements inimical to the League are operating in your organization. Would you agree?"

The factor glared from the screen, looking a little wild-eyed. But after a moment it nodded its elegant head. "So it seems."

"Here's how I must proceed, Factor. I'll dispatch a message drone to Dilvermoon, in case those inimical elements should detonate the crystal before you can find it. Meanwhile, I'll begin my investigations here on the surface. You for your part must immediately institute a blackout of orbit-to-surface communications. You understand the necessity for this?"

The factor was now visibly verging on hysteria. "But, my quotas—"

Ruiz cut him off. "This isn't open to discussion. If the channels remain open, who knows what dangerous instructions might reach those enemies I must deal with here below? The *Vigia* will monitor the spectrum, and release another drone, should anyone aboard the platform violate this order. Signify that you understand."

For a moment, Ruiz thought Prinfilic would defy him, but then the factor nodded, face suddenly grim.

Ruiz cut the transmission.

RUIZ SLEPT FOR a few hours, waiting for dark, and then prepared his disguise with meticulous care. He applied a long-term depilatory to his scalp. He instructed the medunit to apply the temporary tattoos he had chosen during the passage to Pharaoh, then endured the prickly sensations of the inkjets as they passed over his head. Afterward, he looked into the mirror and saw a barbaric stranger. The tattoos swirled over his skull in sinuous fine-lined patterns of clear red and dark magenta, curled down past his brows, emphasizing the sharp jut of cheekbone, the blade of his nose. Narrow eyes glared back at him, glittering with metallic intensity. He tried to smile at himself, but the effort lacked conviction and the smile never spread beyond his mouth. After a moment it metamorphosed into a snarl.

Ruiz shook himself and turned away from the mirror. He dressed in the bizarre finery of a snake oil peddler, many-colored layers of shredded and braided fabric, following the premise that the best disguise is often the most outlandish. The eye, he had found, slips uncritically over the details of an amazing sight. He was confident that no one would identify him as an offworlder. He congratulated himself that his tattoos were artful, and his own coppery skin and black eyes were fortuitously similar to the Pharaohan norm. He donned a half-dozen cheap-looking silver rings—microdevices which would enable him to perform the small illusions that were part of the obligatory social acts on Pharaoh. He applied kohl to his eyes, pasted a beauty star to his cheek, and attached earrings of silver and jet. Among his rags, he hid various weapons and tools, all disguised as Pharaohan religious objects—amulets, fetishes, icons.

When Ruiz was finally ready, he took up the special staff he'd designed and built in the *Vigia*'s workshop, put into his pouch a little splinter gun—disguised as a conjuror's wand—and then shrugged into his merchandise pack, which contained a good supply of the poison-derived drugs that would be his stock-in-trade. He trudged through the *Vigia* to the air lock. Standing in the lock, he gave the boat her final instructions. He breathed in the smells of pangalac civilization one last time, metal and plastic and ozone, machine oil and disinfectant.

He took a disposable rebreather and a set of climbing hooks from a locker. "Okay," he said. "Let's go up. Hover just under the cloud line."

Ruiz felt the tug of acceleration, as the *Vigia* swooped upward. He strapped the rebreather to his face and the climbing hooks to his feet.

Then the *Vigia* stopped and the lock fell open, the ramp just touching the face of the cliff. The corrosive steams of Hell rolled into the lock, and Ruiz darted out, leaping onto the cliffside, hooks humming. The hooks thrust steel rods into the crumbling rock and supported his weight. He turned to look at the *Vigia*, but she had already retracted her ramp and dropped down into the concealing murk, to wait for his return.

•   •   •

HE MOVED UP the few meters to the top of the clouds and paused. Cautiously he raised his head above the murk, into the clear Pharaohan night. Two of Pharaoh's three small moons rode high in the sky, giving enough light that Ruiz could easily see the Worldwall above him, and the nearest demonwatch tower, a hundred meters to his left, cantilevered out from the wall.

No lights showed from the tower; the Watchers kept their balconies dark, so that their night vision would remain acute. He dropped back down into the mists, to consider the situation. He had no great desire to remain on the cliff; monstrous predators might be gathering in the darkness below, climbing the cliff, hungry. On the other hand, he didn't want to find a patrol of demonkillers waiting for him at the top of the Worldwall, either, though that would be the lesser of the two evils. So he took several deep breaths from the rebreather, tugged it loose, and cast it away. Then he surged from the murk and slithered up the cliffside and then the Worldwall, moving over the dark stone as rapidly as a frightened lizard.

He reached the top of the Worldwall without incident, and was congratulating himself on having made a clean entry as he pulled himself over the parapet. But as he unstrapped the climbing hooks from his feet, he heard a quick shuffle behind him. He whirled, to see a tall thin man in the livery of the Watchers rushing at him with a nasty-looking trident. As the man opened his mouth to shriek a warning to the other Watchers, Ruiz swayed aside from the man's thrust and in the same motion struck out with the one set of climbing hooks he had removed. The hooks sank into the man's throat, just above the collarbone, and the shout turned into an unpleasant bubbling sound. Ruiz caught the trident before it could clatter on the stone. The unfortunate Watcher toppled off the Worldwall and fell silently into Hell.

Ruiz crouched under the parapet, hoping the alarm had not been raised.

A few minutes passed, and all remained quiet. While he waited, Ruiz had leisure to regret the killing of the Watcher, who was only doing his job—preventing the Hell monsters from raiding the edges of the plateau and making sure that the Hell gods stayed below. Ruiz felt a deep melancholy, a sensation he suffered whenever his work caused him to hurt an innocent person. He wondered, at such times, why he continued to do what he did, and at the moment he could think of no answer that pleased him. Did the Watcher have a family? Would they be waiting for him to come home from his stint on the Worldwall? An unhappy little drama played out in Ruiz's mind. He saw wide-eyed children watching at the window of a hut; he saw an apprehensive woman, pretending unconcern for the children's sake. He saw weeping and bitter regret—all, all, his fault.

After a while he forced himself to put those thoughts away. He slipped down the steps cut into the inner wall and stole away into the Pharaohan night.

BY DAYLIGHT RUIZ was trudging along a dusty road, which struck straight as a string through a great planting of catapple trees. As the sun rose, peasants came from small huts set back under the wiry branches and began to tend the trees, which were hung with buckets and piping arranged to collect the thin sap. The peasants, thickset round-faced men and women burned almost black by the Pharaohan sun, watched Ruiz with narrow suspicious eyes and would not speak to him, even when he leaned on the stone wall that rose at either side of the road and waved at them. He recalled that except on rare and profoundly celebratory occasions, the peasantry could not afford the pleasure drugs the snake oil peddlers distributed and, naturally enough, resented the idle grasshopper existence of the snake oil men.

He shrugged and went on, until he came to an open area in which men wearing leg irons toiled to remove the stumps of dead trees from the dry powdery soil. Several overseers in white-and-red-checked kilts stood about, occasionally touching the more laggardly prisoners with short limber whips.

Ruiz paused again and beckoned to one of the overseers, a tall cadaverous man with sunken cheeks and the jagged blue tattoos of a second-class coercer. The overseer stared at him, expressionless, for a long moment, then ambled to the wall and stood slapping the butt of his whip into his palm. He said nothing.

Ruiz smiled and ducked his head obsequiously. "Noble coercer, might I trouble you for a drink of water?"

The overseer studied him, then spoke abruptly. "Show me your plaque," he ordered.

Ruiz nodded submissively and fumbled out a small slab of glossy porcelain into which a forged seal had been pressed, and on which a line of graceful cursive characters had been brushed in black slip. All Pharaohans who traveled beyond their home nomarchy were required to carry the plaques, which described their identity and permitted activities. "Here, here . . . all's in order."

The overseer snatched the plaque, examined it closely. After a moment he grunted and returned it. "Can you pay? No charity here; a measure will cost you a full copper nint."

Making a great show of searching through his rags, Ruiz produced a small worn six-cornered coin and proffered it to the overseer. The overseer pocketed it and turned back to his charges, who had slowed their efforts slightly. The overseer shouted irritably at his subordinates; they applied their whips with vigor.

At the far edge of the cleared area stood a battered steam wagon under a ragged canopy. In the small patch of shade was a tripod, which supported a large, red clay water urn. Ruiz vaulted the wall and made his way past the prisoners, who watched him sidelong from red-rimmed eyes.

When he reached the wagon, a small scowling man with a smear of black grease across his forehead appeared from the interior of the wagon, holding a large wrench. From his rough brown robe, identical to the prisoners' garb, Ruiz assumed him to be a trusty. Like the other freeborn prisoners, his tattoos were obscured by strips of shiny pink scar tissue, but enough remained to show that the trusty had once been a snake oil man. Ruiz repressed an apprehensive shudder.

"Ah, good sir," Ruiz said, grinning broadly. "Perhaps you'll help me."

"Unlikely," the small man said, with no change of expression.

Ruiz retained his smile. "Yon noble coercer was kind enough to sell me a measure of water."

The trusty laughed, a short, explosive, humorless bark. " 'Noble coercer,' indeed. You're Rontleses' friend?"

"Not I. I'm just a seller of dreams, just a wayfarer."

"In that case I'll assist you." The trusty put down the wrench and hobbled toward the urn. Ruiz saw that his legs had been broken and allowed to heal unset.

"What did he skin you out of, our noble Rontleses? May milliscorps colonize his crotch." The trusty held out his dirty hand. "Give me your skin, wayfarer."

"A copper nint," Ruiz said, and gave over his water skin, which was empty. The trusty laughed bitterly again, fished a key out of his pouch, and unlocked the urn. He turned a tap and cloudy water flowed into Ruiz's skin. "It's stinkwater, you know," the trusty said conversationally. "Give you the green shits for sure."

Ruiz received the full skin, hoping that his immunizations had been sufficiently comprehensive. "Thank you, good sir," he said, and took a swig. It was, as promised, foul. He repressed the urge to gag. He recorked the skin and hung it about his neck.

The trusty shrugged and relocked the urn. "Don't thank me. Or curse me when your guts turn to slime. I'd have given you some from the overseers' private store, if I'd dared. But I'd rather not have my legs broken again; next time I might not learn to walk so well."

Ruiz declared himself satisfied, at which the trusty looked at him as though a diagnosis of madness had been confirmed. "Well, if one's to be a fool, better a happy fool than a sour one," the trusty said.

"Well said. Perhaps you'd advise me?"

"Why not, so long as Rontleses doesn't notice my absence from the belly of his junk pile."

"What can you tell me of Stegatum? Is it a convivial town?" Stegatum was the capital of the local nomarchy, a center for processing catapple sap and other agricultural products. It lay another five kilometers down the road, and a League agent maintained an inn there.

The trusty made a gesture of dismissal and spat. "Stegatum? It's an armpit like any other armpit. The farmers will show little interest in your wares, but a few merchants and craftsmen scratch out a living there, and, of course, it has the usual glut of dungheap nobility."

Ruiz scratched his chin, as if thoughtful. "Can you recommend a good inn?"

The trusty laughed uproariously, which attracted the attention of the overseer. The trusty sobered instantly, picked up his wrench again, and faded back into the wagon's depths.

Ruiz left, saluting the overseer respectfully as he passed. He wondered what sin the trusty had committed to be condemned to one of the nomarch's slave gangs. The snake oil men were accorded greater latitude than other minor merchants—if less respect. They were commonly held to be mad, due to the constant and necessary sampling of the hallucinogens they traded in, so that their eccentricity was tolerated, and in some quarters even admired. All in all, Ruiz was happy with the disguise he had chosen, but the condition of the gimpy prisoner indicated that it was not a perfect one.

The road passed the last of the catapple plantations and rose into a more pitilessly arid region, a terrain of large gray boulders sparsely distributed over flats of pink quartz gravel. Ruiz followed the track for hours, seeing little but an occasional steamwagon. These freight carriers were driven by gaunt women in faded blue robes, none of whom wasted a glance on Ruiz. He learned quickly to move aside when he saw the first cloud of dust. Twice men passed him riding striderbeasts—tall, bipedal, reptilian creatures, covered by fine scales and moving with a smooth elegant gait. One animal was black and the other a tarnished green, and both wore silver-mounted saddles and jeweled bridles. Neither rider acknowledged Ruiz's greeting, though he saluted respectfully.

By midafternoon Ruiz was descending a potholed side

road into a less barren valley, which contained extensive gardens and, at the far end where the valley was deepest, a huddle of one- and two-storied mud houses, shaded by the feathery fronds of tall old dinwelt trees. On a flat bench just above the village was a public square, the so-called Place of Artful Anguish, a standard amenity in every village and town on Pharaoh. Above that the waste began again.

In the valley, the air was marginally cooler and a bit moister, and Ruiz felt a sense of pleasant arrival.

A half-dozen small boys appeared at the roadside to stare at him with large eyes. They assembled in a line, ranked from tallest to shortest, and they held various bits of homemade paraphernalia, stickhoops and tanglestrings and improvised coin-snaps, with which they had evidently been playing conjuror. Ruiz smiled at them. They edged away slightly, but said nothing.

"Hello, noble young gentlemen," Ruiz said.

"Ain't such," the boldest of them answered defiantly.

Ruiz spread his hands in a gesture of disbelief. "How was I to know, unfamiliar as I am with your lovely environs?"

"Talks funny," said another of the urchins.

"Ought to know we're not sirs. Sirs don't stink of the lizard tannery, or wear cloutcloth. Sirs be riding on strider-beasts." This was contributed by the smallest of the boys, who spoke with careful logic. The others rolled their eyes, and the first speaker tugged the smallest one's ragged hat down over his face.

"He's young yet," the first speaker explained.

"I see," said Ruiz, struggling to control a grin. "Well, perhaps you can assist me, since you seem to be well informed. Is there a decent inn here in Stegatum, for so I hear your lovely village is called?"

The boldest boy rubbed his pointed chin. "Depends what you'd call decent. How swank're your notions?"

"Not impossibly so. A bed free of wildlife, and decent food will satisfy the most extreme of my hopes."

"Then the Denklar Lodge comes closer than the Pougribalt Roadhouse. You staying the night?"

"Such is my plan."

"Smart. You heard of the trouble on the Worldwall? Last night, not thirty kilometers from here, a demon came over the edge and ate a Watcher whole. It'll be running the back country tonight, looking for another dinner. Tonight's a good night to snooze behind a strong door, and the Denklar wins on that count too. Costs, though." The boldest urchin delivered this speech in calm tones of relish.

"Thank you. I'll take your advice." Ruiz hitched up his pack and would have gone on, but the boys watched him with greater expectation than his outlandish appearance warranted. He recalled that they might expect a new bit of conjuring from a stranger who was inclined to be friendly, so he sighed and nodded.

White smiles broke out on the dark faces.

"Watch my hand, then," Ruiz instructed them, and showed them both sides of his right hand, then slowly clenched his hand into a fist. They watched with an intensity beyond their years.

One of Ruiz's rings budded, into the interior of his fist, a tiny bit of memory crystal, which quickly grew into the semblance of a red garnet the size of a thimble.

He opened his hand to show the gem. The boys weren't yet impressed, though they were polite enough to wait for something more notable. "Can't be real," said the smallest boy, dubiously, for which he received a swat on the shoulder.

Ruiz laughed. "No, indeed, it's not a real garnet; in fact, it's the rare and lovely chrysalis of the fabulous ruby-winged flitterbuzz."

"So you say," said the smallest boy, not discouraged. But he looked intrigued, as did the others.

"Watch again," Ruiz instructed them. He cupped his other hand over the garnet, then crushed his hands together. The crystal collapsed into glitter dust, soundlessly, unseen by his audience. His ring extruded another bit of crystal, and Ruiz felt it stir with the semblance of life. After a moment, he opened his hands, and a tiny winged insect straightened its shimmering wings. It sat on his hands for an instant, then fluttered and launched itself upward. It would climb toward the sun until its energy cell was exhausted, and then it would dissolve into drifting powder.

Ruiz flung the glitter dust at the boys, who laughed their appreciation.

"Not bad," the smallest one said.

Ruiz bowed low and resumed his way toward the village.

CHAPTER 6

NISA, favored daughter of the King, reclined on a divan. Blue Hellsilk covered the cushions; looking down, she admired the contrast between that vivid color and the smooth flesh of her naked body. "Sweet," she said with a sigh.

Her favorite bondswoman, Delie, rubbed her feet, slow warm strokes that sent pleasurable chills up Nisa's legs. Allabab, her favorite bondsman, massaged scented oil into her shoulders. His hands were strong and careful, and Nisa gave herself to the delight of the moment.

Allabab spoke softly. "Will there be lessons today, Princess?"

Nisa turned her head so that she could see the cool greens of the King's gardens, visible through an open casement window. The sound of running water came luxuriously to her ears, and she was suddenly very glad to be a princess. "Perhaps," she said. "Perhaps we'll have a lesson in the garden."

Allabab's hands stiffened, became slightly less cunning. But after a moment he resumed his skillful attentions. "That might not be safe, Princess. The garden has unfriendly ears. Sometimes."

Nisa laughed a little. "I'm the favored daughter. Who'd dare listen?"

"As you say, Princess." His voice warmed with anticipation, and his hands moved down her body, as Delie's moved upward—to meet in pleasurable cooperation.

"Oh," Nisa said, dreamily. "It's so nice to be Nisa."

NISA TOOK LUNCH on the highest terrace of the palace. A cooling breeze ruffled the white canopy over her lounge as she looked out over her father's capital. The palace rose from the crest of the hill on which the city was built, so that she could see beyond the city's high walls, far out into the waste.

She ate sweet pinkmelon and little triangles of spiced meat in pastry. The wine was a pale green Sestale, so good that she drank more than she had intended.

After a while, a bit tipsy, she fell to musing on the circumstances that had made her life so wonderful.

Long ago, in the First Days, her ancestors had chosen to travel from place to place entertaining the struggling First People with grubby little illusions—instead of applying themselves to the hard necessities of wresting a living from the ungenerous soil of Pharaoh.

She went to the parapet and leaned against the stone. "You weren't very smart," she said to all the anonymous folk below, the faceless ones who labored to make her life good. "We were." How odd to think that those long-dead vagabonds and their cheap tricks had founded the dynasty of her glorious father—Bhasrahmet, King of Kings, Paramount Lord of all Pharaoh.

But, how amusing!

She laughed. A good thing, she thought, that in the First Days the conjurors hadn't yet grown skillful enough to attract the attention of the gods. Else her ancestors might have been carried to the Land of Reward, and Nisa never born.

"Such a shame *that* would have been," she said. She set

the porcelain goblet on the edge of the parapet and looked down. Far below, small shapes bustled across the courtyard —servants on errands, tradesmen, soldiers.

For a moment, the courtyard cleared. Nisa put her finger to the goblet and gave it a tiny push.

It fell, tumbling slowly in the harsh sunlight, sending back flashes of white.

She turned away before it struck.

THE NIGHTMARE BEGAN in the garden, an hour later. She was instructing Delie from a book of fables, correcting her bondswoman's pronunciation. Allabab watched over Delie's shoulder, waving a fan in slow distraction.

" 'Bhas watches from below,' " said Delie, carefully, pronouncing the god's name in the proper aspirated manner.

A cold presence seemed to come into the garden; it chilled Nisa's back. For a moment, she thought it was the mention of the dread god's name, and was amused at her reaction. Then Allabab gasped and fell facedown, dropping his fan. Delie made a small cry and turned away.

Nisa looked over her shoulder, to see the thin frozen face of the Paramount Priest, watching through the fronds of a pitcher fern. His obsidian eyes were fixed on the book of fables that lay open on her lap. She closed the book, feeling the first touch of fear.

The Paramount Priest stepped from his place of concealment. "So, it's true," he said heavily. Three of the King's personal guard emerged from the bushes, eyes averted.

Nisa could think of nothing to say, so she lifted her chin and waited for the Paramount Priest to speak again.

He sat on the bench, close to her. "Nisa, your father will be sad." He gestured; the King's men jerked her bondservants to their feet and led them away. Allabab went silently and Delie stifled a sob. Nisa could not seem to take her eyes from the Paramount Priest.

He patted her knee with one frail hand. "I'm sorry it's come to this, Nisa, but what choice have I? No one objected to your taking lovers from the underpeople; a woman of your station is entitled to her pets. But one mustn't give those pets the means to power. You knew better. What evil impulse drove you to teach them to read?"

Her throat was almost too dry for her voice to come out. "I'm not sure. It seemed harmless . . . I thought they might enjoy reading the fables themselves; they loved to hear me tell the old stories."

The Paramount Priest shook his head sadly. "First the fables. Then the lore books, then the slaves learn how to break the cisterns and we all dry to death. Surely you were instructed in this progression, Nisa."

"Yes . . . but they were more than slaves. They were friends." Her voice broke, and suddenly she could look away from the Paramount Priest. She looked at the garden, with its deep greens and softly colored flowers, its cool sweet damp, and the tiny lovely sounds of the birds that hopped and flitted through the shadows. She felt a sharp tearing pain in her heart. *All gone now. Not mine any longer. How could I have been so foolish, so arrogant?* she thought.

"Now I must order your 'friends' given to the desert. A pointless waste of expensive stock. And I must give you to Expiation, which grieves me, and will break your father's heart. But I must." The Paramount Priest looked genuinely mournful, and Nisa was moved to pat his hand and smile.

"I understand," she said. But she did not.

CRIMINALS GENERALLY AWAITED Expiation locked in the iron boxes that stood in the Place of Artful Anguish; this torture was part of their punishment. They died in Expiations of standardized form. One whose crime or station was especially notable would be housed in the Temple, under the care of the priests, until a suitably instructive Expiation could be arranged. Nisa's crime and station were both great, and so she was locked up in the Paramount Priest's personal dungeon.

Her cell was austere, but not uncomfortable. Twice a day, she was given a plain meal, and twice a week she was allowed to bathe, using a basin and a rag. The jailers were courteous but silent. Loneliness displaced some of her fear. She received no visitors.

Occasionally her rest was disturbed by the screams of other prisoners being questioned in the room at the end of the corridor. As she had freely admitted her guilt, no such attentions were considered necessary in her case, and so she had much time to reflect upon her follies. She quickly developed a great contempt for the person she had been. Had she acted out of a desire to improve the lot of her bondsfolk? No, she thought bitterly. She was teaching them to read not from some noble purpose, but out of the same idle urge to amusement that might cause her to teach a pet dustlizard to stand on its hind legs and beg for sweetmeats.

A month passed, and then another.

At some point she began to hope, to believe that her father would never let her die a hideous death. She was, after all, *Nisa*.

But he never came. And one day the Paramount Priest arrived, ancient face stiff with resolve, to convey her to the conjurors who would perform her Expiation.

CHAPTER 7

THE Denklar Lodge was a low rambling building, well kept and newly whitewashed, with many muslin-screened windows. The League agent who ran it apparently took some pride in his ostensible occupation.

Ruiz entered the common room, which at that early hour was occupied only by three idlers, who sat together in a dark corner, nursing small tankards of barberry ale.

The proprietor stood behind the low bar, wiping mugs with a dank cloth. At first glance he appeared to be a plump Pharaohan of middle age, bearing the tattoos of the publican's guild. Ruiz's second glance detected subtly wrong details; an un-Pharaohan directness of glance, an indefinably urban stance, a gloss of health.

The man—who would certainly prove to be Vilam Denklar, Agent Second Class—fixed a disapproving look on his face. "Can you pay for what you consume, wanderer? We have little charity to spare in Stegatum."

Ruiz bowed and smiled cheerfully. "As elsewhere. Yes, I can pay, if rates are reasonable."

"Hmph. Well, the rates are posted." Denklar indicated a

slate board on which was chalked a schedule of prices. "Can you read?"

"A little," Ruiz said, squinting ostentatiously at the board.

After a bit, he ordered a barberry ale, which he paid for and took to the side. He sat quietly on a bench and relaxed, sipping occasionally from the mug of ale. After his night and day of exertion, he foresaw little danger of insomnia that night.

Dark fell before Ruiz finished his ale, which had an unpleasant resinous quality and was sour. But eventually his hunger grew to exceed his weariness, so he stirred himself and went into the inn's adjacent dining room. He found a table in a dark corner and sat down expectantly. Time passed, and the room filled with local craftsmen, and a few well-off farmers who presumably preferred the inn's cuisine to that of their wives.

Plates of aromatic stew, loaves of dark bread, and tall tankards began to appear in front of these customers, fetched in by two skinny young slaves. No one came to take Ruiz's order.

The serving boys began to turn uneasy glances toward him as they passed back and forth. Still, they didn't pass closely enough for Ruiz to reach out and snag one, so finally he sighed and rose from his seat. He followed one of them into the kitchen, where Vilam Denklar supervised three sweating cooks.

On noticing Ruiz, Denklar whirled to stare at him in annoyance. "What do you want? I can offer no employment."

Ruiz smiled in a friendly manner. "What about supper? Can you offer that?"

Denklar scowled. "You can pay? I'll take none of your potions in trade. It's a fool who buys oil from a wandering nonesuch."

Ruiz produced two worn silver coins, caused them to ripple across the back of his hand and then vanish. "Will that buy me a supper, a night on clean bedding, and breakfast?"

Denklar no longer scowled, though he didn't smile, either. "Might be so, if they're real. One felk in advance; that buys you supper, if you're not too famous a trencherman. The other in the morning—for lodging and porridge with water and scirfruit."

"A bargain," Ruiz said. "I'll return to the dining room, aquiver with anticipation."

"First the coin."

"Certainly," Ruiz said, and caught a silver felk from the air. He laid it respectfully on the counter and returned to his table.

A few moments later the serving boy set a plate of stew before him. In a thick white gravy floated pieces of pale meat and waxy chunks of some mottled pink and blue root.

Ruiz attempted the authentic cuisine of Pharaoh for the first time, beginning cautiously, and then proceeding more enthusiastically. It was, he decided, not nearly as bad as he might have feared, though rather heavy-handedly spiced with pepper and some unfamiliar bittersweet herb.

When Ruiz was finished, a serving boy came and conducted him to his room. They passed Denklar in the hall, where the innkeeper was berating a charwoman for some minor offense.

"You set a fine table," Ruiz said, smiling. "As good as the Acorn's Ancestor, almost." The Acorn's Ancestor was a widely esteemed establishment convenient to the League's Dilvermoon headquarters, frequented by League crew on furlough. Ruiz fixed a significant glance on the innkeeper, and then winked.

Denklar's mouth fell open briefly, but he clamped it shut and returned to abusing his employee. Ruiz went on.

The room was hardly bigger than a broom closet, but the straw was clean and even the blanket appeared free of vermin. The only window was protected by close-set iron bars; it overlooked the Place of Artful Anguish, which was empty but for several upright man-sized iron boxes. Ruiz lit the small oil lamp that sat on the corner table, set his splinter gun/magewand within easy reach, and pulled off his sandals. His feet were a bit tender, so he rubbed them with a soothing ointment while he waited for Denklar to appear.

A moth with gauzy green wings emerged from some

crevice and circled the lamp. In the minutes that followed, Ruiz finally began to feel the precariousness of his position —alone on a strange and dangerous world, without friends or allies. The feeling was not precisely self-pity, but it was close enough that Ruiz felt somewhat disgusted with himself.

Many times he had found himself in similar situations, and not succumbed to such maudlin thoughts. What was wrong with him? The image of Nacker came to him suddenly. What had Nacker done to him, that he should suddenly feel so vulnerable? He shook his head and tried to empty his mind of distraction. To some extent he succeeded, though he was still conscious of a formless discontent.

When Denklar came through the door, Ruiz snatched up the splinter gun.

"Why do you point your wand at me?" Denklar said heavily. "Will you transform me into a hoptoad?"

Ruiz twitched the wand to the side and fired a splinter into the doorjamb. The masonry shuddered from the impact, and Denklar paled slightly. He raised empty hands. "No offense. Just an attempt at humor. And I hope you don't hold it against me, the way I acted earlier. Just staying in character, doing my job." His voice had changed, become lighter and more fluid, and he spoke in the pangalac lingua franca.

Ruiz frowned at this carelessness. "Can anyone hear us here?"

"No, no. I put you where the walls are thickest—and the window looks out to the Place of Artful Anguish and the waste. The snake oil men sometimes scream in the night, which disturbs the other patrons. Anyone who spends the night in the square doesn't care about the screams of others, or so I conjecture."

Ruiz pointed the wand elsewhere, though he didn't put it down. "Reassuring. I'll have to remember to shriek occasionally."

Denklar grinned, rather unpleasantly. "Not too loud, please. The local muckety, Lord Brinslevos, is entertaining two commoner doxies in the honeymoon suite. If you disturb him, you'll end your career yodeling on an antheap—

and there won't be a thing I can do about it. Touchy, is his lordship. I recommend that you avoid his notice, if possible, though that may not be easy. He's a man for the oil, and he's probably already heard about you."

Ruiz blinked. "I appreciate the advice."

"My job. Now," said Denklar, rubbing his hands together, "to business. Who are you and what brings you to Stegatum?"

Ruiz brought forth his identity plaque and fingered it in a particular way. The white porcelain became transparent, to reveal a glowing golden torc, identifying him as a League agent with Uberfactorial carte blanche.

Denklar seemed impressed. His wide face showed a sheen of sweat, though the air was growing chill. "I see," he said.

Ruiz put the plaque away. "Good. I can tell you this much: I'm here to analyze certain operational deficiencies. And when I'm done, heads may roll."

"Not mine, I'm certain. My job description is simple and exact. I watch for unauthorized technology, I provide housing for League agents visiting the region, and I try to check the worst of Brinslevos's impulses. . . ."

"Oh?"

"Yes, of course—we want life to be hard for the peasants, else what pressure would drive them to excellence in conjuring? After all, it's the only way out, for an ambitious child. But revolutions are too likely to breed unwelcome change, and Brinslevos is particularly careless of his property."

"Ah." Ruiz examined Denklar carefully. No doubt the innkeeper had things to hide; what League employee did not? The crucial question was this: Was Denklar a part of the faction which had tried to eliminate Ruiz, and if so, had the conspirators been able to communicate new instructions to Denklar regarding Ruiz? It seemed at least possible to Ruiz that there had not been sufficient time to formulate a policy and give the necessary orders. In any case, Denklar had reacted to the sudden appearance of a stranger at his inn with no perceptible anxiety, which argued for his innocence—or lack of information. And to suspect every League agent on Pharaoh of duplicity was probably feckless paranoia. Possibly.

Denklar shifted uneasily. "How may I assist you?"

Ruiz allowed him to fidget, while Ruiz maintained a frown of officious suspicion. "Well," he finally said, "I'll tell you later. For now, I'll stay at your inn, sell a little oil, and soak up the lay of the land. Acclimate. You've noticed the blackout from the orbital station?"

Denklar seemed startled. "Actually . . . no. We have spy beads active here, of course, beaming data up to the platform, but very little downlink traffic. This is an unimportant station, after all. Any child who shows any talent for conjuring is immediately sold off to a mage school in one of the major towns, so no serious collecting occurs here." A light seemed to switch on behind Denklar's eyes. "You're here to investigate the poachers, aren't you?"

Ruiz frowned more severely. "My mission is classified. Don't be inquisitive. The blackout I mentioned now includes your uplink; my boat is monitoring the spectrum for violations. It's a very good boat."

"Of course, of course. Well, count on me. What shall I call you, by the way?"

"Call me Wuhiya. Don't alter your behavior toward me, except to permit me to peddle my wares in your common room."

"I wish you wouldn't. Word may get around, and then I'll have snake oil men infesting every corner."

"You can handle it." Ruiz was suddenly very tired. "Go away now; we'll talk more in the morning."

Denklar left, clearly unhappy. Ruiz barred the door, then set out various alarms and mantraps, which might preserve his life if enemies arrived while he slept.

Just before Ruiz was ready for bed, the green moth flew into the lamp and perished in a puff of twinkling sparks.

&&&&&&&&&&&&&&&&&&&&&&&&&&

CHAPTER 8

A hundred kilometers away, in the stone town of Kobatum, a man sat at a table, eyes blank, mouth stretched into a shape of soundless pleasure. Occasionally he jerked and his eyes rolled. On the table before him was a small box of black plastic, from which a flat cable led to a strapped-on inducer at the base of his skull.

Far above, at the edge of the sky, a cloud of minute objects skipped through the first traces of atmosphere. Some took too steep a dive and burned up, but the rest eventually fell safely into the stratosphere.

When they reached thicker air, they sprouted tiny wings and shot off in all directions. An hour later they had scattered to every region of Pharaoh's habitable plateau, seeking out pheromonic beacons.

One settled just inside the man's window. It mated its tiny interface with the receiver that sat on the sill, activating a low insistent alarm, a pulsing note that could not be heard outside the man's rooms.

When his pleasure device timed out, the man noticed the alarm and pulled off the inducer.

"What now?" he said tonelessly, addressing the empty room.

He went to the receiver and punched the button that shut off the alarm. The message from orbit fed itself onto the receiver's small screen, and the man bent to watch it scroll up:

UBERFACTORIAL AGENT ON PHARAOH, PROBABLY DISGUISED AS ITINERANT SNAKE OIL MAN. EXTREME THREAT TO OP-ERATIONS. CARRIES GENCHA DEATH NET. IDENTIFY AND DISPOSE UNTRACEABLY. PROCEED WITH MAXIMUM CAUTION.

Following the message a grainy picture appeared. A lean handsome face stared boldly from the screen—a confident purposeful face.

"Maximum caution," the man muttered irritably. He plucked the messenger from the device and crushed it be-tween his fingers, rolling it into a tiny ball of foil. He flipped it out the window, and sat down to think. In all likelihood, the agent was working someone else's sector, and thus was someone else's problem. *Just as well,* he thought. He pre-ferred his kills simple, direct, intimate. This assignment would require a frustratingly indirect approach.

Still, a kill was a kill, and he began to hope that the agent would be foolish enough to stray into his sector. He laid out his own disguise, which was also the ragged finery of a snake oil peddler. "Apparently," he said to himself, "we think alike." He checked his tattoos, which were bright. He made certain that his weapons were charged and in perfect repair. He set out his stock of snake oil and made sure that none of the vials was too far past its prime. He packed a few little pangalac luxuries—bootleg skinjectors, proscribed neural inducers, black market entertainment skeins—these he'd use to bribe other League agents, when their cooperation was necessary. All these things he arranged in neat patterns on his table, because he was a man who was careful and partic-ular.

Finally, he went to the wall and opened a secret compartment in the stone. In the compartment he hid all the pangalac artifacts he would leave behind. Then he lay on his pallet and rested, waiting for morning. But he did not sleep; he lay in the dark with eyes wide open, his mouth fixed in a trembling smile.

AT DAYBREAK, RUIZ AW awakened to the sound of jingling harness and shouting, sounds which drifted faintly through his window. There was some unusual quality in the shouts, some discordant vitality that attracted Ruiz's curiosity. A glance through his window revealed nothing but the empty square, with its sinister boxes, and the waste, gray and empty under the dawning light. He rose from the bed and went out into the hall, though the mud floor was icy under his bare feet.

At the end of the hall was a curtained window that looked into the inn's courtyard. Ruiz moved the curtain slightly and peered out.

A tall slender noble in black hunting leathers stood in the courtyard, shrieking at two ostlers, who were trying to saddle a huge striderbeast. The beast was highly strung, it appeared, and the noble seemed to be taking a perverse pleasure in making the ostlers' job more difficult, shouting at just the moment the men were poised to clap the saddle on the beast.

"Hurry, can't you, oafs? The sun'll be down before you finish!"

The nobleman's face drew Ruiz's attention. It was typical of the Pharaohan peerage, narrow and fine boned—though in this case distorted by madness. The mouth pulsed, the eyes bulged, and two spots of hectic color emphasized the prominent cheekbones. Ruiz presumed that this was the local nomarch, Lord Brinslevos.

A moment later, when the ostlers seemed on the verge of success, Brinslevos darted forward and struck the striderbeast with his quirt, so that it curvetted away from the man who was trying to control it. The ostlers shot bitter glances at the noble, but made no protest.

Finally, relenting or growing bored, Brinslevos allowed

the saddle to be cinched. He vaulted gracefully onto the beast. He made the beast rear and the ostlers scattered. "Good-bye," Brinslevos shouted, mouth stretched wide with some fey emotion, and galloped forth. The sound of his going slowly died away.

Ruiz turned away from the window and returned to his room, unaccountably depressed. He sat on his bed and gathered his resolve. Finally he turned to making plans.

When he eventually appeared for his breakfast, the dining hall was empty and the porridge had gone stone-cold stiff, but a handsome young woman wearing a dirty shift bustled in and cut him a generous slice. He guessed she might be one of the "commoner doxies" Denklar had mentioned in connection with Brinslevos. She had a dusky bruise on her cheek and moved too carefully, but she seemed cheerful enough otherwise. She occasionally smiled at him, as she went about the dining hall collecting the dirty dishes, and he smiled back.

When he had finished the porridge, he leaned back in his chair and began to pick his teeth with the needle-point bodkin he carried on a chain around his neck. His attention, for some reason, fixed on the doxy's legs. Her legs were long and smooth and brown, and her feet had the healthy beauty of feet that had never known shoes.

He pulled his gaze away and fixed it again on the empty porridge bowl. He was beginning to feel a bit frightened by his undisciplined thoughts. Nacker had certainly tampered with his priorities. He would have to watch himself very carefully, until he could get this over with and get to another trustworthy minddiver. If he lived to see Nacker again, he would have to discourage the freak from exercising his sense of humor at Ruiz's expense. Ruiz shook his head. If he allowed himself to be distracted at a crucial point, he might not get to repay Nacker for his little joke. And wouldn't that be a shame?

He forced his thoughts back into productive channels. First, he'd spend a few days selling oil to the local yokels. He'd try to pick up the texture of Pharaoh; his head was full to bursting with facts and dialects and sociological analyses —but these existed in a cold intellectual void. He needed to know what it was to *be* a Pharaohan, before he could safely move toward his objective. He'd deliberately chosen to emerge in this obscure backwater, to give himself a bit of respite from intrigue. He'd relax and merge more thoroughly with his snake oil man persona, and then he'd go about his business. The mission-imperative twitched in the depths of his mind, causing a tiny stab of pain behind his eyes, but then it settled back into quiescence; apparently it would permit him the delay.

The doxy finished with the clearing up and came to sit at his table without waiting for an invitation. "Hello," she said, flashing white teeth.

"Hello," he said, returning the bodkin to its sheath.

"What a pretty little knife," she said.

"Thank you. My mother gave it to me; she said it would protect me from dangerous women."

"Has it worked?"

He sighed theatrically. "Not recently. But I continue to hope, quite faithfully."

She laughed, apparently delighted. "You're not very gallant."

He fixed a look of comic tragedy on his face. "Alas, I'm not very rich, either."

She hitched her chair closer to his and laid a warm hand on his arm. "I'd make you a special price. One entertainer to another. Or we'll barter."

He smiled. But his anxieties about Nacker and his determination to keep his mind on his business had combined to cool his ardor. "That's extremely kind of you. I might hold you to it."

She apparently sensed his dispassion, but didn't seem to resent it. She patted his arm in a friendly manner. "Let me know. My name is Relia. And yours?"

"Wuhiya. Sometimes known as Wuhiya the Too-Little-Too-Soon."

She laughed again. "Somehow I doubt it. Besides, that can be better than too-much-too-long. For example, last night . . ." Her expression darkened.

But then she smiled and went back into the kitchen,

swaying pleasantly. Ruiz watched her go, feeling a little wistful.

A few minutes later, Denklar bustled in and sat down. "What are your plans now?" Denklar asked, looking somewhat rumpled, as though his night had been restless.

"I'll set up in your common room. I won't work hard at stealing your customers, and if anyone asks, I'll say you're getting a third of what I make."

"Yes. All right." Denklar drummed his fingers on the tabletop.

Ruiz smiled reassuringly. "Be calm, Denklar. I'll soon be gone, and I'll do nothing to excite your yokels."

Denklar gave Ruiz an anxious look. "I hope you're right. I also hope you won't think me disrespectful for saying this . . . but an air of, well, unpleasant deeds clings to you. Trouble and pain."

"Be *calm*," Ruiz said, more sharply. "If I bring trouble, it isn't to you, unless you're an enemy of the League."

LATER, RUIZ CHOSE a place in the common room where he could put his back against a solid wall and see all the doorways. He took a piece of dusty black velvet from his pack and smoothed it over the table—and then began to lay out his wares. The tiny glass vials of oil came in a dozen pale colors, each denoting a different variety of oil. The tops of the vials were flame-sealed, the leftover ribbon of glass swirled and looped into fanciful knots. The rows of vials made a pretty sight against the velvet, glowing like oblong jewels, their topknots glittering.

To the side, Ruiz laid out a selection of pipes, for anyone who couldn't wait for a taste. There was a small water pipe of greenish porcelain, decorated with a stylized carving of a lyretongue lizard. There was a glass bubble pipe, a tangle of frivolous tubing through which the smoke would flow confusingly. There was a simple pipe of brass, its long stem wrapped with colored leather, and a stubby redstone effigy pipe made to resemble a rearing striderbeast.

These things had a certain use-ingrained beauty, and Ruiz took some pleasure in handling them, and admiring the careful craftsmanship that each revealed. He took out his smoker's lamp; the tall silver casting depicted a slender naked woman dancing in flames—which on closer examination proved to be a nest of serpents. The wick emerged from a tambourine she held aloft. Ruiz peered at the tiny face, which seemed to laugh madly. He polished away a bit of tarnish and filled the reservoir, then lit the lamp. It burned with the smoky yellow flame to be expected from a chimneyless lamp, but the fuel was pleasantly scented with sweet musk. Ruiz leaned back, for the moment content to wait.

His first customer drifted in just before noon. A short truculent-looking man bearing the tattoos of the steamfitter's guild slipped in and stood by the door for a moment, apparently allowing his eyes to adjust to the cool dimness of the common room. After a moment, his glance settled on Ruiz, and his dour features broke into a wondering smile, as if the sight of Ruiz and his vials and pipes and lamp were a vista of surpassing beauty.

"Ah," he said, in a delighted voice. "A new oil man." He strode briskly over to Ruiz's table and seated himself. He sat peering at the vials, a gloating expression suffusing his face. "You have the pink gracilic!"

"A connoisseur, I see." Ruiz sat up, arranging his face into a mask of friendly expectancy.

The steamfitter sat back, abruptly frowning. "But I don't know you."

Ruiz shrugged. "Pharaoh is broad. A humble man such as myself can garner only enough fame to cover a small part."

His customer smiled, a bit sourly. "Indeed. Well, we're away from the press of commerce here, so we've had no regular oil man since Efrem displeased the Lord and Rontleses broke his legs. I may buy, if you convince me you can be trusted."

"Why should you not trust me?" Ruiz brought out his plaque, which the man examined carefully.

Finally the man nodded. "It seems proper. But I'm not brave enough to risk bad oil—I don't want to end up frothing and biting the flesh from my hands. Will you smoke with me?"

Ruiz made a lofty gesture of acquiescence. "If I must, to gain your trust and trade. But first, price!"

After fifteen minutes of spirited haggling, they reached a mutually acceptable price for the pink vial.

Money changed hands, and the customer picked up the pink vial in careful hands. "By the way," he said. "My name is Nijints."

Ruiz nodded. "Wuhiya, your servant." He took up the brass pipe and uncovered a small brown stoneware humidor, from which he took a pinch of shredded punkweed. He packed the tiny bowl and waited until Nijints had selected the porcelain pipe and prepared it.

There was a comfortable expectancy in Nijints's broad red face, and he seemed in no hurry. He handled the vial lovingly, holding it up to a beam of light that flickered through the roof thatch. Finally he sighed and tapped the vial's neck against the table edge, until it cracked off. He allowed the smallest possible drop to fall into Ruiz's pipe.

Ruiz fixed a look of proper anticipation on his face, and tipped the pipe toward the flame of his lamp. He drew the sweet smoke deep into his lungs, and Nijints broke into a sunny smile.

"You smoke with decision," Nijints said, and dripped a larger dollop of oil into his own pipe.

The oil filled Ruiz with appealing perceptions. The ranks of vials looked for an instant like blazing suns in the blackness of space. "Starlight is the most dangerous drug," he muttered. Nijints's face seemed almost beautiful in its blunt acquisitive intensity.

Relia the doxy swept into the common room, and Ruiz for an instant was overwhelmed by her grubby perfection. Then, mildly panicked, he clamped down on his sensorium, using expensively acquired cerebral reflexes, and the scene in the common room returned to near normality.

Nijints lit his own pipe and sucked blissfully. For a moment his eyes drooped and he seemed on the verge of passing out, but then his eyes snapped open and he looked about with a heightened intensity. He spotted Relia where she stood scrubbing a table, bent over, her smooth round thighs showing, and his face blossomed with joyful purpose. He capped the vial with a bit of rolled-up leather, and set the burned-out pipe aside.

"You'll excuse me," Nijints said politely, and Ruiz nodded solemnly.

Nijints trotted over to Relia and made arrangements; a moment later both had disappeared into the back of the inn.

Ruiz unclenched his mind and allowed the oil to gild his perceptions again—until the next customer arrived.

CHAPTER 9

T wo days passed pleasantly. Occasionally Ruiz was required by a dubious customer to sample his wares, but gradually the inhabitants of Stegatum assumed his reliability and began to buy without reservation. Ruiz dealt with a variety of townsfolk, and he began to feel a little more comfortable in his role.

However, not many of the locals could afford the prices he set, so on the third day business slowed considerably. Ruiz sat alone for two hours after lunch, awaiting his next customer. No one came, and Ruiz was deciding that perhaps it was time to move on to a larger town, when he heard the clank and hiss of an arriving steam chariot. A moment later a messenger from Lord Brinslevos stamped into the common room, dressed in the Lord's black livery.

The messenger was a tiny man, almost a dwarf. But in front of Ruiz's table he stood as tall as his body permitted him to. "The Lord requires your presence at Brinslevos Keep."

Ruiz quirked his eyebrows. "Ah? And why so, if you'd be so good as to elaborate?"

The small man was impatient with Ruiz's curiosity. "The Lord's requirement is sufficient explanation. No doubt the Lord will reward you for prompt and humble service—or punish you if you deserve it."

"No doubt," Ruiz said gloomily. He began to collect his stock and stow it into his pack. It seemed to him that he had several choices. He could knock the small man on the head and disappear into the waste, there to risk being hunted down by a thwarted and annoyed Lord—and his huntsmen, who, mounted on fast striderbeasts and using coursing beasts, might have little trouble catching him.

He could knock the messenger on the head and steal his steam chariot. That might enable him to escape the local Lord, but it would have the disadvantage of marking him thereafter as a great felon, since only Lords owned personal vehicles, and they took this privilege seriously. Every law-abiding person on Pharaoh would be against him.

Or he could go along quietly, ingratiate himself with the Lord, and move on in a few days. Who knew, perhaps he'd learn something useful at the Keep. It was, after all, the Lords who sponsored the Expiations—the mage plays—that were the planet's paramount art form.

Ruiz sighed. He remembered the mad face of Lord Brinslevos. . . . The memory made it hard to feel enthusiasm for making the Lord's acquaintance.

Still, what other sensible choice was there?

"I must settle my bill with the innkeeper," Ruiz said, when he had finished packing away his vials.

The messenger nodded indifferently.

Ruiz found Denklar in his storeroom, working over a slate of accounts.

"The Lord summons me," Ruiz said, in a hollow voice.

Denklar showed no surprise. "Then you must go. Would you like advice?"

"Of course."

"Then listen. The line of Brinslevos is ancient; the first Brinslevos was a conjuror of the Second Age, almost six hundred years ago. His descendants have grown increasingly strange. The present Brinslevos is eager to take offense, and his catalog of offenses is in constant evolution. But here's a sampling: Don't criticize any aspect of the keep, or the servants, or the livestock, or the cuisine—which is almost unendurable, I must warn you. I think Brinslevos scourges himself with that cooking, so that he can enjoy his sojourns here all the more. Don't be in the slightest degree arrogant; at the same time avoid any whiff of insincere humility. Brinslevos has a nose magnificently attuned to insincerity, for all he's mad. Above all, do not look admiringly at his wives."

"I'll try to bear all these things in mind. Meanwhile, don't give my room to anyone else; I'll be back in a day or two. Here, keep my staff while I'm gone . . . the Lord won't let me take weapons into his Keep, no doubt."

Denklar took the staff in careful hands. "No, he won't."

Denklar said no more, but Ruiz thought he saw a flicker of pity in Denklar's hard eyes, which he found disconcerting.

Outside a somewhat rusty steam chariot waited, long and low, like an elongated cannon shell on four spiked wheels, with a small cab at the front, and a trailing coal carrier at the rear. The messenger directed Ruiz into the cab. Ruiz settled into a threadbare seat and looked about with a degree of interest, since this would be his first ride in a Pharaohan vehicle. The engineering seemed fundamentally sound, if rather flamboyant and idiosyncratic. The castings were embellished by elaborate surface designs, primarily of thorny flowering vines, growing in sinuous energetic patterns. The upholstery had once been luxurious red lizardskin; a trace of the original color remained. Even the bolt heads were made to resemble tiny leering faces; their wide grinning mouths formed the screw slots. Rivets bore a stylized sunburst design. A thousand touches testified to the care and artistry with which the machine had been assembled, but the level of repair was not impressive.

The messenger climbed into the driver's seat, which had been raised by cushions to enable him to see through the cloudy windshield. He darted a hot warning glance at Ruiz, as if daring him to comment. Ruiz smiled blandly. The messenger released a brake lever and pushed a steering yoke forward to feed power to the tall iron wheels.

The machine hesitated briefly, uttered a sibilant protest, and then chuffed away from the Denklar Lodge. Ruiz looked back at the whitewashed building, feeling an odd regret; his stay there had been pleasant and unalarming, all things considered.

The tiny man drove with insouciant abandon, slowly picking up speed as they jolted to the top of the track. When he turned on to the main road, he shoved the yoke all the way forward and the chariot seemed to leap over the washboard road. The springs were not especially effective, and before they'd gone a kilometer, Ruiz's kidneys began to ache. He wondered if the messenger had held his position since early childhood, and if its rigors had somehow stunted his growth. By the time they reached the foot of the mesa on which Brinslevos Keep stood, fifteen minutes later, Ruiz imagined that he might be a few centimeters shorter than when he'd left Stegatum.

The messenger slowed abruptly for the climb up the switchbacks to the keep. The road here seemed in worse repair than the one leading down into Stegatum, and Ruiz was constantly poised to hurl himself from the cab, should the crumbling verge give way under the great weight of the chariot. But they made it safely to a portcullis set into a sheer cliff. The way led through a twenty-meter tunnel cut from the bedrock and then into the main courtyard, where the chariot stopped amid a venting of steam that for a moment obscured the sights of Brinslevos Keep.

When the steam cleared, Ruiz looked about glumly, unable to resist a sudden fit of pessimism. Several iron cages hung from the heights, clasping shriveled corpses. In the center of the courtyard a number of tall sharp poles thrust from a little shrine; their aspect suggested a macabre function, as did their proximity to a three-loop gallows. Ruiz shuddered. Denklar claimed to moderate the Lord's behavior—Ruiz wondered. . . .

"We're here," the messenger said, with an air of grim finality. His small face reflected no joy at the arrival, and Ruiz surmised that Brinslevos was not well loved by his liege men.

"So I see," Ruiz answered.

"Well then, get out. The steward yonder will see you to your quarters and the Lord will summon you when he wants you." The messenger pointed to a small door in the western inner wall, where an elderly hunchback waited, a look of benign idiocy cloaking his lumpy features.

Ruiz alighted from the chariot, and gave the messenger an affable nod. "A pleasure to ride with you," he said earnestly. "A fine machine you drive."

The messenger's face warmed slightly. "Yes, she is. Though she deserves better care than she gets." But then he flushed, as though he had said a foolishly dangerous thing, and his face closed tight again. The chariot chuffed off toward the carriage house, which apparently lay on the far side of the gallows, through a low wide archway.

Ruiz shrugged and carried his pack over to the door—evidently the tradesmen's entrance. "Hello," he said to the hunchback.

The hunchback bobbed his head, swung back the door, and gestured for Ruiz to follow. Ruiz got the impression that the hunchback did not speak.

Inside, they went down a dark hall to a narrow stairway. The steward lit a candle and preceded Ruiz up the stairwell, which twisted and turned in a confusing eccentric fashion. They passed several tiny landings; there were no windows. Finally they reached the floor on which Ruiz would be housed, and the steward unlocked both the door to the landing and the door to Ruiz's room, which was small and musty. Ruiz stepped inside on unwilling feet. Apparently Lord Brinslevos kept his guests in a vertical dungeon. High on one wall a slit of a window admitted a beam of sunlight. A bed frame with a rope mattress, a chamber pot, a washstand, and a tattered quilt comprised the furnishings. Ruiz sighed. The Denklar Lodge seemed in retrospect a haven of comfort and safety. At least, Ruiz thought, the room was dry and no large vermin were immediately apparent.

The hunchback grinned toothlessly and bowed his way out. He closed the door, and a moment later Ruiz heard the clatter of the key in the lock, followed by a more distant rattle as the steward locked the door to the stairway. The locks were a comfort, in a way. They wouldn't long resist

Ruiz's implements, if he needed to get out, but they reassured him as to his safety, at least for the moment.

He dropped wearily to the rope mattress and assessed his situation. He could not shake off a sense of foreboding, which, he thought, was natural under the circumstances. He was in the hands of a man who apparently recognized no limit to his whim, no constraint on his authority—never a healthy situation. Additionally, Ruiz still felt a bit unsettled by Pharaoh's alien ambience, and by his personal uncertainties.

He lay back, fixed his attention on the rough stone of the ceiling. He could hope that Brinslevos observed the Pharaohan custom that allowed snake oil men a greater degree of eccentricity than other low-caste persons. He could hope to be sufficiently entertaining to avoid Brinslevos's disfavor, and at the same time he must be careful not to be so lovable as to be offered a permanent position at the Keep. The thought of staying long was a depressing one, so he put it aside and instead considered the problems involved in catching the poachers.

All over Pharaoh, conjuring troupes competed for fame and for "translation to the Land of Reward." *Translation* was the Pharaohan interpretation of what occurred when a League harvest crew collected a troupe, which occurred whenever the League observers on Pharaoh Upstation decided that a troupe was ripe for collection. The selected troupe was usually allowed one last performance, which almost always took the form of one of the great religious plays called Expiations, during which a victim, usually a condemned felon, was sacrificed to the conjuror's art. Immediately after the conclusion of the play, a League catchboat—made invisible by pangalac technology—moved in and scooped up the troupe. To the spectators, a miracle had passed.

Religion flourished on Pharaoh, as it did on most League-owned worlds. The League found it easy and efficient to exploit the religious impulses of client populations; what better way to conceal the bizarre evidences of its activities? On Cardoon, from which the League exported astonishingly beautiful women, the most beautiful were chosen at

great religious festivals, and then were sacrificed to the gods
—a process that involved loading them into small boats and
sending them down an underground river. League personnel
plucked the victims from their boats, just before the river
disappeared into a vast siphon.

On Mortadinder, famous for the quality of its gladiators,
men and women competed for the gods' favor, playing a
variety of deadly sports. The survivors became saints—and
then product, to be marketed to pangalac worlds that permitted blood entertainments.

On Scarf, scholars strove to outdo each other at intellectual pursuits, for the glory of the gods. The superior were
packed off to monasteries on high crags, from which none
returned—since the monasteries were staging arcas for cata-
loging and shipment.

On Pharaoh, more than religion drove the conjurors to
heights of artistry. Those magicians who weren't quite brilliant enough to win entry to the Land of Reward, yet were
capable of consistently entertaining performances, might
move upward through the otherwise rigid caste system,
might even attain the status of aristocrats. Anyone at all,
even a peasant, might strive for a career as a conjuror.

Ruiz's problem was one of discrimination. With dozens
of major performances on Pharaoh each week, how was
he to pick the one that would be attended by the poachers?
Presumably the poachers had some means of choosing
the best available troupe not yet scheduled for harvest; the
League catchboat had never come in conflict with the
poachers' boat. The League organization here was riddled
by collaborators, obviously.

Ruiz worried at the problem, coming to no conclusions,
until his eyes grew heavy and his thoughts drifted into dis-
jointed speculation. Presently he slept.

By the time Ruiz woke, the sunlight had faded from the
high window. Later, the hunchback brought a meal, one
markedly less palatable than the food at the Denklar Lodge.
Ruiz ate stoically. A long time later, he fell again into uneasy sleep.

.   .   .

ANOTHER MAN WEARING the gorgeous rags of the snake oil peddler arrived in Stegatum at sunset, and rode his weary striderbeast through the sandy streets at a stumbling trot. He pulled up in front of the Denklar Lodge and bellowed for a stable boy. One appeared almost instantly and took the beast to the stable.

The man pushed through the doorway into the common room, jostling a pair of departing farmers, who glared at his back. He went up to the bar and ordered a mug of ale from Denklar. Denklar served him with unusual alacrity, then glanced along the bar, to see that no one stood close.

"What brings you back to Stegatum so soon, Anstevic?" asked Denklar in a soft voice. "I didn't expect to see you again for a threemonth."

Anstevic gave Denklar a searching glance, which caused the innkeeper to recoil slightly. "Business." He tipped up the mug and poured the ale down his throat, belched loudly. He leaned forward and addressed Denklar in a confidential murmur. "I'm going up to my usual room, if it's available. You come to see me later, when no one will connect your absence with me."

Denklar nodded, and a moment later the man was gone, leaving behind a stink of unwashed flesh and overheated striderbeast.

An hour later, when the supper rush was over, Denklar went back into the oldest wing of the inn, where Anstevic waited.

The man sat on the bed, smoking a pipe of raw gray oil, the cheapest and harshest sort. His narrow eyes shifted and glittered with visions, and Denklar was a little afraid. Anstevic had always seemed the most unpredictable of the agents-at-large that passed through on their information-collection rounds.

"Business, you said?" Denklar asked, struggling to keep any trace of mockery from his voice.

"Yes," Anstevic answered slowly. His eyes focused on Denklar for the first time, and Denklar was a bit more fearful. What did Anstevic mean to do, with such a look on his face? It was the look of a man examining a dead reptile about which he was curious. For a dizzy instant, Denklar

wondered when the agent would prod him with a stick, turn
him over to look for the fatal wound.

Denklar shook himself. Crazy thoughts! Anstevic was a
harsh man, addicted to the oil—and probably to more demanding vices—but for all that he was still a pangalactic,
and a League employee. Denklar had no compelling reason
to suspect him of uncontrollably violent impulses.

"What do you want?" Denklar asked, his uneasiness
making him brusque.

Anstevic's strange eyes veiled, and he looked away. "I'm
hunting a man." His gaze snapped back and he stared at
Denklar with a luminous intensity.

Denklar instantly thought of Wuhiya, the Uberfactorial
who had gone up to the Keep that morning. He dissembled,
however, remembering the Uberfactorial's emphasis on se-
crecy. "Oh? Who?"

Anstevic smiled, a curiously ambiguous expression, and
then looked away again. "It's nothing you need concern
yourself with."

Denklar heard these words with profound relief, and so
immediately believed them. "Well, if I can help . . ."

"Of course. But for tonight, all I need is for you to keep
the yokels out of my hair." Anstevic smoothed his hand
over his naked scalp and sniggered. "I'm traveling fast, and
I've no time to devote to oil selling. If anyone asks, tell them
I'm traveling to buy, not to sell."

"Yes, no problem," Denklar said, forcing enthusiasm into
his voice. "We're in luck there. Another oil man just came
through and spent a couple of days. He took everyone's
money, before Brinslevos called him to the Keep."

Anstevic stood and clapped Denklar on the shoulder.
"Well, we're sorry for the poor wog, eh? When did he go up
to the Keep?"

Denklar laughed uneasily. "Just this morning." He wondered why he had mentioned the Uberfactorial at all—he'd
been too eager to seem friendly, he supposed. He was again
uncomfortable. But he reassured himself that if by some
unhappy chance Anstevic *was* looking for the Uberfactorial,
then he might have learned Wuhiya's whereabouts from any
of the tosspots who frequented the common room. And this

way, Anstevic might not think that Denklar had been deliberately uncooperative—just discreet. To change the subject,
he said, "As I recall, you never had any difficulty with Brinslevos."

Anstevic gave him a comradely hug, which made the
bones of Denklar's shoulders grate together painfully.
"You're right. Brinslevos and I always get along famously.
That's because we're two of a kind, don't you think?"

There seemed no safe answer to that question, so Denklar
ducked his head and chuckled nervously.

"Well, now I must rest for a bit," Anstevic said. "But I
do have something for you." Releasing Denklar, he went to
his saddlebags, which hung from a peg. He rummaged
briefly, drew forth a small package. "Here," he said, hand-
ing it to Denklar.

Denklar unwrapped it, found a black datastrip, of a sort
which the League prohibited to its agents on the surface.
The sensie pornography encoded on the strip was Denklar's
one indispensable vice, and he smiled gratefully at Anstevic,
who was his only source of fresh material. Anstevic had
given Denklar the smuggled-in playback unit, years before.
Denklar considered this vice to be the only thing that made
his life on Pharaoh bearable.

"The latest and hottest from Dilvermoon," Anstevic said.
"Now, let me rest. I'll have to be on my way in an hour or
two—though you may see me again soon . . . or maybe
not."

ANSTEVIC THE ASSASSIN filled his pipe again, when the
fat innkeeper was gone. The situation could hardly be more
to his liking. Brinslevos was a notoriously volatile Lord.
Who would suspect Anstevic of involvement in the death of
the Uberfactorial? One day he'd punish the innkeeper for his
imperfect helpfulness, but not tonight.

Denklar would have to live awhile, unfortunately. When
the Uberfactorial met his end, there must be no associated
violences for any investigators to find. They might question
Denklar, but the innkeeper would be anxious to conceal
Anstevic's visit, lest they discover his contraband. And in a

few months, Anstevic would return to Stegatum and snip off that loose thread.

The oil showed him pleasant visions—knives ripping soft bellies, garrotes sinking into soft throats, the innkeeper's blackened face frozen in fear and disbelief. He enjoyed this satisfying picture for a few minutes, until his pipe had grown cold and stale.

Then he gathered his gear and went out to the stables.

CHAPTER 10

B Y MIDNIGHT, Anstevic had reached the top of the mesa on which Brinslevos Keep was built, and hobbled his striderbeast in a small pocket among the rocks. He took a slipsuit from his saddlebag and exchanged his oil man rags for the near-invisibility of the suit. When he switched it on, he became no more than a flicker of shadow on the moonlit stone, and he walked boldly up to the mesa top sally port and picked the lock.

He gained entry without difficulty; the port was guarded only in times of siege, and since the League's acquisition of Pharaoh some thirty generations past, no wars had been permitted to disrupt the smooth delivery of product to the League slave pens.

His knowledge of Brinslevos Keep was superficial, but in past visits he had left locator beacons in various parts of the Keep, and now he tuned his finder to the one in Brinslevos's private chambers. He took an infrared safelight from his pocket and adjusted the slipsuit's goggles, then set off through the red-gleaming darkness. He met no one else in the corridors.

Fifteen minutes later, he was opening the ark in which Brinslevos kept his pipes and his punkweed. The ark was a fanciful silver effigy of an arroyo lizard, all jaws and teeth, whose head split open to reveal a storage cavity. He lifted out Brinslevos's humidor of punkweed.

From a pocket of the slipsuit, he drew an atomizer and sprayed the weed. He stirred it to distribute the poison evenly, then returned the humidor to its ark and closed the jaws. The ark made a tiny click, and Anstevic froze. From the Lord's sleeping chamber came a mutter and a sigh. Silence.

Minutes passed while Anstevic waited, but he heard nothing further, and he finally drifted out of the Lord's chambers.

When he was back among the rocks in which he had hidden his striderbeast, he pulled back the hood of the slipsuit and laughed with a pure and childish delight. It had been so easy. Brinslevos would insist on buying the Uberfactorial's wares, and then Brinslevos would die. His guards would hang the Uberfactorial from the battlements immediately—following the odd Pharaohan religious dictum that a victim suffers a year in Hell for every hour that his assassin survives him—and then Anstevic could return to the reliable pleasures of Kobatum, mission accomplished. He would have to wait until that night to confirm the agent's death, but no matter . . . the hard part was done. As the dawn washed the mesa top with pale color, Anstevic made himself comfortable under an overhang that would provide some shade at the hottest part of the Pharaohan afternoon.

IN THE MORNING the door slammed back and the hunchback ushered a grim-faced coercer into the cell. Ruiz sat up on his cot and was surprised to recognize Rontleses, from whom he'd bought water his first morning on Pharaoh.

"Greetings, noble coercer," Ruiz said politely.

"Stand when you speak to me," answered Rontleses.

Ruiz scrambled from the cot. "As you command."

Rontleses looked dusty and tired, as though he had just arrived from the catapple plantations. "I'm required to instruct you. Tonight you'll attend the Lord. He'll sample your oils, and you'll accompany him on his journey. Be very careful what you allow him to take. If he becomes ill, he will assume you have poisoned him, and you will suffer a terrible death. The Lord's executioner is an imaginative man."

"I'll bear your instruction in mind at all times," Ruiz said sincerely.

"See that you do."

The coercer spun on his heel and left. The hunchback brought in breakfast, which if anything was more unappetizing than supper had been. The rest of the day passed slowly, unenlivened by anything more entertaining than mild gastric distress. Finally Ruiz dozed.

THE RATTLE OF the key in his door woke Ruiz, and he sat up abruptly. His head swam for an instant; then he was ready. The ray of sunlight was gone and the room was dark. He sensed that many hours had passed, that it was very late. Ruiz slid from the bed and over to the wall, poised to deal with any enemies that might appear.

But it was only the hunchback steward, who poked his unlovely head through the doorway. He said nothing, but he grinned and made gestures with his smoky lamp, indicating that Ruiz was to follow.

Ruiz picked up his pack and went with great reluctance. He felt more than ordinarily oppressed by the circumstances; he felt sure that he had exerted less control over the situation than he should have. He might have dragged his feet, except that the hunchback moved briskly and the lamp's yellow light was the only illumination.

The steward conducted him through a maze of rough tunnels, through echoing rooms, and through hallways of tatty magnificence, until they reached the audience room of Brinslevos Keep.

A hundred torches flared dramatically along the tapestried walls, but the hall was empty of courtiers. Threadbare carpet marked a red path across the black porcelain tiles to the gilded throne on which Brinslevos sprawled. Behind the Lord, poised in an attitude of baleful curiosity, stood the

Lord's conjuror and executioner, a short man with a round bland face and a lipless mouth, who wore a black robe and carried an ornate ivory wand.

"Come, come," Brinslevos called out, in his oddly pitched voice, which vibrated with mad gaiety.

Ruiz paced over the carpet with all seemly haste and went to a knee before the throne. "Your servant," he said, in low tones.

"Yes, yes," the Lord said. "Rise. Show us your wares. By the way, what is your name?"

"Wuhiya, great one." Ruiz opened his pack, and two boys in the nomarch's livery trotted forth from the anteroom, carrying a table, which they set beside Ruiz. Ruiz nodded his thanks, and laid his vials on the table. They made a fine sparkling display in the torchlight, and the Lord came down from his throne to inspect them.

For an instant, Ruiz looked into Brinslevos's eyes, which glowed with some unreadable but intense emotion. Ruiz was abruptly terrified, though nothing of his fear reached his face—or so he hoped. Here, he thought, would be a truly dangerous man, were he not mad. And even so . . .

Ruiz stood back humbly, and the Lord fingered the vials, an artlessly avid smile on his narrow face. "Interesting, interesting." Brinslevos selected a vial of green latigar. "Describe the effects of this one, good Wuhiya."

"It is the venom of the latigar dragon, great one, processed by the artifice of the Jings, who range down the slopes of Hell on the north side of the world. The dreams the latigar brings are subtle and introspective, much concerned with the nature of reality. An oil beloved of philosophers."

Brinslevos dropped the green latigar, chose a vial of blue-purple cansum. "And this?"

"The venom of the cansum constrictor, great one—morphed by a process known only to the cave-dwelling Inklats, who wear no tattoos and feed their snakes on human flesh. Very rare. Very expensive. It brings dreams of mortality; it shows the face of life for what it is, a mask on a skull. The skilled dreamer can learn to value the mask, or so it's theorized."

"You've never taken this oil?"

"No, great one."

Brinslevos weighed the vial in his elegant hand. "Then we will embark on a voyage of discovery together, Wuhiya."

The Lord's conjuror frowned and gave Ruiz a glance of cold dislike. But he said nothing.

BRINSLEVOS HAD GONE, leaving Ruiz to wait in the empty audience room. He repacked his vials, then spent a few uneasy minutes shifting from foot to foot. The Keep was uncannily silent, except for the sputter of the torches. When the hunchback steward finally came to fetch him to the Lord's chambers, he was almost relieved. The hall had a dark ambience, a trembling aura of ancient horror, as though unspeakably ugly deeds had occurred on the black tiles.

The steward took him through another maze of twisting corridors. Ruiz began to think that the Keep was a great deal larger than he had originally estimated. Apparently the majority of its spaces had been carved from the bedrock and the battlements he had glimpsed from the road must be only the tip of these great subterranean works. Ruiz tried to memorize the turns, but by the time they arrived at their destination, he was unsure of the way out.

The Lord Brinslevos had furnished his chambers in eccentric fashion. The walls were hung with hunting trophies —so thickly that the rough stone was almost completely obscured. Some were notable, and Ruiz wondered if the Lord had personally killed them. Here was a pangolin swarter, great-tusked head lifted in red-eyed challenge. There was the hide of a greenback Helldemon, covering ten meters of wall. In the far corner stood an enormous stuffed river lizard, rearing on its hind legs, nightmare jaws gaping. The floors were covered by deep soft carpets, that swirled with pale hues, peach, celadon, ivory. Fat cushions, covered in cloth-of-gold and beaded with ruby spangles, were scattered in random heaps; here and there were low tables in red and black lacquer. It struck Ruiz as an odd combination, as though a strong-minded taxidermist had moved in with a relentless interior decorator.

Brinslevos sat upon a cushion by a table covered with the paraphernalia of the oil smoker. The Lord gestured for the steward to leave, then beckoned to Ruiz, who stepped forward.

"You do me far too much honor, great one," said Ruiz.

"Nonsense." Brinslevos looked up and his face pinched. "Sit down—don't stand there looking down at me. Have you no respect?"

Ruiz sat hastily, before the annoyance on the Lord's narrow face could mature into rage. "My apologies, great one."

Brinslevos glared at him for an instant, and Ruiz looked down at his hands. He was unhappily aware that he was in a great deal more danger than the night he had climbed up from Hell into Pharaoh. The Lord was far more unpredictable than a Helldemon, and possibly more lethal, as the vast hide on his wall seemed to testify.

"Well, no matter," Brinslevos said. "I'm a tolerant man; I grant almost everyone one mistake. If I love you, I might grant you two, though I don't advise you to test my affection yet."

"Yes, great one." As he spoke, Ruiz looked Brinslevos in the eye and smiled pleasantly, remembering Denklar's advice—that the Lord found excessive humility as irritating as arrogance.

Brinslevos laughed. He looked for a moment like a child, innocent of malice—a trick of his madness, or so Ruiz presumed. "So. Let us smoke."

Ruiz nodded, and from his pack he drew forth the simple brass pipe he favored and packed it with punkweed. He wondered that he was as calm as he seemed to be; perhaps Ruiz Aw was mad, too, to be smoking oil with a dangerous lunatic. But now there seemed no way out.

Brinslevos opened a silver effigy box made in the shape of an arroyo lizard and took a porcelain waterpipe from it. He filled the pipe from his own humidor of weed, then added a drop of the cansum oil, first to his and then to Ruiz's pipe.

The Lord ordered the lamps dimmed, so that the visions would have no difficulty in suppressing reality. Unseen hands saw to this, so that the room was filled with gloom and the bizarre shadows cast from the dead creatures on the walls.

Brinslevos waited until Ruiz had held the bowl of his pipe over the flame and drawn deeply; then he followed.

Lavender smoke leaked from the Lord's high-bridged nose. After a long moment he released his breath suddenly, and so did Ruiz.

"Ahh . . . sweet," said Brinslevos. Strangely, the Lord now seemed calm, as though the oil had reversed some polarity in his head, tipping him toward sanity.

Ruiz felt a tide rising in his body, a tingling flood of unease. His expensive reflexes clamped down automatically, damping the swing toward hallucination. He shook himself, forced those reflexes to relax slightly, so that he could appear to accompany the Lord on his trip into otherness. It wouldn't do for the Lord to suspect Ruiz of some sort of trickery—this was a world full of hands that were quicker than the eye.

"Tell me what you see," Brinslevos ordered, after several more puffs.

"Yes, great one," said Ruiz. He opened the floodgates of his sensorium a little wider, and waited.

Evil dreams scrabbled through on little clawed feet.

He took a deep breath and shuddered it out. He began to babble. "I see myself, a servant in a house where two beautiful monsters dwell. They are less human than the Helldemons who crawl up the wall of the world, but they speak in soft breathless voices, they wear garments of spider velvet, they smell like the desert, clean and dead."

"What do they look like, Wuhiya?" The Lord's eyes were like moonstones, a lambent pale gray.

"Like perfect corpses. Their skins are white as the finest porcelain, without a wrinkle, smooth and hard. They have long hair, like black smoke, the male and female both. Their faces seem human, but under the clouds of their hair each hides a hundred eyes, which watch in all directions. Sometimes I see the glitter of these eyes. . . .

"Their fingers are knives, unless they are icicles."

"Ahhh . . . ," sighed Brinslevos, leaning back and closing his eyes. "You have the voice. Use it."

Ruiz gave himself more freely to the dream, began to see more clearly the dark things he imagined. He spoke the shapes the drug showed him. "Their feet are perfect, narrow, high-arched, perfumed. They walk like human beings, but where they set their feet down, roots strike deep, tiny white wires, racing downward like worms born of lightning, to take strength from the ground. When they lift their feet from the ground the worms fall away and die, invisible.

"The beautiful monsters wear fine scarlet sashes about their hips, so that their genitals are hidden. Now they remove their sashes and I see only smooth bright metal between their legs. I don't know what they wish me to do, but never have I been more afraid." For an instant it was true, and he struggled against terror.

Ruiz fell silent, and neither spoke for a long time. It was so quiet in the room that Ruiz heard his heartbeat, measuring out the seconds.

Sweat streamed down Brinslevos's face, and he muttered inaudibly. Then the Lord said, in a stronger voice, "I hear the grinding of machinery in the darkness—first the rasp and rattle of tiny cogs and then the pumping of many small pistons. The sound grows and changes, until it becomes a steel music, and I know that a great machine, unseen in the night, rises on all sides of me, up to the stars and beyond. I seem to float, light as smoke, in the center of this machine, which now seems so huge that no world could support it. I can see nothing but the flicker of starlight through the girders and levers and wheels.

"At first I thought myself at the center of the machine, but now I understand that I am trapped in one tiny pocket of it, and that a million others float here, too, each in his own separate cage. It *is* a cage; I feel that now, and I wonder why I am being kept."

Brinslevos moaned, a sound of puzzled agony that threatened to pull Ruiz into the Lord's vision. Ruiz damped his reaction to the drug and swam up from the depths.

Brinslevos spoke urgently, in a rising panic. "Why? Why! The gears grind faster and faster, until the darkness shudders with the motion, and I can hear nothing else, not even my thoughts. I grow heavier, I start to sink, toward the danger below, a gnashing beast of metal, with cogs for jaws and rods for muscles. It's hungry and I carry no weapon, I am naked and cold and weak." Brinslevos twisted and flung out his arms. "Something's gone wrong. . . ." He screamed, a sound that completely sobered Ruiz. The Lord's face was suddenly distended with terror, as if some awful creature had forced its way under his skin and was trying to push out. His eyes bulged with insupportable horror, his mouth strained to wring the last bit of sound from his scream—he seemed to be unable to draw his next breath.

Any moment, servants or guards would come running, and what would Ruiz Aw tell them? "I'm sorry; I seem to have poisoned your Lord, excuse me now."

Ruiz leaned forward and pressed his left pinky ring against the Lord's corded neck. A full-spectrum antidote and strong sedative jetted into the Lord's carotid, and the Lord fell back unconscious, face relaxing.

An instant later, something exploded against the back of Ruiz's head, and he knew nothing for a while.

CHAPTER 11

RUIZ woke slowly to the sensation of heat and confinement, and the bitter smell of rust. His head thumped with a regular rhythm, a stabbing pain behind the eyes. He groaned and sat up in semidarkness, to discover that he was naked.

His senses swam for a moment, and he touched the back of his head gingerly. Blood was crusted on a split in his scalp, but his probing fingers found no evidence that his skull was cracked.

Where was he?

Beams of hot light penetrated his prison through chinks in the welded iron that surrounded him. Carefully, he rose to hands and knees and put his eye to one of these cracks. His heart sank. He was in the Place of Artful Anguish.

One of the other iron huts was visible through his chink, and above it flew a black pennon, indicating that it also contained a condemned criminal. Ruiz wondered who the other was, and why that unfortunate had been selected to share Ruiz's punishment.

Useless to think about it. His immediate concern was escape, which must come soon, before the performance in which he would Expiate his sin against Lord Brinslevos. Already he could feel the uneasiness of the death net, tugging against its anchorages in the depth of his mind. He would live only until the situation was irretrievably hopeless; then he would die, and the uninformative circumstances of his death would be transmitted to the League. Ruiz shook his head. Bad enough to die painfully, worse still to die pointlessly. He knew nothing, except that a conspiracy of some sort flourished on the orbital platform, a datum that the League might logically have assumed without the event of his death.

He shifted his thoughts from the gloomy avenue they had begun to follow. The situation was far from hopeless; surely when Denklar heard of his predicament, the innkeeper would communicate with him, and then it would be a simple matter of the innkeeper fetching the packet of pangalac devices hidden in his room. Ruiz had only to exercise patience, and to survive his time in the iron hut. It would grow hot, no doubt, but surely the Lord's executioner preferred lively victims to ones already half-cooked.

As if in answer to his surmise, a pair of stout women came into view, laboring under shoulder yokes and large buckets. They set the buckets down next to the other occupied cage with theatrical sighs of exertion, and presently began to pour water into the pan-shaped roof of the cage.

"Air-conditioning," Ruiz muttered, and shortly he heard the trickle of water on his own roof.

"Hey," he shouted. "What foolishness is this? I've done no wrong. Call the Lord, tell him I'm innocent."

One of the women chuckled sardonically. "The Lord is feeling poorly; in fact, I hear your Expiation must wait a day, until he feels well enough to give his complete attention to the performance. Myself, I haven't much sympathy for you—since you botched the job. So many fine poisons exist. What madness possessed you to dose the Lord just enough to make him ill? If you'd succeeded in murdering him, they'd have hung you from the battlements and that would have been that—a clean death and a quick one."

"Ill-considered of me," Ruiz said in an agreeable voice. "And the other prisoner?"

The woman laughed again, and this time it was a sound of pure pleasure. "That's Rontleses, who didn't see you make the switch that poisoned the Lord—as was his responsibility. What's worse, his gimpleg trusty has reported to the Lord that several days ago you and the coercer talked together in low voices, at an unlikely spot out in the catapple plantations. So the Lord suspects a conspiracy between you and Rontleses, though none of his advisers can imagine why you should thus plot."

She leaned close to the iron. "In Stegatum, opinions differ. Though you blundered away your opportunity to rid us of Brinslevos, at least you've taken Rontleses to his death, which pleases almost everyone but Rontleses."

"Well," said Ruiz. "Every blessing is mixed. For my part, I'd prefer not to accompany Rontleses."

"No doubt," said the woman, whose voice seemed to come more faintly, as if she was leaving. "They undertake Rontleses' Expiation tonight, and yours tomorrow night, so you can look forward to at least one more day of life. Who knows, perhaps he'll speak under the question, convince the Lord of your innocence. Probably not. Rontleses is a hard man. He'll be pleased with your company in Hell, even if you *are* innocent."

Ruiz heard no more. He sank down, clutching his aching head.

VILAM DENKLAR STOOD in the room formerly occupied by Wuhiya the oil man. He peered from the window that overlooked the Place of Artful Anguish, wringing his hands. He was being forced to an unpleasant decision, but he could see no way out. The agent in the iron cage was an Uberfactorial; no doubt he carried a death net. Were Denklar to ignore his plight, and allow the agent to die for his foolishness—as Denklar would certainly do were the idiot of less exalted rank—the news of his inaction would immediately reach the League. Soon thereafter, implacable persons would come calling. "Denklar," they would say, "tell us why you did nothing to save the Uberfactorial." And what would he answer? They would judge him incompetent at best; at worst, a traitor.

So engrossed was he in his thoughts that he failed to hear the light step of Anstevic behind him, until a hand fell on his shoulder. He spun, to see Anstevic, looking dusty and red-eyed, as though he had spent an uncomfortable night in the waste. He opened his mouth to curse at Anstevic for so startling him, but the assassin clutched Denklar's throat with one hand, sealing off his wind. In Anstevic's other hand was a long dagger, thin as a wire. This he slipped into Denklar's open mouth, so that the point pricked his palate. Denklar tried to pull away, to no effect. He tried to shut his mouth, but the wireblade was as rigid as an iron bar, and forced his jaw down cruelly.

"You have questions," Anstevic said softly. "They must wait, possibly forever. First I'll ask mine, and I hope you can give the right answers."

Denklar nodded, a tiny careful movement, and Anstevic smiled. "Good," he said. He withdrew the dagger from Denklar's mouth. "Quietly now, tell me what has happened."

Anstevic's grip loosened slightly and Denklar drew a deep shuddering breath. "This morning men came from Brinslevos Keep, with Rontleses and the snake oil man. Wuhiya, he calls himself."

With horrifying speed, Anstevic picked Denklar up by his shirtfront and threw him against the stone wall, where he hit with a dull thud. Anstevic jerked the dazed innkeeper to his feet and spoke in a harsh voice. "Do not dissemble. Tell me who the oil man really is."

"All right, all right. He's a League agent, Uberfactorial. I meant no harm—he told me to tell no one—but remember, I mentioned him before, I'm a loyal friend, Anstevic."

Anstevic smiled encouragingly. "Go on."

"I don't really know what happened. After they put the prisoners in their cages, they came into the inn and ordered breakfast. They said the oil man had tried to poison the Lord, which makes no sense. He's an Uberfactorial, after all; if he'd tried, he'd have succeeded, surely. Rontleses will die, they said, because he was on duty last night, watching from concealment to see that no treachery occurred when the Lord and Wuhiya smoked together. I can't understand it at all."

Anstevic muttered something under his breath. "Bad luck," he said ambiguously.

"Yes . . . bad luck." Denklar began to see a positive aspect to Anstevic's unexpected presence. "But I'm glad you're here. You can get him out of the cage and away from Stegatum much more easily than I—it's more your line of work, isn't it? I'm an innkeeper, not a man of action."

"Umm . . ." said Anstevic. "Have you contacted him? Has he managed to send any messages to you?"

"No, no . . . I was just considering how best to proceed."

"Good, very good. A pity, in a way, that the Lord survived. Eh? Then they'd have dealt with him at the Keep, and we'd have been out of it. But the Lord believes in public displays, so I suppose we must act." Anstevic chuckled, apparently in a good humor again.

Denklar began to relax. The matter was out of his hands and into more competent ones—a great relief.

The wireblade slipped through the soft flesh below his chin, through his palate and into his brain. Anstevic gave a dexterous twist.

Denklar knew an instant of cold stinging astonishment, and then he was dead.

THERE WAS LITTLE blood. Anstevic rolled the corpse under the bed, and sat down to wait, pipe in hand.

THE MORNING PASSED, and Ruiz gradually recovered his equilibrium. He explored his cage, but found no encouragement. The cage was stoutly constructed, with heavy forged fastenings and a solid door, locked with a massive padlock. The padlock's keyhole faced the small grid set into the door, by luck. Had he a piece of wire, he might have tickled it open, but he was naked and the cage was swept clean. The cage grew hot, despite the water, but not unbearably so. Ruiz sat cross-legged in the center of the cage and concentrated on his situation. As the pounding in his head eased, he was able to think more clearly about the events that had led him to the Place of Artful Anguish.

The Lord had been poisoned, though not by Ruiz. The Lord was not well loved in Stegatum and the surrounding nomarchy. No doubt the Lord had many enemies, one of whom had seized the opportunity to assassinate Brinslevos in such a way that Ruiz would be blamed. It served no great purpose to wonder who or why; what was important was this: Ruiz was still alive. Presumably Denklar would help, and Ruiz could escape under the cover of night. And then Ruiz would be on his way. *Unless,* Ruiz thought, *Denklar was part of the conspiracy that had first revealed itself aboard the platform.* This was a disquieting idea, and led to a train of further unpleasant speculations. Perhaps the Lord had been poisoned not by the Lord's enemies, but by Ruiz's. In this case, Denklar might do nothing, except perhaps to laugh as Ruiz was taken out of the cage to his death. No, no, that was unlikely, because he had revealed himself as an Uberfactorial to Denklar, and so Denklar must assume Ruiz to be equipped with a death net. Even if Denklar *was* a conspirator, he would be foolish to dare the League's investigators, who would be aware of the circumstances of Ruiz's death as soon as it occurred.

If instead Brinslevos had died, and Ruiz had been executed immediately, such a plan could have worked well. *Had* that been the plan?

Ruiz shook his head; such speculation was pointless. For the present, he must compose himself to wait for Denklar's help, which in any case would not be forthcoming until after dark. When he was free, he would question the innkeeper vigorously. The thought was pleasant and calming.

The afternoon passed in heat and silence, and Ruiz was astonished to find himself bored. That the imminent prospect of a painful death could not divert him from boredom for a few short hours seemed to him a frightening and ominous thing, though only abstractly. He pounded his fists against his forehead. "Alertness, alertness, Ruiz," he told himself.

As the sun sank to the level of the surrounding hills, the citizens of Stegatum began to appear, strolling about the Place of Artful Anguish in couples and small groups, as though it were a peaceful park. Children ran here and there, occasionally stopping to fling a stone at the iron cages, which made a fine loud clang. Rontleses presently began to bellow lurid curses. Ruiz said nothing, plugging his ears with his fingers, and consequently the children spent most of their stones on Rontleses' cage. Their parents looked on with solemn approval. No one attempted to speak to Ruiz Aw.

When the sun was down and twilight was fading, the citizens went in to supper, and a crew of laborers brought a small wheeled stage into the square, leveled it, and then set up a variety of unpleasant paraphernalia on it. There was a tall iron frame, well supplied with straps and chains and hooks, a coffin-shaped box, a long table with dark stains dried on its edges.

Ruiz felt a chill, and found himself no longer bored.

When darkness completely covered the town and the air had grown colder, a rank of torches was lit behind the stage. Peering from a crack in his cage, Ruiz saw the citizens of Stegatum gathering for the night's entertainment. The square was filling up; presumably the peasants of the outlying districts had heard about the execution, for there seemed to be many more folk present than lived in the town. The spectators crowded close about Ruiz's cage, and several adolescent boys climbed to the top of the cage, where their hobnailed boots created a splashing din. Apparently he was to be ignored, for the present.

When the square was almost full, a steam chariot arrived, somewhat larger and fancier than the one that had fetched Ruiz to the keep. The crowd became very quiet. The chariot parked before the stage, and its midsection cantilevered open to reveal Lord Brinslevos, lying on a luxurious couch, with a fur coverlet pulled up to his chin. The Lord seemed pale and tense. After a moment, he raised his arm and made a peremptory gesture. "Begin," he said, in a weak voice. He looked once toward Ruiz's cage, and Ruiz thought he saw as much puzzlement as anger in the Lord's glance.

The Lord's conjuror, who wore robes of inky black, appeared on the platform, and the torches grew brighter. "Citizens of Stegatum," he said, in a well trained voice. "Welcome to this Expiation and Exemplification." He bowed with a flourish. "Bring us the subject!"

Two soldiers in black livery opened Rontleses' cage and dragged him out. He had fared less well than Ruiz during the heat of the day; his legs would not at first support him, and his eyes stared blindly, without comprehension. When one soldier offered him a drink from a leather cup, he clutched at it, drained it in two gulps.

Just outside his cage, Ruiz heard a chuckle of quiet satisfaction from a person he could not see. The person whispered, "He's too mad with thirst to refuse the philter, which will make him docile and at the same time abrade his nerves, so that he feels each agony more intensely. Ha, ha, it couldn't happen to a more deserving man."

Ruiz shifted to another crevice, and now he could see in profile the pleasant features of Relia, resident doxy at the Denklar Lodge. She turned to glance toward him, and said, "Are you in there, Wuhiya? I think I see the gleam of your eye."

"Yes," he answered. "I'm here."

She shook her head sadly. "I'm sorry to see you. You seemed a decent sort, for an oil man. What possessed you to give the Lord bad oil?"

"I don't know. . . ."

A short silence passed, during which the soldiers half-carried Rontleses onto the stage. They secured his naked body to the iron frame, and he seemed to recover some of his self-awareness, glaring with burning eyes at the crowd, and the Lord.

Relia sighed. "Later I'll try to bring you a water reed, so you can defy the philterer when your turn comes tomorrow night."

"Thank you," he said, but she had moved away from the cage. *A compassionate woman, Relia the doxy,* he thought—but he hoped he'd be gone before she brought him the water.

The performance began, and Ruiz watched with morbid interest.

First the conjuror warmed up the crowd with a series of small tricks, humiliating and painful, but not yet mutilating. He pretended to squeeze the coercer's head, and brown vapor seemed to jet from the victim's ears. He appeared to discover several large venomous insects here and there about the coercer's body, which the conjuror retrieved fastidiously with tongs, though not before they had bitten Rontleses painfully, so that the victim shrieked and writhed with astonishing energy. Then, from Rontleses' straining mouth, he began to pull a shiny pink egg, which proved a bit too large to extract. He dithered over the problem with the egg half-protruding from the victim's face. Rontleses turned first red and then blue, when the conjuror pinched his nostrils together, ostensibly to get a better grip on his face. Eventually, the performer tapped the egg with his wand, and it hatched into a greasy cluster of white segmented worms— some dripped off and some seemed to wriggle down Rontleses' throat. Rontleses coughed out worms and drew a great shuddering breath. His face had already changed, in some basic way, so that he seemed a different man entirely.

Ruiz felt sick to his stomach, but he couldn't turn away.

The first major episode of Rontleses' Expiation began. The conjuror flung a thin white silk over the former coercer, who sagged in the middle of the frame, apparently exhausted by the preliminaries. The folds of the silk settled over the victim like fog, and by some trick of arrangement, seemed no longer to be hiding a human shape, but something monstrous, something pregnant with ugliness. The torches guttered low for an instant, motion rippled the silk —then the conjuror whipped it away.

Rontleses had suffered a terrible metamorphosis and now resembled a huge spider with a half-human face. By some means, the ligaments of his legs had been stretched or severed to allow his legs to be twisted up behind his head and over his shoulder. His toes pointed downward in an unnatural manner; they jiggled feebly, and his arms waved spastically from beneath his buttocks. Four artificial limbs had been attached to his abdomen; these flipped about with more energy than his natural limbs, and after a moment Ruiz saw that they were animated by snakes held within the pale leather tubes. The reptiles struck at each other, and at Rontleses' flesh, with indiscriminate enthusiasm.

Rontleses could not scream, apparently because the spider mask he now wore over his lower face also functioned as a gag. But his eyes were wild with pain, and he jerked his head violently to and fro, adding to the theatrical impact of his new form.

The conjuror bowed low to Lord Brinslevos. "Thus do we see the Expiant in his true shape, an insect who would sting his Lord's hand."

The Expiation proceeded.

The conjuror poured onto Rontleses' body a hundred insects, which burrowed into the victim's skin and disappeared, until the conjuror clapped his hands and shouted an arcane word, whereupon the insects emerged and flew away. The exit wounds formed a bright red message in the angular Pharaohan script. It seemed to be an apology, but it was legible only for an instant, before the blood ran down Rontleses' torso and blurred the letters.

An intermission ensued, while the conjuror treated the victim for shock and stanched the blood.

When the Expiation resumed, the former coercer hardly seemed human, except for his eyes, which now appeared to view the world with as much bewilderment as pain. He hung from his frame and accepted the further indignities inflicted upon him with more docility than his executioner considered proper. Fire was employed, and knives, and various irritant venoms, and once again Rontleses writhed with as much vigor as his broken body allowed. Clever barbarities were enacted upon him, for perhaps another half hour.

In the end, Ruiz could no longer stand to watch, and so missed the moment of Rontleses' death, which was marked by a silence from the crowd. The silence seemed so portentous that he stood and, peering from his cage, witnessed the finale.

The corpse of Rontleses sat up in its coffin and pointed a pallid finger in Ruiz's direction.

Its mouth dropped open and then moved with a fair semblance of life. "Wuhiya the snake oil man is to blame," the corpse shouted, in a metallic buzzing voice that seemed entirely appropriate to its speaker. "Wuhiya has killed me, but he'll commit no more mischief." Its dead lips pulled back from its broken teeth in a grim parody of a smile. "Ha, ha."

Ruiz wondered what sort of apparatus animated the corpse, and whose voice issued from the torn lips. The eyes were dull, and looked in slightly different directions; that was the weakest part of the illusion, in Ruiz's opinion.

"Wuhiya plotted to destroy my Lord, from jealousy and madness, and he clouded my mind with his poisons, so that I failed my duty, and deserve no less than I've received. But I have my Lord's forgiveness, and I go now to the Land of Reward without regret." The corpse dropped its quivering finger, inclined its head respectfully toward Lord Brinslevos, and then fell back into its coffin.

The show was over. A murmur of disappointment ran through the crowd, and someone spoke close at hand. "The Lord was easy with Rontleses. Too bad; he deserved far worse, and now the oil peddler will suffer in his stead."

Ruiz shuddered. If he had just witnessed leniency, of what did harshness consist? The datasoak had glossed over some of the particulars of Pharaohan criminal justice; so much was certain. He felt the death net tug at his life, a bit more strongly than before, and for an instant he was almost tempted to give in and spare himself even the possibility, even the *contemplation* of such pain, such degradation. But then he shook himself and took a firmer grip on his unruly emotions.

Denklar will be here soon, he told himself, and forced himself to believe it.

CHAPTER 12

BUT Denklar did not come. Laborers took Rontleses' coffin away, and the square emptied. The temperature dropped, until Ruiz stood shivering in the center of the cage, unable to bear the icy touch of the metal on his naked body. He wrapped his arms around himself and hopped from foot to foot, minimizing the time each foot must spend in contact with the iron, and also attempting to generate a bit of internal warmth.

Hours passed, and the lights of Stegatum went out, until the town lay silent and dark under the starblaze. Still Denklar did not come. Ruiz's teeth chattered and his spirits sank.

Long past midnight, he heard the scuff of careful feet just outside the cage, and he suppressed a laugh of hysterical relief. But the steps seemed lighter than Denklar's could be, and a voice too soft and melodious to belong to the innkeeper spoke from the darkness. "Wuhiya? I've brought a water reed. Here."

A slender tube slid through a chink in the iron, and Ruiz took it gratefully. "Thank you; you're kind."

"It's little enough," said Relia the doxy. "I'd do more if I could, but what help could *I* be? Here's another one; keep it till you need it." She slipped another reed through the chink.

Ruiz snapped off the end of one reed, and allowed the slightly sour watery sap to drain into his mouth, which was dry as ashes, both from the effect of the day's deprivation and from terror. The fluid tasted wonderful, and for a brief instant he was entirely content. The sensation dissipated almost as swiftly as it had come. "Relia," he said, leaning against the cold iron, peering out. "Tell me, have you seen Denklar this evening? How did he seem?"

Relia sniffed. "He always seems the same, but tonight? I can't say. He's gone; no one knows where. The cooks were most put out, what with all the extra custom tonight, yokels in for the killings and so forth. Very odd, if you ask me— Denklar's always on hand when silver's to be had."

Ruiz's spirits plummeted again. Where was the innkeeper? Had he run away, for some reason beyond Ruiz's comprehension? Or was there something else wrong, something that hadn't yet occurred to him? A conviction grew in him that the latter explanation was somehow the true one, but his day in the cage and his witnessing of the coercer's Expiation had combined to slow his wits in some subtle way. He pounded his forehead with his fist. *Think, Ruiz Aw,* he exhorted. But nothing came.

"Well," said Relia, in a voice of soft regret. "I'll have to go in now; the night's cold and I'm not dressed for it."

"Wait!" Ruiz cast about for a purposeful course. Relia constituted his only avenue of action. "You said you'd help if you could."

"Yes. But what could I do?"

"Could you bring me something else?"

"Perhaps. The cages aren't watched at night. No one is clever enough to unlock them, from the outside or the inside."

"Good. Good. In my room, the one I slept in before I went to the keep . . . I left a packet of religious articles, hidden in one of the bed's pipes. Could you fetch it to me?"

Relia stirred uneasily, and Ruiz sensed her reluctance.

"I'd do the Lord in the eye, if I could do it and suffer no grief," she said. "I hate him, as would anyone with a heart. But I don't care to Expiate my feelings here."

Ruiz put his head against the iron, striving for a voice of calm persuasion. "No, no. Nor do I."

"I guess not. I don't want to see your tall pretty body all opened up on the stage; a waste that'll be." Relia chuckled throatily, a sound which under the present circumstances Ruiz found a bit grotesque.

"As you say," he said fervently. "Can you bring it?"

She drew a deep breath. "I'll try. Why not? How big is it, this packet?"

"Not large; it will fit through the chink, though you might have to hand it in a bit at a time. It's wrapped in a brown oilcloth, and has a number of little metal fetishes, which mean a lot to me. Don't play with them," Ruiz cautioned. "They're sacred." The bits in the packet, if activated inadvertently, might easily kill Relia before she could bring them to Ruiz.

"I'll try," she said again. She started to leave.

"Wait! Have you got a bit of wire about you? A pin, perhaps?"

She seemed to consider. "It'll do no good, Wuhiya."

"It'd occupy my time; I'm too cold to sleep."

"All right. Here's a rusty hairpin, which no one could say was mine if you're discovered with it. Still, if I can't bring your fetish bag . . . promise me you'll push the pin out the chink before it gets light. Or if you decide to open a vein, wipe the blood off before you push it out, so they'll think you used your teeth."

With trembling fingers he took the pin, which was long and slender and springy, and perfect for his purposes. "I promise."

RUIZ STRUGGLED WITH the lock for an hour, until his sore fingers were numb with cold and exertion. But the lock remained obdurate; its apparent crudeness concealed wards of unusual cleverness. Finally he desisted and admitted defeat. *Not surprising,* he thought, *that the locks should be good, on a world full of magicians.* He lapsed into a brief period of despair, but then he recalled that Relia would be bringing his tools soon. Soon.

He kept hoping, until the Pharaohan sky began to grow light.

STEGATUM WOKE EARLY, and tradesmen clattered back and forth across the square, rousing Ruiz from his apathy. He found that he looked forward to the heat of the day after the icy night; such was the shortsighted instinct of the body.

He was watching the light strengthen over the town, conscious that he might never see such a thing again, when a peremptory rap brought him across the cage to the shadowed side. He looked out and saw nothing, and then thought to apply his eye to a lower chink. There he saw the smallest of the boys who had greeted him on his arrival into Stegatum.

"Hello," he said.

The boy watched him earnestly for a moment. "We're sorry you'll die."

"Me too."

"It ain't a good way to die . . . though they say you'll bring a good rainstorm."

"Do they?"

"Yeh. They say your Exp'ation been put off till tomorrow night, so the Lord's foolkiller have time to come up with some fine new tricks. Not a drop did fall, for the coercer's dying . . . old stuff. We seed it all before."

"Old stuff, huh?"

"Yeh. It's no easy job, being the Lord's foolkiller, 'cause we got so many fools here, so the Lord's always having to do 'em down. Hard to come up with new 'lusions."

"I suppose." The conversation was disheartening on one level, but also a great relief. He might live another night, if the boy could be believed. Then again, the boy might only be reporting a rumor.

The boy showed no signs of departing. "Say," he said tentatively. "Since you not be needing your tricks, maybe you could show me how you did that gem and bug trick you shown us. I never saw that one before."

A notion occurred to Ruiz. "Perhaps I could. But I need my apparatus, and they took everything."

"Oh," said the boy regretfully, and started to turn away.

"Wait! I have an idea."

"What's that?"

"Well . . . listen. Did you see Relia anywhere about, this morning?"

"Denklar's whore? Nope. Didn' see him neither. Maybe they run off together." The little boy snickered in a manner much too old for his years. "Why?"

"Hmmm. Let me think."

He thought. Denklar gone? Relia gone? The only two people who were in a position to help him were missing. What did that suggest? Perhaps someone was actively working against him, someone he didn't know anything about.

"What's your name?" he asked the boy.

"Brumbet."

"Brumbet, eh? A promising name. You want to be a conjuror, then?"

"Who don't? But if I can't be a conjuror, I won't be an oil man. Who wants to hear voices all day, and spend the night having bad dreams? Then like as not I'd end trussed up on the stage, like you done." The small boy delivered this speech in phlegmatic tones.

"Good thinking. I wish I'd been as smart as you when I was your age. Tell me, Brumbet. Seen any new faces around town?"

The boy guffawed. "Yeh. Town's full of 'em, here for the killings."

"Hmmm. Well, what about before . . . say, a couple of days ago?"

The boy rubbed his chin in a curiously adult manner. "You mean, like t'other oil man, the rich one?"

"Right! When did he come?"

"Night you left, and then he went away again, but he's back now. Though I ain't seen him."

"How do you know he's here, then?"

Brumbet looked scornful. "His striderbeast's in the stable. You think I smell like this 'cause I spend all day shoveling moonpoppies?"

"I hadn't noticed. What's he look like?"

"Tall man, but not 'risto-faced like you. Though he's got a striderbeast and you don't. Still, he looks to be a lizard-cutter, you ask me. Up to no good, but too mean to get caught. Not like you."

"Mean man, eh? Where do you think he might be?"

"Don't know, but could be Denklar put him in the back corner, same room you stayed in, away from the decent folk. Maybe he's there, sleeping off a binge."

"Maybe. Maybe so. Well, that's a problem. I left my little bag of tricks hidden in that room, before I went up to the keep. If they're still there . . . well, I could show you how to work a couple of them, if I'm still here tonight."

The boy leaned close and his narrow face was alight with anticipation. "For real? I'll fetch your tricks; you tell me where to find 'em."

Ruiz forced himself to sound reluctant. "Well, but what if the mean man is in there? I'll show my tricks to you, but I'd rather they rusted away than go to a stranger."

"No worry. I'll wait till he goes to the shitter, or to supper, or I'll yell 'Fire!' in the hallway." The boy grinned. "I ain't stupid, no matter what my brother says."

"All right," Ruiz said. "I'll tell you where to find the tricks, and you bring them to me. You mustn't play with them before I show you how to work them—they're dangerous, some of them."

Brumbet curled his lip. "I told you I ain't stupid."

Ruiz remembered that he was on Pharaoh, where illusions could be very grim indeed, and nodded. "I believe it. Be very careful of the tall lizard-cutter. He might well be even meaner than you think."

THE DAY PASSED slowly. The women came to pour water on the roof, but this time they were disinclined to gossip.

As they were reattaching their buckets to their yokes, Ruiz asked them if he was to make Expiation that night. They exchanged pitying glances.

"No," said the woman who had spoken with him the day before. "The Lord's executioner researches novelties."

"Ahh . . ." Ruiz said glumly, concealing his elation.

The women left and Ruiz waited.

NIGHT FELL, AND no one came to set up the stage. Ruiz was briefly wilted with relief, then taut with hope and dread. Where was the boy? Had he disappeared down the same hole as Denklar and Relia?

An hour after sunset, he heard a patter of small bare feet and the rasping breath of a frightened child.

"What is it?" he whispered.

No reply came for a moment, but then a small quavering voice spoke. "Dead things," Brumbet said. "The room got dead things in it. I waited till the man went down to supper, an' crawled over the roof and in the hall window. There was dead things under the bed, two of 'em, a fat man and a girl, but I wouldn't look at the faces."

Ruiz's heart sank. "Did you get the tricks?"

" 'Course—they hid right where you said. I ain't stupid. Didn' go to Provost's hut neither. Dead things'll keep till you show me. Maybe I won't need to tell anyone, 'cause they're starting to stink."

"Good thinking. Well, give me the tricks."

Brumbet seemed to consider. "Now wait. How do I know you'll show me all?"

"You're smart. Tell you what: I'll do one at a time, and then give them back to you."

"All right. Which first?" The boy unrolled the bundle, and metal bits glimmered in the starblaze.

"Hmmm," Ruiz murmured, pretending to consider. "First, a simple passing-through-metal illusion."

Brumbet sniffed, unimpressed. "Everyone knows the ring trick, even babies."

"This version has a clever twist. Give me the fluted cylinder . . . yes, that one. And the silver half-ring, and that thing that looks like a pipe with lugs at one end."

Somewhat reluctantly, Brumbet passed the pieces

through the chink. When he had them all, Ruiz began to feel alive again.

He snapped the pinbeam laser together and burned off the lock in a shower of pink sparks.

He stepped out into freedom and drew a deep breath. The square was deserted, and he detected no rustle of alarm from the town. Brumbet stared up at him, shock masking his small features.

Ruiz snatched the bundle of tools from the boy.

Brumbet started to protest, but Ruiz looked at him and the boy skittered back, as though he had seen something dire in Ruiz's face.

"Never mind," said the boy, suddenly resigned. "You're a mean man, too, meaner than he is—I see it now. I ain't stupid."

"No, you're not. I'm sorry to have deceived you, but it was necessary. I'm grateful, too, but I can't reward you just now."

Brumbet sniffed. "I be young yet. Next year you wouldn't a tricked me."

"Probably so. Go home, Brumbet, and say nothing to anyone. Else I'll have to hurt you," advised Ruiz absently. He was already thinking of the man in the inn, and how best to capture him. He happened to look down at Brumbet one last time, and was startled by the contempt he saw in the small face. Then Brumbet ran away.

NO LIGHT SHONE from the window. Perhaps his enemy was still at supper. Though Ruiz would have preferred to confirm the man's whereabouts, he was still naked, still a condemned felon, and he could conceive of no safe way to reach the dining room. So he jumped, caught the edge of the window, and pulled himself up cautiously.

The smell of death was strong, but nothing moved in the darkness inside the room. Ruiz cut away the bars with his pinbeam and slithered in. No one attacked him.

He stood motionless for a moment, extending his senses, reaching out for any evidence that the room was booby-trapped or otherwise dangerous. He heard nothing, felt no vibration, saw no gleaming telltales. He twisted the pinbeam's vernier, so that it gave a soft red glow, and examined the room thoroughly.

The man's saddlebags hung from a peg. These Ruiz did not touch, fearing alarms or mantraps. He found no other obvious security measures, and marveled at the man's confidence or ineptitude. He found the bodies of Denklar and Relia, jammed together under the bed, which showed evidence of recent use. The innkeeper had been dead for a day or two, Relia for a shorter time—her body showed cuts and bruises and other signs that her death had not been an easy one. Ruiz permitted a chill anger to fill his heart.

He squatted against the wall by the door, and readjusted his pinbeam. He felt no exhaustion; rather, his body sang with the need for violence, and he waited eagerly, growing more impatient with each minute that passed.

By the time heavy steps came down the corridor toward the room, he felt more like a feral animal than a human being. He felt his face; his lips were skinned back in a grin, so that his cheeks ached. He reached for calm and was partially successful.

The assassin threw back the door and swaggered inside heedlessly. Ruiz almost laughed at the man's foolishness. To so disregard the possibility of Ruiz's vengeance—incredible! The light from the hallway was perfectly adequate to Ruiz's purposes. Without rising, he swept the pinbeam through the man's spine. Before the legs had begun to collapse, he put a beam through one elbow, then the other.

The man fell facedown, legs paralyzed, arms useless. He screamed, a high breathless sound, expressing almost as much surprise as pain. Ruiz advanced cautiously, ignoring the screaming, relying on Denklar's assurances regarding the room's soundproofing.

He turned the assassin onto his back, using his toe, pinbeam aimed at the man's forehead.

"We meet at last," Ruiz said, full of the purest joy.

The man gulped air and stopped screaming. In the dimness, his face was unclear.

"What shall I do with you, now I have you?" Ruiz mused pleasantly.

The man remained silent, except for the hiss of his breath.

"Can't you speak? If you'll tell me why you've done these things to me, and to the League, I can promise you an easy death. Otherwise I'll leave you for Brinslevos. He'll be distressed by my escape, but he'll have you—I was careful with the beam and you'll live another day or two. I imagine he'll be happy to uncover a conspiracy of oil men, and one's as good as another, eh?"

Finally the man smiled. "You won't give me to Brinslevos."

"Why not?" Ruiz leaned forward, full of interest.

But the man twitched and died, as suddenly as the technician had aboard the orbital platform.

This is a frustrating thing, Ruiz thought. All his energy drained away, and he sat down to rest and consider. The assassin's death had the same texture as the technician's death. Coincidence? Probably not. He thought of the Gencha, and wondered.

After a bit, he shook himself and lit the lamp. He searched the room, finding nothing new. He approached the saddlebags with elaborate caution, but found them unprotected. *Such insouciance,* Ruiz thought, marveling. The pack contained a water flask, a sack of dried meat and fruit, a bundle of oil vials—less complete than Ruiz's had been. Beneath a false bottom he found a collection of pangalac skinjectors, several neural inducers, and a bandolier of entertainment skeins. Under these trade goods, at the very bottom, he discovered a dataslate.

He drank from the bottle, hoping that the dead man's apparent lack of subtlety was real and that the water was unpoisoned. He activated the slate and probed its architecture carefully. The slate's access security was rudimentary, and Ruiz easily penetrated it. The slate held nothing but a list of conjuring troupes. Appended to each troupe's file was a list of personnel, a synopsis of the troupe's major illusions, a schedule of upcoming performances, and a priority number.

Ruiz studied the listings with intense interest. One troupe was identified with a priority number higher than any of the

others. In three days, the troupe would perform a great Expiation in a town named Bidderum, a hundred kilometers to
the south.

Luck indeed, he thought. Here was a member of the
poachers' organization, beyond a doubt. He wondered how
this list would compare to the official League list. Beyond a
doubt, the lists would not be identical.

He would be at Bidderum in three days.

He overcame his distaste and stripped the corpse, and
then dressed in the assassin's rags. The assassin had carried
a number of weapons concealed under his rags; these Ruiz
took also, as well as the man's identity plaque. He picked up
the saddlebags and slipped out of the room.

The inn was quiet. Apparently the folk of Stegatum were
abed. Ruiz reached Denklar's apartments without meeting
anyone, and retrieved his staff.

In the stable, Ruiz had a bit of difficulty saddling the
assassin's striderbeast, which apparently smelled the death
on its former master's clothes.

But finally he was safely away from Stegatum, riding over
the waste under the moon, and the sensation of escape, of
freedom, was as fine a feeling as he could remember.

CHAPTER 13

RUIZ AW squatted in the meager shade of a mud wall, waiting for the parade. Sweat trickled over his body, though the sun was sinking fast.

The townspeople of Bidderum filled the street leading into the square. They kept a cautious distance from Ruiz, respecting his strangeness. To encourage them, he fixed a leer of affable madness on his face.

Ruiz felt the hard-packed clay of the street tremble under his feet. As the crowd condensed on the shady side of the street, he heard the gasp and whistle of steam thumpers, and he stood up in the properly respectful attitude. The parade toiled up the street toward him, moving at a slow dragstep that matched the rhythm of the thumpers. The thumpermen passed, three abreast, the huge steel feet of their machines slamming down on the street with jarring force, in perfect unison. As the thumper rebounded into the air, each man stepped forward smartly, wrestling his machine ahead, straining at the long handles braced to it. It was clearly no job for weaklings, for the men, all brawny specimens, sweated and struggled as they marched their smoking ma-

chines into the central square. In earlier times the
thumpermen would have carried great balks of timber to
shake the earth. *Progress,* Ruiz thought, and chuckled.

Behind them came several dozen musicians in the traditional Pharaohanic mourning garb, which consisted of
masses of thorny shrubs bound to the torso with leather
straps. Ruiz saw that they were of all ages and sexes, and
that many exhibited entertaining deformities. All held eccentric musical instruments in their hands, but marched in
silence. It was an artistic and well-balanced group, and the
thorns were cinched in so that the blood ran in thin striations down each lean dusty body, an effect which indicated a
first-class production budget. Dancing about the perimeter
of the orchestra was a cadre of clowns, jugglers, minor
mages, streamer tossers, and glitter flingers.

The last mourner, a much-scarred ancient with a particularly large and uncomfortable collection of thornbushes,
preceded the steam engine that drew the stage. This engine
was in the shape of a scarab, plated with damascened steel
and turning man-high spiked driver wheels.

The stage it pulled was skirted with flashing metal-thread
tapestries, showing scenes from the Pharaoan mythos.
Mounted on a central platform was a grand gilded sarcophagus, carved with various beasts, demons, and the several
Pharaohan gods of redemption and resurrection. On the
four corners of the stage stood the members of the phoenix
troup. Each held a ritual pose, as still as the jounce and
sway of the stage would allow. Three were older men in the
fanciful costumes of senior conjurors, and one was a young
woman of great beauty. She had the pale olive skin and fine
coppery-black hair of the Pharaohan nobility, and wore the
linen robe of the intended phoenix. As the stage jerked past
she looked directly at Ruiz Aw, but then her gaze swept
past, impersonal and unseeing.

He found that he had dropped his lunatic grin, just for a
moment.

Behind the stage trudged three fat doctors, there to cer-
tify the death. They wore over their shoulders the tanned
hides of large arroyo lizards, with skull and toothy upper
jaw worn as hats. This symbolized the chancy nature of

their calling, though Ruiz supposed that the costume was also a gesture of professional respect. The lizards provided many patients.

Ruiz Aw bent his head and stared at his dirty toes. The datasoak had given him the outline of what was to follow. Reluctantly, he joined the crowd filtering into the square.

NISA, FORMER FAVORED daughter of the King, concentrated on her balance as the stage jolted toward the Place of Artful Anguish, willing all other thoughts away, pushing her mind into a safe golden corner, feeling nothing but the throb of life in her veins. The drug made it easier; she remembered the way the philterer had made it for her, stirring the fine red granules into the pale wine. He'd handed the goblet to her with an air of ceremony, and in his faded old eyes she'd read both envy and compassion.

Since that moment, she had only broken bits of memory, like the dreams or nightmares of a restless sleeper.

. . . The gowners, washing her with sweet oils, while she stood, passive, arms lifted, eyes closed, feeling their subtle touch on her body, caressing, teasing.

. . . Flomel, helping her to mount the stage, dark eyes burning in his narrow face. He pulled her toward her station as if she floated above the scarred wood of the stage. "You will be magnificent!" Flomel whispered to her fiercely, holding her face in his long clever fingers.

. . . The heat, the dust, the smell of the people in the narrow streets of Bidderum, the stench of refuse from the alley mouths. She breathed it all in, as if it were fine perfume, filling herself with sensation one last time.

Just before the stage rumbled into Bidderum's central square, she caught sight of an extraordinary figure in the crowd that lined the gate. He was garbed in the fantastic rags of a snake oil peddler, as tall as if he carried noble blood, with a face like a daybat, sharp and imperious. He was so unexpected a sight that she was briefly shocked from the grip of the drug. Her eyes looked into his for a moment, and his glance reminded her of the mirrored hall of her father's palace, where Nisa could look into the polished metal and see herself growing smaller with each new reflection. His eyes were hard as glass, but just for a moment they softened.

She allowed her gaze to float away. Were she not promised to Expiation, were she at home in her father's palace, she would probably send her guards for the strange casteless man, and so would have yet another folly to Expiate. Then the drug pulled her under again, and she thought no more.

THE SQUARE OF Bidderum was broad and level, surrounded by earthen walls that gave increasing shade as the sun dropped toward the west. Ruiz elbowed his way through the press, ignoring the muttered curses that followed his progress, until he reached a low buttress that provided an excellent vantage. He unceremoniously displaced a group of urchins who were already established there, swinging his staff cheerfully until they fled, cursing him. He hitched up his rags and settled back on his heels to wait for the opening act.

To his left a stocky woman, wearing the clay-spattered apron of a potter, talked with her neighbor, an ancient with the tattoos of a scribe. "Mark my words," she said, speaking loudly into the ear of the scribe, "this is an unhealthy sort of entertainment. Things were different in your day, eh?"

"Yes, yes. I sometimes think the young are too ambitious."

"Too ambitious? You put it gently, venerable Dudmose." Her hairy brows knit into an expression of righteous concern. "Others might call this blasphemy. I've yet to witness a phoenix, and this is the fifth attempt in Bidderum this tenyear. And the King's daughter besides; where will it end?"

The scribe hawked up a wad of phlegm and spat untidily. "I stand by my statement."

Then the two were swept away by the eddying crowd, out of eavesdropping range.

The square was packed, not only with townsfolk, but also with many farmers and artisans from the outlying regions of the nomarchy. On the far side of the square, Ruiz could see a bright pavilion, full of local nobles, drinking wine and smoking oil. A platoon of the nomarch's guards stood before the pavilion, sweating in leather corselets and iron helmets. The soldiers watched the commoners enviously, particularly those who had come equipped with wineskins, food hampers, and one-legged stools.

A ripple ran through the crowd as the senior mage stepped from his place to the apron of the stage. He was a wiry man of late middle age, and his tattoos emphasized dignity and artful restraint. His voice was a fine resonant baritone. "Citizens of Bidderum, I greet you in the name of the King of Kings, to whom is given life forever: Bhasrahmet, son of Halakhum—Bhasrahmet, called the Great, who has graciously permitted this attempt to portray the deepest mysteries of our calling." From the air the conjuror produced a gilded wooden tablet, sealed with the indigo chop of the king. With a flourish he presented it to the waiting captain of the guard, who relayed it briskly to the pavilion. The nomarch of Bidderum, a slender, nervous-looking young Lord only recently elevated, took the license and gestured his approval.

The conjuror bowed deeply. He turned to his two fellows, clapping his hands together with a sound like wood striking metal. They leaped forward in a flutter of rich gowns, leaving the woman motionless at the back of the stage. The lesser mages touched hands ceremoniously, and as they drew apart, a wand of polished black wood appeared to grow between their hands. Their leader seized the wand and struck it to the stage. Crimson light flared and a veil of red silk shot up, to be deftly taken in midair by his two assistants. Trailing the swirling cloud of fabric they ran back and flung it over the woman, where it settled over her still form. The leader made a series of arcane motions with his wand, culminating in a dramatic slash in the direction of the shrouded woman. In a glitter of golden sparks the shroud collapsed to the floor of the stage. Ruiz leaned forward, watched the empty shroud disappear into the cracks of the flooring, running like quicksilver blood.

The three performers linked arms and began to spin in a tight circle. As their speed increased the leader began to whirl his wand overhead, making a moaning sound. A great tube of shiny blue cloth rose slowly around the spinning mages, lifting higher and higher until they were completely hidden. It rose higher still, until it swayed over the platform like a vast serpent. The stamping of the mages' feet and the shriek of the wand were clearly audible. When it seemed from the sounds that those within had accelerated to a humanly impossible speed, the tube belched forth a small cloud of metallic glitter and collapsed empty to the stage.

During the lengthy intermission that followed, Ruiz Aw leaned back and tried to get comfortable against the hard mud of the buttress.

The blinding pinpoint of the sun sank behind the toothy crags of the Senmut Hills. With twilight, torches flared into life on the stage and the nobles ordered braziers lit in the pavilion against the swift chill.

With full dark, two snag-toothed ruffians attempted to dispossess Ruiz of his perch, but he rolled his eyes maniacally at them, and set his staff to output subsonics in the most tooth-grinding register. The ruffians faded away with gratifying speed, making curse-warding gestures.

The mourner-musicians, who were arranged in ritual ranks between the stage and the pavilion, began to play a portentous dirge. On the stage the lid of the gilded sarcophagus rose. When the heavy stone lid had rocked back completely on its stops, the three mages leaped out. There was a final screeching crescendo from the orchestra, then silence.

The three stood in a row at stage front, arms raised, each wearing dull black robes, their features concealed beneath the fantastic masks of the Dead Trinity. Central was Bhas, the dry god, god of death and heat and choking dust. The lower half of his mask was an insect's complicated mouth; the upper half, with its armored eyes, was the skull of a deadly lizard, one that carried venom in the spikes of its crest. The mask was edged with plumes of yellow and rust, signifying barrenness.

Flanking Bhas were his two sons by the lost goddess Nekhret, deity of improvidence. On his left was Thethri, god of famine, masked as a starving child. On his right was Menk, god of slavery, with a man's eyes but a dog's muzzle.

Behind them a fourth figure emerged from the sarcophagus, lifted on a hidden piston; the goddess Hashupit. In the first moment Ruiz hardly recognized the phoenix. The embroidered robes of the goddess enclosed her, a rich pale gem in a finely wrought setting. In Pharaohan theater, gods are introduced in masks, but not goddesses.

Her fine-boned face was alive now, as if the pleasure of the performance had overcome her dread.

Pipes skirled and the dark gods tore off their masks, revealing smaller masks that clung tightly to their heads, even uglier and more realistic than the overmasks. They flung the overmasks into a heap at center stage and pranced in a circle, while the goddess ignored them. A puff of green smoke obscured the masks and when it cleared the pile heaved with unpleasant movement. The mages drew aside and stood like statues. The heap burst apart with a hiss and a shriek of pain. A jackal-like creature scrambled free, dragging its hindquarters, pursued by an armored lizard. In a bound the lizard was on the jackal, crushing the foxy head with one snap of its jaws.

As the lizard fed, the scrabble of insect feet was clearly audible over the crunch of flesh and bone. Ruiz was surprised to see the audience closest to the stage drawing back in a welter of overturned stools and spilled wineskins. Then he saw the first of the bonan, an insect with a painful, but not dangerous sting. The wings of these were so heavily gilded that they could make only short flights at the shrieking crowd, but they made a fine glittering display as they shot through the torchlight.

It was not until the last bonan was crushed underfoot and the crowd had regained some composure that the lizard lurched toward the edge of the platform. There were some genuine wails of fear at this development, and even some rapid movement in the nobles' pavilion. But the lizard disappeared down a trap just a meter from the edge. A faint shriek from within the stage drew several gloomy mutters from the nearest spectators.

Through all this savage movement, the phoenix looked on calmly, a faint inward smile in her eyes.

Thus began the performance of the traditional play called *The Withering of the World.*

IT WAS IN the Green Time, before the Mistake, when the land was covered with sweet grass and water ran naked under the sky. The Three were in their great banishment, prisoned in Hell, far below the edge of the world. The Three had festered there for a million years; and so above all was tranquil.

The goddess Hashupit walked one day along the edge of the world, alone. This was long before the building of the Worldwall, so that she could stand at the very edge and look out over the poisonous clouds.

She heard a dry voice, tiny, calling as if from a great distance. "Hashupit, cool, pale Hashupit," it said.

She paused and looked out across the gulf of Hell, for the voice seemed to come, however impossibly, from the void. But she saw nothing, only the thick steams of Hell. After a time she felt a touch of fear, the first time she'd felt that emotion during the long eons of her existence. She heard nothing more, so she shrugged her perfect shoulders and returned to her father's palace.

The next day she didn't walk, nor the next.

When finally she resumed her walks, she stayed away from the edge of the world. Yet when she heard the voice again it was stronger, and beneath its arid rasp she felt the unmistakable resonance of power. "Hashupit—sweet, cool, cloud-haired Hashupit," it said, then the voice drew a breath, a bellows firing a forge. "I can show you a clever trick."

She waited a safe distance from the brink until almost dark—then she fled home feeling a mixture of panic and curiosity. A million long years had worn away since Hashupit had had a new admirer.

RUIZ WAS AMAZED at the texture of the performance. With delicate, controlled gestures, the phoenix acted the part of the goddess, soft and foolish, so effectively that Ruiz was not distracted by the primitive mechanisms of the play. The illusion was remarkable.

The three magicians clustered together on the lower level of the stage. From the huddle a thin orange paper snake occasionally shot skyward, symbolizing a poisonous thought directed at the favored gods above. The snakes sailed up into the night and then fell among the spectators, who ripped them open for the cheap beads and candy within.

Ruiz's staff shuddered in his hand, signaling the movement of a large metallic mass nearby, and Ruiz jerked his attention from the play to the staff's readout, disguised as a nacre inlay. It flickered unsteadily. But a moment later the indicator faded to normal. Ruiz frowned. Either the staff was reacting to a chance orientation in the metal-bedizened crowd—or they had very good dampers on the vessel he hoped to board.

In any case there was nothing he could do yet, and he sank back into the performance.

NOW HASHUPIT CAME to the edge of the world every day, but the voice was silent.

But a week later, when she'd almost lost interest, it returned, with a power like avalanching dust.

"Hashupit—smooth-skinned dewy Hashupit, have you forgotten me?"

"Who are you?" she asked, as bravely as she could.

Below the edge of the world Bhas paused at the top of his climb, mightily pleased. The fair gods above had truly forgotten him. "I am the spirit of this place," he replied. "I can be pleasing."

"Just show yourself," she said.

RUIZ SAW THE player pull a black silk hood down over the horrible features of Bhas. He mounted the upper stage with a clever slither. He stood before Hashupit, and from his fist sprouted a bouquet of poisonous pink thistles, arranged with black razorgrass.

HE PRESENTED AN interesting appearance to the goddess. He was tall, elegantly thin, and though his black garments were unfashionable, she saw that he dressed with a dandy's attention to detail.

"We meet," he said, bowing low. He handed her the bouquet. "From the foothills of Hell, for you."

She took the bouquet, but the blossoms stung her, and when she dropped it the razorgrass sliced her fingers.

She was angered, and a red shimmer filled the air. "This is my father's world," she said. "Be off with you, before I call him to devour you."

"As you wish," Bhas said. "But first, allow me to make amends, please." He raised his hand high, and the red glow of her anger was pulled from the air into the cup of his hand. In an instant a silver bowl lay there and Bhas proffered it to her.

"Here, lovely Hashupit, lave your pretty fingers here," Bhas said, in courtly tones.

Her anger had been pulled away from her so quickly that she was disoriented and pliable, and without thinking she put her hand in the clear fluid. The blood from her fingers swirled in the bowl and the fluid began to darken, from claret to thick purple to black. Hashupit felt an intolerable pain in her hand. She jerked it out. "What have you done?" she gasped.

Bhas laughed, a cruel dry croak of amusement. "Poor Hashupit," he said cheerfully, "you mustn't depend upon your father in this. If you seek his aid, your fingers will never be pretty again. Look now, Hashupit."

She looked and it was almost worse than the pain. The skin was dark and mottled, the fingers swollen into five ugly sausages.

"You'll pay . . ." she said, but Bhas gripped her arm in a hot dry hand.

"I have paid, no, never doubt that," he crooned, low and malevolent. "But that time is over. Remember, if you go to your father, it will be much worse. Think of the wrinkles, the sagging flesh of age, the ugly bones beneath." Then he released her and she stumbled away as fast as she could go.

At the palace, she went up to her apartments, hiding her hand in a fold of her dress, going by little-used ways. She met none of the other gods and godlings, for which she was grateful. The pain in her hand had subsided to a dull ache, centered in the joints of fingers and wrist. She looked fearfully at it, then held it up before her eyes.

In those days, the gods were above decay—immortal, for all they knew. Hashupit stared at her hand, withered, knobknuckled, blue-veined, spotted with the discolorations of age. She made a small, unbelieving sound and fainted to the gold-leafed floor of her bedroom.

CHAPTER 14

SWEAT ran down Ruiz Aw's face, though the air was now quite cool. He found himself unprepared for the play to end so soon. The phoenix lay still on the gilded stage, a cast away blossom. The audience seemed to hold its collective breath. A black curtain swirled up from the stage apron, concealing the scene.

Moments later it dropped to reveal Hashupit, both hands wrapped carefully in rainbow gauze, waiting at the vast table of her father, the god of gods, Canesh.

SHE STOOD WELL back from her father's huge devouring mouth. He would never consume her purposely, but his mouth was so vast and his hunger so great that accidents were possible. Her father's arms, long and knotty as thorn trees, swept the sacrifices into his maw. As fast as he cleared the table, new heaps magically appeared, bullocks, bushels of sweet fruit, countless fowl, piles of ripe grain, pigs large and small—all sent to him by his priesthood, who saw value in keeping the most powerful and capricious of the gods fully occupied. Everything disappeared down her father's throat, but though his jaws worked ferociously, he never quite caught up with the flow. Some of the food spilled and was carried away by mortal servitors, tiny as insects under the table of the god.

"Father," she greeted him, intending to confess her foolish actions and rely on his power to set things right.

"Daughter, it's pleasant to see you," replied Canesh, in rumbling tones.

Hashupit felt an unpleasant tingle in her wounded hand. "Father," she began, "a very strange thing has happened to me." She stifled a shriek as her hand spasmed in agony. She held it below the table edge, where her father couldn't see, and looked. Creeping up her wrist was a hideous line. Above was the polished skin of the goddess; below was the liverish withered flesh of age.

She remembered the demon's warning.

"I . . . I might have an ache—a stomachache, the mortals call it. Is this possible, Father?" The line of corruption halted just above her wrist, but gave none of its ground back. Hashupit felt close to fainting again.

Her father eyed her for a long moment, his jaws slowing slightly. Then he smiled. "It's only because you're such a picky eater that you've never noticed that gluttony takes vengeance even on the gods." Canesh rumbled a laugh. A belch enveloped Hashupit in a pungent cloud, and she held her breath. "Too much amberberry nectar, eh?"

"Perhaps that's it," she said. She managed a wan smile and withdrew from his dining hall.

RUIZ WATCHED THE phoenix, back in her chambers, unwind the rainbow gauze from her hand, slowly and methodically. He shuddered with disgust and pity as she raised her disfigured hand, though the datasoak told him that she'd been painblocked before the hand had been deep-fried in hot oil and then desiccated in a crude vacuum dryer. The hand was a hideous claw, and the phoenix looked at it in disbelief before fainting again.

The curtain fell on the first act—though in this case it fell upward from the stage, magically suspended from the night air.

During the brief intermission, Ruiz fixed his eyes on the ground and tried to think of anything but the phoenix and her pain.

The curtain dropped to begin the second half of the play. The phoenix knelt at the feet of the senior conjuror, his god-mask still concealed in black silk. At the far corners stood the two other mages, also masked. The torches around the perimeter of the stage alternated darkness and light, pulsing through no visible agency. The tableau held motionless for a long, long moment before Bhas raised his arms in jerky greeting.

HASHUPIT FOUND BHAS waiting for her at the edge of the world. She lay her head against his feet, sobbing. "Oh please," she said, "please, what can you want of me?"

The dry voice of power spoke gently. "Ah, lovely Hashupit, I only mean to help. The pain is necessary—necessary to ensure your future happiness. It's true!"

Hashupit wordlessly raised the claw, shaking.

Bhas was silent for a long moment, looking down on her, as if with fondness. Then he spoke, and his voice resonated with curiosity and pity, or so it seemed to Hashupit. "Hashupit," he asked, "how is it that you've never mated? Never in these long eons?"

For a moment she forgot the pain, and she straightened her back into a haughty line. "How can this be your concern?"

Bhas seemed to grow taller, wider, darker. His voice rolled over her, suffocating her under its power. "You forget yourself, Hashupit. My concerns are what I make them."

ON THE STAGE the torches fluttered faster, and from the orchestra rose a low discordant wail, a raw sound that scratched at Ruiz's nerves.

·   ·   ·

THE SONS OF BHAS sidled closer. In the tracks of Thethri, god of famine, tufts of withergrass sprang up, writhing with a spastic urgency. From the footprints of Menk, god of slavery, grew a rank tangle of corpsewort, and the perfume of that ugly flower rolled out over the audience, a musty putridity. The goddess rose and drew back, noticing the two for the first time.

"And these weirdlings, who are they?" she asked, with as much of a sneer as her trembling lips allowed.

Bhas touched her hand and punished her with pain, pain that seared up her arm and clutched at her heart. She fell to the ground, rolling from side to side, striking at her claw with her good hand, as if to punish the source of her torment. When finally the pain eased, she sat up and looked at Bhas with eyes that held no more rebellion.

Bhas smiled beneath his mask, and it was as if the black silk was disturbed by the scurry of maggots. "These are your choices, Hashupit," he said, gesturing to his sons. "One will be your mate, the mate that was promised you when the world was young. As you were promised, lovely Hashupit, to us. Your father never told you of that bargain, did he?"

"No," she said. She could not bear to look at the awful trio, but their godly emanations touched her like a hot dirty wind; the black intensity of Bhas, the empty greed of Menk, the hopeless desperation of Thethri.

"But it's true, oh yes." Bhas stepped to her side. Twisting his thin powerful hand in her hair, he jerked her to her feet. She was too weak to resist, or even to support her own weight, so she hung from his hand like a trophy. "May I," said Bhas, "present my beloved sons?" He gestured with his free hand. "This is my firstborn, Menk."

Menk executed a servile bow, as stiff as a reanimated corpse. Hashupit shuddered, and Bhas gave her a small shake of admonishment. "And this," he continued, "is Thethri, the younger of my children."

Thethri didn't bow; rather, he stretched his arms out in a pleading gesture. Where the robe fell away from his arms, they appeared almost fleshless, bone covered with tightly stretched skin, and his fingers were talons.

Hashupit finally found the strength to stand, and Bhas

released her and stepped behind, resting his elegant hands on her shoulders. "You must choose," he whispered in her ear. "You have no choice but to choose. If you resist me you won't die, but you will wish to. You'll be forced to hide your hideousness in the deepest cavern you can find, lest those who once praised your beauty destroy you in a fury of loathing. Eh?"

Hashupit found it impossible to doubt him. "Are there no brides for your sons in Hell?" she asked, in a tiny defeated voice.

Bhas laughed, and his hands clenched on her shoulders, digging into her flesh. But the small pain was like a caress, compared to the agony of her hand. "Oh, perhaps there are," he answered, "but the Hellmaids are hard and rough in comparison to you, ripe Hashupit."

As if to punctuate his words, the pain in her hand flared, so that she almost passed out again. "Yes," she said. "I will choose."

RUIZ SHIVERED IN the increasing chill. He watched, completely absorbed, as the play progressed.

He watched as she chose Thethri. He watched as the gods unmasked, and Hashupit swooned yet again. In a swirl of blue glitter, the scene changed to the palace of Hashupit's father. The action of the play accelerated as Hashupit allowed Bhas and his sons within the gilded halls, where sweet fruit hung from branches that grew from the cool white stone, where new wine flowed from every courtyard fountain. The conjurors performed marvels of deception, shifting the scene as deftly as in any pangalac holodrama, while the beauty of the phoenix grew ragged, pressed between pain and horror. Her face bleached whiter with each passing moment, her hair grew lank with sweat. The Dry God and his sons prowled the corridors and gardens, and where they passed, death followed, stilling the fountains and withering the blossoms.

Ruiz felt a cold dread. Despite his conditioned detachment, he had begun to see the phoenix as something . . . human. Something more than an anonymous victim on a backwater client world. As she twisted and struggled, moving down the narrowing corridor of the plot, closer and closer to her death, it became more and more difficult for Ruiz to watch. Her eyes seemed to turn inward, the fullness of her lips was cramped into a tight line of misery, but through it all, she performed her role flawlessly, admirably, still the foolish sweet goddess.

The climax of the play approached. Ruiz stirred himself, descended from his vantage point. He began to slide through the crowd, as if in a trance, encountering no resistance from the citizens of Bidderum, who were even more caught up than he. Ruiz worked his way closer to the stage, his training taking over, while his mind continued to be held by the play and its marvels and terrors.

IN THE PALACE of Canesh—where before all had been cool delight—dry ruin spread. Bhas moved at will, corrupting all within, even the sacrifices on which Hashupit's father fed, so that the greatest of gods grew deathly ill. Canesh had barely enough strength to scrape the decaying scraps into his maw, and as Canesh weakened, all of Pharaoh approached death. Menk and Thethri stalked the land, infecting the world with their own special horrors.

As for the goddess Hashupit, she sat at the far end of her father's feasting table and watched, thinking of her mating ceremony on the morrow. She had no faith that she would survive long after that, after Bhas had secured his triumph, and in any case, Pharaoh would be dust, utterly and forever.

RUIZ STOOD AT the apron of the stage, waiting. His staff trembled in his hand. But he was so transfixed by the play that the staff had to increase its signal to a painful tingle before he responded and dropped his eyes to the indicator. Metal was moving nearby, a mass suggestive of the craft that Ruiz watched for. He looked back over his shoulder, striving to pierce the gloom beyond the cressets, though he knew that such a craft would have excellent visual shielding. He felt a familiar tightening between the shoulder blades, and he should have taken steps to purge the spell of the play from his mind. The indicators zeroed again, and he relaxed minimally. The poachers were evidently willing to wait for the end of the play.

FOR THE LAST time, Hashupit stood at the south edge of the world, looking down into Hell, her silk slippers touching the crumbling verge, where a heavy man would not dare stand. A hot wind lifted her cloud of fine hair and brought the scent of her body to her. She wore her favorite gown, so fine and sheer that her elegant flesh showed clearly beneath. Her ruined hand was wrapped in satin ribbon, cinched by strings of black sandpearls. She was, again, a magnificent sight, a believable goddess.

From the north came Bhas, to perform the ceremony of joining, the final cementing of his power. From the east staggered Thethri, bridegroom, holding his bloated belly as if it might fall off. From the west came Menk, a jealous witness to the ceremony. They slowly converged on the goddess, who shifted just a bit closer to the edge.

Bhas cried out in alarm, "Take care, beautiful Hashupit; the drop is far. You would not care for the steams of Hell, nor would I care to descend after you."

Thethri made a faint gurgling sound and extended his skeletal arms toward her.

"You see," Bhas said, "your husband-to-be is concerned. Please, come away from the edge."

She held up her hand, the one wrapped in ribbon. "I'm no longer so beautiful, am I?"

"No matter," Bhas said, edging closer by imperceptible stages. "Thethri is not particular."

"So I guessed."

Bhas stopped, just out of reach of Hashupit's arms. He eyed Hell's void uneasily, then stepped back a bit. "Menk," he ordered, "bring her away from the edge."

Menk folded his massive arms. "No, Father; I have no stomach to begin another million-year climb. You must fetch her yourself, or perhaps Thethri will do it." Menk laughed, a soft throaty snigger.

The end came swiftly.

Thethri tottered forward with a strangled cry of desire, and the goddess welcomed him with open arms. Bhas darted forward, too late, as the two toppled off the edge of the world, Thethri shrieking fear, Hashupit smiling like a bride, clinging tightly.

ON THE STAGE, plinths shot high, carrying Bhas and Menk upward out of the light of the torches, giving the illusion that Thethri and Hashupit were falling. Their bodies, supported by some unseen means, twisted and fluttered in the draft of a wind machine below the stage. In a moment they had "fallen" to the level of the first steams of Hell, represented by colored veils released into the blast. These veils were rippled by rising floods of darker and darker color as the two fell deeper and deeper into Hell—pure white yellowing gradually into pale sienna, darkening into the crimson of arterial blood, the purple of stained steel, and finally, the deepest black. Just before the torches guttered to their dimmest, while Thethri went windmilling on down to disappear into the depths of the stage, the goddess was struck by a ledge that slammed up to meet her. Her body bounded high, limbs loose, then fell back into a motionless heap.

Ruiz hoped fervently that the impact had killed her, or at least rendered her unconscious. He looked on, horrified, as she began to stir feebly on the stone.

Then she jerked, and her eyes bulged, and her face twisted out of that mask of unnatural beauty into the face of an ordinary woman in agony. She began to scream, but the sound was choked by the thorny leafless stem that burst from her mouth. Her body shook in the final moments; then the vines thrust through her abdomen with small geysers of blood.

She lay still, finally. The vines writhed upward and burst into flower, covering the corpse with great, white, sweet-scented double blooms.

Ruiz was shaken. The phoenix had been executed with a stiletto vine, an ephemeral species that grew on the upper slopes of Hell, seeds of which could be won only by slave Helldivers.

The lights came up and revealed the senior conjuror standing above the corpse of the phoenix, flanked by his two fellow performers. He began the traditional coda.

"And so the goddess Hashupit met her doom in Hell. But by her sacrifice we are spared Famine, and by her sacrifice the power of the remaining two of the Awful Three is diminished, so that our lives are bearable. Never must we forget that Thethri is climbing the walls of Hell, and will someday return, if the priests watching at the Worldwall are not vigilant."

The three performers bowed, and Ruiz saw a curious emotion in their eyes. He understood suddenly and strongly that these men expected translation to the Land of Reward. They had given the performance of their lives, the culmination of all their craft and faith, and they knew it. Only the frail magician who'd played Thethri seemed to feel any doubt that he wanted his reward, though emotion was hard to read in the tattooed wilderness of his face.

Ruiz's staff buzzed insistently. He fought his way through the last layer of the silent crowd.

"As Hashupit herself will rise one day, for not even death is forever," the conjuror finished, as Ruiz flung himself onto the stage, sprawling before the bier of the phoenix.

RUIZ HAD TIME enough to see shock and outrage begin to form on the thin aristocratic face of the senior conjuror. Then the catchbubble formed around the stage, and the stun field struck. The conjurors dropped as if poleaxed, and even Ruiz, despite his conditioning, felt as if unseen hands were stuffing thick cotton into his ears, as if his skin no longer was connected to him, as if his eyes were full of opaque jelly. He lay motionless for what seemed years. Then he stirred, trying to locate his extremities, trying to decide which way was up. After a time, he sat successfully, shoving one of the unconscious conjurors off his legs.

Ruiz moved in a fugue. Had more of his personality remained operative he might have been cursing his stupidity and inattention. As it was, the only strong current in Ruiz's mind was the emotion with which he'd viewed the conclusion of the phoenix play, a deep melancholy regret, centered on the ravaged body of the phoenix. As his vision cleared marginally, all he could see was her still form.

The light in the transport bubble was pervasive, a hard violet-tinged radiation that allowed nothing to remain hidden. Ruiz found his staff, got unsteadily to his feet, staggering and almost tripping over the body of the mage. Trailing his staff from one hand, he approached the bier where the phoenix lay. His head was filled with a sourceless buzzing, his bones shook in the grip of the slaver's unshielded drives; thought was impossible. He stood looking down at the phoenix. By no stretch of the imagination could she be considered beautiful now. The blossoms had wilted and fallen over her like coarse yellowing snow, and the vines themselves were already far gone into decay.

Almost absently, Ruiz dropped the staff and began to pull away the vines. They were crumbling into black slime, but the portions rooted in her body were still solid enough to come out in one piece. They made a terrible little sucking sound as they pulled free, but Ruiz noted that the wounds themselves were rather small. There was no great quantity of blood.

He arranged her so that she looked more comfortable, and closed her eyes. He was still not capable of real thought, but it seemed to him that there was more that he could do. Along with that feeling came anxiety, an anxiety that Ruiz somehow related to time. It seemed that there was something that he must do soon, if he was to do it at all. Ruiz chased the thought through the darkened depths of his mind, but it was as elusive as an eel. Finally his eye fell on his staff where it lay beside the bier. The anxiety stabbed deeper. He picked it up, handling the polished wood as if touching it for the first time. His hands made a curious twisting motion, without his prompting, and the staff separated.

Several items fell out of the hollow in the head of the staff, and Ruiz bent to sort idly through them, dropping the staff again as his attention wandered.

Then, obeying some impulse that made only dim sense, he picked out the medical limpet and an ampoule of general-purpose replicant gel.

The buzzing in his head grew louder, and his movements even less certain. Finally, with a frown of ferocious concentration, he laid the medical limpet against the waxy flesh of the woman's neck, near the site of the worst damage. Readouts flared crimson, and tendrils shot from the limpet to curl protectively around her skull. A long moment later, other tendrils emerged, to quest into the other wounds made by the stiletto vine.

He broke open the ampoule and smoothed the gray gel gently over the torn flesh. The gel had a sweet smell that mixed unpleasantly with the stench of the rotting blossoms. There was enough gel to coat the disfigured hand as well, so he unwrapped the ribbon and forced himself to do it. He watched, shuddering with weakness, until the gel was absorbed, and then he noticed that the limpet's angry flash had faded toward amber. The woman's chest began a shallow rise and fall, and her skin was less gray.

Blood roared in his ears, and his vision darkened. He used the last of his strength to gather the scattered contents of the staff, replacing them in the secret compartment; then he snapped the staff back together. His legs gradually refused to support him and he collapsed to the stage. A moment later the staff rolled from his hand, and he slept with the rest of the cargo.

RUIZ AW WOKE first. Had it been otherwise, had some unmodified primitive thrown off the stunfield first, Ruiz would have been astonished.

His naked body rested against warm metal and plastic; above was a glare of light that hurt his crusted eyes. The air smelled of disinfectant and urine. The subliminal moan of the drives was gone from his bones, and that inspired his first fully formed thought. *We're here,* he decided, *wherever here might be.*

CHAPTER 15

COREAN admired her droneship as it sat cooling in the center of the landing ring. The *Sinverguenza* was a good little ship; it boasted an autonomous brain, the revenant of a famous Bansh Pilot of several centuries past. It was fast for its size, its systems were thoroughly redundant, and its graceful hull was plated with a lovely pale violet armor.

The ship seemed to be in good condition after its passage down from the orbiting security platforms. The life support indicators showed a full cargo, every coffin in use. The stock would have to be weeded; it always needed to be weeded.

But everything was fine, she was sure. She disliked any joggle in the smooth pleasant flow of her life. Others might seek the life of a slaver for adventure, for the delights of domination, or for even darker reasons.

Not Corean. She was a slaver because it was the most profitable trade open to someone of her background. Wealth insulated her from the terrors of her youth—the dimly remembered time when she could only dream of sufficient food, comfortable shelter, and sanctuary from the press gangs that had roamed Dobravit's steel warrens, where long ago she had been nothing more than an uncontracted snuffer.

And, of course, her wealth could buy her such wonderful toys: her face, her Moc bondwarrior, the services of beautiful helots. And she had other avenues of pleasure. She valued the sensual delights of a fine meal; she owned several master chefs. She was a connoisseur of the nonlethal chemical pleasures, rich wines from a hundred planets, the infinite varieties of smoke, the rare and subtle psychoactives gathered in the raving jungles of Posset. Her deepest pleasures were taken in her bedroom, and here again her profession served her. She was content with her apartments here on Sook, burrowed deep into the safe bedrock. Her neighbors and fellow slavers were no threat; the Pung who owned and operated the pens kept order. Though her operation was one of the smaller ones in the compound, her facilities were adequate to her purposes.

It pleased her that her good little ship was back safely, with a fat cargo, a cargo that she could exchange for yet another increment of safety.

She stood and stretched. In the screens, a half-dozen Pung guards were cautiously approaching the cooling hull, alert for any sign of trouble, though trouble was unlikely. Trouble was for the incompetent or the unlucky, and she was neither. "Come, Marmo, time to count," she said.

Marmo rose from his station in the corner of the command center and hovered on his floater. Her aide functioned with the aid of numerous antique prostheses, though it made him look like a poorly designed droid, bizarrely patched here and there with human flesh. He offended Corean's eyes, but he was not only a valuable adjunct, he was the closest thing to a friend that she permitted herself, so she did not insist that he alter his eccentric appearance to a more pleasing one.

As they left the command center, her Moc bondwarrior paced behind, silent but for the scrape of its claws against the steel deck.

EVEN THE MUSCLES of his eyes refused to function at first, but gradually they recovered, and Ruiz Aw was able to bring his surroundings into focus.

He lay naked in a deep metal trough that was unnervingly reminiscent of a morgue tray. A broad band of monoplast fit snugly across his chest. The sides rose above his line of sight, so that he could see nothing but the metal of the ceiling, set with bright glowstrips and uncomfortably close. A net of unbreakable monoline covered the trough. The interior was inlaid with cleansing jets and sensors.

The only sound was the faint hum of ventilators.

He concentrated on recovering the use of his body. Gradually it began to respond—a twitch here, a tremble there. Ruiz had time to begin thinking. He listed the positive aspects of his situation: He was not dead, he was not in an interrogation cell, he was on the way to finding out who the poachers were. When he considered the negatives, he was momentarily depressed by the length of that list. The stunfield . . . that was the backbreaker; his expensive cerebral shunts had not saved him from being caught. A ghost memory tugged at him for a moment—had he managed to do something before succumbing? No, no, he decided, the stunfield had been much too good, ferreting out the strand of his consciousness where it hid.

Why, then, did he feel that twinge of anxiety? It was reminiscent of a feeling that he'd had after his rare but notable binges, the suspicion that he'd done something memorably foolish—something that he couldn't remember, but that others certainly would.

He started to flex his muscles, as inconspicuously as possible, trying to move blood and feeling back into them. Prudence demanded that Ruiz be ready if a course of action offered itself.

Ruiz heard the first feeble groans and whimpers from the rest of the cargo rising into the air on both sides of his trough. He decided it was safe to move, and he found he could do it. He rubbed the dried discharge from his eyes, and concentrated on remaining calm. His fellow slaves were making no effort to do so. Ruiz heard a chorus of fear all about him, as the others discovered their alien surroundings, wailing, shrieking, cursing, praying. As their muscles recovered from the stunfield, the sounds of thumping and flailing from the metal troughs became deafening. Their new surroundings didn't correspond in even the slightest detail to the Pharaohan version of the Elysian Fields, where they all had expected to wake after the success of the phoenix play. Would the gods trap them first in unresponsive bodies, then in steel coffins? Would heaven smell like piss and vomit?

As time passed, the curses began to outweigh the prayers, at least in volume.

Ruiz began to join in, not wishing to seem unnaturally calm, in case the cargo hold was under observation. His natural inclination was to curse, but he prayed instead, hoping to present a docile affect. He writhed about in as panicky a manner as he could manage without risking injury to his long-inactive muscles.

He became so involved in his performance that he almost missed the first touch of the trank gas. But when he noticed, he began to pray with less fervor, and gradually feigned quiescence, though the gas was too unsophisticated to defeat his conditioning. Still, the gas imbued him with a certain artificial optimism, and he had to make an effort to retain a realistic degree of gloominess.

Soon the hold was quiet again.

With a slight lurch and the whine of servos, Ruiz's pan began to move. It slid slowly forward, then began to tilt. In moments Ruiz was standing upright, leaning forward against the slight elasticity of the monoline net. He could now see that his pan was part of a transport rack made up of a half-dozen similar containers. Across the corridor were tiers of identical racks, still horizontal.

Some of the other captives in his rack had also sagged against the net and were making happy faces at Ruiz. He mugged back at them and awaited developments.

Somewhere a hatch cracked, and Ruiz sensed the pressure increase, as a thicker richer air flooded in. He heard the footsteps a moment before the inspection party entered the hold.

There were three: a human woman, who seemed to be in charge, a human man, and a Mocrassar bondwarrior. The sight of the Moc extinguished any immediate hope of escape. Its size was unusual, even by Moc standards: the enameled designs on its grasping limbs spoke of great age and high lineage. The immense insectoid wore a soiled Elizabethan doublet, modified to fit its six-limbed body. Ruiz could tell that the crusted fabric had once been fine. The Moc's midlimb manipulators were fitted with built-in energy tubes. It stank like a barrel of drowned cockroaches.

The man was a much-cyborged specimen, his legless torso mated to a floater console, one arm replaced by a multipurpose weapons mount—now equipped with a nerve lash. His skull was a metal carapace; only below the level of his nose did his face remain flesh. A segmented metal collar replaced his neck. He was a holodrama picture of a pirate, too colorfully authentic to be quite believable. Still, he twitched the nerve lash in a practiced manner.

But after the first moment it was the woman who captured all of Ruiz's attention. She was tall; she possessed the unremarkable perfection of form available to any pangalac with the means—slender, with small high breasts and long smooth muscles. Where the simple white shipsuit exposed her skin, it was the rich color of old ivory, with an almost iridescent polish. Her hair hung down her back in a businesslike braid, heavy as a black snake. It was her face that made her unforgettable. Ruiz recognized the hand of Arlaian the Younger, that master lineamentor, whose works commanded vast fees. The eyes were a simple blue, the brows dark and slightly tilted, the lips full, colored a natural coral. But from these unpretentious components, Arlaian had formed one of his great masterpieces. It was a face that spoke of power, above all else, power untempered by any soft emotion, power that was its own justification. It was a face that demanded worship, and Ruiz felt a sudden surge of sensation in his loins, a reaction that he swiftly damped. In his present state of undress, such a reaction would be a fatal giveaway, evidence that he was relatively immune to the gas. At the thought of what might then happen, Ruiz had to exert himself to prevent his testicles from trying to withdraw into his body.

Ruiz's trough was near the far end of the rack, so he had

time to observe the trio as they moved along the rack slowly, discussing the other specimens.

She had a voice like a bell, sweet and high and precise. She spoke the pangalac trade language, with a trace of Dobravit accent. "Marmo," she said, addressing the cyborged pirate, "you'll have to spend some time on your grabfield algorithm. The bubble is snatching too many by-standers. It's a serious loose end; the League catchboats are never so sloppy. We don't want to give rise to any new religious movements, do we? Pretty soon the peasants will be crowding the stages, hoping to be taken to paradise, and we'll have a destructive overload. Besides, why collect trash?" She stopped before a pan containing a peasant with the facial tattoos and the heavy muscles of a journeyman stonecutter. "This one, for example. See his tattoos? Of what use is he to me? Ours is a high-ticket trade. This one isn't even worth processing." The peasant lolled his face against the netting, smiling vacantly and making pawing gestures at her.

She studied him dispassionately. She flipped a safety cover off a switch and pressed. The interior of the pan flared white. A moment later the ashes trickled through the floor grating and were gone.

"I'll give it my full attention, Corean, soon as we have these safely in the pens," the pirate replied, in a rich boom-ing bass. She gave him a glance, then reached to a pressplate on his console. When he spoke again his voice was markedly smaller. "The Bansh brain refuses to do the culling—you know how intractable it can be, in certain respects—so that I must run the algorithm on the auxiliary systems. Another difficulty is that if we make the bubble too small we run the risk of losing some portion of the troupe or its equipment."

"Do your best, then," she said, moving on.

Marmo rubbed his mouth with the back of his one flesh hand. "Perhaps," he said, "perhaps I can develop a utility that recognizes tattoo patterns. We have a fairly extensive data base to work with. That way the culling could be done before the bubble closes."

She nodded.

Before they reached Ruiz's pan, two more of the captives

had been burned, and Ruiz found it hard to maintain his guise of innocent idiocy. He could smell the woman's perfume, a sweet edge cutting through the odor of burned flesh, the various stinks of the hold, and the overpowering musk of the Moc. In a sudden perceptual inversion, that flowery scent seemed to epitomize death, or at least death of the pointless and unexpected sort. Although he knew there was nothing he could do, his hindbrain howled and gibbered for escape. When she stopped before him, he was almost paralyzed with fear. He struggled to show nothing more than a dazed and affable curiosity. He saw a flicker of distaste cross that magnificent face, and then some other, less definable emotion—but she didn't reach for the destruct switch.

"Another cull," said Marmo. "A snake oil peddler, by his marks. Probably brainburned and diseased." And Marmo flipped open the switch cover.

Corean struck Marmo's hand away with an effortless flick. It happened so quickly that Ruiz had no time to react.

After a very long moment, she turned away, saying, "Mark this one for my personal coffle. Perhaps we'll make a comfort boy out of him; he has an interesting look to him. Salable, or I'm no judge of stock. Anything to cover the overhead, eh?" She reached through the net and marked his shoulder with a spot of blue dye, evidently an identifying mark.

Relief shuddered through Ruiz. *Still alive, still alive.* . . . He was in no immediate danger from the death net; it would not trigger until he had been positively identified as a League agent by his captors. He'd be allowed to go on collecting information for as long as it was safe.

His relief lasted until the inspecting party reached the far end of the hold. He sensed a sudden crackling tension in the hold and he heard the woman Corean curse, a short burst of invective in the gutter argot of Dobravit. Ruiz rolled his head around on the net, so he could see.

She reverted to pangalac. "What the hell is that?" she hissed, pointing into the pan at the end of the rack.

Ruiz could see a single knee pressed against the net, an unusually smooth and pretty knee. For some reason the sight resurrected in Ruiz that anxiety he had felt on awakening.

"It's a medical limpet, I think," the pirate said, in uncertain tones.

"I can see that! What's it doing on my ship? It's pangalac! What's it doing wrapped around the neck of some Pharaohan slut?"

Ruiz was abruptly certain he had made a massive mistake somewhere during the journey. He struggled to remember, but the trank gas interfered with his thinking just enough that the memory eluded him. What had he done?

The pirate made no answer to Corean's perhaps rhetorical question. "So," she snapped, "query the ship, you idiot."

"At once," said Marmo. He fumbled with a touchboard that flipped up on his floater console. When he looked up he said, "The ship is unhelpful, Corean. When it sent motiles to separate the Bidderum cargo from its gear, the woman was as you see. Her life functions were much more marginal then, however, and the ship decided to allow the limpet to remain with her."

"Is it lying, Marmo?"

The pirate shrugged. "Well . . . I can't say. The Bansh was a great womanizer, by its own account, and the woman's appealing. The Bansh is so old and so well armored into itself that I would consider it capable of such a lie. Perhaps it attached the limpet . . . but I don't know where it would have gotten such a thing."

Corean turned cold eyes on the cyborg. "This is an ambiguity that I will not tolerate. Find out, Marmo."

Corean slapped a touchplate at the side of the pan and the net withdrew. She reached in. Her hand came back into view carrying the limpet, writhing, its tendrils tipped with red. Ruiz's heart squeezed, for reasons he didn't understand. The pretty knee quivered, then relaxed.

"You'll make it your job to get to the bottom of this, Marmo. And we'll have to stop burning the culls; we'd better keep them until we know who put the thing on her. Meanwhile, keep her with the others. She's handsome, for a Pharaohan; we'll find an appropriate use for her." Corean threw the limpet to the deck, crushed it under her heel.

The limpet expired with a brief mournful buzz.

Ruiz looked away before his interest could be noticed.

The rack began to move. As it slid out of the droneship onto a donut-wheeled transporter, he saw the next rack tipping out for inspection.

OUTSIDE, COREAN FIXED Marmo with malevolent eyes. "It's the pretty snake oil man. He has a dangerous face."

"I'll kill him immediately," said Marmo in subdued tones.

"Idiot! What if he's a League agent? What if he carries the death net?"

"We'll freeze him down and put him on a long-hauler."

"No. We need to know more. Watch him. Maybe he'll show us what he is."

THE LANDING RING was heavily hardened, so that Ruiz Aw could see nothing but concrete and steel, lit by glaring blue spotlights. The roof was a furled iris of black metal. Standing about the ship were dozens of small gray humaniform aliens, members of a species not immediately familiar to Ruiz Aw. They were squat and powerfully muscled, with loose warty skin, and a crest of faded magenta quills atop their broad flat heads. They wore ragged uniforms of great former splendor and carried themselves with careful dignity. Ruiz searched his memory. Pung? The name seemed right, but he could recall no details.

They released him from the transport rack after carefully leashing him with a nerve collar. They marked his palm with a temporary stock number and conducted him to an elevator, which dropped deep into the depths of the compound, to a solitary cell carved from the bedrock. Instead of bars, a crystal plate hummed and snapped in the doorway, a constant edgy sound. Repellent waveforms made it difficult to approach the door, and Ruiz knew that touching the crystal would bring excruciating pain. It was a simple secure setup, and Ruiz's professional approval was aroused, to his personal irritation. The only furnishings were a bed of softstone, a nutrition tap, and a drain in one corner. They gave him no clothing, but the temperature in the cell had been set to the human comfort range.

As the effects of the trank gas wore off, Ruiz finally remembered his actions immediately after the snatch. He was overcome by panic, which he allowed to rage unchecked for a therapeutic interval. How, he asked himself, how could he have been so foolish and impulsive as to revive the phoenix? How?

Eventually, he reasserted control. Nothing connected him to the phoenix. The rest of his pangalac technology, like all League covert gear, had been designed to resist analysis, to reject fingerprints, and to gene-scramble telltale tissue. Presumably it was working, or he would already be identified as the interloper. Even if he were to be identified as a pangalac, his case wasn't hopeless; his shield persona, that of a minor free-lance slaver, would survive any but the most skillful brainpeel.

If his captors knew who and what he was, then he was already dead. But it served no useful purpose to consider that particular possibility, so he must put it from his mind and act as though he had a fair chance of survival. True, he was without his usual resources, but certainly his case might be worse. After an hour had passed, he grew bored and then curious about the other prisoners.

He stood as close to the doorway as comfort allowed, looking across the bright corridor to the opposite cell. At random intervals the other cell's closure field fell briefly into phase with his own, and he could see his fellow prisoner, the senior of the conjurors who had performed at Bidderum. The conjuror's hard black eyes fixed on Ruiz's with an expression so malevolent that Ruiz stepped back, then away, out of sight.

More hours passed. Ruiz roamed the confines of his cell, using the few amenities, always conscious of the possibility of observation. With that in mind, he acted the terrified primitive—but one capable of restraining his hysteria. Ruiz was not anxious to be labeled a nonteachable. He'd been too impressed with Corean's casual culling of her slaves.

Ruiz could find no memory of a slaver named Corean—

not surprising, in spite of the large amounts of credit that Ruiz had spent on datasoaking. There were, after all, countless slavers among the pangalac worlds. But not many could afford a face like hers, and Ruiz surmised that it was an unregistered work of the great lineamentor who had carved it. That in itself was an indication of the wealth and power of Corean; vast amounts of both would be required to coerce an artist of that stature to work anonymously. It was a somewhat intimidating thing to muse on.

When two of the gray Pung guards came for him, he was feigning sleep on the softstone bunk. He heard the snap and rattle of the charged doorplate die away, then the sigh of pneumatics as the door whisked up.

Ruiz heard the cautious plop of the guards' large discoid feet as they entered the cell, and he smelled the faint fish-oil scent of their bodies.

"Sleeping like a sprat," one muttered in the pangalac trade language.

"As you must have been when you put him in here," the other said in a sharper tone. "The bitch gave definite instructions: blue mark in solitary cells, the rest in the Old Trari Tree paddock. You keep pluckheading around like this, she'll have your quills."

Ruiz heard a hiss and rattle; he assumed it signaled offense. Ruiz opened one eye slightly and saw the first guard swelling his throat sac. "Pluckhead, am I?" it shrilled. "My quills are thoroughly attached. See? The blue mark is on him, as I told you. The bitch simply changed her mind. And anyway, there's no harm this way. As long as the special stock stays in cells, no harm. Now, if I'd gotten it the other way around, as you did last Windday, then I'd be concerned. Have you forgotten the episode?"

"How was I to know the muckling little widge was a cannibal?"

Further acrimony was prevented by Ruiz, who appeared to awaken. "Demons!" he shrieked in Pharaohan; then he leaped into the corner, where he pressed himself trembling against the stone.

The guards rolled their protruding eyeballs at each other. The larger one shook out a net and bared its teeth in what was intended to be a reassuring manner. "Come along quietly, gangly norp," it said, motioning toward the doorway.

Ruiz observed that energies snapped and whispered along the strands of the net. Not wishing to be stunned, he peeled himself off the wall, gathered his dignity, and left the cell, mugging fearfully.

They moved through what seemed miles of subterranean corridors, before coming out into the daylight. The walls were still high, the way narrow, closed over with buzzing snapfields, but Ruiz turned up his face to be bathed in the sun. From a hundred clues—the hot light, the pull of gravity, the richness of the air, the smell of salt, the fragrance of the unseen vegetation—Ruiz knew with reasonable certainty that he was on Sook, a notorious refuge for pirates and slavers and an assortment of other monsters. He felt a thrill of expectation and fear.

If he could somehow escape and launch a message torpedo to the League's Dilvermoon headquarters, his job would be finished and the mission-imperative that drove him would dissolve, taking the death net with it.

But it was far more likely, he thought, that the net would instead take him to his death.

CHAPTER 16

THE narrow passageways twisted and turned as they continued through the warren.

Hundreds, perhaps thousands of unlicensed slavers must maintain facilities here, as well as pirates, kidnappers and bootleg fleshtinkers. In the course of his work, Ruiz had visited many of Sook's slave pens and shipping depots, but nothing looked familiar to him, nor did he remember an operation staffed by Pung guards. He wasn't surprised; Sook was vast and the Shards, the planet's alien owners, vigorously suppressed attempts to map the surface —and that deliberate obscurity was another attraction for the criminals who based their operations here.

Here and there observation ports were set into the walls. The ports were ancient, caked with dust and clouded with scratches, but Ruiz could see enough to be amazed at the diversity of the merchandise. Within the paddocks were beings of most of the races Ruiz was familiar with, and some he had never seen. The majority of the specimens were human, or near-human.

He saw a Noctil presentation group, the lessers ranked

carefully about their primary on a small grassy knoll. The primary was a lean vulpine woman with a great mass of fiery orange hair; the color of the lessers' hair cooled from the center out, until those on the edge of the setting had sleek blond heads, and plump vulnerable bodies. The primary was orating. Ruiz was impressed by the fluid pattern that the setting formed, the manner in which each gesture of the primary was taken up by the lessers, repeated and interpreted all the way to the edge. He would have stayed and watched, had it been possible; here was a valuable property indeed. But the guards hurried him on.

Each observation port was a window into strangeness. He saw a pack of Parbalong clone yodelers, a herd of wood gnomes from Sackett's World, a strong collection of fancy marine-adapted humans from the ocean world Cholder, sporting in a deep green pool—and many others. Most of the specimens were exceedingly fine. The compound was impressive in both size and scope.

By the time they arrived at the Pharaohan paddock, Ruiz had fallen into a subdued and thoughtful mood.

A port pierced the wall next to the doorway, and Ruiz looked inside while the larger of the guards fumbled in its pouch for the molecular seal that operated the door. The landscape within the paddock approximated a small Pharoan oasis, without the fields and catchment system. A dusty compound huddled in the center of the paddock, surrounded by the feathery foilage of dinwelt trees.

The door hissed upward, revealing a security vestibule, lined with storage bins, closed at the far end with another door. "In you go," said the guard, flipping the nerve net at Ruiz's heels.

Ruiz moved with respectful speed. Once inside, the other guard opened a bin and hauled out a tunic of coarse brown fabric and tossed it to Ruiz. Ruiz put it on, and then the sandals the other guard handed him.

The guards inspected him. "Looks authentic to me. Didn't the other ones want to shave their heads?"

The other guard laughed, a choked whistle-gurgle. "He doesn't have to, so it appears. A natural pluckhead; can you believe it?"

Uneasiness touched Ruiz. He hoped no one else would notice that he did not have to perform that particular Pharaohan grooming ritual. His depilation was good for a few weeks yet, but his tattoos would fade before the depil wore off—another problem.

One guard touched a control panel. The first door dropped, and a moment later the inner door popped open. The guards shooed him cheerfully out of the lock. The door slid shut behind him with a clang.

Ruiz stood alone, the light of Sooksun beating on his naked head.

He looked about curiously. The paddock seemed to cover a roughly circular area of slightly more than a hectare. The walls were high and smooth, made of the same meltstone masonry as the rest of the compound. The tops of the walls were protected by snapfields that reached high above the compound, forming a faint lacy pattern in the air where they intersected with other fields. The glowing fields would be quite beautiful at night.

He set off down the path to the compound at the center of the paddock.

He resolved to pass himself off as an innocent Pharaohan bystander, to step lightly with his fellow slaves, to collect information but give out none, to fit in as seamlessly as possible, to wait for an opportunity to improve his circumstances. After all, this was his profession, which previously he had practiced with reasonable skill. He shook his head, feeling a bit pessimistic.

Taking care not to touch the corrosive fronds, Ruiz edged past the dinwelt hedge into the compound's central square. It was deserted in the noontime heat, but after a moment a burly man with the tattoos of a guildmaster emerged from one dark doorway. "Man or demon?" he demanded of Ruiz, in a voice hoarse with suppressed terror.

Ruiz stood quietly for a moment, adopting an unthreatening posture, open hands held at his side.

"More than man, less than demon, or perhaps the other way about. Sometimes it's difficult for me to tell," he said cheerfully.

The man squinted at Ruiz, then relaxed. "It's just a snake

oil peddler, by his tattoos and speech." At this reassurance, a half-dozen other Pharaohans emerged into the square.

"Oh yes," Ruiz said, "I'm the dream merchant, but alas, I'm fresh out of dreams. Perhaps this is the dream, eh? Certainly it's stranger than any realm I've visited on snake-back."

"You spoke true, Guildmaster Dolmaero," said a thin fellow with a blind eye and the tattoos of an animal handler. "I thought never to welcome such a one, but he's an easier sight than those warty gray horrors."

They studied Ruiz with tired red eyes. Finally Dolmaero spoke. "What is to be our fate? Have you word of this?"

Ruiz spread his arms in a gesture of puzzlement. "I'd hoped," he said, "that you could tell me."

Faces fell. After a bit the Pharaohans turned and shuffled within. Last to go was Dolmaero, who paused and said kindly, "There is the dwelling of the casteless." Dolmaero pointed across the square to a building that showed signs of long disuse. "Twice a day the demons come to summon us to feed. You must wait your turn, but there will be plenty to eat." A look of private sorrow touched Dolmaero's broad face. "There is no snake oil here." Then he disappeared, leaving Ruiz alone in the square. Ruiz had the uncomfortable sensation that many eyes watched him from the shadowed doorways that fronted the square. The remainder of the conjuring troupe was housed here, perhaps forty or fifty men and women who—working the traps and slides and pulls that made the illusions possible—had been beneath the stage when the catchboat had taken them.

Ruiz shrugged and walked to the door of the indicated building. The hanging wilifiber strands that once had protected the interior from noxious flying insects were tattered to uselessness. He pushed them aside and entered.

Within, it was dark and a bit cooler. In the moment it took for Ruiz's eyes to begin to adjust to the gloom, he sensed that the hut was, unexpectedly, occupied. He sidled aside from the silhouetting light of the doorway, all his senses reaching out. In addition to the musty scents of dust and mud and timber and ancient leather, he caught a thin organic waft—the smell of sickness. As his eyes adjusted,

Ruiz made out a line of dilapidated cots against the wall. One was occupied by a still figure.

Ruiz moved cautiously forward. The woman on the cot lay still a moment longer, then twisted uneasily, as if tormented by a fever dream. A tiny moan escaped the pale lips of the phoenix.

Ruiz sighed and sat down gingerly on the nearest cot, which supported his weight with only minor ripping sounds.

Here was the tangible evidence of his foolishness. He sat for a long silent while, watching her troubled sleep. She represented an anomaly to his enemies, a source of suspicion, a focus for their paranoia. Ruiz was among them, a potentially fatal infection, and this woman was the first tangible symptom. For a time he weighed the notion of smothering her—no one would be able to say she had not simply succumbed to her wounds. When she was gone, perhaps his mistake might be forgotten.

Later, Ruiz could not remember just when he discarded that hopeful idea. He watched her sleep, watched the sweat bead on the sweet contour of her upper lip, watched her dark lashes flutter against the flushed translucent skin of her cheeks. Almost as an afterthought he assembled the logical support for his decision; the girl was already entered into the inventory banks of the slavers—her death or disappearance would remind them of the troubling question of her presence on the slave ship.

Finally he put his hand to her forehead and felt the fever burning bright in her. "Too hot," he whispered, as if she could hear. He rooted about in the debris at the back of the hut and found a cracked plastic bowl and a wad of filthy rags. He went outside, located the watershed. Inside, in addition to the traditional bathing pool, he found a universal tap, the kind installed by slavers who couldn't be sure what sort of hands their property might have.

When the rags were washed clean, he carried them back inside. She shifted feebly when he pulled off her rough tunic, but she was more than asleep.

The slaver should have left the limpet awhile longer, he thought.

He washed her as well as he could, and then continued to

bathe her with the tepid water. He felt no sexual stirring as he passed the rag across her handsome body—she was still too ill to be beautiful, too close to death. But there was pleasure of a more detached sort in touching her; it was like running his fingers over a fine carving. Her skin was as smooth as polished wood, the topology of her body cleanly modeled. The scars of her brief death were only faintly visible in the dim light of the hut. The replicant gel would continue its work until they were gone entirely. Even her hand was healing cleanly, restored to youth.

For the remainder of that afternoon she slept. Occasionally Ruiz was able to squeeze a trickle of water into her mouth, using the cleanest rag. She was able to swallow, and her lips looked less parched. Ruiz began to take an odd guilty satisfaction in his nursing. When he realized this, he became angry with himself, but he continued. She began to look a bit more comfortable, and she seemed to rest more easily.

As the sun was setting, a tone rang out in the paddock, and Ruiz looked out to see a robocart trundle into the square, trailed by a gray guard holding a nerve lash ready.

The other Pharaohans emerged from the buildings. Ruiz was surprised by their numbers; there were at least fifty Pharaohans, mostly men, all commoners. The conjurors were apparently being held in the high-security cells below, as befitted more valuable stock.

The Pharaohans watched silently until the guard waved them forward. As they surrounded it, the robocart opened, revealing steaming tubs of Pharaohanese edibles: sand-mussel stew, hot pickled vegetables, a gray mush of ground jemmerseed. The slaves dipped reluctantly into the provender, with no great evidence of appetite.

When all were provided, Ruiz approached, and the others drew away. He saw that the food was only superficially Pharaohanese; it was, in fact, synthetic, crudely textured and colored and flavored so as to resemble familiar fare. Ruiz took a disposable plate and piled it high with the most digestible-looking choices.

With his mouth full of tasteless pseudo-barley and stringy synthalizard, Ruiz approached Dolmaero, who leaned against a wall, chewing stoically. A bit farther along the wall, a tall angular man with the tattoos of a coercer squatted, glaring at Ruiz with scornful eyes. The man had enormous hands, which he curled into hooks as Ruiz neared Dolmaero. Ruiz stopped at a respectful distance.

Swallowing with some difficulty, Ruiz spoke politely. "Honorable Dolmaero, favor me with your wisdom."

Dolmaero looked at Ruiz, his heavy jaws working. He grunted, which Ruiz took to be permission to proceed.

"It was kind of you to inform me this afternoon," Ruiz continued, "but perhaps you'll be generous again, and tell me of the woman who lies in the House of the Alone."

Dolmaero looked away and Ruiz thought at first that Dolmaero would not answer. Then he looked back at Ruiz with hard eyes and spat a bit of imitation redstem on the ground. "She was brought here by demons. She was barely conscious. I instructed the women to move her to the House, that our souls not be tarnished by her death."

"It may be that she isn't dying," Ruiz said.

"Her wounds were terrible," Dolmaero said. "Were you at Bidderum when she died?"

Ruiz was momentarily taken aback. Somehow he was not prepared for that question, so he dissembled.

"Her wounds seem minor, now. Who knows what amuses the gods?" Ruiz said.

Dolmaero laughed bitterly. "Wherever we are, it's not the Land of Reward. And now, get away. Your familiarity infringes on my dignity."

The tall man rose and assumed a threatening posture, his face a mask of disapproval and eager violence.

Ruiz shrugged and returned to the robocart to reload his plate. He carried it back to his hut, and as he stepped inside he sensed that the phoenix was awake.

"WHO . . . WHO IS there?" she asked in a tiny dry voice.

She was attempting, without much success, to sit up. Ruiz hastened to help her. Setting the plate aside, he lifted her so that she rested against the wall. She appeared confused, as was natural for one who had undergone a death, however short.

"Don't be afraid, Noble Person," Ruiz said softly, reassuringly. "It's Wuhiya, a simple seller of dreams, who attends you."

Her eyes snapped wide open. "This is the Land of Reward?" she asked in a stronger voice. "Where is the light, where the godservants? I hear no music. What has happened?"

Her lips trembled, her eyes filled with imminent tragedy. She looked at Ruiz and recoiled, clutching to her the rough tunic that had fallen away when she sat up. "You're casteless," she accused. "Oh, what's gone wrong?"

Ruiz felt a strong impulse to comfort her—but how? She huddled back against the wall, her eyes darting about the disordered hut.

"Try to calm yourself," Ruiz said. "True, this isn't the Land of Reward, but things might be worse. We're alive; here is food and water and shelter from the sun. And you'll soon be feeling better."

She was hearing nothing he said. "My servants . . . such a terrible dream . . ." she muttered, her voice growing weak again. Her fingers pulled at the tangles in her hair, and the cloth that covered her torso slid down, exposing her scars, still faintly puckered in the smooth skin of her belly. She looked down absently and saw them. Her eyes widened, and she opened her mouth as if to scream, and then her eyes rolled back in her head.

"You faint a lot," Ruiz said, catching her before she could thump her head on the wall. Ruiz arranged her as comfortably as possible on the cot, then bathed away the sweat of her exertions. It was best to let her sleep, he thought. He settled down to his dinner, now cold. He ate mechanically, but he finished every scrap. He began to feel stronger, for the first time since Bidderum.

He sat beside her far into the night, long after he could see nothing but a shapeless darkness where she lay.

•   •   •

IN THE MORNING , she still slept when the robocart made its appearance. Ruiz came out to get his share of breakfast. The other prisoners were still distant, though Dolmaero favored him with a curt nod. Ruiz found a sunny section of wall away from the others. The food was not tasty, but doubtless it was sufficiently nourishing to maintain slaves in salable condition. It probably contained a multitude of beneficial additives, and Ruiz returned for another helping when he was done. When next she woke, he'd attempt to get some food into the phoenix.

Dolmaero eyed Ruiz as he heaped his plate full again, and he had the sensation that Dolmaero watched him with more suspicion than before. The tall coercer, who seemed to be Dolmaero's dog, stood up and made as if to approach, his nostrils flaring with combative anticipation. Ruiz smiled disarmingly and returned to his hut.

The phoenix still lay quiet, but she breathed easily, and when he touched the back of his hand to her forehead, her skin was cool. He set the food aside for later.

While he waited for her to wake again, he pulled off his tunic and began to exercise the kinks from his body. He discovered, unsurprisingly, that the passage in the slave ship had sapped much of his strength and suppleness. With each slow movement, he found unexpected little pains, dangerous small weaknesses. He twisted and pressed, stretching the ligaments, pitting muscle against muscle. He found, after a while, an intense pleasure in the familiar dance, and his abused body began to respond, moving faster and faster, until the world was a spinning blur, and his heart pounded.

When he was finished, his skin ran with sweat and his muscles were tingling with hot fresh blood. He wiped away the sweat with a rag and dressed.

He sat down beside the phoenix, breathing deeply, mind empty, happier than he had been in weeks.

She was awake. She watched him with wide eyes, as if he were some strange performing beast, encountered in a menagerie.

"Noble Person," Ruiz said carefully, "you're awake? That's good. Would you care for some breakfast?"

She made no response.

"Perhaps a cup of water?" Ruiz asked, getting up to fetch it.

"Yes," she finally said, cautiously. "I'm very dry."

He helped her to sit again, though she shrank from his touch. Then he handed her the cup. She seemed not to notice when her tunic fell away from her breasts. She drank the tepid water greedily, keeping wary eyes on Ruiz.

When she finished she held out the cup for more. Ruiz took it and said, "Wait a bit; see how your stomach receives it."

Her eyes flared briefly, as if she were about to remind him of his station, but then she seemed to remember her surroundings.

Ruiz was pleased by her composure; it indicated an attractive strength. "I'm glad," he said, "that you're calmer today."

"Have you told me your name?" she asked after a bit.

"Wuhiya of Sammadon," Ruiz said, sketching a bow, "late of Bidderum."

Her gaze darkened and Ruiz wished he hadn't mentioned Bidderum. "Ah, Bidderum," she said. Her voice became distant. "Bidderum, a dismal place. Though not so dismal as this. And I was in better health there, for a while."

She looked down then at her naked belly. The scars were almost gone, only faintly visible in the dim light of the hut. She gasped and rubbed her fingers over her flesh. "Look," she said. "Did I die? Was I resurrected? The Land of Reward, where we were to be reborn perfect—I'm not perfect but I heal. I heal."

Her eyes were full of wonder when she turned them back up to Ruiz.

"This isn't the Land of Reward," Ruiz said, suddenly uncomfortable. He saw no point in theological discussion, so he lied as gracefully as he could. "You were badly injured, but you didn't die. The doctors in this place are excellent beyond our experience; thus you mend rapidly."

She giggled, which astonished him—there seemed no hysteria in the sound, just a sweet skeptical amusement.

" 'This place,' you say. You make it sound as if we were no longer in the lands of Bhasrahmet. What other lands are there?"

This was a difficult question indeed, and Ruiz turned it over in his mind before answering. "We are far from Pharaoh, Noble Person. Very far."

Before he could think of anything else to say, she spoke, and her voice was fearful again. "Are we in Hell, then? But we cannot be; the steams there would melt the flesh from our bones."

"This isn't Hell, either," Ruiz reassured her. "I'm not sure I can tell you. . . ."

She touched his arm gently. "Can you tell me anything?"

Ruiz suppressed, with amazement, a mad impulse to tell her of his offworld origin. He was distracted by a sharp knock against the door frame.

"Come forth," spoke Dolmaero's harsh voice.

She took fright again, shrinking back against the mud wall. Ruiz smiled reassuringly, and went to the door.

When he stepped through, Ruiz confronted a ring of guild elders, who glared at him with uniform expressions of outrage. Dolmaero was closest; the big coercer stood beside the Guildmaster. The coercer seemed eager; Dolmaero looked unhappily determined.

"What is your name and village, casteless one?" Dolmaero demanded.

"I'm honored by your curiosity. I'm Wuhiya of Sammadon."

"With whom do you speak, Wuhiya?"

"Sir?" Ruiz feigned incomprehension.

"Inside, witless one! Who speaks?"

"Ah." Ruiz allowed understanding to spread over his face. "You mean the noblewoman who lies ill."

Dolmaero's broad face paled. "She still lives, then," he said, as if to himself. He stood rubbing his chin, an unhappy man. Finally he seemed to reach a decision—though from the set of his mouth, it was not a decision he took pleasure in. "You must fetch her out," he said to Ruiz.

"Ah," Ruiz said, with forced friendliness. "You wish to

house her in a manner more suitable to her rank; am I right?"

Dolmaero made no reply, though his face set into a more dour expression. Then the coercer drew a long cord of twisted fiber from his tunic and wrapped it around his huge fists, smiling.

CHAPTER 17

Ruiz Aw looked at the coercer, then at Dolmaero. "Honorable Dolmaero," he said, pretending astonishment, "you don't mean to harm the noblewoman?"

"She is an abomination!" Dolmaero stepped toward Ruiz. "Bring her forth! It's unnatural, an affront to the gods; she should be dead. We all saw her when the demons brought her here." He looked at the others for confirmation, and their heads nodded like so many puppets. "Her wounds still oozed! Had the gods raised her, she would be perfect. Unnatural, unnatural." Then, as if to himself, Dolmaero said, "She must complete her part. The elders have decided." The Guildmaster looked down; regret flickered across his broad face.

Ruiz felt trapped, pulled between two impulses. Common sense dictated that he give up the phoenix. Suppose the paddock was observed? No lowly snake oil man would think to oppose a Guildmaster.

Dolmaero lost patience before Ruiz could make up his

mind to pursue the sensible course. "Casmin," Dolmaero said, turning to the coercer, "bring her out."

Casmin shuffled forward quickly, grinning, and Ruiz saw that the coercer's teeth were filed to points and stained red. Ruiz retreated before Casmin's outstretched arms, backing into the hut.

In the gloom inside, Ruiz turned to glance back toward the woman. She had apparently heard everything. Somehow she had managed to crawl into the farthest corner. She was trying feebly to hide beneath some rubbish there.

Ruiz had no time to admire her determination to live. He had badly underestimated Casmin's speed. As Ruiz started to turn back, the coercer was on him, dropping the loop of fiber over Ruiz's head.

Casmin jerked him close, tightening the loop just enough to cut off Ruiz's wind. "I'll tell the master you resisted, shithead," Casmin whispered in his ear, chuckling with delight.

Casmin began to dance him about, so that the scrabble of their feet would be audible to the listeners outside.

"Casmin?" Ruiz heard Dolmaero ask. "What's going on?"

Before Casmin could respond, Ruiz snapped his head back into Casmin's nose. Cartilage broke with a wet crunch and Ruiz felt hot blood spray his neck, but though Casmin's grip loosened slightly, he didn't let go. Ruiz lashed an elbow back into Casmin's ribs. The coercer made a small shocked sound as the ribs splintered, and tried to push Ruiz away. Going with the movement, Ruiz bent at the waist and reached between his legs; he grabbed Casmin's testicles and squeezed, using all his strength. With a high-pitched, breathless screech, Casmin collapsed, unconscious.

"Casmin?" Dolmaero sounded more worried. "Casmin, you are only to bring out the woman, do you hear? Restrain your enthusiasm, Casmin."

Ruiz burned with adrenaline. He smiled what he thought was a merry little smile. He picked the coercer up by one leg and the scruff of his garment, and tossed him out through the dangling fibers that covered the door, into the sunlight.

He stepped lightly after him, to see the guild elders staring in horrified amazement at the prone, twitching body.

"Don't worry, honorable Dolmaero," Ruiz said in a pleasant cheerful voice. "Casmin will restrain his enthusiasm." He dropped Casmin's strangling cord in the dust. "I suggest you all follow his example."

No one spoke, so he went back inside.

Her eyes were huge in the dimness of the hut. She huddled in the corner, and for a moment she seemed as afraid of him as she had been of the coercer. "It's all right," he said as he went to her. "No one will harm you." *Not for a while, anyway,* he thought—but he put the thought away immediately.

He lifted her and carried her back to the cot. She said nothing, though she clung to him more tightly than was necessary.

After a while she slept again, without uttering another word. Ruiz sat beside her and mopped Casmin's blood from his neck, thinking darkly about his own folly. His only chance of survival, after all, was to remain anonymous until he found an opportunity to escape. The phoenix was a dangerous distraction, had already led him to commit two acts of conspicuous foolishness.

What was wrong with him? For some reason, Nacker's shapeless face swam up into his mind's eye.

Abruptly Ruiz felt a great weariness—prompted partially by his exertions and his less than optimal physical condition —but due more, he supposed, to his astounding behavior. That idea led directly to another: Was he growing too complacent for this profession? Or, worse yet, too old? The fact that he had survived so long in such a risky business was, he reminded himself fiercely, no guarantee at all that his life would continue.

It could end right here, in this ratty pen. He lay back to rest awhile. Casmin's friends might attempt to avenge his humiliation, but Ruiz doubted it. It was difficult for Ruiz to imagine a stolid craftsman like Dolmaero creeping up to slit a throat. Besides, coercers of that stamp usually had no friends outside their own caste—only masters and victims.

HE WOKE WHEN the robocart sounded the tone for the evening meal. The phoenix was sitting on the edge of her cot, watching him, looking much improved.

Her cheeks were pink with well-being rather than fever. She'd fingercombed the worst of the tangles from her hair, so that it flowed smoothly down her back, a river of coppery black. A twisted scrap of blue cloth bound her tunic to her body in a more flattering shape. Ruiz was amazed and horrified that her movements hadn't awakened him—a lucky thing that no enemies had come upon him.

"At last," she said.

Ruiz rubbed at his eyes. "I'm glad you're feeling better."

"It's a miracle, isn't it?"

There was a mocking undertone to her voice, and Ruiz stared at her for a moment. "Yes," he agreed, "a miracle."

Her brows drew down. "Don't humor me, Wuhiya. This isn't Pharaoh or the Land of Reward either, and I wonder if you're a snake oil peddler." Anger showed strongly on her face for a moment, but she controlled it and even attempted a smile. "Can you tell me? Do you know where we are?"

Ruiz got up and went to the door. He temporized. "It's dinnertime. I'll go fetch us some food; you'll need it."

"I'll go with you," she said, standing with remarkable ease, considering her recent condition. She went past him, and out the door.

He caught up to her just outside, where she stood looking across the square at the gray humanoid guard and the robocart, frozen in terrified amazement.

She clutched at his arm. "What is that?"

Ruiz took a deep breath. Sooner or later she would have to start learning about her new life. "They call themselves Pung. They operate this . . . this . . ." Ruiz stopped, at a loss for words that seemed kind enough. Then he decided that false kindness wouldn't help her to survive, so he continued with the truth. "This is a slave pen, Noble Person."

She looked at him, her eyes wide with shock, then outrage. "No!" she said. "No! Do you know me? Nisa, I am Nisa, daughter of Bhasrahmet, King of Kings." Her face crumpled and she stumbled back inside the house of the casteless.

Ruiz sighed. He wished her an easy bondage. With her beauty and intelligence, she might find a place with an indulgent owner. It bothered him that he could formulate no better hope for her.

NISA FELL FACEDOWN on the filthy cot, heedless of the ancient stains. Her throat was full of panic, but she refused to cry. She pounded at her temples with her fists, as if she could drive this unacceptable reality from her. She seemed to be doomed to a greater Expiation than she'd bargained for, lost in an alien place, surrounded by contemptuous enemies and monsters, her only friend a casteless man whose opacity matched his strangeness. He spoke with the semblance of proper respect, but she was somehow sure he thought himself her superior—an almost incomprehensible idea to a favored daughter of the King. He treated her as she might have treated a sickly pet glistle. And the hideous way he'd disposed of the coercer, as if the destruction of Casmin had been a source of deep joy. . . .

In that brief terrible dance, Wuhiya had seemed not quite human, a soulless beast, like one of her father's hunting dirgos, set loose on some helpless quarry.

And yet with her he'd been gentle. And in unguarded moments, his eyes sometimes lost that flinty glitter, his mouth softened from its habitual tense line.

She grew less agitated, thinking about her protector. Who was he? More to the point, what was she to him?

THE PHARAOHANS DREW back when Ruiz approached the robocart, this time more in fear than in loathing, which was at least mildly satisfying. As he dipped up the pseudo-food, Ruiz felt Dolmaero's eyes on his back—not in anger, as he might have expected, but in speculation.

Casmin was nowhere to be seen. The Pung guard watched Ruiz incuriously; it seemed no complaint had been made.

When Ruiz brought their dinner back, the phoenix was huddled on her cot, her face to the wall. Her shoulders quivered, but she made no sound. Ruiz put her plate on the floor.

THAT NIGHT RUIZ sat outside, watching the snapfields—sheets of pale green fire fluttering up from the walls. Suddenly he bent forward, rigid with interest. A section of the snapfield on the western perimeter had winked out, leaving a patch of darkness. He counted the seconds; shortly the field popped back on with a shower of off-phase sparks.

Over the following hours it failed several more times, always over the same section of wall.

He allowed himself to hope. It was a fine feeling, and soon he felt calm enough to go in to sleep. He settled on the cot next to the phoenix, who stirred but did not wake. "Pleasant dreams," he whispered, just as though she were a real person, and not just a character in this dangerous play.

RUIZ WOKE REFRESHED from his short night's sleep. Nisa still lay on her cot, but from the regular rise and fall of her breasts, Ruiz saw that her slumber was healthier.

He took off his tunic and exercised. This time he felt a little stronger, a little quicker, and he pushed his body a little harder. The phoenix woke while he was finishing. Her eyes were large with some complex emotion, but she said nothing.

Ruiz dressed and went out. The soft early morning light slanted across the paddock, throwing long shadows. It was too early for the robocart, so Ruiz walked to the wall nearest the security lock, intent on evaluating the paddock's security system. As he loped through the cool air, it occurred to him to wonder why it had taken him so long to get started. It occurred to him that his sudden incompetence had much to do with the woman. Ruiz shrugged, dismissed the idea.

The wall itself was a substantial impediment to escape—six or seven meters high, and built of smooth gray meltstone. Ruiz noticed where some small burrowing animal's digging had exposed the roots of the wall to a distance of half a meter. No deterioration was visible, above or below ground level. Ruiz assumed that the barrier was deep enough to preclude escape by tunneling. He turned his attention to the lock itself.

To his disappointment, he was able to identify the mechanism that controlled the door. It was a Feltmann molylock, unpersuadable with any equipment he was likely to construct using the unpromising material he might find in the paddock.

Ruiz was bent over, absorbed in his examination of the lock, when the door whipped up. Inside the security lock, the Pung guard stiffened and brought up the nerve lash it carried. At the far end of the lock, another alert Pung stood, a widefield stun cone ready.

Ruiz stepped back hastily, smiling a harmless smile. The guard glared at him for a moment, then signaled the robocart forward. Ruiz turned away and walked back toward the huts, his back crawling. But the guard didn't use the nerve lash. At least, Ruiz thought, the Pung didn't seem to be a vindictive or sadistic group, as slavers frequently were.

Ruiz carried a breakfast plate inside to Nisa. She was sitting up, face composed. He smiled when he set the plate down next to her, but she looked away. He felt an odd twinge of unhappiness.

Ruiz went back outside to eat his breakfast and settled in a patch of sunshine, where a crumbling mud wall made a comfortable seat.

To his surprise, Dolmaero approached as he was finishing the tasteless meal.

"May I sit?" Dolmaero asked.

Ruiz nodded. "Of course, Honorable Dolmaero. How may I serve?"

Dolmaero settled his broad frame on the wall, and chuckled ruefully. "I don't think you need be so concerned with the proper form of address between us. You're evidently not what you appear to be." Dolmaero shot Ruiz a shrewd glance. "Nor am I what I once was."

Ruiz made no reply.

Dolmaero peered at him with good-humored intensity. "Casmin will live, it seems, though at present he takes no pleasure in that."

"Good news," Ruiz responded, ambiguously.

Dolmaero laughed with genuine amusement. "Well," he said, "I must apologize for my henchman's rashness, though I think it's safe to say he's even sorrier than I am."

Ruiz was forced to smile.

"Listen," Dolmaero said, "I approach you against the advice of the elders, who are convinced you're a ravening beast. I don't think so. I think you are someone who knows more of our situation than we do, and I intend to appeal to you for information. Where are we, for example?" Dolmaero gestured at the sky, where Sooksun would rise above the walls. "Where's the sun of old? At night the stars are unfamiliar; small clots of light litter the sky, like so many tiny moonlets, but there are no moons."

Ruiz looked at Dolmaero with sudden respect. Here was a primitive with a supple mind. He shook his head and started to reply, but Dolmaero held up his hand. "Wait," Dolmaero said. "I must tell you, the decision to put down the phoenix was a poor one, prompted by despair. Be assured, no more such decisions will be made. If nothing else is clear, we can be certain that the gods have turned away from us, so I'll waste no more time hoping for their mercy or kindness. Instead, I ask for yours. Please, tell me what you can."

Ruiz considered. It could do no harm, he thought, to tell the guildmaster of his experiences following the unloading of the drone. "I know little enough, but I'll tell it. I was taken at Bidderum. After I woke in the iron coffins, I was taken below the ground, deep below, and put in a dungeon there for some hours. Was this your experience?"

"No, no, we were brought to this enclosure. I myself remember little of the iron coffins, except for a smell of overcooked meat. You remember more?"

"My memories are confusing," Ruiz said honestly.

Dolmaero's bright eyes searched Ruiz's. "What of the dungeons?"

"The lights were magical. I was given no clothing, but it was neither warm nor cold. Little else occurred."

"And then you were brought here?"

"Yes," Ruiz replied. "I had the impression that a mistake was made. The only other prisoner that I saw in the dungeons was the conjuror, the one who took the semblance of Bhas in the play."

Dolmaero's eyes crackled with interest. "You saw Master Flomel?"

"Is that his name?"

"Yes. What of Master Kroel or Master Molnekh? Did you see them, too?"

"No."

"Umm." Dolmaero seemed lost in thought. Then he said, "Some among the elders believed that only the masters were translated to the Land of Reward, while we lesser folk were forced to bide in this land of Expiation. Apparently they're wrong. I'm not sure this is hopeful information."

A long silence ensued, during which Ruiz finished his meal.

Dolmaero sighed. "I believe that your story is longer than the one you've told, but I don't blame you for keeping your own counsel. We've given you little reason for trust, so I thank you for your news." He got up, with an effort. He stood looking at Ruiz for a moment with both puzzlement and interest. Finally he said, "Your tattoos are interesting to me, if I may comment on them without incurring your animosity."

Ruiz nodded slowly.

"Well," said Dolmaero. "They seem to partake of several traditions, in a manner that I've not seen before. Furthermore, and I mean no insult, they seem a trifle pale. An interesting variation." Then, in an apparent non sequitur, Dolmaero said, "A study of obscure legends is a pastime of mine. You know of the discredited Cult of Saed Corpashun? Bhasrahmet has several times expunged the cult. But a few devotees survive, and claim that men from the far stars occasionally walk Pharaoh."

Ruiz allowed no emotion to reach his face, other than polite interest. Dolmaero nodded in a friendly manner and walked away. Ruiz was amazed. Here was a canny primitive, indeed. And if Ruiz's tattoos were losing their brightness already, there was little time left to engineer an escape. He returned to the hut in a sober frame of mind.

Nisa was standing by the door, holding her empty plate. He smiled cordially as he stepped by her. His intention was to sit quietly for a while and consider the possibilities of the situation, to try to rearrange them into a shape that offered a chance of escape.

As he passed, however, she reached out and tugged at his arm. "Wuhiya, will you help me?" she said.

He stopped reluctantly.

"I'd be very grateful if you'd take me to the bathhouse. I'm afraid to go by myself. You know why." Her eyes were large, her small smile appealing; Ruiz saw that she was holding on to her dignity with difficulty. When he didn't reply immediately, her lip began to tremble.

Ruiz sighed. "Of course, Noble Person, though I don't believe anyone would molest you, now."

Her eyes brightened, and she smiled. "You may call me Nisa," she said. "I will appoint you a Royal Friend."

He had to laugh. She took no offense, apparently mistaking his amusement for simple pleasure.

AT THE BATHHOUSE, two men and an old woman left hastily, rolling their eyes fearfully. Ruiz watched while Nisa dropped her tunic and scrubbed her body with a handful of soapweed, then rinsed away the filth of her illness with dippers of cool water from a crock. He took a surprised delight in the pleasant lift and jounce of her breasts as she lathered her mass of dark hair, in the way the sudsy water ran down her pale flesh, flowing in the hollows, shining on the convexities. For the first time, Ruiz perceived the phoenix as more than a lovely but pitiable object. An urgent desire kindled in him, so that he could not look away from her.

NISA FELT HIS eyes on her as she washed. After a while she felt his desire, and so she began to shift her body for his benefit, moving in the ways that gracefully emphasized the line of her breasts, the soft sweep of her thighs. At first she was hardly aware that she was being provocative. After all, his status was only a bit higher than a slave's, and with slaves and peasants one did not provoke, one commanded. Too, with his sudden violence and his alien beauty, she was not even sure if she believed him to be human. He seemed undismayed by this world of demons—was that natural?

She avoided looking at him, pretending that she didn't feel the touch of his gaze. As she rubbed the soapweed slowly over her body, the coarse tingling touch of the fibers woke a trickle of heat between her legs, and it grew more difficult for her to suppress an occasional shudder of pleasure. She became aware of an aching tension in her breasts.

Still he sat quietly in his shadowed corner. Abruptly, her mind formed the image of Wuhiya at his exercises, his body flowing from one position to the next in a blur of hard beautiful flesh.

NISA SEEMED TO pay no attention to him, until she was finished and relaxing in the bathhouse's deep cistern, as was the Pharaohan custom.

He could see nothing of her but one small hand where she held the side of the tank. He tried to quell his desire, to regain a cautious perspective, but his desire refused to cooperate. It painted pretty pictures in his memory, until he could think of nothing but Nisa.

"And you—do you plan to wash?" she asked, in a soft voice.

"Why not?" he answered. He soaped and rinsed in the prescribed Pharaohan manner, and it was very pleasant to rub away the dust and blood and sweat. He felt clean for the first time since he had left the *Vigia*. He stood on the step at the tank's edge, looking down at her for a moment. She floated on her back, eyes closed, her hair a cloudy swirl, her breasts like white water flowers. Ruiz sighed, and then slid into the tank.

"How long may we stay?" she asked, without opening her eyes.

They were alone in the bathhouse, and Ruiz speculated that word had spread through the paddock: The undead phoenix and the mad casteless slayer were using the facilities. "As long as you like," he said.

"Good." She smiled and arched her back, so that her breasts emerged deliciously from the water.

Ruiz felt a little out of breath.

She allowed her legs to sink and turned to face him. He could almost feel the warmth of her body through the water that separated them. He floated silently, heart thumping.

"Did you see?" she asked in a wondering tone. "The scars . . . gone."

"Yes, I saw."

"Truly, you were right about the doctors here. Though now I'm not so sure that I didn't dream the scars. The scars . . . and what went before."

Ruiz was uncomfortable with that line of thought, but before he could think of a way to divert her, she pushed her shoulder lightly against his. Her skin seemed so exquisitely smooth . . . it was difficult for Ruiz to hold any other thought in his mind. But he didn't shift away, and in a moment she pressed more firmly against him. Her face was very close to his; he felt her breath on his cheek, sweet and warm.

"Wuhiya, you were at Bidderum, I remember you at the gate. Did you see my death? No, don't tell me. It was too ugly. If I didn't die, I came close enough to satisfy the gods, and now I'm guiltless."

He felt no curiosity about her crime; all his curiosity was focused on her body. What would it feel like to run his hands over those lovely contours, to touch her inner heat? He had the eerie sensation that she heard his thoughts—they were so close now—but she didn't draw away.

"It's odd, but I feel more alive now, in this terrible place, jostled by commoners who'd like to see me dead, than I can ever remember feeling in my father's palace." Her voice was slow, musing.

A long moment passed, and then he felt the tips of her breasts touch his chest. "Will you touch me?" she whispered. "Here, where the wounds were." She took his hand

and drew it across her belly. He found that she was as pleasant to touch as he'd imagined.

He wanted her with a fixity that amazed and horrified him. What was wrong with him, that he could so forget his precarious situation? She sensed something of his ambivalence and drew back, eyes wide and hurt.

"What is it? Is it that I am still dead? That I'm rotting and don't know it yet? Do you fear a taint?" Her voice broke on the last word. "Will the grave infect you?"

He thought she might cry, for the first time, and it came to him that for reasons he could not understand he would find her tears unbearable.

"You're alive. There's nothing of death in you, Noble Person." He touched her taut waist, pulled her close again.

She resisted for only an instant. "Show me this, make me believe it," she said. "Make me know I'm alive." She gripped his hips with her strong thighs, and pulled his head down so that he could kiss her breasts.

Afterward, he would remember the slow surge of the water as he moved inside her, and her upturned face, eyes closed, lip caught between small white teeth.

Shining through chinks in the bathhouse walls, the sunlight dappled her with golden glimmers.

But also he would remember that, although she was skillful and eager, there was in her lovemaking an odd detachment, a certain impersonality in the melting looks she gave him, a curious restraint to the soft sounds she made. By all the rules of his existence he should have found that detachment reassuring, but it made his heart ache a little.

THROUGH SOME REMNANT sense of propriety, she insisted that she must leave before he did, and he saw no reason not to humor her. As Nisa stepped out into the sun, Ruiz heard her gasp. He went to the shadowed doorway, where he could watch and not be seen by those who stood in the square.

First he saw Corean the slaver, dressed in the same white shipsuit; her uniform, he supposed. Beside her stood the Mocrassar bondwarrior, the cyborg, and the conjuror that

Dolmaero had called Master Flomel. Half a dozen Pung guards stood to the side.

Master Flomel caught sight of Nisa, and he jerked to attention, delight spreading over his narrow face.

"Why, it *is* you, dearest Nisa," Flomel shouted jovially. "How glad I am that you survive." There was no doubting his sincerity.

"Secure her," Corean said, and the two nearest Pung moved with startling speed. They clipped a monoline coffle drop around her throat and led her away, out of Ruiz's sight.

CHAPTER 18

THERE was nothing to be done. She was gone and it was time to start worrying again about his own precarious situation, time to stop worrying over the fate of some client world primitive. Still, Ruiz shivered with anger—anger at the slaver, anger at his own helplessness.

But it might have been worse. Flomel the conjuror was here, and Ruiz might have blundered out into the square and been noticed. He remembered the way Flomel had stared at him in the low-level cell, and the look that Flomel had given him, back in Bidderum, when Ruiz had flopped onto Flomel's stage. Flomel had the look of a good hater. Ruiz was fortunate not to be in the hands of the conjuror, who would then surely tell the slaver about the blasphemous actions of the snake oil man, and then . . . where would Ruiz hide?

While Ruiz watched, the Pung herded out a delegation of the guild elders, headed by Dolmaero, who looked uncomfortable, but in control. In contrast, the others seemed terrified to the point of catatonia. They were, it seemed, most fearful of the Moc, and Ruiz silently commended their grasp of the situation. His own knees turned to water whenever he looked too long at the great insectoid warrior.

Ruiz found it difficult to analyze Flomel's relation to Corean. It was almost as if the conjuror was unaware that he was property. Flomel spoke. "Dolmaero, Asewil, Tegabides, how glad I am to find you well." Flomel used his orator's voice, rich and sonorous.

Dolmaero stepped forward boldly, then bent his knee in a perfunctory bow. "Master Flomel," said Dolmaero, without great warmth, "we're happy to see you safe."

Flomel seemed oblivious to the undertones in Dolmaero's voice. "Thank you, good Dolmaero. You must be wondering what's going on."

"Yes, of course."

Flomel paused and shot a somewhat anxious look back at Corean, who stood with her assistants, displaying no impatience. Apparently she preferred to deal with her property as uncoercively as possible.

Corean nodded, and Flomel turned back to the elders. "First," he said, "I introduce our new patron. You're privileged to meet Lady Corean Heiclaro, a Noble Person of this region, and a sponsor of follies and serious drama."

"A great pleasure," Dolmaero said, sweeping low in a more sincerely servile bow. The other elders imitated him, shakily.

Flomel continued. "There are many puzzling things about our arrival here, I know, but suffice to say, we're not among gods or devils. Your confinement to these quarters is purely for your own protection, by the way; there are creatures in the outer corridors who have uncertain temperaments."

Tegabides, a small round man with a perpetual expression of doubt, spoke bravely. "If yon monstrous bug is not a devil, what is it? And the fairness of the Lady Corean compels one to think in terms of goddesses, to say nothing of the magical manner in which we arrived in this unknown place."

Flomel paled slightly. He spoke in a confiding tone. "It's not good to speak rashly, Tegabides. The tall armored warrior is Dalfin, a member of the Mocrassar race, and our

Lady's bodyguard and executioner. These things have been explained to me in detail; at present I have no time to go into them with you."

Tegabides seemed truculent, but Dolmaero laid a calming hand on Tegabides' arm. "Let's listen carefully to whatever Master Flomel *does* have time to explain."

Dolmaero's self-possession under these strange circumstances amazed Ruiz. He himself shook with rage and fear, and he was from a culture that took for granted much stranger things than Moc bondwarriors. But Ruiz excused himself; the phoenix was gone. He felt a shocking, irrational degree of loss.

"Come," Flomel said. "Dolmaero is wise, as always. Lady Corean graciously permits us to go to the shade house to discuss these important matters." Flomel turned and performed a deep theatrical bow, which brought a cool smile of amusement to Corean's perfect lips. Then the conjuror herded the elders before him, and they disappeared from Ruiz's sight.

Ruiz shrank back into the deepest shadows. How would the slaver pass the time? Would she call forth the stock for evaluation? Would she check the facilities for proper maintenance? Would she inspect the bathhouse? Ruiz watched in mounting apprehension as she stood quietly in the sun.

The Moc might have been a grotesque statue. The cyborg seemed to be playing a game on one of the dataslates built into his floater console.

Long minutes passed. Ruiz sweated.

At last Flomel returned, trailed by the guild elders. The elders seemed a good deal more cheerful, except for Dolmaero, who looked slightly ill.

Flomel approached Corean and spoke in wheedling tones. "Noble lady, Guildmaster Dolmaero asks a favor."

"What is it?" Corean asked without inflection.

Dolmaero spoke. "There is an injured man. Could you speed the healing of his hurts, as you did for the phoenix? Or, at least, ease his discomfort?"

Corean came forward and the Moc moved after her, its great leaping limbs slowly pistoning. "Bring him out," she said.

Dolmaero gestured and a moment later two men carried out an improvised litter. On it was the coercer, whose face was one vast bruise, radiating from his flattened nose. Casmin drew a sharp breath when he saw the Moc, then winced.

Corean stood over him, a look of detached curiosity on that incredible face. "How was he hurt?" she asked.

"He fell," Dolmaero said quickly, before anyone else could answer, and Ruiz remembered to breathe again.

"He fell?" She turned to Flomel. "How well do you know this man?"

"Well, indeed, Lady. He was warded to our family when he was only three. A loyal man, who deserves your help." Flomel stared at Casmin, taking in his injuries with growing puzzlement.

"Describe the part this man plays in one of your productions."

Flomel looked defensive. "Ah, well, noble lady, he actually plays no direct part. His services are among the perquisites of my position. He provides protection against evil deeds, and instruction to recalcitrants."

Now her amusement seemed definite. "In other words, he twists arms at your behest?"

Flomel made no answer for a long moment, and then nodded jerkily, features stiff with suppressed annoyance.

"Then he no longer performs any essential function," she said, in that sweet clear voice. "Still, I'll ease his discomfort."

She bent over the litter. At the tip of her index finger, a shimmering tongue of disrupted air appeared. The burbling sound of a sonic knife came clearly to Ruiz's ears. With a graceful sweeping gesture she sliced Casmin's throat open, down to the spine, then danced nimbly back from the blood. The elders scattered like frightened chickens.

She nodded to the Moc. It pointed a midlimb at the corpse, which still twitched. A plasma lance whooshed white fire and heated the remains to crumbling incandescence. Most of the troupe fled indoors. Only Dolmaero and Flomel stood their ground, staring.

When nothing remained but smoking ash, Corean left

without ceremony, taking along a pale Flomel. Before she passed out of Ruiz's line of sight, Corean glanced directly at Ruiz's place of concealment, expressionless.

When the slavers were gone, the Pharaohans came forth and stood about in the square in little arguing knots, avoiding the blackened spot at the center of the square. Dolmaero seemed not to be taking part in the general discussion. He sat on the low wall, staring at nothing in particular.

Ruiz waited a long while before he came out of the bathhouse and joined Dolmaero.

Dolmaero looked at Ruiz without speaking.

"I'm sorry about your man," Ruiz offered.

Dolmaero made a gesture of dismissal. "Don't be concerned. Casmin was always a jackal. Away from the restraining influence of his guild, it would have been only a matter of time before he'd have begun to practice his ugly pleasures on the innocent. And how would I have controlled him?"

"Still . . . I appreciate your not revealing the source of his injuries."

"I told no lie," Dolmaero said heavily.

"No, I suppose not. Did Master Flomel say what they intended for the Noble Person?"

Dolmaero looked at Ruiz, and Ruiz sensed that evil news was coming. Dolmaero seemed reluctant to deliver it. "Yes," Dolmaero finally said, "he went into that a little. I'm not sure you want to hear what he said."

"Tell me," Ruiz said.

"Do you remember when I said my decision to put the phoenix to death was a mistake? Now I'm not so sure. It might have been a kindness, had you not interfered. Master Flomel plans to use her in an upcoming performance."

"A performance?"

"Yes, so he said. It seems we will perform for an audience of the mighty, to whom the goddess-woman is simply an agent. I don't understand the details, but there will be bidding for our services."

Clever of the goddess-woman, Ruiz thought, sickened. She would put the troupe on the block, and they would do their utmost to bring her a high price, thinking it their opportunity to impress the influential of their new world. She practiced the slaver's art skillfully.

"And so," Dolmaero continued, "the girl will be required to die once more. I wonder; will she again be revived? How many times could that be done? Do you know?"

Ruiz was silent. Not in his most pessimistic appraisal of Nisa's future had it occurred to him that he'd saved her only to play the phoenix once again. But now that he considered it, it made perfect sense. She had been brilliant in the play. And she could be so again, for many more performances, until her sensorium was so damaged by the death trauma that she could no longer act her part. Long before that, Nisa would lust for the peace of a real death.

"Many times," Ruiz answered, giving much away, but at that moment not caring. "Tell me, Dolmaero, when do your rehearsals begin?"

"Soon, I think. Master Flomel mentioned that the stage would be brought within the week. There will be a period of repair and restaging; then we begin. Perhaps the girl will return then."

Dolmaero watched Ruiz struggle with his thoughts, and Dolmaero's small bright eyes softened in sympathy. He patted Ruiz's arm gently, then heaved his bulk up and went away.

THAT EVENING, RUIZ filled only one plate. The house of the casteless seemed very empty. Just before dark, a boy brought a small oil lamp to the door. "From Master Dolmaero," he said, and handed it to Ruiz. Ruiz was touched by the Guildmaster's gift, and he burned the lamp far into the night, sitting on Nisa's cot and watching the tiny flame. But when the last of the oil burned away and the lamp went out, he rose from the cot and went out to walk the wall. His nocturnal explorations were aided by the absence of any other explorers; the Pharaohans did not go outside their walls after sunset. On Pharaoh, many hungry creatures hunted by night. He went about his business under the assumption that no one watched the paddock; if they did, he couldn't understand why he had not already been taken.

Again, he found the section of wall where the snapfields occasionally failed. The failure was random, occurring once or twice an hour. The duration of the failure averaged between fifteen and forty-five seconds. Twice that night, however, the failure lasted less than ten seconds. If Ruiz were caught at the top of the wall when the field resumed, he would fall off the wall in pieces. It wasn't an optimum escape route, but it was, so far, the only possibility he'd found. Of course, the other side of the wall might just be another paddock, not an access corridor. Ruiz could think of no good way to tell in advance; the harsh buzz of the fields made listening impossible.

It took him all the next day to braid a rope from the leather fragments he found in the house of the casteless. That night, he tied to the rope a slender stick, weighted at one end with a rock. He went to the defective section of the wall. When the first failure occurred, he heaved the stick over the top of the wall, hoping that no one watched from the other side. He pulled the stick back slowly. By watching the arcing tip of the stick, faintly visible against the starfields as it tilted over the rounded top, he was able to determine that the wall top was smoothly curved, innocent of angles where a grapple might catch. He sighed and pulled the rope down.

On the next darkening of the field, he tried it again, and before the field returned he got a fairly good idea of the shape of the wall top. Just for good measure he tried it one more time, but this time the field returned prematurely, and the rope fell down minus the stick. Ruiz heard it hit the ground on the other side, and he cursed. He could only hope that no one would notice the stick, with its tag of homemade rope, or pay enough attention to it to wonder where it had come from.

His next task was to fashion a hook that fit the contour of the wall top closely enough to hold his weight. This took the better part of a day. Ruiz cobbled it together from bits of wood salvaged from the cots, and bound the hook into rigidity with strips of wet rawhide. He dried the assemblage on the roof, in the hot sun. When he was finished, he had an object that looked as if it had been sawn from the end of a giant shepherd's staff. Ruiz attached the braided leather rope and his escape apparatus was complete.

The drawback to this particular technique, he thought, was that the hook couldn't be tested in advance. Once Ruiz managed to hang the hook on the top of the wall, he'd have to go up the rope to retrieve it.

So it was time to decide. Should he go immediately, escaping into the unknown territory of the compound, or should he remain in the paddock awhile longer, mending his strength? Complicating the decision was Ruiz's completely impractical urge to see Nisa again, though there was nothing he could do for her that wouldn't jeopardize the job he'd been hired to do, to say nothing of his life. He could not even give her a merciful death without accepting certain exposure. She was a valuable part of the troupe; Corean would take a dangerous interest in any harm that befell Nisa.

When Ruiz considered it, however, it did seem strange that the slaver had shown so little interest in the source of Casmin's injuries. And why had she allowed Nisa, a valuable item, to be penned in the paddock, ill and vulnerable to superstitious peasants? Ruiz could make no useful inferences, so he took a deep breath, shook his head, and put all thought of Nisa from him.

On the day that Ruiz completed the hook, Flomel came again, late in the afternoon. Ruiz was in the house of the casteless, adding to the length of his rope and inspecting it for weaknesses. He heard voices in the square, and he went cautiously to the door.

Flomel stood in the middle of the square, conversing with Dolmaero and the other guild elders. Two Pung guards stood by, their bodies expressing patient boredom. Ruiz could just barely hear what was being said.

"But how will they bring it?" Dolmaero spoke, puzzled, and he gestured in the direction of the small personnel lock.

Flomel pointed overhead with a theatrical flourish. "Look," he said. "See the beams, those silvery threads? The Lady's minions will hang the stage from those beams and float it down into our practice quarters. Don't ask me how. There's a lot about these folk that none of us understands."

You could say that, Ruiz thought, with a certain vengeful relish.

Dolmaero looked diplomatically dubious. "As you say, Master Flomel. And when will Masters Kroel and Molnekh join us?"

"Very soon, very soon. Now, I anticipate a problem with the girl. In Bidderum she was magnificent, but then she was an Expiant, no? Naltrehset, we'll have to rely heavily on your philters to make her amenable, but to an extent she must cooperate willingly. Dolmaero, you worked most closely with her before. Have you any suggestions?"

Ruiz became even more intensely interested in the conversation. To Ruiz's eye, Dolmaero seemed to sink slightly into himself. "Nothing comes to me at the moment, Master," Dolmaero said, looking aside.

A man with pinched features and a subservient whine spoke up. "Master," he said, "what of the casteless one, the one that protected her from Casmin?"

"What is this?" Flomel asked, his narrow face darkening. "Who is this casteless one, and why was it necessary to protect the phoenix? Who wanted to harm her?"

Dolmaero answered. "Before we knew you were safe, Master, before we understood anything of our situation, the elders decided, by guild ballot, that the survival of the phoenix was unnatural and possibly an affront to the gods." Here Dolmaero paused, looking uncomfortable. All eyes turned toward the house of the casteless, where Ruiz hid. Reluctantly Dolmaero continued. "The casteless one, Wuhiya by name, a snake oil seller by profession, he cared for her, since she was mistakenly lodged in the house of the casteless. No doubt he recognized her value. At any rate, I sent Casmin in to fetch her out for judgment, and Casmin—you know how he was—Casmin attacked Wuhiya. Wuhiya defended himself. You saw the result."

Flomel rubbed his chin. "I should be pleased, I suppose. The girl is far more important to the troupe than Casmin was, though I'll miss his rough-and-ready humor. Had you restrained your religious impulses, none of this would have happened." Then Flomel's eyes widened, and rage suffused his features. "Wait," he said thickly. "Is this Wuhiya the same oil-sucking wretch who threw himself onto the apron at Bidderum, spoiling the finale?"

Flomel started for the house of the casteless, his long fingers crooking into claws. *"Is he the one?"* Flomel shouted.

Dolmaero hurried after Flomel. "Wait, Master. Do nothing rash, I beg you." He caught up with Flomel at the doorway, where Flomel had paused, staring past the fluttering insect-guards into the darkness inside. Ruiz Aw, meanwhile, was pressed against the wall, out of sight, wondering what he could do if Flomel attacked him or denounced him to the guards. They might not take Flomel's accusations seriously; on the other hand, they might take Ruiz before Corean, where Ruiz would be hard-pressed to explain his eccentric behavior. But Flomel stopped, his breath whistling between his clenched teeth.

"Come out, dust rat," Flomel hissed. "Come out and be rewarded."

Ruiz made no sound.

Dolmaero reasoned with the conjuror. "Master, you can't think to sully yourself with this one's worthless blood. Besides, look what happened to Casmin."

Ruiz heard nothing for a few seconds.

Then Dolmaero continued. "Listen, I have an idea. The phoenix is obviously attached to this Wuhiya. He nursed her, he saved her from Casmin's cord, and they were observed in passion at the bathhouse."

Flomel gasped. "You joke, Dolmaero! She's a princess, or was before she became an Expiant."

"Nevertheless, it's true, Master. I don't know the reason; it seems incomprehensible to me, too . . . but what doesn't, these days? At any rate, we can use her regard for the wretch to secure her cooperation in the play."

Flomel seemed to be considering. At last he said, in calmer tones, "You've given me good counsel once again, Guildmaster. I'll petition the Lady for a more effective coercer. Perhaps she will loan me the great bug. Just the sight of that one should frighten her into helpfulness, and if not, we'll pluck fingers from the oil peddler until she takes the point."

Then the voices moved away, discussing the logistics of the rehearsals, supplies to be requisitioned, the choice of material to be performed, the changes required in the stage. Ruiz's thoughts ran cool and distant, and he could feel the death net tug at him, a warning tension. He sagged against the wall. Just when the situation seemed worst, it deteriorated again.

Flomel was gone by the time the evening meal arrived. Ruiz took his dinner to his accustomed spot. To his surprise, Dolmaero joined him.

"Well, friend Wuhiya," Dolmaero said, "I must apologize to you again. You heard?"

"Yes. Flomel's a vindictive little fart, isn't he?"

"He takes his art seriously; what more need be said? He's a bad enemy. But I hope you'll believe I was trying to do my best for you. I just couldn't think of anything better."

Ruiz looked at Dolmaero, appraising. Ruiz's profession was one that bred cynicism, but in Dolmaero's broad face, Ruiz saw only concern and weariness.

"I believe you," Ruiz said. He seemed to concentrate on his meal, but he was thinking about the night ahead.

CHAPTER 19

W HEN the Pung took her away, Nisa still felt a certain pleasurable lassitude, and so she was slow to fear. The monsters were gentle, and that seemed so incongruous that she walked between them to the personnel lock without thought of escape.

"Where are you taking me?" she asked the monsters, when she finally found her voice. But they were silent, though the one on her right showed a mouthful of needle teeth. Was it a smile meant to reassure her?

At the lock, the door startled her when it slammed up into the arch of the opening, and she tried to run away. The monoline collar bruised her throat when she hit the end of the lead, and she fell to one knee, gagging. The larger of the two Pung guards helped her to her feet. The skin of its hands was cool and hard—not unpleasant, but so strange that she shuddered. Thereafter, she went along, docile.

After a time she took an interest in the sights.

She began to understand the size of the compound after they'd been walking the corridors for half an hour. Her father's palace was a collection of hovels, in comparison. The walls of the corridors were made of a slick gray-white sub-stance that reminded her of unglazed porcelain. The walls were several times the height of a man, and the way narrow, so that only a ribbon of sky was visible above. It was very quiet, as though whatever life existed behind the walls was muffled by their thickness.

She couldn't help looking into the observation ports as they passed the other paddocks, and a sort of detached hor-ror grew in her as she stole glances at the beings penned within.

Some seemed to be human, though not any sort of human with which she was familiar. They came in every shape, size, and color—white as ice, black as charcoal, tall massive crea-tures, small nimble ones. They wore strange garments, and many bore strange disfigurements. Most of the men did not shave their heads. Some were naked, some wore garments of such magnificence that the person within seemed to disap-pear. These otherworldly people wore inexplicable expres-sions, used bizarre gestures; even their postures seemed alien.

The monsters she saw were less disorienting, since she had no expectation that she would understand anything about them. She saw a pen of creatures that resembled irrin, flightless birds of the Pharaohan drylands, except that these had massive brain cases that hung back over their molting shoulders. They huddled in a landscape of flat sand and low bushes, in small motionless groups, powerful legs folded un-der them. There was something piercingly sad about them, hopeless and resigned. Their great golden eyes were opaque with loss. Nisa felt tears sting her eyes, just from that one glimpse.

But there were other monsters that inspired no pity. In one pen she caught sight of a colony of swift reptilian predators that ripped at the still-moving body of an old woman. They had sly goat-eyes, and they seemed to be aware of Nisa as she peered through the cloudy glass of the observation ports. She shuddered and looked away.

"When will we get wherever we're going?" she asked. The guards paid no attention, and she began to suspect that they didn't speak her language.

She wondered how the guards could find their way through the labyrinth. There were so many turnings and junctures. The great number of beings she had seen indicated that the compound was a place of great activity, but she saw no others in the corridors, until they stopped at a three-way intersection to allow a coffle and its guards to pass. The coffle was made up of a dozen exquisitely matched women, somewhat human in appearance, chained neck to neck, wearing short kilts of silvery metal scales and nothing else. Their skins were toned a pale celadon green, their milky hair long and knotted into complex braids. Their wide lavender eyes looked at Nisa as though she were some odd freak.

Nisa felt acutely the demoralizing effects of her dirty sackcloth tunic and tangled damp hair, and she started to drop her head in shame. But she was still the daughter of the King of Kings—a risen phoenix—and her chin lifted. She stared back at the freakish women, lips set in as haughty a sneer as she could manage.

In a moment the women were gone down the corridor, and Nisa and her guards continued.

They finally reached a long wall set with many doors. As they approached, one door folded back, revealing a very small room. Nisa couldn't imagine any good reason why she should go in there with the Pung guards, and she pulled back against her leash, tugging at the thin clear strand with her hands.

The larger guard showed its teeth again in that frightening smile, and gestured. Nisa shook her head stubbornly. "Please," she said. "Why must we go in there?"

The guard released a rumbling sigh and took her by the arm. Effortlessly he propelled her inside. When the other guard was wedged in, the door shut.

Nisa felt a need to whimper, but she forced it down. The alien smell of the guards thickened in the tiny space. Abruptly, she felt as if she were falling and then a whimper did escape her tightly clamped lips; but she noticed that the guards seemed unperturbed. So she assumed that death was not imminent.

A moment later the elevator slowed and stopped, and that sensation was almost as distressing.

The door folded back.

Her first thought was that she had miraculously been transported to her uncle Shimanekh's harlotry, a place she'd visited more than once, disguised as a visitor from the provinces.

The ceiling was low overhead, as if to concentrate and compress the scents of pleasure. Nisa smelled a hundred subtle odors, sweet wine, pungent smokes, the deep note of human bodies in heat. The room was huge. To each side walls were visible, but the far end of the room was lost in darkness.

Nisa observed a similar range of luxuries—deep carpets and soft fabric, highlighted with the glitter of precious metal and rare stone, everything to please the touch as well as the eye. The furnishings were eccentric: here a divan with cloven feet, there a love seat with snakeskin cushions. She examined a chair with grotesque ebony finials—infant vampires, their tiny mouths stretched wide, exposing long canines. Nisa shuddered, and looked away.

Nisa heard, low and far away, a thread of atonal tinkling music. Other than that, silence filled the room.

But if there were a recognizable aura and purpose to the place, also there were unfamiliar things, things that shocked her with wrongness, things that she could hardly bear to see. There were, instead of the erotic statues that Shimanekh favored, strange glittering wraiths, pale blue, translucent, locked in almost-frozen sexual ecstasy, but moving in slow life. It was as if ghosts copulated in the niches along the walls.

And the lights. On Pharaoh the brightest lights, the only lights other than naked flames, were the gaslights that lighted her father's palace and a few of the wealthier temples. But here were lights of every hue and intensity, tiny colored lights attached to sleek metal panels everywhere, vast globes of soft pastel luminance, sharp pools of white glare.

She and the Pung seemed to be the only inhabitants of that vast room.

The guards took her to a high-backed chair padded with pale brown leather. They attached her leash to a sturdy iron ring that was built into the arm of the chair, and there they left her, returning into the little room. The larger one waved genially, and she waved back. She was almost sorry to see them go.

She sat alone in the chair for what seemed at least an hour. Her fear was gradually eroded by the advent of boredom. She examined her surroundings with interest; her eye was drawn to a design in the leather of the chair. After a moment she realized that it was a tattoo; in a moment more she recognized a pattern favored by the highlanders who lived on the secondary plateau north of the capital, and she realized what sort of animal had furnished the leather of the chair. Suddenly the touch of it was greasily intolerable and she stood up, still tethered.

A woman came for her, finally. She was enormous—tall, broad, and muscular, with great thrusting breasts and vast hips. The woman wore a gown of transparent silken stuff, and knee-high leather boots, polished black. The only tiny thing about the woman was her face; her features clustered tightly together in a broad expanse of smooth flesh. She wore an expression of simpering madness, and she jerked roughly at the lead as she led Nisa into the dim depths of the room.

At the far side, on a couch piled high with velvet cushions, Corean waited. She was naked to the waist, and attended by two smooth creatures of uncertain degree of humanity.

The monstrous insect stood behind her, in a darkness between the lights, still as a statue. The big woman unsnapped the leash, and Nisa rubbed her sore neck.

"Come to me," the woman called, in a voice like music. She smiled and Nisa moved closer, as if sleepwalking. She stopped just out of reach.

Corean patted the cushion beside her, smiling. The creature on her right hissed, and Nisa saw that they were some sort of human-shaped cats. Their faces had a foreshortened look, their noses were black stubs, and their teeth were white and jaggedly sharp. A gloss of short black fur covered their otherwise naked bodies, except for muzzles and pink palms.

A look of vexation touched Corean's perfect face and she made a shooing gesture. Immediately the two attendants slunk away, seeming to flow from the couch. Nisa heard a tiny snarl as one passed her, and she saw a casual hatred in the bright eyes.

Nisa sank into the soft cushions, and Corean shifted to make room for her. At close range Corean's beauty was even more devastating. Her skin seemed almost poreless, and it had a silky gloss that made Nisa want to touch it, just to see how so unusual a substance might feel.

"Nisa," Corean said, "I can't say how happy I am to see you. Did you know, you are the first phoenix I've ever met?"

Nisa could say nothing. Corean's scent was subtle, a warm ghost of scent, so tantalizing that it made Nisa want to bury her nose in Corean's flesh, to find where that delicious odor was strongest. *Stop it,* she said to herself. *Have you learned no lessons at all?*

"Well, you are. I've seen other phoenix troupes, oh, many of them, but no other phoenix has lived." Corean smiled again, showing small sharp teeth. "If they had, I wouldn't have been half so pleased by them as I am by you. Flomel tells me much about you. That you're the daughter of a King. That you are the finest phoenix that he has ever worked with, dignified, beautiful. Full of that brave acceptance that means all to the connoisseur of phoenix plays." Corean seemed to be orating a carefully composed speech, though her voice never rose above an intimate purr.

Nisa responded to the one oddity she'd felt in that speech. "I'm the only one that lived? Why would that be? Wuhiya says . . ." She trailed off, sensing that she was on treacherous ground.

Corean leaned forward, so that one small white breast touched Nisa's arm, a soft caress. "Wuhiya says . . . ?" Corean prompted. "Go on, Nisa."

"Wuhiya, he's the man who cared for me when I was sick," she temporized.

"Yes?"

"Well, he said, when I asked him why I was alive, why the scars were going, he said he thought that they must have very good doctors here. Is that true?" Nisa was a little less rattled. "And can you tell me, where am I?"

Corean sat back, a flash of irritation crossing the perfect features. It was only for the briefest instant, but Nisa was suddenly not so completely overwhelmed with Corean's beauty.

"One question at a time, Nisa. Yes, we have very good doctors here, but the other phoenixes were dead before they reached us. Perhaps you are specially favored by the gods. That could be it. Or perhaps you had help that the other ones never got, a hidden friend. What do you think?"

"I don't think of it at all if I can help it," Nisa answered honestly.

Corean laughed, a soft practiced sound. "So? Well, as to your other question, here is Sook, the Bargerell Plate, the Blacktear Pens, my apartments." A pause. "My couch," Corean said.

"Oh," Nisa said. Much of what Corean had said made no sense to her. "I've never heard of Sook. Is it far from Pharaoh?" In her childhood, Nisa had had a constant companion, an old woman who'd cared for her, soothed her hurts, and told her fanciful stories about magical lands that rose above the mists of Hell, far around the breast of the world.

"Yes, far. Now tell me: What of this Wuhiya? What manner of man is he?" Corean moved closer again, and Nisa felt Corean's interest intensify. "Has he any other theories about you? Or me?"

"He has not mentioned you. In fact, he says very little, so I don't know what I can tell you about him." Nisa paused to look into Corean's blue eyes, saw a warning there. Nisa took fright, spoke on in a quavering voice. "Wuhiya is strong. He hurt a coercer, Casmin, very badly, when Casmin meant to kill me. And Casmin was held to be a mighty man; he killed three men in the Blooding Festival last spring, they say." Nisa had a sudden sinking feeling that she'd betrayed the strange man who had made such delightful love to her in the bathhouse. "But he didn't finish Casmin, though Casmin was helpless."

"Merciful, is he, do you think?" Corean asked.

"He pitied me," Nisa said.

"That, I think, is only one of the emotions he feels for you," Corean said. She laughed again, and moved closer yet, until she was pressed against Nisa. Her breath was spicy. "Did you," Corean asked, "enjoy your bath?"

Nisa didn't know how to answer, but she felt a blush climb in her face. Corean took her chin, and turned Nisa's head until she was looking directly into Corean's eyes, those eyes like hammered blue metal. Corean kissed her, all soft moist lips, and then Nisa felt the touch of Corean's tongue, a light tingling stroke.

"You still taste a little of death, Nisa," Corean said. "But it's all right. That's not a bad taste, to me."

Corean's perfect face was still heartbreakingly beautiful —and that, Nisa thought, was a terrible, incomprehensible thing.

Corean drew away and signaled the giantess. "Take my guest to her quarters, and give her a helot to see to her comfort." The woman moved forward with the leash, but Corean frowned and said, "She won't need that."

AT THE WALL , in the night, Ruiz waited for the snapfield to fail. As he waited, he twirled the hook moodily. He thought unwillingly of Nisa, who had already caused him so much trouble. And who, though she was gone beyond recall, continued to trouble him. A rational being—such as Ruiz Aw—formed his attachments based on rational factors: intellect, or a commonality of interests.

Here he sat, however, mooning over a woman from a world that, with extraordinary luck and a thousand more years of Terran tech seepage, might become eligible for limited membership in the lowest rung of the pangalac culture. It rankled.

In his darkest moments, Ruiz Aw worried that he was no better than any other foolish romantic.

The snapfield failed, cutting short further maundering, and Ruiz stood up. *Well, now,* he thought.

He flipped the hook up the wall, and it arced over, trailing the leather rope. He gave a jerk; the hook caught, and he swarmed upward. At the top he straddled the wall, jerked the hook loose. As he did, he took a split second to look about, and his heart sank. The compound was vast, covering thousands of hectares. And worst of all, there was no corridor below, just another paddock, shaped like a bowl, much bigger than the Pharaohan pen, and at the center a lake, glowing with a soft blue light.

"Ah, well," he said. He was acutely conscious of the snapfield rail, cold against his crotch. He made his decision, pulled his leg over, flipped the hook loose, and dropped off the wall into the strange paddock.

It was a long drop, but he rolled out of the impact along a grassy lawn. The reengineered bones of his legs absorbed the shock successfully. As he sprawled to a stop, Ruiz heard the sizzling whump of the returning snapfield.

He crouched under a low bush. The paddock was lush and green, the darkness alive with the songs of night birds. The bush he hid beneath was starred with tiny white blossoms and released a scent of cinnamon and apples when he brushed against it. He waited patiently for long minutes, until he was reasonably sure there would be no hostile reaction to his arrival. He watched the snapfields that surrounded this new paddock, and was disappointed to see that they all appeared to be in perfect order. He could only hope there was another way out.

Finally he retrieved his rope and hid it in the fragrant bush. He headed downhill toward the center of the paddock.

The woods that covered the upper slopes of the bowl were parklike, manicured, and made for easy walking even in the pale starlight. Sook had no moons, unless one counted the myriad of tiny glints from the Shard orbital stations, the weapons platforms that enforced the peculiar laws of Sook.

Ruiz moved cautiously, making less noise than the occasional zephyr that fluttered the leaves. The trees, Ruiz noticed, had silver leaves, with an almost metallic reflectivity, so that when disturbed they scattered the starshine in tiny pinpoint sparkles. It was a pretty effect. The woods had a restful, lulling effect, and Ruiz supposed that subsurface harmonic generators were skewing his perceptions. If the security technology of this paddock matched the sophistication of its design, he was probably already discovered. But Ruiz took heart. The Pung seemed to be running a simple and unpretentious operation here; perhaps that simplicity extended to the security measures, which would be their responsibility and not that of the paddock's leaseholder.

As he neared the lake, the woods gave way to gardens, somewhat informal and rustic, but beautifully maintained. Here he heard voices, and he quickly hid behind a nearby statue, which depicted a native of Corvus carved in some glassy black stone. The wings of the statue drooped in an attitude of defeat, providing Ruiz with a perfect lurking place.

Two figures came toward him through the darkness of the garden. They murmured together as they strolled the path of white stone, and Ruiz saw that they were a man and a woman, amorously involved. Mentally Ruiz urged them past his hiding spot; perversely they settled on the bench in front of Ruiz's statue.

"I speak my mind," said the young woman. "Your compassion is the wonder of the sept."

"Compassion? She's my soul companion." The young man's voice was light, teasing.

"A travesty. What could the Septarch have been thinking of, to pair you with her? She is drab, her hair springs forth like a nest of sea spines, she dances the fulgura like a frog in hip boots."

The young man laughed. "Your opinions are quite colorful. But in some respects I'd have to agree. Certainly you show more understanding of my qualities than ever she did."

"Yes. . . ." And for some minutes Ruiz was forced to listen, at close range, to the consummation of their tryst. At some point in their exertions, they rolled off the bench onto the grass. Presently they slept.

Ruiz pondered. Their clothing was scattered invitingly about the nearby shrubbery. His own crude tunic was certain to draw attention at the center of the paddock. Quickly he stripped it off. He crept about collecting the young man's garments, and shortly he was appropriately clothed, though the jacket was tight across the shoulders and the pants too short. A broad velvet cap covered his naked scalp and obscured Ruiz's fading tattoos.

Ruiz drew a deep breath and set off for the lakeshore.

Above him, invisible in the soft darkness, Corean's spy bead followed.

CHAPTER 20

COREAN gave all her attention to her spyscreen. She watched Ruiz assembling the snoring swain's outfit, and laughed.

At her side, Marmo the cyborg rested on his floater, uncommunicative. But when Ruiz, equipped in his stolen garments, turned toward the lakeshore, Marmo spoke. "Are you certain this is wise? The Farelord Preall takes his little world seriously. He'll be put out if your unknown damages it."

Corean kept her eyes on Ruiz's progress through the garden. "Preall is nothing to me. Besides, Preall fears me, as he should. If the unknown should take a sledgehammer to Thera, if he should poison the sea meadows, if he should net Preall's darlings and hang them all on hooks and take holos for the folks back home and write on all the walls, 'This is Corean's fault,' Preall wouldn't say a word to me. And if he did, I'd tell him to complain to the Pung. After all, it's their compound. They're the ones who maintain the snapfields."

"You're right, yes," Marmo said. His vocoder was turned down to a whisper. His lips pursed.

On the screen, Ruiz sidled delicately through a patch of shoreside bushes.

"Look, Marmo. He's an elegant sort of snake, isn't he?" Corean smiled.

"He doesn't appeal to me. You knew he was the one, back when he saved the phoenix from the yokels—why didn't you deal with him then? Freeze him down, ship him off Sook, and leave him where no one will ever find him. It's always worked before."

"Ah, but Marmo, what if he's too quick for us? What if he manages to die before we get him frozen, and a signal goes out? What then?" She shrugged. "And anyway, he's entertaining to watch."

An uncomfortable silence ensued. Corean knew she was right to treat the unknown with caution. If he was a League agent, as seemed likely, there was an excellent chance he was fitted with a death net; if she were to simply kill the man the consequences might be fatal for her. At the moment of death, a burst of data would flood the tachyon strata, activated by the unknown's death trauma. The burst would carry the unknown's location and the immediate circumstances of his death back to the League.

But there was some doubt that he was a League agent. The preservation of the phoenix was a deep enigma. That the unknown had acted in so quixotic a manner was very puzzling. Either the unknown was an arrogant blunderer, with no grasp of the gravity of his situation, or else he was no blunderer at all, just a being so supremely sure of himself that he could afford to flaunt the survival of the phoenix in his captors' faces. In any case, it was disquieting in the extreme that the unknown had resisted the stunfield long enough to attach the med limpet to the phoenix. She would have thought such a feat impossible. Certainly she had paid enough for that technology, supposedly the very latest, proof against any known conditioning system. These uncertainties made Corean reluctant to act against him until she understood the situation better. So she had set her traps and now she watched, waiting for the unknown to announce his identity.

If it turned out that he was only a beautiful predator,

then she wanted him. She could brainpeel him, and eventually make him safe. And then she would keep him forever in her collection of beautiful things.

RUIZ REACHED THE shore. Looking down into the waters of the lake, he saw a mariphile's vision of fairyland, a fantasy city under the water, glowing up through the green depths. The city was built to an eccentric plan, with a complexity of spires and balconies, constructed of some pale translucent stone bright with an inner light.

There was something infinitely enticing about the city, which Ruiz attributed to the harmonic generators. Ruiz felt a strong urge to join the revelry that swirled among the towers and courtyards and pavilions of the submerged city. Tiny human figures swam far below, flitting lazily from building to shining building.

Ruiz felt a touch of optimism. If appearances could be relied on, he had stumbled onto some wealthy being's plaything, a permanent installation maintained on Sook for the diversion of the owner and his guests. Escape from here might be feasible, because of the greater volume of traffic in and out.

Ruiz examined the surface of the lake, which had a dense, viscous, unwatery look. He nodded, stood up, stretched, and allowed himself to fall face first into the lake.

As he had expected, he didn't get wet; there wasn't even a splash. The surface layer, a semiliving protein, flowed around him and bonded to his skin and clothing, preventing the penetration of the fluid, which was not water and carried a hypersolution of oxygen. Ruiz breathed in, and the bond layer passed oxygen through to him. The bond layer ensured survival, comfort, and even sartorial correctness; his cap remained tightly attached to his skull. The fluid provided Ruiz with a small negative bouyancy, so that Ruiz drifted gently downward toward the city. The fluid was just cool enough to be comfortable, though it took him some moments to grow used to the odd talcum-powder slipperiness of the fluid against his skin.

Through the fluid he could hear music. A dozen small

orchestras played softly below, and the murmur of many voices carried oddly through the fluid. Ruiz floated toward a large pavilion, directing his descent with small flicks of his hands. The pavilion's roof was formed to resemble a starfish, and each spiny projection on the roof was tipped by a tiny sparkling light. The lights pulsed and rippled to the music that played within.

Ruiz touched down just outside the railing that rimmed the dance floor of the pavilion, where a number of filigree booths gave a little privacy to tired dancers.

He rested for a bit by the railing, watching the dancers. They danced a complicated figure, swirling in slow grace. The men were uniformly dashing, the women as beautiful as they were haughty. All wore mannered expressions so uniform that the effect was unsettling, as if Ruiz watched one couple in a hall of mirrors instead of the dozens who filled the domed interior.

Ruiz recognized the touch of Cleve of Sook, a minor master in the art of the grown culture. This example of Cleve's work, though probably not among his most original designs, would still fetch a pretty price in the Pit on Dilvermoon. Ruiz wondered if it was stolen, that being the only reason he could imagine for the culture's presence here in an obscure slave pen. He shook his head. Grown cultures always made Ruiz Aw uneasy, for reasons that he had never been able to give a definite shape to. Perhaps it was due to the sense he had, when among the dwellers of such a culture, that the artificially instilled behavior that directed every thought and mood of the dwellers was dangerously brittle, so that the uncontrollable humanity of the dwellers might at any moment erupt in terrible acts.

The act that unfolded while Ruiz watched, however, was certainly part of the programmed ambience of the culture. Two young men at the center of the figure, both striving for a fashionable extravagance of gesture, chanced to bump elbows. Immediately they whirled to face each other, interrupting the flow of the dance. The music trailed off uncertainly; the two spoke harshly to each other, though Ruiz couldn't make out the actual words. The other dancers formed a globe around the two, and from the avidity of the watchers' expressions, Ruiz understood what was to follow before it happened, though it happened very quickly.

Both whipped willow-leaf daggers from their sleeves at the same instant, as though controlled by the same brain. The first slash and parry were almost a continuation of the dance; the fluid they swam in enforced grace even in the extreme of combat. But then it was over, and the victor pulled his dagger from the throat of the loser. A small crimson puff of blood escaped before the bond layer sealed the corpse. The loser floated quietly in the center of a rapidly emptying pavilion.

Many of the couples were swimming upward toward the surface, faces taut with unconcealed lust. The nature of the bond layer made it inconvenient to perform the more basic human functions, including sex, because the bond layer did not pass nongaseous matter. Doubtless, air spaces were common in the city's private areas, but Ruiz couldn't deny the lure of the starlit gardens.

A hand touched his sleeve and he turned as quickly as he could in the fluid.

A stout man with a sly appraising face floated there, watching Ruiz with tiny eyes. "You're a guest of Lord Preall also, eh?" the man said, emitting a cloud of tiny bubbles. The tiny eyes widened when he saw Ruiz's tattoos.

Ruiz collected himself. "Of course," Ruiz said in his most autocratic tones.

The man relaxed, apparently satisfied that no painted savage would speak in so assured a fashion. "I introduce myself," the stout man said. "I'm Highfactor Fhuniac Bolard, of Moover Station."

Ruiz revived a former incarnation, one he'd used on an ill-fated mission to Tronkworld. "Yuhi Nolto Macchia, Scion of the Kruger Macchias." Ruiz smiled coldly. "We have more intriguing entertainments on Kruger, I must inform you."

The Krugerites were a notoriously bloodthirsty, eccentric, and testy race, who brooked no interference with their personal whims. Ruiz could almost see the gears turning in Bolard's brain. The stout man was thinking that inviting such a guest was an act of conspicuous foolishness on the part of Lord Preall—quite inhospitable to his other guests, in fact. But after a moment Bolard decided to put the best face on things; it was, after all, the only feasible course. "Dancing, killing; I agree with you, not well done," Bolard said nervously.

"You presume to put words in my mouth," Ruiz asked in quivering tones.

"I? Never, Scion."

"That is well. Of dancing I have little opinion. But killing can be immensely entertaining, when performed with skill and élan."

"Yes, of course. Well put, Scion." Bolard was now thinking only of getting away, and Ruiz took a certain grim amusement in pressing him. From the moment Ruiz had leaped onto the stage at Bidderum, others had pushed; Ruiz had yielded. There was an ugly but undeniable pleasure in doing the pushing, for a change.

Ruiz spread a feral grin across his face. "You are a frequent visitor to Preall's little domain? Good! You shall be my guide, as this is my first visit. I am sure you'll not disappoint me."

Bolard concealed a look of resigned despair. "You honor me too much, Scion," he said hopefully.

"Not at all," Ruiz said, taking Bolard's doughy arm in a grip so vigorous that Bolard was not quite able to avoid a wince. "Where shall we begin, good Factor?"

AS COREAN WATCHED, she chewed delicately at her lower lip. "He's convincing," she murmured to herself. "Yes, he is. I wonder, Marmo, could he really be of the Macchias? No, no, of course not. But still, he's good, isn't he?"

Marmo was listening, as he always was. "Freeze him, lose him. You know my view," the cyborg said. He was playing one of his endless games, his crystal eyes fixed on the larger eye of his dataslate.

Corean shot him an annoyed look. "Patience. We'll wait for him to show us what he is, or for the situation to begin to get out of hand. Right now, we have him where we want him, no?"

"I suppose so," Marmo said, with a rasping sigh.

"Here is what we watch for, Marmo: any sign that he is a League agent. Or indisputable evidence that he is not. Or any sign that he's about to get away. Until then, we just watch." Corean rose gracefully from her chair and shook back her long jet braid. "You have the duty now, Marmo. Run your assassin past him at the first opportunity. I'm going to bed. Disturb me only if you see something important occurring." She swept out. At the door, she looked back, to see Marmo staring thoughtfully after her, his photoreceptors gleaming.

AS TIME PASSED and Ruiz refrained from killing him, the factor relaxed somewhat, and became a passable guide. They passed other visitors to the submerged city, which Bolard called Thera. Ruiz glared fiercely at these others, who thereupon paddled in the opposite direction. Fortunately, none of them seemed to be the owner, who might have investigated a hard-looking guest he did not recognize.

One of the first buildings they approached was a dining hall, and Ruiz directed Bolard toward it, prompted by a sudden gnawing in his stomach. Long hours had passed since his last meal of pseudo-Pharaohan cuisine, and his exertions since then had been considerable.

When they emerged in the hall's air space, the bond layer flowed away from them in sparkling rivulets. Ruiz took a deep breath, more satisfying than the rapid, shallow respiration that the bond layer demanded, and the odor of rich pangalac foods filled his nostrils. They were alone in the hall, except for a dozen robot servitors who waited by the dispensers. "Come, Bolard, I will try Preall's table," Ruiz said.

Bolard looked more enthusiastic than he had since he had made the mistake of speaking to Ruiz. "A fine idea, Scion," he said, licking his lips. Ruiz guessed that Bolard was one of those fat folk who perpetually hungered, despite the availability of appetite conditioning, because such condi-

tioning made gluttony no longer enjoyable. And here was
Ruiz, ostensibly an irascible Macchias, the perfect excuse
for indulging. Ruiz could almost hear Bolard explaining the
situation to himself: *But the Scion might have been fatally
offended, had I not joined him at the table. . . .*

Well, Ruiz was not one to deny his victims their pleasures, as long as he wasn't inconvenienced. He fell to eating
with insistent enthusiasm, and encouraged his prisoner to do
the same. Soon Bolard's good humor was restored. Preall
served a fine banquet, with choice food from many pangalac
worlds, brought by the robots in unending rivers: rare
meats, savory sauces, pastries light as sugared air.

Ruiz tasted a bit of everything, but refrained from gorg-
ing. Matters were proceeding suitably, but should an emergency arise, he must not be comatose with food and drink.
Besides, an unbidden memory arose, of the phoenix play
and the devouring mouth of the god of gods and the banquet
that appeared as magically as this one did. That led to the
memory of Nisa lying still with the stiletto vine violating her
flesh.

Dark thoughts diminished the pleasure of his dinner.

Ruiz grew morose as his appetite waned, and Bolard noticed. "Well, Scion," Bolard said timidly, "what would you
like to see now?" The factor wiped greasy hands. "Perhaps
the game rooms? The euphorium, or . . . would you like to
visit Lord Preall's peach pit? The harlots are imaginative
and skillful, they say."

Ruiz spoke sourly. "At present, none of those appeal."
Time, he thought, to restore the fat factor to a malleable
terror. He leaned close to Bolard, spoke with a leer. "Let us
return to the subject of killing. Tell me, Bolard, is artistry
available, not simple butchery?"

Bolard's chins trembled. "Oddly enough, Scion, I believe
that the night's entertainment commences soon."

Ruiz was not surprised. The culture had the flavor of a
barbarian conceit, where intensity in all the emotions was
encouraged, where any number of abstract concepts such as
honor and status and duty were artificially elevated to a
higher status than life. "Take me to the place," Ruiz said,
with a barely perceptible touch of weariness.

Bolard was pompous, but he was no fool, and a calculating sidelong glance told Ruiz that Bolard was thinking too much, and that Ruiz had made a serious mistake in revealing any distaste.

But Bolard smiled and said, "This way, then, Scion."

He smiled with a very near approximation of his original servile smile, but Ruiz resolved to keep a close eye on Bolard.

At that moment a burly scarfaced man in the somber uniform of the Lawbirth proctors stepped up into the hall. He looked at Ruiz as if inviting conversation. Ruiz looked back at the uniformed man with as unsociable a glare as he could summon, and after a moment the man turned away, shrugging.

Reentering the fluid, Ruiz and his guide swam downward, toward the roots of the city.

MARMO WATCHED WITH one eye, as the spy bead showed the unknown as he and his captive went deeper.

Marmo's ploy had been a long shot, so he was not unduly frustrated by its failure. Had the unknown rushed up to the false proctor with his tale of being kidnapped, then the proctor, who was one of Corean's best coercers, could have burned down the unknown without further ado. But the unknown was apparently not an innocent bystander; he knew he was on Sook, where no pangalac law reached.

The unknown was clever and resourceful, but all humans were fools in Marmo's eyes, which was why he served a woman who in her own way was no more human than Marmo, who had managed to burn away most of his soft, fallible flesh in several centuries of pirating among the stars. Sometimes he wished he were still plying his former trade, which was cleaner in some ways than his present one. But age comes to all beings, and this was a useful and amusing form of retirement.

There were undignified aspects to his present employment, of course. He chafed, for example, under Corean's instructions not to act against the unknown, who had demonstrated an amazing arrogance. It was, after all, Marmo's expertise that the man had circumvented, not once, but several times. He had resisted the stunfield; he had attached a limpet to cargo that should have been spaced before the ship had left Pharaoh's system; he had managed to get aboard in the first place. It all cast an uncomplimentary light on Marmo's expertise. Corean had said little after her first outburst, but Marmo was sensitive regarding his handling of the ship, or any of the other mechanisms in his care.

They were, after all, his brothers and sisters.

So he watched carefully with one eye, and with the other he watched the progress of the endless game he played against his own coprocessors.

His interest quickened when he saw the unknown and his guide disappear into the vault of resurrection.

RUIZ AND BOLARD sank through a deep pit faced with black granite, through a dim murky layer of brown-tinted fluid, and then into a vast spherical arena. Bright air-filled galleries lined the inner surface, and they were full of folk, both dwellers of Thera and visitors of many races. Held at the center of the arena by slender pylons, a roughly spherical, multifaceted form of pitted metal rotated sluggishly in the current that constantly flowed, around and around. Each facet held a narrow door, proportioned to pass a full-grown person. There were dozens of facets.

"Scion, you would honor me by sharing my personal box." Bolard led him to a fluid lock, and from there into a corridor that spiraled through the skin of the arena.

Bolard's box was rather smaller than the majority of those Ruiz had glimpsed, but it was comfortable enough, with a wide couch that looked out through a crystal band into the arena.

Bolard ushered Ruiz inside with much ceremony, but to Ruiz's straining ears, there was a false note to Bolard's subservience. No matter, Ruiz thought, he'd just have to keep a close eye on the factor until a way out presented itself.

"The entertainment begins now," Bolard said, with a raspy grunt of anticipation.

A circular door at the bottom of the arena irised open,

and the combatants floated up into sight. These were two of the handsome, haughty women of the drowned city. They wore iridium mirrors on their left forearms and carried energy projectors in their right hands. Otherwise they were naked, but for spiderweb skin designs in orange biolume. Ruiz watched their faces, but could detect no sign of fear.

They scissored their legs slowly, until they'd risen to the level of the equatorial viewing boxes, and faced each other across ten meters of fluid. At the sounding of a deep thrumming tone, the duel began.

It was ugly. The projectors fired a short-range heat beam. Each woman at first deflected the beams of her opponent with great skill, but before long, beams began to miss the mirrors and strike flesh. The meat cooked from their bones while they still lived and struggled. After a time the combatants concentrated only on protecting their eyes and the muscles that pointed the projectors and squeezed the triggers.

The current in the arena carried their twisting bodies around and around, past the galleries where the watchers pressed themselves against the glass. The exhibition ended when one woman was blinded, and the other beamed her into a bubbling mass, before expiring in apparent triumph.

Ruiz sat, impassive, conscious of the occasional sly glances that Bolard cast his way.

"Now watch," said Bolard. "This is the amusing part."

Attendants stroked swiftly into the arena and removed the remains. Then an expectant interval ensued, and Ruiz looked where Bolard pointed, where two facets on the central artifact glowed with a pale red light.

Soundlessly, the doors popped open, expelling two figures in a cloud of tiny bubbles. They tumbled forth, and Ruiz saw that they were clones of the two women who had just died. For a moment they both seemed confused, floundering weakly in the current. They saw each other, and now Ruiz did see anger. The two women struggled toward each other, and would have torn at each other with bare hands, had attendants not separated them and carried them away.

"Hereditary enemies," Bolard said with a chuckle. "The womb can mature a clone about every six weeks. These two will be matched against each other afresh, as long as the womb survives. The only time they're happy is when they're allowed to get on with the business of killing each other. It will be a long six weeks for those two." Bolard laughed again. "I suppose the funniest part of it is that they consider themselves to be the luckiest of beings, blessed, immortal, better than we who come to see them die."

There were more duels, for hours, and Bolard grew merrier as Ruiz sickened. But finally it was over, and robot strainers swept through the bloody soup that now filled the arena.

"Did you enjoy the entertainment, Scion?" asked Bolard.

Ruiz shook himself, and turned his eyes to the factor. "It was inventive at first, if you enjoy spectator sports."

Bolard looked just the least bit uncertain. "Scion?"

"Does watching ever bore you, Factor? Don't you long to dip your own hands in hot gore?" Ruiz fixed a bloodthirsty rictus on his face. "I do."

Bolard had gone pale. "Lord Preall reserves that for himself and his closest cronies, I'm afraid, Scion. Er . . . are you among those?"

Ruiz said nothing, but Bolard must have seen something frightening in Ruiz's eyes. "Well, it has been a great pleasure, Scion, but now I must be getting back to my ship. We lift for the Archplate at dawn."

He stood, edging away. Ruiz got up and slid swiftly to the door. A long moment passed before Ruiz spoke. "I'll walk along with you for a bit, Factor."

Bolard gathered his dignity. "As you wish," he said.

MARMO FORGOT HIS game. He activated the line to Corean's quarters. "Corean," Marmo said in his artificial voice, "he's going to the landing zone with the merchant."

CHAPTER 21

RUIZ kept a tight grip on Bolard's plump arm as they left the box and followed a ring corridor built into the arena's shell. As they walked, other departing guests joined them, until the corridor was crowded with weary revelers. They gave Ruiz no more than an occasional curious glance. Ruiz contained his disgust.

Ruiz saw that the merchant's doubts were flourishing. Even a less astute observer might have developed reservations by this time. In any case, the merchant was still afraid of him, and that was the important thing, more important than shoring up the Macchias identity. The fear showed in Bolard's rolling eye, in the sweat that beaded on his neck, in the way he hunched his shoulders, as if fearing the impact of a knife.

Ruiz decided to accelerate Bolard's doubts and fears, and he adopted a different persona, that of a dangerous maniac. Now Ruiz began to roll his own eyes, and smiled wickedly —and, with the sort of antic enthusiasm favored by madmen, said things like "Bolard, I like you!" or "Aren't we having a fine time?" And then he would clout Bolard on the back or give him a bone-cracking hug.

Bolard's answering smile grew sicklier each time.

A hundred meters ahead, the ring corridor came to an end at a ramp, where the guests were stepping onto waiting freefloat platforms. These sank from sight, to be replaced by empties. At the ramp two large men waited. They wore matching tunics and trousers of a subtly military cut. Ruiz identified them immediately as security, and he tightened his grip on Bolard, who squeaked.

Ruiz's leisurely pace, however, did not alter as they approached the guards. "Tell me of your ship," he said to Bolard, giving Bolard's arm another squeeze.

"It's a Terratonic Personal, Scion. Not fancy, but it suits me. Another time perhaps, I can show you about, if you like, though there's not that much to see."

Ruiz cursed under his breath. The fat merchant's boat was only an insystem runabout, not much good to Ruiz. It had doubtless been dropped from a stellar ferry. Even if Ruiz got the boat into the atmosphere, escape would be uncertain. He'd still have to find a friendly launch ring and convince Sook's alien owners to permit him to wait aboard one of their platforms until a League vessel called. He wrenched his thoughts away from the problem and gave his attention to the immediate problem: the guards.

The guards were too well trained to oppress the guests with impolitely direct glances, but their eyes missed very little. Their body language betrayed a rising tension as he and Bolard approached the bubble ramp.

"Friend Bolard," Ruiz spoke into the merchant's ear. "Do you have anything to tell me? Think carefully!"

"Whatever do you mean, Scion?" Bolard's voice cracked in alarm.

"I mean this: You would certainly want to help us avoid any trouble, would you not? After all, we'd surely face it together, eh? Two such comrades as we?"

The guards were definitely alerted by some anomaly. They loosened the nerve lashes that they wore holstered at their belts, making the movement seem a casual meaningless gesture. They drifted apart, so that no attack could reach both of them in the same instant. They no longer glanced at Ruiz, even indirectly—a failure in subtlety, Ruiz thought.

And yet they did not seem fearful or overly anxious, as if the situation they saw developing was one they dealt with every day. The readiness seemed more a routine response pattern than the result of any genuine alarm.

"What is it, Bolard? What do they know?" Ruiz asked. Bolard was silent, but his face gleamed with sweat. Ruiz transferred his grip on Bolard's arm to the other hand and draped a friendly arm across the merchant's pudgy shoulders.

Ruiz smiled the most terrible smile in his repertoire. "I'm about to hurt you, Bolard. Don't stumble, or cry out, or I'll kill you now." Ruiz dug two fingers into the factor's ear. He twisted the ear, exerting a fair amount of his strength. Bolard did stumble, but he stifled a gasp. Ruiz stole a glance at the guards, who were only a dozen meters away. They took no apparent notice. Ruiz released the pressure on Bolard's ear.

The merchant drew a shuddering breath. "They think you're a dweller from the city. You don't carry a guest implant, do you? Please, don't hurt me again. There's no way you'll get past them. Release me and I'll use my influence, I'll help. . . . Please."

So they thought Bolard was trying to smuggle out a prettyboy. That misconception gave Ruiz an acceptable edge; the guards would be expecting trouble from Bolard, not Ruiz. As they drew abreast of the security men, Ruiz stroked Bolard's round head affectionately.

One guard stepped forward, a flat-faced man with oddly colorless eyes. "Sir," said the guard, reaching out a detaining hand to Bolard, "did you know that the Dwellers Below are not permitted to leave the city by this route?"

Bolard opened his mouth to protest his innocence, as Ruiz acted.

He shoved Bolard into the guard with enough force to send them both crashing down into a flailing heap and leaped toward the other guard. The heel of Ruiz's hand smashed into the guard's sternum before the guard had the nerve lash halfway clear of its holster. The guard jolted back, thumped into the wall, and fell bonelessly to the floor, unconscious or dead.

The nerve lash rolled free, and for an instant, Ruiz was terrified that it would get away from him. But his lunging fingers closed on the lash just in time to prevent it from skittering on down the hall.

Ruiz bounded to his feet as the first guard threw Bolard to the side. Ruiz whirled his lash to extrude the clinger-stingers to maximum length, shoved the vernier up with enough force to jam it at lethal output, and pegged it straight into the horrified face of the guard. The stingers struck and wrapped tight; the lash made an ugly thrumming buzz. The guard managed one stifled shriek as the lash burned out his brain—and then he fell back dead.

The other guests huddled against the walls, looking everywhere but at the bodies on the floor. The ones who were still close to the arena fled back inside, and Ruiz surmised that he had very little time before the management learned of the events in the corridor. He scooped up the other nerve lash and thrust it through his belt, after making sure that the safety was securely locked down.

Bolard lay on the floor and stared up at Ruiz. The whites of the merchant's eyes showed all around, and the look on Bolard's face had gone beyond mere terror. "Who . . . what are you?"

"Just another pretty face," Ruiz said cheerfully. He hauled Bolard roughly to his feet. "Shall we go, sweetie?"

Ruiz dragged Bolard along at the best speed the fat merchant could manage, to the bubble ramp. They stepped onto a waiting freefloater, and sank slowly toward the hangar floor.

COREAN WAS BACK, tousled attractively with sleep. She tore her eyes from the screen reluctantly. "He's good, amazingly good. It's a mortal shame we've got to terminate him, don't you agree? At least in the abstract?"

"You know my opinion. It hasn't changed," Marmo replied. The cyborg was at a tactical dataslate, metal fingers tapping, directing Corean's Moc into position.

Corean favored him with a sour look. "Yes, of course, Marmo. Necessity rules us. Still, don't you feel even a tinge of regret that we must destroy such a beautiful animal?"

"No."

Corean sighed. "Your circuits hold no poetry, Marmo. But in practical terms, then. What if he is not a League agent? What if we could secure his loyalty? What then?"

Marmo looked up, and Corean could read no emotion in that metal beetle-back of a face. "Impractical," Marmo said. "Risky."

THE PLATFORM DROPPED through the upper reaches of Lord Preall's guest hangar, too slowly to suit Ruiz. He possessed no long-range weapon; if the Lord's men attacked him now, it was all over. But Ruiz saw nothing to alarm him, beyond the line of curious faces that hung over the ramp, watching their descent. No one followed.

But a moment before the platform landed on the durcrete floor of the hangar, a distant alarm bell began to ring. A moment later it was joined by a cacophony of other bells, sirens, whistles, horns—and the approaching sound of feet running in military sync. Ruiz jerked Bolard from the bubble to a temporary shelter under the burnished wing of a Uriel Jumpshuttle parked close to the lower bubble ramp.

The hangar was divided into heavily hardened revetments, half-arches made from gigantic monomol pipe. At first Ruiz couldn't imagine why the owner had provided his guests with parking spaces that would deflect the power of a small antimat grenade. Then he realized that the revetments were designed to contain destruction within their walls. Apparently Preall had enemies clever enough to use a guest's spaceboat to smuggle a bomb into Preall's playpen.

The craft of departing guests still moved swiftly along the taxiways, their immediate destination a great tunnel cut through the far wall of the hangar. Ruiz presumed that the tunnel led eventually to the surface outside the pens.

Bolard was staring at nothing, and Ruiz realized that he was losing the merchant to shock. He gave Bolard a shake, hard enough to make Bolard's teeth click. "Where is it?"

Ruiz hissed. He shook the merchant again. "Where is your boat?"

Bolard was slow in answering. Ruiz considered breaking a finger, or otherwise stimulating the merchant, but then Bolard said, "The next row over, almost to the end."

Too far, it might be too far, but Ruiz had little choice. There were few successful spaceboat thieves; so valuable an object as a spaceboat would be protected by extremely sophisticated devices. If Ruiz attempted to board one of the closer crafts, he would not only fail to get it moving, but in all likelihood he would be captured and held for disposal by the boat's security systems. It came down to time; Ruiz might attempt to take a boat without the owner's cooperation, had he enough time, but time was presently in short supply.

"Is anyone aboard?" Ruiz demanded.

"No, no one is aboard." The question seemed to heighten Bolard's anxiety.

"Come," Ruiz said, and forced the merchant to his feet.

They ran along the edge of the revetments. At any moment, Ruiz expected to feel the hot touch of a particle beam, cooking through his body. Surely Preall must have automated security in the hangar, though Ruiz had seen nothing that looked like a weapons emplacement on the ride down.

Bolard began to gasp, shrill whistling sounds of distress, clutching at his chest. "Stop," Bolard sobbed, "please, my heart bursts, please, stop."

Ruiz dragged him along. "Die later. Run now."

The sound of pursuing feet was louder now, and Ruiz glanced back over his shoulder. He saw a squad of security men spreading out behind him; all seemed to be armed only with nerve lashes. Ruiz mentally applauded the caution shown by the owner of this little entertainment complex. Presumably Preall was so concerned with the possibility of assassination that he permitted no heavy weapons within his preserves.

Miraculously, they appeared to have a chance of reaching Bolard's Terratonic. And in the same moment Ruiz made that optimistic assessment, he spotted a boat of the right make three revetments up, a somewhat battered specimen recently recolored with a coat of garish red patina. "That the one?" Ruiz asked.

Bolard's face was purple; the merchant was beyond speech, but he nodded weakly.

"Rest soon, rest soon. Hang on, friend Bolard, and all will be well," Ruiz said, getting a fresh grip on the merchant and hauling with renewed vigor. They reached the revetment that sheltered Bolard's craft, just as the pursuing security men got close enough to start throwing immobilizer-gas grenades. The first of these fell short, but the bursts of fast-dissipating green vapor were dire signals of what was shortly to come. Ruiz himself might resist the gas for seconds, but Bolard would go stiff the instant the vapors touched him. And Ruiz still needed the merchant.

There was a personnel gate set into the kinetic mesh that curtained both ends of the revetment. Ruiz snatched at Bolard's wrist, jammed the merchant's palm against the entry idplate there.

The gate cycled aside with infuriating languor, but as soon as it was open enough, Ruiz dragged Bolard in. The merchant got stuck briefly, then popped through as the gate widened and Ruiz yanked. Ruiz hit the closure and the gate reversed, almost in the face of the approaching security men. The kinetic mesh was fine enough to prevent the guards from throwing more immobilizer grenades, and Ruiz had a few moments respite.

"Come on, come on!" Ruiz hustled the merchant toward the Terratonic, taking most of Bolard's weight. Bolard's feet paddled weakly at the ground as they neared the boat.

The Terratonic had a standard idplex sensor beside the lock, and Ruiz hoped it was as straightforward as it appeared. He propped Bolard up before the idplex, and said, "Now, friend Bolard, get us in. Quickly! I'm not patient." To emphasize his point, Ruiz twisted cruelly at Bolard's wrist. The merchant's head snapped up, and he pawed at the idplex, punching in the access code.

"Good, good. Continue," Ruiz said, giving Bolard an encouraging pat.

Bolard turned eyes to him that were devoid of hope. "You'll kill me anyway," he said.

"No . . . how could you think so? I don't want to hurt you, but if I must, I must. All will be well; just get us inside." Ruiz threw an apprehensive glance at the kinetic mesh. The security men were attempting to attach a master-image to the idplate. In a moment they would succeed.

Bolard smiled ingratiatingly, a ghastly expression. "Yes," he said, "I trust you. . . ."

He staggered, and then stepped up and put his eye against a sensor. Apparently Bolard favored the retinal holotattoo as a means of identification, not a bad choice, technically speaking. Disconnection from the optical nerve would destroy the image, so a knowledgeable thief could not simply gouge out the merchant's eye and present the gobbet to the idplex.

The moment that it took the idplex to recognize and respond to Bolard seemed to stretch into an eternity. Ruiz's body sang with adrenaline. The security men finally got the masterimage locked onto the idplate of the revetment as the airlock plug withdrew, and Ruiz boosted Bolard inside. Ruiz scrambled after. He hit the closure bar just as the security men burst into the revetment.

As the lock snapped shut, Ruiz waved cheerfully at the guards, who showed clenched faces and brandished useless nerve lashes.

"All right," Ruiz said to Bolard, who watched him with bulging eyes, "to the cockpit."

COREAN THUMPED MARMO'S console in her excitement. "There," she said, "didn't I tell you? He evaded Preall's best men; he hardly worked up a sweat. Don't you find it interesting, Marmo? To watch a man like that?"

"I find it unsettling, more than anything else. Besides, he looked pretty sweaty to me, and he relied overmuch on luck, in my opinion. Now it's up to us. And if Preall's men had taken him, we'd be worse off than we were before we started this, ah, impetuous maneuver." Marmo floated quietly, projecting noninvolvement.

"You're a dry stick, Marmo," Corean said, sitting back,

as the spaceboat pulled out of the revetment, scattering the guards. "Is the Moc ready for him?"

"It waits in the control room at the end of the egress tunnel, as you ordered." Marmo shifted on his floater. "Tell me, what will you do if he carries the death net, and manages to expire before the Moc freezes him?"

Corean grew less animated. "The *Sinverguenza* is always ready. I'll take what I can, and leave. They won't catch me easily. And I would give up this face, if I had to. What would you do, Marmo? Would you come with me?"

"I? Who knows?"

RUIZ DIRECTED THE boat along the taxiway. He could see no sign of barriers at this end of the exit tunnel; perhaps they were at the other end, if any existed. That would make strategic sense, and was a hurdle he'd have to leap when he reached it.

In moments he entered the brightly lit entrance. The guards had fallen behind, and now, as Ruiz glanced at the rear vision screen, he saw them stopped at the tunnel apron, a forlorn group. Ahead the lights abruptly ended, and the tunnel became pitch black. Ruiz lit the running lights, locked the boat's pilot to the guidance strip, pushed the speed up to maximum taxi, and turned to Bolard, who slumped in the cockpit's jump seat. The merchant's color was better and his breathing was quieter, but Bolard's eyes still had a glaze of hopelessness.

"So," Ruiz began, in conversational tones, "how do you feel?"

For a moment Bolard didn't answer, and Ruiz thought the merchant might abandon dignity completely and weep. But then Bolard seemed to collect himself. "I'm better, though still near death, I think."

"Nonsense. I don't want your life. Help me to escape, and you'll be rewarded handsomely for your inconvenience."

Bolard grew less apathetic. "Reward? And to what authority would I apply for this reward?"

"For your own safety, I won't say yet. Rest assured of

this: Cooperation will bring generosity; obstruction will bring pain."

Bolard probed at his tender ear. "Yes, I see."

Ruiz smiled disarmingly. "Let's put that unpleasantness from our minds now. Together we'll succeed; together we'll enjoy the fruits of success. Tell me, what weapons do you carry on board?"

"Weapons?" Bolard seemed genuinely puzzled. "A factor has no use for weapons. We trade only on Peacebond worlds."

"Oh? Then what are you doing on Sook?"

"A much-needed vacation. And I remind you that a pangalac being on legitimate business here need have little fear of violence, if he follows proper procedure."

"True," Ruiz agreed. And offhand, he could think of no business that was considered illegitimate by the Shards, the aliens who enforced the laws of Sook from their orbital platforms.

Bolard appeared to be projecting injured innocence with suspicious energy. Ruiz eyed him sharply, and switched tacks. "How long before we reach the end of the tunnel?"

"Perhaps fifteen, twenty minutes, at our present speed—which seems excessive to me, by the way."

"The boat's pilot keeps us moving at the same speed as the traffic ahead of us," Ruiz pointed out. "The guilty seem to be fleeing. What can you tell me about the security systems at the far end?"

"Very little. The tunnel surfaces at a launch ring, out in the jungle. There are maintenance buildings there, but no other facilities that I noticed."

"You observed no barriers, no blast doors?"

Bolard shrugged and spread his hands in a gesture of helplessness. "The boat was on auto from the time I left the Shard platform. I'm no pilot. Perhaps there are such things there; I don't know."

Ruiz considered. The launch ring would be unavailable to him, of course, but with any luck he could make a run overland until he found a ring that was willing to heave him out of Sook's gravity well. He rose from the command chair. "Come, Bolard, let's take a look around your little boat. I understand that some Terratonics have been modified to carry small cargos. That right?"

Bolard went pale again. Ruiz had to lift him to his feet and march him back to the passenger lounge of the Terratonic.

The boat had indeed been modified for cargo, and when Ruiz saw the cargo secured in the converted hold, he lost what little sympathy he had retained for the fat merchant. Crammed into the former lounge was a stasis rack, filled with six frozen members of the Cleve culture, and Ruiz was certain that they were three pairs of matched hereditary enemies. Ruiz now saw the reason why Preall kept his culture here on Sook; not because it was stolen, though it might be, or because Preall's guests craved the privacy of a Sook address, but because Preall was violating copyright laws by selling off bootleg clones of the culture.

"Naughty," Ruiz said, shaking a monitory finger at Bolard. Then he took the merchant by the collar and completed his search of the boat. Unfortunately, Ruiz discovered that the merchant had been telling the truth about weaponry. There was nothing useful on board.

Back in the cockpit, Ruiz settled Bolard in the jump seat again, then secured the merchant carefully to the seat with a roll of adhesive restraint webbing from a supply locker in the hold. Bolard's eyes showed relief at this indication that Ruiz planned no immediate mayhem. He would have spoken, but Ruiz stretched a piece of webbing across his mouth and patted him reassuringly on the head.

"Well, now we'll just have to wait and see what develops," Ruiz said.

Ruiz sat back, clearing his mind. The boat rolled down the tunnel on its pneumatic casters, and the minutes passed.

Ruiz saw a tiny glitter of light far ahead. They approached the end of the tunnel rapidly, and the light swelled into a half-disk. A boat, the last one ahead of Ruiz's, climbed over the edge and disappeared into the glare. Ruiz thought to himself, *I might just make it out. How strange.* Then the half-circle became a crescent, narrower and narrower, as a blast door levered shut. Ruiz pounded the control panel with his fist, hard enough to make the dust rise from the crevices. "Shit," he said.

The opening shrank to a thin arc of light and then closed completely. Ruiz knocked the controls back into manual and slowed the boat. He boosted the running lights as high as they would go, and rolled to a stop before the massive blast door.

He saw no activity. To one side, a maintenance corridor opened in the meltstone tunnel lining. An illuminated sign read: EMERGENCY PERSONNEL EGRESS. To Ruiz's eye, it might as well have read: RUIZ AW TRAP. He sighed. What other choice did he have? No matter what reception Preall had managed to arrange for him, Ruiz would have to leave the pleasantly appointed cockpit of the Terratonic. He turned to Bolard. "Well, friend Bolard, our paths part at last."

Bolard's eyes bulged and he struggled against the webbing. "No, no," Ruiz said soothingly, "don't worry." He grasped Bolard's fat neck with both hands, his fingers probing for the carotids. "I told you I wouldn't hurt you. You'll sleep for a while. I'll leave the air lock open for Preall's men; they'll eventually get here." Ruiz bore down. Bolard relaxed and slipped into unconsciousness, a look of sheepish gratitude on his broad face. When the merchant was thoroughly under, Ruiz broke his neck with a quick twist.

"I don't know why I didn't just let you be afraid," he told the dead man, thinking of the ones who slept in the hold.

CHAPTER 22

RUIZ sat for a few moments beside the merchant's corpse. All his attention was focused on the corridor that led away from the blast doors. Was it a good enough trap?

In his favor was the general ineptitude shown by Preall's men, and the fact that the tunnel ended out in the jungle, at a distance from the pens. Perhaps Ruiz had only to contend with the security forces resident at the launch ring; perhaps Preall had not yet been able to supply reinforcements. It was possible that Preall's major forces were still back in the pens, fumbling through the intricate maze that led to the wall.

Or were even now traveling through the tunnel toward him. The thought galvanized Ruiz into movement. That he had not considered the possibility before frightened him; he just wasn't concentrating.

Ruiz wheeled the Terratonic about and set the brakes. He ran the thrusters up, until the little boat trembled. He killed the running lights, locked the pilot to the guidance strip, overrode the safety monitor, and hit the touchbar that opened the air lock. A final question occurred to Ruiz: Were the frozen clones in the hold equipped with their customary weapons? He went to see.

He shut down the stasis trays. As he had hoped, the Dwellers carried their little leaf-shaped daggers in their forearms, in toughened sheaths of living flesh. But the Dwellers were like so many brittle sculptures, held in the field that damped the molecular energy in their bodies, and it would take too long to thaw them. He cast about the hold for something hard and heavy, and found a chunky creeper-cleaner nuzzling for dirt in one corner.

The arms of the Dwellers shattered readily under its weight, but Ruiz's cheek was grazed by a shard of frozen flesh, cutting him slightly.

Soon two daggers lay loose in a jumble of glassy red fragments. Ruiz picked them up in a fold of his cap. They smoked and grew furry with hoarfrost. He dropped them, still wrapped in the cap, into his boot.

In a moment, Ruiz stood beneath the belly of the boat, under the maze of conduits and servo lines exposed by the open lock.

Ruiz tried to look two ways at once: at the corridor, from whence an unpleasant suprise might at any moment leap, and at the darkened depths of the tunnel. Far away down the tunnel he seemed to see a tiny white light, like the light another boat's running lights might make at that distance.

He reached up and tugged violently at the brake servo line, which resisted only for a moment and then tore away in a shower of sparks. Ruiz threw himself to the side, and the rear casters of the boat passed over the spot where he'd been standing an instant before.

By the time he picked himself up, the twin blue glows of the Terratonic's thrusters were already far down the tunnel.

MARMO WATCHED THE screen. The unknown was standing at the tunnel end, watching the departing spaceboat with a disquieting look of satisfaction on his hard handsome face. Marmo turned to Corean with a whine of tiny servos. "I begin to see the source of your fascination," he told Corean, who watched with an expression disturbingly similar to the unknown's.

"Oh?"

"Yes. You are a pair."

Corean refused the distraction, saying nothing.

"Have you rehearsed what you will say to Preall when he comes to you, complaining that one of yours destroyed a substantial portion of his security force, killed a customer, and blew up his tunnel?" Marmo's voice betrayed no more than a polite interest.

"How will he guess? Preall knows my stock. Have I ever before traded in assassins?"

"Ah," Marmo said, returning his attention to the screen. The unknown was running toward the corridor now, long springing strides.

"What about the security men the Moc killed at the ring? I doubt that Preall will accept that their wounds were made by anything human. I remind you, Corean, you're notoriously the only leaseholder of the Blacktear Pens who commands the services of a Moc."

"Marmo, you're tediously and repetitiously concerned with Preall's happiness. I am not," Corean said. Her tone quivered at the edge of ugliness. Marmo felt an involuntary cringe creeping along his circuits, and said no more for a while.

The two of them watched in silence.

Eventually Marmo summoned enough courage to continue the conversation.

"Perhaps you would indulge my curiosity," he said. "Since we've begun this risky maneuver, I haven't really understood why."

Corean kept her eyes on the screen. "I explained all that, Marmo, before we started. I told you then, I wanted to learn as much as I could about the man, before we took the risk of freezing him. Otherwise I'd have done it in the pen."

"Ah, yes. For what reason did you wish to learn about him? It seems to me that our response would be much the same, no matter who he turns out to be. If he's a tourist, kill him. If he's free-lance, kill him. If he's League, kill him carefully. If we'd just killed him carefully at the beginning, that would have covered all the possibilities, and we might have saved ourselves much uncertainty."

"Marmo, you're too logical. I know that's what I pay you for . . . but have you no curiosity?"

Marmo made no further appeals to logic. For some reason, Corean was unwilling to admit that she wanted the unknown for a toy—though this was abundantly clear in the flush of her cheeks, in the sparkle of her eyes, and in the eager stance of her body.

RUIZ STEPPED INTO the corridor. The initial section was empty, as it had appeared from the Terratonic's cockpit. The walls were featureless gray meltstone, finished smooth as glass, with lume strips installed at knee height and head height. The greenish light revealed that the corridor ran straight for about a hundred meters, then angled abruptly to the left. Whatever reception had been prepared, it waited around that turn.

Ruiz moved forward swiftly, making little sound. He covered the distance in seconds, conscious of the destruction that might fill the tunnel at any instant. At the turn, he eased carefully up and listened, straining for some clue to what lay beyond.

He heard nothing. Making up his mind, he took out the nerve lash, and rolled around the corner. As he did, a shock wave arrived at the end of the tunnel. It buffeted him as he tried to regain his feet in the still-empty corridor, and then the sound of the explosion reached him. Ruiz rolled helplessly, until he fetched up at another bend, jolting into the wall with enough force to knock the breath from him.

He didn't notice the tiny fitful buzz of the disabled spy bead that lay a short distance down the corridor.

MARMO STABBED AT the touchplate of his spyscreens, but the screens stayed blank.

Corean looked at him. "When will we see him again, Marmo?"

"When he enters the bunker, so I would suppose."

Corean gave Marmo another look, lambent with appraisal, and Marmo was suddenly reminded of his place. "Yes, certainly," Marmo said hurriedly. "I have an additional spy bead there."

"Can we move it to the foyer?"

"Not until he opens the door." Marmo was carefully diffident. "But after all, what can he do in the foyer, except go into the bunker?"

RUIZ GOT TO his feet, wincing. Apparently no enemies would attack him from the tunnel. He looked along the featureless corridor and saw that it ended in a broad foyer. At the far side of the foyer Ruiz saw a series of side-by-side closed doors. A strip sign over the doors flashed: LAUNCH CONTROL BUNKER. He approached gingerly. Anything might be lurking in the ends of the foyer to either side, out of sight.

When he reached the foyer, he cautiously extended the lash past the edge, wiggling it enticingly. When nothing pounced, he followed. To one side the foyer ended in blank meltstone. But on the other side, a steep ramp rose to a surface door. Ruiz moved silently past the closed foyer doors and up the ramp, but when he got to the surface door, his heart sank. The thick metal door had been spot-welded to the frame. A warm draft of air slid in under the door, air filled with the green scent of freedom. He leaned against the door for a long moment, thinking pointless wishful thoughts.

Evidently he was being herded into the bunker. Ruiz wondered what sort of surprise he could contrive for whoever waited within. He returned to the linked doors of the bunker, this time giving each a careful examination. When they were all open, the foyer wall would become a broad portico. Each was operated by a separate touchbar. To the left of the first door, a control cluster opened and closed all the doors simultaneously.

Ruiz examined the cluster carefully. He fished out one of the daggers, now warm enough to touch without loss of skin. With great care, he inserted the tip of the dagger into the almost invisible top seam of the cluster. He chipped delicately at the seam, until the cover separated. He managed to catch the cover before it hit the floor.

He assumed that the bunker could be locked from within, but obviously someone wanted him inside. Else why all this? So the doors would open. The only tactical edge he could dredge up at this point would be to surprise them by opening some of the doors prematurely. If nothing else, it might confuse their field-of-fire assignments for an instant and give him a chance to get among them. He thought for a moment, then took the dagger in the insulating fold of his cap again, and traced the contacts for the two rightmost doors. He hesitated for a moment, thinking that his options had been narrowed with disturbing skill. But then he dismissed the notion. Why would Preall, whoever he was, be interested in Ruiz, who had no interest in Preall? And who else could have arranged this?

Then he put the dagger across the contacts.

Sparks flew, and Ruiz jerked the dagger away. At the other end of the foyer the two doors slammed up, shaking the wall as they hit their stops. Ruiz instantly jammed the dagger into the contact that operated the first door, pounding it in with the heel of his hand. He launched himself at the bottom of the door, and it responded just as he reached it. He rolled under the rising edge.

He saw a sight that should have frozen him with amazement, long enough for the Moc to freeze him with the ice gun it carried strapped to its exoskeleton. The Moc was braced against the thrust of the gun, firing a blinding burst through the first two doors Ruiz had opened. Motes of frozen gas glittered in the path of the ice gun, and then the air rushed in to fill the void with a thunderous crack.

But Ruiz's momentum and expensive reflexes carried him behind a massive bank of launch monitors. He registered the impression that he was alone in the bunker with the Moc, just as the Moc's second volley crashed into the monitor bank, causing an ear-splitting shattering of delicate components. Ruiz scurried for cover, but what hope was there? The Moc was so much faster and stronger, and Ruiz was armed with a ludicrously inadequate dagger. And he heard the rumble of the doors closing, locking him in with the Moc. Any physical contest between unamplified human and Moc was a ridiculous mismatch.

The Moc was a flicker of movement among the monitors, and the next volley missed Ruiz by inches, shattering an expanse of crystal that looked out at Preall's launch ring. Ruiz had no time for reflection; all his capabilities were devoted to the task of avoiding the Moc. At some deeper level, however, Ruiz realized that this was the same Moc that had accompanied Corean, and Ruiz felt an ashamed amazement, that he had been so easily duped, so easily led to this hopeless confrontation by the beautiful slaver. And to what purpose?

The insectoid warrior was slightly hampered by the bulk of the ice gun, or it already would have been over.

But it soon would be over, no matter what Ruiz might do. He flipped, dodged the next blast, rolled frantically under a desk, only to confront the Moc in the next aisle. He whipped the nerve lash into the Moc's mandibles, but though Corean's bondwarrior vibrated and roared, the lash diverted the Moc only for the instant that Ruiz needed to roll back under the desk. Behind him, Ruiz heard a snap as the Moc bore down on the lash with its terrible jaws—and then the earsplitting crack of the ice gun again.

COREAN STOOD, GRIPPING the edges of the screen, as if it were a grave she was being pulled into. "Oh no, oh no," she said, "what went wrong?"

Only instants had elapsed since Ruiz had entered the bunker and the Moc had fired in the wrong direction. Corean's face was livid with rage and panic. "What happened?"

She was further enraged when she noticed that, despite the destruction of her safe world by this bizarre bad luck, Marmo was laughing loudly. She turned to him, murder in her eyes. He saw, and stopped abruptly. "Corean," he said. "He's not dead. If he carried the death net, he'd be dead."

And so it seemed.

·   ·   ·

THE ICE GUN had touched him lightly on the last shot, and now Ruiz wriggled desperately through a portion of the bunker where the consoles were so crowded that the Moc could not follow him directly, but could only bound over, firing down from the top of the arc. The warrior was remarkably accurate in that awkward moment, but Ruiz was devious, faking one way and rolling the other.

It was, however, almost over. The Moc got closer with each blast, and Ruiz's cold muscles were responding more slowly. He felt the tug of the death net in the roots of his mind, as it prepared to send his obituary across the galaxy. In Dilvermoon, the gnomes of the League sat at their tachyon filters, waiting for his small field of data.

Oddly, the thought that filled his mind in that moment of extremity was of Nisa, the lost phoenix, the manner in which the sun had dappled her naked skin in the bathhouse, like the stroke of soft golden paws, the sun patting her body delicately.

Ruiz automatically diverted some of his failing store of energy to fighting the onslaught of the death net, and that slowed him even further. His vision was beginning to go gray.

"Wait." The voice was the soft perfect voice of Corean. And miraculously, the Moc stopped.

Ruiz was in a dream world of fading contrasts, slipping away from life in the ocean of his mind. It took long dreadful moments for him to understand that the Moc was no longer pursuing him with the ice gun, that helpless capture was no longer imminent—and longer still before the death net stabilized and sank its anchors again. Ruiz lay as if already dead, drained of all purpose and much of his core body heat.

But his ears functioned for another few seconds, and he heard with drifting astonishment Corean's instructions to the Moc. "Watch him, detain him here if he attempts to leave. Do not injure him. I'll be there shortly."

IN THE AIRBOAT, Marmo fumed. "What can you be thinking of, Corean? Granted, the man is not a League agent—he carries no death net. But you've said it yourself, over and over, he's dangerous."

For a minute, Corean did not bother to reply. She was concentrating on steering the boat through the occasional high-altitude snapfields that spiked the sky over the Blacktear Pens. But when they cleared the perimeter wall and were racing above the purple jungle, she set the pilot and turned to the cyborg, her brows drawn together in irritation.

"This discussion is overdue. In the first place, we're in a dangerous business. He could be very useful to us. I shouldn't have to remind you that we can make him utterly harmless."

"But," Marmo objected, "our next scheduled slot at the Enclave isn't for almost a month. Would you leave a two-step viper loose in your bedroom for a month, knowing that you could pull his fangs thereafter?"

"I don't plan to keep him in my bedroom."

"Are you sure?" Marmo had rotated away, as if intent on observing the jungle's canopy.

Corean was briefly charmed. The old pirate had never before shown any sign of resenting the diversity of Corean's sexual amusements. Did Marmo now wish to share her bed? The possibility was difficult to credit. Corean doubted that such an erotic conjunction was even possible; her usually facile imagination failed her, and she smiled.

"I don't want him yet," she said, as if it were the truth. "I plan to restore him to the company of the phoenix. Flomel claims we can use him to gain her cooperation."

"Ah," Marmo said noncommitally.

"And, we'll brainpeel him first, just to be sure."

"That would be wise."

They landed beside Preall's launch ring, across the tarmac from the shattered ports of the control bunker. Corean walked swiftly, threading her way through the tattered lumps of carrion that had been Preall's ring crew, before the Moc had annihilated them. Marmo floated silently behind, a pulse gun attached to his metal arm. As they approached the bunker, a hatch levered open, and she could see the Moc waiting inside, motionless.

Inside, the devastation wrought by the ice gun was impressive. The observation ports lay in crystalline drifts, knee-deep under every empty casement. The banks of monitoring instrumentation were heavily damaged. The ice gun was designed to capture living protoplasm without damage, but the less flexible innards of the machines were everywhere ruptured. At first she couldn't see the unknown, and she felt a pang of disappointment. Was he crushed beneath that tier of collapsed flux gauges? But then she saw him, wedged partly under an intact plastic chassis.

"Is it safe?" she asked the Moc. The bondwarrior made a sign of assent. Corean picked her way through the debris, to the spot where the unknown lay. She knelt over him, a bit shocked by his appearance. It was difficult to reconcile this gray-faced, dull-eyed creature—who watched her with no hotter emotion than mild curiosity—with the demon who'd killed and destroyed with such fiery efficiency just minutes before. She reached out a tentative hand to his face. It was like touching chilled metal. Her eyes widened. He had been grazed by the ice gun at some point in the struggle. That the man had continued to resist, to resist a Moc, after that . . . it was in the nature of a minor miracle, and Corean felt a touch of awe.

She stood quickly. "Bring the autogurn from the boat. We've come near to killing him, after all."

IN THE BOAT, Ruiz's perceptions slowly returned to normal, under the stimulation of the autogurn's heated cover and the perfusor cuff that cycled restoratives into his bloodstream. Shapes assumed meaning and color, and gradually he heard voices and caught Corean's subtle perfume.

"In one respect, at least, this has worked out well." Ruiz identified the mechanical inflections of the cyborged pirate.

"And what is that, Marmo? I'm eager to learn of your approval, since in every other respect you've found fault with my plans."

Ruiz took delight in the sound of Corean's voice; it caressed the ear, as her face pleasured the eye.

"It's this, then. Preall will never believe that it was you

who visited such destruction on him. It was too extreme for any but an act of vengeance or madness. I'll see to the repair of the snapfields immediately, and there will be no evidence to tie us to it."

"Good."

With returning warmth came a comfortable lassitude. Ruiz resolved sleepily to think about recent events at a later time, when his mind would be clearer.

He slipped slowly into a healing oblivion.

CHAPTER 23

THE rooms to which the giantess conducted Nisa were at first glance more spartan than any dwelling she had ever known.

The giantess pressed one beefy hand to a small rectangle of pulsing light at the side of a metal door. The door jolted aside with a gasping sound.

Darkness lay within, and Nisa was afraid to enter. The giantess shoved her impatiently.

As soon as Nisa crossed the threshold, soft white light flooded the room.

"Oh," she said, dismayed. Surely Corean hadn't meant for her to stay in this featureless box. There was nothing at all in the room. The ceiling glowed brightly, banishing shadow. On the far wall, a doorway opened to another, smaller room.

Nisa turned to her escort. The large woman was turning away, blank-faced. "Wait here," she told Nisa. She stepped out, and the door clashed shut.

Nisa stood in the center of the box, too overcome with strangeness to move. By degrees her amazement left her, and it was as if only that astonishment, like the stuffing in a scarecrow, had been holding her up. She slumped to the hard floor and set her face in her hands. She made no sound, but presently tears began to leak through her fingers.

Finally her eyes ran dry, though her nose continued to drip. She rubbed at her face, and pulled her fingers through the worst of the tangles in her hair.

The open doorway into the next room drew her. She rose and went over to it. It was equally featureless, as she could see by the light spilling from the first room. As she stood peering in, she heard the gasp of the door and whirled.

An exotic creature entered the box with a curious prancing stride. Nisa's first thought was, *How elegant.* Her next was, *How strange.* Her visitor was tall and broad-shouldered, with tumbling ringlets of auburn hair, wearing a knee-length shift of some light, clinging white fabric, patterned with random flecks of warm color. Below the hem, the calves were strong and smooth. The slender feet wore thin sandals, laced with lavender ribbons. Small high breasts thrust against the robe, and rounded hips swayed as the visitor moved. The naked arms were strongly muscled, the hands long and fine, the well-shaped nails striped with delicate bands of color. The chiseled face was mercurial: at one moment as innocent and open as a young child's, the next suffused with a dark cynical calculation.

It spoke. "A burning paramount pleasure to serve you, noble lady." The voice gave no clue to the creature's gender; it was a melodious contralto.

It swept into a low bow, legs straight, curls brushing along the floor. "One rises as far above one's station as Sooksun at his apex rises above the jungle, to introduce oneself: One is called Ayam."

Nisa scarcely knew how to respond to such flowery abasement. "Hello, Ayam," she said lamely.

Ayam bowed again and again, apparently overcome by hysterical joy. "Oh," Ayam cried in a throbbing voice, "one swoons at the undeserved honor of your greeting, noble lady. One swoons with delight and wonder, both at the generosity of the noble lady, and the wisdom of my great mistress, whose name need not be spoken by such as Ayam—"

Ayam seemed willing to go on in that vein for a long time, but Nisa made a gesture of impatience and the stream of hyperbole cut off.

"Why are you here?" Nisa spoke sharply.

Ayam wilted, collapsing into a mound of misery on the hard floor. "Oh, noble lady, Ayam is devastated, that one has failed so terribly to inform the noble lady properly, oh woe, woe—"

"Ayam, please!"

Ayam pulled itself together and wiped at its lovely eyes, though Nisa had seen no actual tears on Ayam's smooth cheeks. "Yes, of course," Ayam said in tones of shaky restraint. "Noble lady, Ayam is your helot, here to serve in any small capacity one can, to make you comfortable, to ease your ills, to fetch and carry, to warm your bed, to answer any request—"

"Yes, yes," Nisa cut off Ayam's speech. "Well, we won't be very comfortable here, will we?" She gestured at the barren room.

Ayam's eyes widened in theatrical shock, but it suddenly came to Nisa that the helot was amused. "Noble lady," it said. "This is one of the finest of my mistress' apartments, which you may shape perfectly to your needs. Allow one to show you, though, of course, one is unworthy to instruct the noble lady in the smallest—"

"Never mind that," Nisa said. "Show me what you mean, Ayam."

The helot stood, abandoning its pose of abjectness. "From the floor, then," it said. "What manner of floor covering does my lady prefer?" Ayam stepped to the door, beckoning with one elegant hand. "Come, noble lady, place your hand here." Ayam gestured to a hand-sized rectangle of metal set into the bland plastic of the wall.

Nisa put her hand cautiously to the plate, to feel a tingling warmth. She started to pull away, but Ayam nodded approvingly and said, "Just so. Now, if you will, think of how you would most like the floor to look, to feel. Would you prefer carpet, or pandawood puncheons, or cool earth? Just think, noble lady."

Nisa wondered if the helot were mad, but then she con-

sidered that many strangenesses had come to seem usual to
her since she had taken the path of Expiation. So she closed
her eyes, and imagined that the floor was covered in the rich
fur of the dust otter. She felt a tickle under her feet, and
opened her eyes in astonishment. The hard floor was sprouting a downy coating! As she stared, it thickened into glossy
carnelian fur. She noticed that the texture against her toes
was not as soft as the real fur; as she thought it, the fur
silkened into a perfect counterfeit.

Nisa was charmed and fascinated. She spent the following hours converting her cell into an opulent jewel box, with
Ayam's enthusiastic assistance. The other room was a bathhouse, and Nisa changed it into a luminous grotto, all porcelain and glass.

She caused the wall to sprout a vast canopied bed, heaped
with silken coverlets, curtained with the finest gauze. At this
point she detected a covert look of appraisal from Ayam.
She considered only briefly before wishing a small alcove in
the corner for the helot's bed. Ayam watched impassively,
but Nisa thought she'd caught just the tiniest trace of disappointment on that smooth face. That look afforded Nisa a
small satisfaction—that she was desired by this elegant creature—but the helot was just too strange, far too strange.

Besides, she had become aware of a confusing and novel
distaste whenever she contemplated taking another stranger
into her bed. The hard enigmatic face of Wuhiya was in
some way connected to the confusion, but she could not
imagine how.

SEVERAL DAYS PASSED , first in pleasant diversion, then
in increasing boredom. Nisa bathed endlessly, enjoying the
extravagance of the never-failing water, the rich soaps and
lotions, the unfailing attention of the helot. She slept. She
ate her meals from a cupboard in the wall that served her
whatever she desired. She wished a vast wardrobe of fine
gowns in colors that suited her.

Despite these diversions, she grew more and more restless. No one came, and the company of the self-abasing
helot grew tedious. Ayam's advances grew less subtle, more

pressing. After her bath on the third day, the helot offered her a massage, which she accepted. The massage was a highly developed art form on Pharaoh; she lay on a heated softstone slab, eyes closed, smiling with nostalgic anticipation.

She heard the rustling sounds of the helot's undressing with no alarm—the sweet massage oil would stain Ayam's beautiful shift.

She felt oil pour across her back in a warm stream. The helot's strong hands moved across her flesh, stroking, squeezing, pummeling gently. Nisa gave herself to pleasure.

Gradually, however, Ayam's clever fingers began to stray into more intimate areas.

"What are you up to?" Nisa asked, though it was obvious.

The helot's muscular thighs gripped her hips and the fingers teased deeper. She half-rolled under the straddling helot and opened her eyes.

Ayam's nipples were erect and a flush of ardor mottled its breasts. Its erect penis lifted above a small vagina, where moisture glistened.

Nisa shut her eyes. "No. Get off me," she said, in a voice full of fascination and revulsion.

The helot did so, babbling apologies, to which Nisa did not respond. Thereafter she was more cautious with the helot, and it grew slightly less deferential.

WHEN, A DAY later, the door to her cell finally opened, the sound startled her. The ugly giantess pushed a wheeled litter inside, and on the litter was the motionless body of Wuhiya.

The giantess shoved the litter, and it glided smoothly up to Nisa. "Here," the giantess said. "He'll be your guest for a while. Leave him alone; the limpet will awaken him when the damage is repaired." The giantess left.

Nisa bent over Wuhiya. She was at first certain he was dead. No, he was alive, but he looked terribly ill, his skin gray, the muscles sagging in unhealthy relaxation. She touched his face, and then pulled her hand away, a little repelled. His flesh was cool, too cool. On his neck was something that looked like a metal spider; on it lights burned amber. From it slender throbbing tentacles writhed out and sank into his neck. Nisa wondered if she had looked this much like a corpse when Wuhiya had first seen her, and the thought triggered a flush of tenderness. Wuhiya had tended her; now she would tend him.

Nisa pushed the litter across the cell, until it rested beside her bed. She instructed the room to grow an extension of the curtains around the litter, so that he would be with her even when she slept.

When she finished, she felt the helot's eyes on her, appraising. "Ayam," she said, "you will treat this man as my honored guest, do you understand?"

The helot bowed deeply. "Yes, noble lady. All is clear."

Nisa frowned. Was the helot mocking her? No, she must be imagining it. She turned all her attention to Wuhiya.

RUIZ WOKE IN fairyland, or so it seemed to him. Pastel silks diffused a soft warm light, sweet fragrances filled the air, and hovering over him was the transformed face of Nisa. The black cinnamon hair of the phoenix was cunningly swirled and plaited with strands of glittering gems; her heart-shaped face was painted with great skill; she wore a simple tunic of some sheer fabric that touched her body lightly. When she saw that he was awake, her face lit with a glow that warmed him in places that had been cold for longer than he could remember.

"Wuhiya," she said, breathless.

Ruiz's body trembled in the grip of the antisedative, and he felt the small sucking pains of the limpet's withdrawal. His throat was full of disuse, and at first he couldn't make any intelligible sounds.

"Where is this?" He heard a frightening weakness in his voice.

"You're safe, Wuhiya. This is my apartment. Isn't it pretty?"

Ruiz was confused. His last memories were of the Moc and its ice gun, the tearing sensation in his mind as the death net threatened to trigger, the precarious sense of reprieve as it stabilized. The translation to this perfumed luxury disoriented him in a way that was only half-pleasurable. The limpet finished its withdrawal and fell away from his neck. He wanted to reach up and rub the spot, but his arm would not respond. Then, slowly, life began to burn back into his muscles. The pain twisted his face, and he saw his distress mirrored in Nisa's pretty features. "It's all right," he croaked. "I'll be better soon."

She smiled and wiped away the sheen of pain-induced sweat with a cool cloth. The gesture was a curiously practiced one, and Ruiz understood that Nisa had been caring for him.

Sentimental tears trembled on his eyelashes; he cursed his weakness, but it was all he could do not to sob with relief. He wondered again at Nacker's manipulations, but now he felt no indignation. Whatever Nacker had done, however the minddiver had meddled, the result was not without merit. Ruiz's heart was raw, true, but what did he expect? Nacker had somehow cut away the calluses of a hard lonely lifetime.

Then another face floated into his misted vision, a striking androgynous face, alight with malicious curiosity. Ruiz's vision cleared abruptly and he frowned. Here was an unpleasant manifestation indeed. "What's this?" he asked.

Nisa patted the creature's broad shoulder. "This is Ayam, the helot that the Lady Corean gave me when I became her special guest."

Ruiz closed his eyes. Not only was he locked in a cell with one of Dilvermoon's treacherous race, but the cell was in Corean's private apartments. He wondered how matters would next worsen. Then he remembered that Corean now knew for certain that Ruiz was no Pharaohan, and not even a pangalac tourist, innocently scooped up with the phoenix troupe.

Ruiz could look forward to a brainpeel. He hoped his shield persona would hold up.

THE FOLLOWING DAYS saw Ruiz's recovery completed. Nisa was touchingly solicitous, though occasionally her pa-

trician background would surface obnoxiously. Ruiz dealt
with these imperious outbursts by ignoring them, and soon
Nisa would regain her good humor.

The herman Ayam was a constant source of anxiety for
Ruiz. He observed with a suprisingly vivid sense of relief
that Nisa had assigned Ayam a bed separate from her own.
The herman's hostility toward Ruiz was apparently not obvious to Nisa. She didn't seem to be able to grasp the idea
that the helot was dangerous.

"But," she would say, bewildered, "Ayam's only a slave.
What harm could come of that? Ayam is here for our conve-
nience."

Ruiz could think of no discreet way to point out to Nisa
that although they also were only slaves, he had high hopes
of being harmful. The cell was certainly monitored. So he
would say, patiently, "Nisa, Ayam may be a perfectly gentle
being, but it springs from a race that bred itself for treachery. Dilvermooners are in demand for all sorts of nasty jobs
—extfam tapeworming, dynastic subversion, psuedopols—
you name it, a herman can be found to do it."

Nisa, puzzled by these unfamiliar crimes, would glance at
Ayam, who would shrug and look hurt. And Nisa would
shake her glossy head and give Ruiz a reassuring pat, the
sort that frightened children receive from indulgent parents.

Eventually he persuaded her to completely enclose
Ayam's cot with a sturdy shell, locked externally. Now at
least it was possible to banish the helot from sight. Ayam
went cheerfully enough, to Nisa's relaxed perceptions, but
Ruiz caught poisonous glances, whenever the herman was
ordered away.

The privacy yielded benefits, as soon as Ruiz was sufficiently recovered to take an interest in lovemaking. Thereafter Nisa was no longer bored. The hours passed pleasantly
under the colored silks of Nisa's bed. Ruiz was as happy as
he could be under the circumstances, though he wondered
continually what Corean planned.

There was time for Ruiz to learn a little more about Nisa.
She seemed to enjoy telling Ruiz about her life as the daughter of the King, though she avoided the subject of her Expiation, and whatever crimes had led to it. Her stories involved

parties and Rain Carnivals and midnight swimming in the cisterns, and Ruiz's eyes occasionally glazed over as she spoke. It saddened him to think that the soft pleasant life she had led as a princess might have cheated her of the toughness she would need to survive as a slave.

But then he would remember the stage, and the path she would walk on it, and he would fall into a silent mood.

She asked him about his own past life, but he laughed and teased and evaded her questions. He did admit to being a tradesman, in a business beyond the stars. When she pressed him, he said that he was a sort of talent scout. He fended off her few questions about life in the far worlds, and, in fact, she showed remarkably little curiosity. He surmised that she found the subject distressing, that she preferred not to think about the universe beyond Pharaoh. He felt no inclination to upset her; let her take comfort where she could.

He told her his real name, since Corean would peel that out of him whenever she got around to it.

"Ruiz Aw. A curious name," she said, rolling the unfamiliar syllables on her tongue.

Ayam was locked away, and Ruiz and Nisa naked in her bed, when Flomel arrived. The door gasped open at the most indelicate moment possible, and Flomel bustled in, accompanied by the giantess.

"Nisa," Flomel called. "Where are you?"

He stood puzzled for a moment, his greyhound head questing about the cell. Then he noticed the quiver of the canopied bed. He stepped briskly across the floor and parted the silks with his wand. By that time Ruiz and Nisa had separated somewhat and had pulled a coverlet over themselves. Flomel's eyes widened, and he gasped, much louder than the door.

"What is this?" Flomel's lean features were purpling, and he shook with rage.

"Get away from my bed," Nisa snapped, as outraged as the magician. Ruiz remained silent, gathering himself.

No one moved for a moment, until the giantess said, "Where's the herman?"

She stepped into the cell with a heavy confident tread, her tiny features drawn together with suspicion. "Where is it?"

she asked again. She looked in the bathroom, then she looked in the bed. She took hold of Ruiz's arm with a massive hand and drew him from the bed effortlessly. She pulled him close and spoke again. "Where is it? The Lady will be very unhappy if you've damaged her property."

Her breath was foul, and the dead devotion in her tiny eyes was unnerving. Ruiz pointed with his free arm. "There," he said. "Ayam has its own little room. Isn't that nice?"

She gave him a casual shake, rattling his teeth, and released him. He caught up a sheet and wound it around himself. The giantess went to the alcove and unlocked it.

The herman fell into the room, floundering. Ayam had apparently been listening at the door seals. But it recovered its balance and dignity almost immediately. "At last," Ayam gushed. "Mighty Banessa, you come to the rescue of this poor oppressed servant. One casts oneself at your awesome feet in abject gratitude."

"Shut up," the giantess said impassively.

She turned to Flomel. "Proceed," she ordered.

Flomel drew a deep breath. He seemed to have regained his self-control, though a glitter of strong emotion still showed in his eyes. "Nisa," he said. "How is it you cheapen yourself by dallying with this casteless one? Please, remember who you are. I appeal to your sense of propriety."

Nisa was still flushed with anger. She sat up in the bed, pulling the coverlet around her. "You, Master Flomel, should remember who I am! And your own caste. I'm no longer an Expiant, subject to your whim."

Flomel seemed surprised. "No longer an Expiant? How is this?"

Nisa smiled. "My Expiation is finished. And here I am, resurrected."

Flomel considered this, long fingers stroking his chin. He studied Nisa with hooded eyes. "Perhaps," he said, "you're storing up new sins. Your misadventures with the casteless one are, if I remember correctly, somewhat akin to the sins that gave you into Expiation in the first place."

"We're no longer in the lands of my father, Magician. Different rules here, as any fool would know. And you're wrong to call Ruiz casteless. I don't know his lineage, but it's higher than your own. Of that I'm sure."

Flomel looked as if he might take his wand to Nisa, and Ruiz stepped around the corner of the bed, close enough to the magician to stop him if necessary.

"Enough," the giantess said. "No more squabbling. Explain what is required. The Lady Corean expects punctuality. We depart for the pen shortly."

Flomel drew a deep breath. "As you say," he said. "Nisa, my apologies. I cannot help looking on you as a child of my own flesh, and I sorrow over your mistakes, as your real father would, were he here. But now to business. We begin rehearsals for the new play, today."

Nisa recoiled, shocked. "The new play?"

"Yes, yes. The new play. The performance that will assure us an influential patron in this new world. Have you not been told?"

"No."

"Well, as before, you'll be the central character. A great honor, no?"

Nisa sat back suddenly, her face crumpled. "As before. . . . No, the Lady Corean would never permit such a thing."

Flomel smiled. "It's the Lady Corean who sends me here."

"No, I can't." Nisa looked at Ruiz, appealing to him for help, but he could think of nothing to do or say. Her eyes dulled and she looked away. He felt a terrible sadness, and an anger so intense that he trembled with it. The images of her first death rose in his mind, unbidden. He had to make a violent effort to keep his face impassive.

He was still searching for some word of comfort for Nisa, when the giantess spoke again. "The woman must dress now, unless she wants to go naked to the pens." She turned to Ruiz. "You also."

Nisa rose from the bed, and went slowly into the wardrobe.

·   ·   ·

RUIZ WALKED BESIDE Nisa. Her face was like stone, and she moved as if already drugged for the performance. Behind them, Flomel marched, swinging his wand and puffing a little with the exertion. The giantess trudged in the lead, and a sour unpleasant odor followed her. Ayam the herman brought up the rear, exclaiming at each new sight, discussing at length its boredom in Nisa's rooms. The herman's relentless voice was like needles in Ruiz's ears, but he suffered in silence.

They reached the Pharaohan pen. Through the observation port, he could see that the stage was already set up, and the guildsmen swarmed over it like maggots over a gaudy corpse. Nisa drew a sharp breath, and then looked into Ruiz's eyes. "I won't, not again," she whispered.

Ruiz was speechless. He gripped her shoulder, squeezed. She put her hand over his for a moment, then turned to Flomel.

"You," she said bitterly, and drew a gem-encrusted set of sewing scissors from her sleeve. She sank it into Flomel's belly and ripped up, opening him like a fish for cleaning. He stumbled back, collapsing into Ayam, who fell. Nisa darted away down the passage.

Banessa swung her giant frame around just as Nisa disappeared around the bend of the corridor. A flicker of irritation crossed her immense face, the first expression that Ruiz had seen in that large face. Ayam was hooting, hysterical, trying to push Flomel off its chest. Flomel was busy dying, a glazed look of amazement in his eyes.

The giantess detached a seeker from her harness, and Ruiz's heart sank. The seeker was a cruel device, capable of following a scent trail for miles, programmed to herd the quarry back to its owner with small doses of an insupportably painful venom.

"Wait," Ruiz said. "I'll fetch her back."

The giantess looked at him with the merest trace of amusement. "Yes," she said. "You understand the seeker? Yes. This one I tune to you." Banessa chuckled. "Best hurry." She unhooked another seeker. "And this one for her, should you lose her."

The seekers buzzed in her hands, eager to be off. A drop of venom trembled at the end of a stinger.

Ruiz ran.

Nisa's long legs had carried her a considerable distance before Ruiz saw her, dodging into a side passage. He blessed the luck that had brought him within sight of her before she'd gotten lost in the maze. He increased his pace and turned the corner, to find her waiting for him.

"I thought you'd get away, too," she said, smiling and holding out her arms.

But when he reached her, she must have seen something in his face, for she paled and jabbed at him with her scissors. He disarmed her easily. "Why?" she said in a broken voice.

"It wouldn't have worked, Noble Person."

"Shut up," she whispered, and struggled to break away from him.

Ruiz was forced to take her wrist in a gentle comealong grip, before he could turn her back the way she had run. She said nothing more, but her eyes were opaque with hatred. Moments later the seekers arrived, snarling, to convoy them back to the paddock.

CHAPTER 24

A T THE portal Corean waited, her perfect face incandescent with rage. Behind her Marmo monitored the limpet that held Flomel's guts together. Flomel lay on a floater, breathing with effort. Flomel's eyes were open; they rolled toward Ruiz and Nisa, and then away. A pair of Pung guards waited silently by the portal.

Ruiz released Nisa, and she stumbled away from him, her eyes large with betrayal and shock. Ruiz could only stare impassively at her, though he wanted to explain, to say something to soften the accusation in her face. One of the Pung took her by the arm and snapped a monomol leash around her neck.

Banessa stood by, massive arms folded. Ruiz went to her, and proffered the bloody pair of scissors. The giantess took them, showed them to Corean, then folded them between her huge fingers into a harmless lump of metal. She toggled a switch on her harness, and the seekers slapped back into their holsters.

Corean stepped close to Ruiz, nostrils flaring, white showing all around the irises of her eyes. "You," she said.

"Somehow this is your fault, isn't it? I should kill you now and be done with it. Marmo was right!"

Ruiz stood mute, sure that any response he could make would turn out to be the wrong one. Out of the corner of his eye he saw that on Nisa's face concern had replaced some of the hate, and his heart lifted slightly.

Corean stood rigid for a moment; then she lashed her hand across Ruiz's face. Ruiz had an instantaneous vision of Corean cutting the coercer's throat with her finger knife, and he wondered what his eyes would see after his face fell off. But it was just a stinging blow.

Corean flicked her hand, as if shaking off some unpleasant substance. "No. I'll get some use out of you yet."

She turned to Marmo, who looked up and said, "We'll be able to ship the magician in a day."

"Good, it's not a total disaster, then. The rehearsals we'll put back until they return. I'd feel better about the trip, though, if the Moc weren't locked in its molting cell." She seemed to be speaking to herself, but Ruiz pricked up his ears at the implication of a journey.

She turned to the giantess. "Banessa, you'll be in charge of security. See that nothing like this happens again. These will go: the girl, the three conjurors, the Guildmaster. And this one." Corean gestured at Ruiz. "That is, he'll go if he survives the peel. Take him back under and prepare him."

Marmo made an approving sound. "A wise decision," he said. "I'll see that he's properly wired."

Banessa fastened a collar to Ruiz. As the giantess led him away, Corean said, "Leave the girl here, with Ayam to keep an eye on her. Ayam, see that nothing further happens to the magician."

COREAN WATCHED THE readouts as Marmo guided the probes into the unknown's skull, using an injector prosthesis. The cyborg was extremely deft at this work, and Corean had little fear that her attractive enigma would be damaged during the procedure. She wished, however, that she had spent more credit on peel technology. Her tech wasn't state-of-the-art anymore—but what was, in a galaxy so full of diversity that no one could possibly keep abreast of every new development?

The unknown's tattoos had almost completely faded away, leaving only traces. The body seemed recovered from the icing; the burnished copper skin had regained its glow, and the nails on the strong hands were pink and shiny.

Marmo finished. "He's yours," the cyborg said, and floated away.

Corean set the analog helmet on her head, taking care not to muss her hair. She leaned back, closed her eyes, and squeezed the deadman switch.

She broke through the meniscus of his mind in a thrash of bubbles. She stabilized just under the silvery surface, observing the life that teemed there. Thoughts arrowed back and forth like shoals of agile fish. Below, in the blue depths, larger artifacts undulated, rich, dark, intriguing.

Corean floated for a long time, taking in the flavor of her unknown's mind, a savory, complex soup. The pleasure she took in this reassured her that she had made the correct decision in preserving him. "Waste not, want not," she whispered to herself, delighted.

She got down to business.

"Who are you?" The message went rippling out like a waveform in a pond, though this was an ocean-deep pond.

The answer came back. "Ruiz Aw."

"Ruiz, who owns you?"

"I'm a free agent, chartered out of Lanxsh."

"What is your business?"

"I deal in select humaniform stock."

Corean felt a tingle of satisfaction. A slaver! Ruiz's business was the one most likely to be helpful to her, further vindication of her good sense in preserving the man.

But she was cautious, so she probed deeper, below the verbal level of Ruiz's mind. And in corroboration she found a well-defined inversion layer of memory: the harsh images of a thousand slave pens, the unmistakable stinks of confined humanity, the sound of nerve lashes buzzing on flesh, the cries of auctioneers in the markets of a thousand worlds. The deeper she probed, the more vivid these memories became, but the experiential pressure increased even more rapidly, and soon Corean gratefully rose to a less painful level. She could not doubt the reality of those memories. And nowhere in the memories she disturbed was any trace of the Art League, no indication that Ruiz possessed the subservient, authority-oriented personality that was usually attracted to League work.

"And what were you doing on Pharaoh?"

This was an important question, and Corean watched alertly as Ruiz gathered his thoughts to answer. "I was there to steal magicians. I didn't expect to be taken myself." The response contained dense undertones of fear, embarrassment, caution, and an intense desire to avoid punishment.

Corean laughed. "Don't worry," she said, projecting reassurance. "It's all for the best." She felt Ruiz's mind relax slightly. She took up a different line of inquiry. "Why did you save the phoenix?"

Ruiz's mind roiled with unmistakably genuine confusion. "I don't know. But . . . she performed so well in the play. And she is good to look at. It must have seemed a waste, though I don't remember much of the time after the boat caught me."

This was not so satisfying a response. "And Corean," she asked acidly, "is she good to look at?"

"Yes," came the answer instantly. A red tincture of lust stained Ruiz's depths, washing away her irritation at his previous answer.

Satisfied, Corean released the deadman switch and returned to her own body. She sat for a moment, admiring Ruiz Aw, thinking about what they would do together when he returned from the Enclave. She told herself that the pleasure would be as great as it might be now, that any other difference she might feel existed only in her own perceptions. But, she wondered, was a toothless tiger still beautiful?

RUIZ WOKE TO the sound of quarreling Pharaohans. He was on the familiar dirty cot in the house of the casteless. That he was awake was proof that his shell persona had survived Corean's peel. He seemed to be spending an unreasonable amount of time unconscious, though, an unhappy thought that touched off a reverie of self-pity, in which Ruiz gave himself over to feeling herded about by an unkind fate. This assignment had been characterized from the beginning by a distressing lack of control on his part. In retrospect, he had planned his escape attempt through the marinarium with a ludicrous degree of optimism, and the execution of the plan . . . the kindest observer would probably have described his efforts as having a certain hysterical exuberance.

The only sweet spots in the whole fiasco were the times he had spent with Nisa, who was a living symbol of Ruiz's current ineptitude.

He sat up, his stiff muscles protesting.

No, Nisa was more than a symbol. She might hate him now, but she was intelligent; perhaps she would listen to his explanations. He went out into the square.

Most of the troupe seemed to be there, except for Flomel and Nisa. The elders formed a gesticulating circle, with Dolmaero at the center. The two lesser conjurors listened at the edge of the group of arguing elders. The others stood around in sullen groups, whispering.

"Quiet!" Dolmaero's face was red; Ruiz had never seen him look so exasperated. "It makes no difference what you would or would not do. Do you not yet grasp the situation? We are owned!"

A fish-faced elder spluttered. "Owned? We're not slaves; we belong to an honorable guild. How can we be owned?"

Dolmaero looked as if he regretted his outburst of candor. "Well, perhaps *owned* is not the correct term, Edgerd. But we are at least prisoners, can you argue that?"

"No, but whose fault is that? You're our Guildmaster; why have you done nothing to protest our status? What use, to have a Guildmaster who can do nothing for his guildsmen?" Edgerd clenched his scrawny fists. A mutter of agreement ran around the plaza.

No one had yet noticed Ruiz in the shadow of the doorway, and he did nothing to draw attention. The air of the plaza was charged with incipient violence.

A heavy-shouldered youth with the tattoos of an assistant lizard tamer pushed forward. His meaty face was tight with frustration. "Yes!" he shouted, and Dolmaero drew back. "What use indeed. We live in these hovels, we are forced to eat this alien sludge; now they force us to rush this new production into being, without proper sacrifices and observances, without any firm payment schedule, without any of the customary relaxations and stimulants to which we, as artists of the first rank, are entitled. And why?"

"Tell us, Nusquial." Other shouts of encouragement came from the crowd.

"Because we gave the finest performance ever seen in the southern nomarchies? Because our fates are harvested away from the soil of Pharaoh? Because we've fallen among demons? No! I don't believe it!"

Ruiz was fascinated. Nusquial had obviously been erroneously trained as a beastmaster. The boy had a fine gift of rhetoric. The Pharaohans were captivated, eager to hear his words.

"No!" Nusquial shouted. "I say it's because our Guildmaster, the once-Honorable Dolmaero, has failed us. Has he interceded with the demons who hold us captive? Has he? Has he requested those comforts that are our just due? Why must we simply accept the miserly dole that Dolmaero seems to think proper? There is strength in our unity; that is the message that a hundred generations of our guildfellows send us. It's our power not to perform that Dolmaero will not use."

Nusquial jumped forward and took Dolmaero by the arm. The Guildmaster recoiled in shock, but the husky lizard tamer held him fast.

Nusquial's face burned with violent energy. The two conjurors drew away, putting distance between themselves and whatever unpleasantness might occur. Nusquial dragged Dolmaero through the circle of elders, toward the west wall of the plaza, and Ruiz noticed that some of the elders seemed troubled. But the other members of the troupe seemed united in their anger with Dolmaero.

Reluctantly Ruiz followed. His natural inclinations and training urged him not to get involved. But he felt an unnerving certainty that he would be wise to act. In the first place, Dolmaero was an intelligent, resourceful man, and the troupe would need such a leader very badly in years to come. And Dolmaero had been kind to Ruiz. In the second place, if the troupe destroyed a valuable member of Corean's new property, her rage would fall heavily on the troupe. Some would inevitably splash on Ruiz, if he made no effort to head off the disaster.

Nusquial shoved Dolmaero up against the wall, stepped back, and took up a piece of rubble. Dolmaero held himself straight, maintaining an impressive but useless dignity; all eyes were on Nusquial. The crowd pushed close. Nusquial held the chunk of stone high, like a trophy. He didn't notice Ruiz threading the crowd behind him. "With this," Nusquial declaimed, "we make a change for the better. With this, we wipe out the stain on our honor, in the time-honored manner. With this, we show our captors what manner of men we are." Before Ruiz could reach him, he threw the stone with all his strength. Dolmaero ducked away, but the stone glanced off the polished top of his head, and the Guildmaster went to his knees, blood sheeting over his face.

Others bent for stones. In the midst of this, Ruiz tapped Nusquial lightly on the shoulder. Nusquial turned, his face full of feral excitement. Ruiz hit him two slashing blows, one on each ear, so quickly that the sound of the blows merged. Nusquial's eyes went dim, and he fell like a tree, to lay face up in the dirt, quivering.

In the sudden silence, Ruiz stepped forward. He looked down at the prone lizard tamer, then nudged him tentatively with a toe. Nusquial lay as if dead. Ruiz drew back his foot and kicked him in the ribs. The sound of breaking bone shivered the air.

Ruiz turned to the crowd. "Good afternoon," he said pleasantly. He slowly scanned the circle of white faces; no one seemed disposed to be rash. Ruiz smiled.

"A bit of wisdom, paraphrased from an ancient sage of the Home Worlds," he said. " 'Let he who is without good sense cast the next stone.' "

A clatter of dropped masonry sounded in the plaza, and the crowd evaporated.

Dolmaero, on his knees, was trying to find a way to stand up. Ruiz helped him over to the shady side of the stage. He

settled Dolmaero there on a bit of scaffolding erected by the
stage painters, and went for a clean cloth and a basin of
water.

Dolmaero said nothing while Ruiz wiped his face, though
he winced and vented a small curse when Ruiz clamped his
fingers down on the wound to stop the oozing blood.

When Ruiz was finished, Dolmaero lifted weary eyes to
him. "Once again, you've saved the rubes from their own
foolishness."

Ruiz shrugged, smiling. It wasn't the sort of remark that
called for a response. After a bit, Dolmaero smiled back.
"Not," he said, "that I'm ungrateful. But tell me, what
made you exert yourself?"

"The same thing that should be motivating your flock,
Guildmaster. The fear of Corean's displeasure."

Dolmaero nodded. "Yes. In my own provincial way, I've
stumbled on that truth. Strange that something so beautiful
should be so deadly, eh?"

Ruiz laughed. "I'll point this out, though doubtless
you've already noticed: Many of the deadliest things are
beautiful. For example, take the Lady Nisa."

"Nisa? I would have thought her utterly harmless, except
to herself."

"Harmless? Ask Flomel about that when next you see
him. She took up a pair of sewing scissors and did a thorough job of airing his innards."

Dolmaero's eyebrows climbed to the top of his forehead.
"So the mage is dead?"

"No. The quacks here are very good. And fast. I have it
on good authority that we'll all be traveling together soon.
Where, I don't know."

Dolmaero digested this information at length. Finally he
said, "You're a source of strange predictions, Wuhiya."

"Call me Ruiz," Ruiz said.

"Ruiz, then. Is that truly your name? Never mind. Your
tattoos have washed away, I see."

Ruiz rubbed at his face. "So. Well, I apologize for any
offense my naked face may give."

Dolmaero clapped him on the back and grinned broadly.

"You could paint yourself blue and eat with your feet, without offending me in the slightest. I'm truly in your debt. Besides, a naked face frightens. I would guess that causing fear is part of your trade. Whatever that might be."

Dolmaero got up, puffing with the effort. "But now," he told Ruiz, "I'll have to see to young Nusquial. He was always a hothead, which is why I made him a lizard man when he wanted to be a mage. Some don't wear power as well as you wear yours." He went off across the square, before Ruiz could ask him where Nisa might be found.

But he found her easily enough, in the bathhouse, attended by three ancient women—gowners, Ruiz supposed. Nisa stood on a low stool, while the women tried the drape of a rich red velvet against her. Bolts of other fine fabrics lay about in disarray. When Ruiz entered, the gowners failed to notice him at first, and he watched as they pinned and marked and debated in shrill cackles. Nisa looked at him, her arms lifted from her sides to accommodate the gowners, her face set, her eyes distant.

Against the cistern, Ayam lounged, watching the gowning. Ruiz glared at it, but it gazed back blandly, undisturbed.

When the gowners finally looked around and noticed Ruiz in the shadow of the entryway, they dropped their fabrics and pins and chalks and tapes, and fled out the back door with a chorus of small wheezy shrieks.

Ruiz hoped their hearts were strong. He had no wish to cause any further casualties among the properties of Corean.

"May we speak?" he asked.

She regarded him with little apparent interest, then spoke in a slow detached voice. "Why not? You've frightened away the couts. Besides, you can do as you please; you've demonstrated that, have you not?"

Ruiz stepped closer. Nisa still held her arms out rigidly, as if she had forgotten that they belonged to her. Ruiz saw that her pupils were pinpoints; she must be almost blind in the dimness of the bathhouse. He felt a surge of anger. "Has the philterer been busy already?"

"Yes. It's better this way." A spark of faraway amusement lit her face for a moment. "But I think they'll not be as happy with my performance this time."

Ruiz looked into her face, saw nothing more of Nisa there. In her present state, there was no point to explaining his actions outside the paddock. Better to wait for a time when she could understand, if she would. Besides, Ayam was Corean's creature, sure to report, with an unflattering twist, anything he might say to Nisa. He turned and left.

A DOZEN PUNG guards came for them in the morning. They were herded into the center of the plaza: Ruiz, Nisa and the Dilvermooner, the two assistant mages, and Dolmaero.

Kroel, the mage who had taken the part of Menk, god of slavery, struggled briefly with the Pung who had collected him. The Pung touched him lightly with the nerve lash, and Kroel fell to the ground howling and writhing. Kroel was a short broad-chested man with heavy features and tattoos in an antique, mannered style.

The other mage, Molnekh, a cheerfully cadaverous man, helped Kroel to his feet and dusted him off. "Now, now," said Molnekh, "is this dignified?"

"Dignified!" Kroel was still whimpering. "Dignified, you say? What is dignified about this abuse? I believed when we were reunited with the troupe that our torments were ending."

"I, too, was hopeful," Molnekh said, facing the Pung and baring his long yellow teeth in a fawning smile. The Pung gestured with its lash, and the two joined the others without further incident.

Shortly, Banessa came through the portal. Behind her a Pung dragged a truly wretched creature, a humanoid of indeterminate age and gender, in the last stages of starvation or some wasting disease, hairless, clad in nondescript rags. The giantess carried a handful of coded monomol detention collars, and Ruiz's heart fell.

"Attention," said Banessa. "You'll be going on a short journey. You must all wear these security devices—no exceptions."

"Excuse me, large person," said Dolmaero. "Can you tell us where we're going?"

"That's irrelevant," the giantess said. "The name would mean nothing to you."

But Ayam giggled and said, "I can tell you a little. You'll be going deep into the ground. You'll meet some fascinating people, and when you come back up, you'll be so nice, so cooperative. The Gench—"

Banessa swung her huge fist at the herman and knocked it down. "Shut up," she said.

Ruiz barely noticed. His knees had gone weak, and he could feel the wrenching movement of the death net in the depths of his mind. A terrible tension filled him, as though the net had been set to trigger at the first mention of the Gencha. He remembered, dimly, what Nacker had said: ". . . a silver bullet, aimed at some monster . . ."

He was dizzy with the effort of resisting the net. Dolmaero noticed his distress and took his arm. "Are you unwell?" Dolmaero asked.

No! he shouted at the net. *Wait! Just a while longer. I'm going there, I'm going, and I'll be able to learn where they are.*

As though the net had heard him, it stopped its slide toward oblivion, so abruptly that for a long moment Ruiz seemed to hang over an abyss, looking down into endless blackness. His vision dimmed, and he could hear nothing.

Then it was over and he was standing in the square again.

"I'm fine," he said, shaking off Dolmaero's hand. "Nothing wrong."

But things had gone terribly wrong. He knew now why he had been sent to Pharaoh. The League was interested in the curtailment of poachers, true enough. But the League was far more interested in catching rogue Gencha, who were vastly more valuable than any human stock. The League had known that he would end up on Sook. And once he had reached Sook, they had hoped he would be sent to the rogue Gencha practitioners, who specialized in the making of organic machines from living beings.

He would die before that happened to him, for which he

was thankful, but the others would come back from the enclave without souls, without that inner direction that marks all sapient beings. For the rest of their lives, they would exist only to please their owners.

He couldn't bear to look at his fellow prisoners.

ONE AFTER THE other, the entire group was collared, except for Ayam. The herman stood apart from the rest, smiling.

Ruiz touched the slick monomol that circled his neck snugly. It was not a highly sophisticated tech; for that he could be grateful. It carried a locator beacon, a sedative ject, and a decap explosive. With a little time and the right tools, he might be able to get it off. He fed himself hope, as though he were a small fragile fire. He gradually regained a bit of his mental equilibrium.

Banessa carried the control console hung on a ribbon of lavender velvet between her enormous breasts. Ruiz wondered how her thick fingers could accurately work the delicate controls of the unit. He discovered the answer when she activated the collars. She flexed her hand and slender claws of bright metal slid from the ends of her fingers. With these, the giantess tapped away, and Ruiz felt a thrumming vibration as his collar activated.

Banessa's tiny dead eyes rested on each of them in turn. "A demonstration," she said. "You must learn this lesson." She tipped back the head of the starveling with the butt of her nerve lash. Around its neck was a collar like theirs. Its eyes rolled back in its head, and it slumped, almost falling when Banessa took away her lash.

"First," she said, "the collar will tell us where you are, so no matter how far you flee, we'll catch you. Second, if we don't want to take the trouble to catch you, we'll do this." She gestured to the Pung, who pushed the wretch away. The slave stumbled and staggered a half-dozen paces away; then Banessa clicked a claw against her console.

They heard a small report, like an ax hitting a log of some hard ringing wood. The slave's head popped off. The body fell, the head rolled away, and a small flow of blood sank into the sand.

"Remember this," Banessa said, dropping the console back between her breasts. She retracted her claws, then gestured to the Pung guards. "We'll go to the airboat."

Everyone stepped lively.

CHAPTER 25

THE boat was a standard low-level, low-speed model, suited to the laws that governed movement over the surface of Sook. Heavy monomol armor covered its squat frame, and a ruptor turret capped the control blister.

They filed aboard, Ayam leading the way, Banessa following behind. The giantess oversaw the securing of the prisoners to low metal benches on either side of the cramped portless hold. The herman did the work with relish. Ayam seemed to take particular pleasure in cinching Ruiz's straps tight. Its strong arms bulged, hauling at the straps, and it smiled its unpleasant Dilvermooner smile. Banessa inspected Ruiz's bonds and made the herman loosen them slightly.

"Your owner values this one," the giantess said in her odd buzzing voice. "Damage him and she'll take it out of your own precious hide."

Ayam was sulky. "One will never understand the Lady's preferences, though, of course, one is ill-equipped to advise the exalted Corean."

"Keep that in mind." The giantess moved along, found no fault with the rest of the straps.

Ruiz sat with Dolmaero on one side and the two mages on the other. Molnekh was closest to Ruiz, the sniveling Kroel at the far end. Nisa was secured across the narrow aisle, still flat-eyed with whatever drugs the philterer had dosed her with. He gave her a tentative smile, but she stared back without any discernible emotion.

They waited. The warm humid air of Sook filled the hold, and the prisoners sweltered. Ayam settled beside Nisa, and amused itself for a bit by peering into her drugged face. The herman touched her where her tunic had rucked up, smoothing its fingers across her knee. Ruiz glared. Ayam glanced at him, smiled maliciously, and slid its fingers a little higher. Nisa took no notice. Ruiz looked away, and eventually Ayam tired of its game and went forward to the control blister. Ruiz could hear a mutter of voices, and he thought he recognized the artificial tones of the cyborg, Marmo, raised in impatience.

A clatter on the cargo ramp announced the arrival of Flomel, strapped to a floater. Ayam rushed down to take the floater from the Pung guard who had delivered it, and the herman secured it to the empty bench next to Nisa. Flomel looked much improved, though the limpet still laced his belly. He craned his neck and realized that Nisa was sitting beside him.

"Help!" he shouted, in remarkably vigorous tones. "It's her—keep her away; she wants to kill me!"

Ayam laughed and patted his face. "Not to worry, O exalted sir, her claws have been clipped. This lowly one will see to your safety." Ayam fastened a control collar around the mage's bony neck. "Here's a valuable amulet for you. No, no, don't thank me!"

When the herman had gone forward again, Dolmaero spoke. "Good to see you so lively, Master Flomel."

Flomel turned his head to take in the opposite bench. "It's a miracle, Guildmaster. There's nothing like feeling your guts slipping through your fingers . . . gives you a new appreciation for life. Though I don't recommend it as a routine physick. Is she truly safe?" Flomel jerked his head at Nisa.

"Yes, I would think so. The philterer has done well with her. She should be calm enough."

"Good, good. Have you any idea where we're bound, Guildmaster?"

"The herman told us a little, but we all hoped that the Lady Corean had taken you into her confidence."

Flomel looked uncomfortable. "Apparently the Lady has been quite busy. Otherwise I'm sure she'd have instructed me at length. But from the remarks of my attendants, I gather that we're going for some type of orientation or training, to better fit us for our new life in the pangalac worlds." He sniffed. "Though I can't imagine why the casteless one is being sent with us. Another mystery, eh?" Flomel looked at Ruiz, eyes glittering.

Dolmaero leaned forward. "The pangalac worlds? What are they, exactly?"

Agitation surfaced on Flomel's face. The monitor lights on his limpet flickered toward amber. With a tiny hiss, the limpet injected a soporific, and calm washed over Flomel's lean features. "I must rest now, Guildmaster. We'll talk later."

Flomel's eyes dropped shut, and presently he began to snore.

Except for Flomel's noisy exhalations, silence reigned in the hold again.

When the boat's engines came up to speed, filling the hold with a metallic whine, the Pharaohans shifted uneasily in their bonds.

"What's that sound, Ruiz? It sounds like a thousand headsmen whetting their axes." Dolmaero's voice cracked nervously.

"The engines—nothing to be alarmed at."

Molnekh turned to Ruiz with a look of startled interest. "How is it," he asked, "that you are so knowledgeable? I mean no offense, understand."

Ruiz shrugged, but Dolmaero spoke. "Perhaps he's from one of these 'pangalac worlds.' You can see he's no Pharaohan." Dolmaero nodded at Ruiz's naked face.

"Ah?" Molnekh smiled. "Perhaps you would be kind enough to tell us what you know of our fate?" The mage touched his control collar with a bony finger. "Of course, I recognize the slave collar."

Before Ruiz could reply, Corean swept into the hold, followed by Marmo.

"All set?" She seemed distracted.

"Yes. One last time, I ask you if this is wise. Wait two weeks and the circuit collector will be here. Does it make sense to accept the cost of shipment, the security problems, when all this could as easily be their problem, not ours?" Marmo gestured with his prosthetic arm, now fitted with a nerve lash.

"One last time, I will tell you why. We cannot start the rehearsals until they've been processed. Time presses. And, as you know, there is at least one dangerous creature in this cargo." She favored Ruiz with a smile almost affectionate. "Do your job, Marmo, and all will be well."

"As you say."

Corean stroked Ruiz's shoulder. "Be good," she said, bending close. She kissed him lightly on the cheek.

She turned to Nisa with a frown. She studied Nisa's drug-frozen face. She patted Nisa's sleek head in a proprietary manner. "Won't we all have fun when you get back?" Her tone was bright. She cast one last look about the cargo hold, and left.

Marmo fixed his sensors on Ruiz. "Yes, do be good," the cyborg said. "I would love an excuse to be done with you." He rotated, floated forward.

The boat left the ground with a lurch and stagger, then lifted slowly until it cruised over the pens at an altitude of a hundred meters. The Pharaohans paled.

"Don't worry," Ruiz reassured them. "This is a safe mode of travel."

"If you say so, Ruiz." Dolmaero's voice shook slightly.

Kroel whimpered. Molnekh leaned a skinny, comforting shoulder against his fellow mage. "Now, now, Kroel. The outworlder says we'll survive. That's good enough for me." Molnekh winked hugely at Ruiz. Ruiz smiled back, amused by Molnekh's resilience in these alien circumstances. He found himself warming to the cadaverous mage. Molnekh seemed the best and bravest of the conjurors, despite his apparent frailty. Ruiz wondered how the timid Kroel had managed to play, so effectively, the powerful god of slavery.

The engines whined, they flew out over the purple jungle, and the hours passed. Ruiz fell into a drowse, his head tipping forward onto his chest.

He woke when he felt the jolt of landing. Ruiz looked about alertly.

"You do awaken swiftly," Dolmaero said.

Nisa was watching him, her eyes huge. Only traces of the drug's confusion showed on her face. "You're a prisoner, too," she said.

Ruiz smiled, shrugged. She did not smile back, and after a moment she looked away.

Banessa descended into the hold, trailed by Ayam. "Lunch," the giantess announced. The Dilvermooner unsealed their straps, contriving to pinch Ruiz painfully in the process. Banessa watched impassively. Her clawed fingers hovered over the collar controller.

They left Flomel sleeping in his floater, but the others walked down the ramp into a grassy clearing.

Sook's sun burned down brilliantly on the feathery pink grass, struck a blue glitter from the surrounding jungle. Beneath the sinuous trees, a noisy darkness crouched. Alien scents tingled Ruiz's nose.

The Pharaohans, oppressed by this strangeness, clustered together at the base of the cargo ramp. Banessa gestured with the controller. "Remember the lesson. And the ruptor. It will kill anything that crosses our perimeter, coming in or going out. Besides, there's nowhere to run to." She looked at the jungle, a touch of dread on her vast face.

Presently Ayam passed among them with self-heating packets of standard shipfare. Ruiz showed the Pharaohans how to pull the activator strip, and they marveled. Ruiz wolfed his down, though it was bland amorphous stuff, and he advised the others to do the same. "Eat when you can, sleep when you can," he said, smiling. "That's the secret to successful travel."

Only Kroel refused his portion, and Ruiz split it with

Molnekh. The bony mage ate with an excellent appetite, despite his skinniness. "I've had worse," Molnekh said, smacking his wide lips, when he'd scraped the last bit from the container.

Ruiz touched Nisa's arm. "You should stretch your legs," he said. "You may not have another chance soon."

"Yes," she said, and they walked slowly in the boat's shade, not quite touching. "Tell me," she said finally. "Tell me why. Was it those metal wasps? Did Banessa send them to fetch me back?"

"One of them. The other was for me. The sting would have been terrible, like nothing you've ever felt." He put his arm lightly around her waist. "There was no chance, Nisa. Though it was a fine try."

She pulled away from his touch.

The Dilvermooner saw them, frowned, and spoke to the giantess. "Time to load," Banessa said.

Before the straps were replaced, Banessa allowed the prisoners to use the boat's recycler, one at a time.

THE BOAT FLEW on. Ruiz dozed off lightly now and then. The others eventually relaxed enough to do the same, except for Kroel, who sat hunched with terror, eyes wide and rolling.

At the next stop, the boat sat in the long grass of the uplands when the prisoners stumbled forth. The air was cooler, and a light breeze rippled the grass. The sun was setting swiftly behind a wall of jagged peaks, far away over rolling steppes. The vista was empty except for a herd of browsing creatures, tiny in the distance.

Banessa leaned her great bulk against the ramp and watched as the herman carried out her instructions. From the upper end of the ramp, Marmo scanned the grasslands, a splinter gun cradled in his manipulators. Ayam brought out an armload of perimeter sensors and dropped them every few meters, marking a hundred-meter circle centered on the boat. The herman was clearly nervous, and returned to the boat with a sheen of fearful sweat on its face. Ruiz surmised that the long grass held predators, though it was hard to imagine a predator that could evade the ruptor turret's sensors. Perhaps Marmo was overcautious.

The hull of the boat extruded a security light. It lit a circular area at the side of the boat, and Ayam set a group of self-rooting leashes around the edges. The leashes spun noisily in the grass, then like great worms sank their tendrils deep into the soil.

One by one Ayam attached the prisoners to the two-meter whips of the leashes. It came to Ruiz last, and as it locked the whip to Ruiz's collar, it leaned close and whispered, "One has the responsibility of the graveyard watch tonight. One plans to visit your tent; be ready. Or perhaps one will visit the woman first—one puts you next to her, so you may listen, and anticipate." The herman smiled and pinched Ruiz's cheek painfully.

Ruiz's fingers ached for the herman's throat. The giantess was watching, with her hand over the collar controller. He did not believe he would lose his head if he acted up. But he would certainly be sedated, and thereafter any opportunities that appeared would be lost.

Ayam passed out supper, which differed in no discernible way from lunch. As the prisoners ate, the herman unloaded tubetents from the boat, and activated one by each leash. They puffed up like huge white sausages; then both Ayam and Banessa went inside the boat. Marmo remained, his metal face slowly scanning the darkening grasslands.

Nisa seemed lost in thought, picking at her food. She went into her shelter without speaking, though she gave Ruiz a very small swift smile.

Dolmaero squatted in the grass, eating his supper, making a wry face with each bite. "I rely on your assertion that this is edible, friend Aw. Otherwise I would fear to be poisoned."

"I make no guarantees."

Dolmaero laughed. "You're a cautious man. Tell me, why do we stop? Does the flying egg depend upon the sun's light for its power? Or do terrible beasts roam the night skies?"

"It's the Shards," Ruiz said. "They permit no movement above the nightside surface. No night flights."

"The Shards? Who might they be?"

Ruiz realized he had spoken without his customary restraint. But . . . Dolmaero might find a description of Sook entertaining, perhaps even useful, if they somehow escaped before the Gencha took them.

"Dolmaero," Ruiz answered, "do you know of the Acasta, in the King's city?"

Dolmaero finished the last bite of his supper. "Oh, yes. The quarter where anything may be found, for a price."

"Yes. Well, this planet, which is called Sook, is the Acasta of the outworlds."

"Sook . . . it has a low ring to it."

Ruiz glanced about. No one else was paying attention. "Sook is the slave world, the world where bandits are born, where old pirates go to die."

"So? Then the Lady Corean is a bandit? Slaving is not permitted in the worlds?"

"Oh, she's a bandit. But slaving is legal on most of the pangalac worlds. She's doing something else that isn't legal —she's stealing slaves that belong to others."

"Ah? Who did we belong to, before?"

Ruiz concealed his uneasiness at this question. Once again he had underestimated Dolmaero. "I don't know," he lied.

Dolmaero considered this, eyes bright and noncommittal. "And the Shards—who are they?"

Ruiz glanced up at the sky, where the glitter of the orbital platforms outshone the stars. "Sook belongs to the Shards; they make the rules here, what rules there are. They permit no large craft or large fleets of small craft to ground on Sook. They allow no high-speed air transport, no heavy weapons, no large-scale settlement. They watch. From up there, Dolmaero." With his hand, Ruiz indicated the swarming lights of the platforms. "Otherwise they don't care what happens here, so long as the taxes are paid."

Dolmaero gazed upward, mouth hanging open in wonder. "What are they like? Are they like you, Ruiz?"

Ruiz laughed uneasily. "No. They're not even human. Much stranger than the Pung. Imagine a river lizard with a dozen arms, and in the palm of each hand, whispering mouths with poisoned fangs."

Dolmaero shuddered. "Do they ever come down?"

"Never. But the platforms carry terrible weapons. They could reach down and turn me to a puff of smoke without disturbing you in the least."

"Where did they come from? Why do they permit criminals to use their world?"

"No one knows. The guesses I've heard . . . maybe they're a very old warrior race, tired of conquest, but still trying to maintain their way of life. They collect entry fees from visitors, a lucrative business. Or they think they're running a game preserve. Or perhaps they simply find our antics entertaining."

They sat silent for long minutes. At last Dolmaero said, "And they watch? They can see us now?"

"They can. But whether or not they're watching at this very moment . . . that I don't know."

Dolmaero looked at him, eyes wide. "I believe I'll sleep now." The Guildmaster crawled into his tubetent.

Ruiz saw that he was the only prisoner still outside. He sighed and went to bed.

He woke in a thrash of terror, soaked with sweat. A moment passed before he remembered where he was. He breathed in ragged gasps and his heart thumped, as if he had been running.

When he was calmer, he heard a quiet scrabbling sound, a sound unlike the other sounds of the night.

Ruiz put his head cautiously through the tent flap. From the wheel of the stars, he judged the time to be well after midnight. He listened. The sound came again, from Nisa's tent. He craned his neck to look up at the boat. No one stood guard at the top of the ramp.

Adrenaline fired into his blood. He squirmed from his tent, shook off the last of the dreams. Was the cyborg watching from the boat's control blister? If not, he might have a chance.

He could not quite reach the corner of Nisa's tent; the leash was too short. The sounds from inside the tent took on a thrusting sexual rhythm. Ruiz reversed his body and hooked at the tent with his foot. It caught in a loop of cord, and Ruiz gave a great tug.

The tent slid toward him. Ruiz flipped again, and as the herman's angry face emerged from the flap, Ruiz caught its throat in his hands.

"Hush, Nisa, not a sound," he whispered urgently. Ayam slapped at Ruiz with its powerful arms, but Ruiz bore down, crushing its larynx under his thumbs. The herman thrashed, clawed at Ruiz's face, weakened. As it expired, quivering, semen spattered on Ruiz's stomach.

With a shudder of distaste, Ruiz threw the corpse aside. "Nisa," he whispered. "Are you all right?"

A muffled sob came from her tent.

"Nisa! Give me its things. Quick!"

He heard her move; a moment later the herman's blouse and slacks flew out, followed by the stun rod it carried on watch.

Ruiz searched the pockets in a frenzy of impatience, darting an occasional glance at the boat. It remained dark and silent; he began to hope the others were asleep or inattentive.

In the last pocket he found a key and unlocked his leash. He shoved the herman's corpse into his own tent, then scrambled into Nisa's.

In the dark, he could barely see her, huddled at the back of the tent. Her eyes were wide, staring. "It's dead?" she asked.

"Yes. Listen carefully. I'm going to try to take the boat. I'll unlock your leash; I don't have the key to the collar. If I succeed, everything will be fine." He used the key and dropped it in her lap, patted her foot gently. "If I don't come back in half an hour or so, or if you hear a big fuss inside the boat . . . you might want to think about running for the perimeter. A hit from the ruptor would be quick and clean. No pain. Do you understand what I'm telling you?"

She nodded.

He turned to go. She reached out and covered his hand with hers for an instant.

AT THE FOOT of the ramp, Ruiz paused for a moment and listened. Nothing. He sauntered up the ramp, rolling his hips like Ayam, in case the boat was equipped to detect motion signatures. At the ramp's top end, the lock hung open and dark.

He leaned against the cool metal, took a firm grip on the stun rod, and ducked inside. The hold was empty, unlit except for a small red light by the lock mechanism. He went silently to the end of the hold, where a ladder led up toward the crew quarters and control blister. Ruiz mounted the ladder, raised his eyes cautiously above the passageway sill.

He detected no obvious sign of the cyborg or the giantess, but a light showed from the aft-running passageway, back toward the crew quarters. He could see no obvious security cameras or other security sensors. He began to feel lucky.

Ruiz considered. He needed Banessa first. Her collar controller was the biggest danger. Where was she? If she was with Marmo, the situation was hopeless. Did they seem like boon companions? No.

Ruiz decided that Marmo would prefer the company of the boat's computer, up in the control blister. Banessa might then be in the crew quarters. He slipped down the passageway aft.

Banessa's cabin was the last one, and the only unlocked cabin. The door stood slightly ajar, so Ruiz applied his eye to the crack.

The giantess lay naked on her back, her enormous feet toward Ruiz. The massive curve of her belly and breasts prevented him from seeing her face, but he could see the distinctive horned shape of a sensie helmet on her head. Was she awake? Would she be too involved in her sensie to react swiftly when he made his rush? Was she equipped with a subcutaneous insulator field, to protect her from the stun rod? All too probable, he decided—skin fields were a standard slaver precaution.

He noticed an earthy pungent odor. The giantess moaned, pumped her hips, and her knees fell open. Ruiz suppressed an insane urge to giggle. He hefted the stun rod. An idea came to him, an ugly idea, but just possibly an effective one. Ruiz shrugged. Banessa was a slaver and a murderer. He thought, *Now is not a time for chivalry.* He thumbed the stun rod's trigger, cranked it all the way up.

Ruiz swept the door open, plunged forward, socketed the stun rod between Banessa's great thighs, where—he hoped—she was unprotected by the deadening mesh of the skin field. He threw himself away from her, but she was helpless, shaking, heels drumming against her bunk. She retained enough control of her body to extrude her claws and slash her arms back and forth, but her eyes stared blindly and her mouth was open in a scream that she had too little breath to make.

Ruiz dodged the claws, rolled behind her bunk, found the ribbon from which the collar controller hung. He crossed his wrists, wrapped the lanyard around both fists, wrenched it tight around her throat with all his strength. He gave thanks that the ribbon was stronger than it looked.

Minutes passed before the giantess grew still. Ruiz got up slowly, his hands numb. He was glad that it had not been a fair fight; he was beginning to feel very lucky indeed.

He took the controller, doubled the loop, and hung it around his own neck. Then he searched the cabin. He found a number of odd things: a locker full of absurdly undersized lingerie, a box full of illegal sensies of the most depraved sort, a big jar full of severed human penises, floating in blue-tinted preservative, several drawers full of antique weapons. But nowhere could he find the key to the collars.

Marmo will have it, he hoped. He refused to believe that Corean had kept it to send later by separate courier, though that would make sense. He refused to consider the notion, because Corean would have another and more powerful transmitter back at the pens. She would surely explode the collars herself should the boat fail to reach its destination.

He rummaged through Banessa's weapons. He took a slender spring-loaded stiletto, tucked it into his shoe. He found a beautifully made bola, its bronze weights shaped like little skulls. He looped it through his belt. He found an old splinter gun with yellow ivory grips and a dead battery; reluctantly he set it aside. In the last drawer he found a truly anachronistic weapon, a chemical-propellant handgun, a revolver of blue steel that fired nonexplosive slugs. He flipped out the cylinder; miraculously there were cartridges, the brass green with age. He checked each cartridge carefully, discarded one with an obviously corroded primer. Perhaps one or two of them might still fire.

Lastly, overcoming his revulsion, he retrieved the stun rod, but it had apparently burned out.

He crept out into the passageway. The struggle with the giantess seemed to have gone unnoticed. He checked the other cabins, found them still locked. He would have to be content with the weapons he had found.

Ruiz moved as silently as he could, balancing caution with speed. He remembered the advice he had given Nisa, and he felt a twinge of alarm for her. How much time had passed? He shook himself, pushed those thoughts away, concentrated on the task at hand.

The passageway ran forward to the bow salon. Just before the salon, a ladder led up into the control blister. Here Ruiz paused for a moment to gather himself.

Ruiz went quietly up the ladder, peeped into the control blister. The cyborg stood by the armorglass port, motionless, gazing out over the dark steppe. The overhead lights were off. Dozens of green and amber telltales glowed on the main board, cast flickering reflections over Marmo's polished carapace. The cyborg carried no obvious weapon, though his right manipulator was hidden from Ruiz.

Ruiz took a deep slow breath, closed his eyes for a moment. He took the ancient revolver in one hand, the bola in the other.

CHAPTER 26

Ruiz rose into the control blister, whirling the bola. Marmo turned swiftly, and to Ruiz's horror, the cyborg held a splinter gun. Ruiz released the bola. The bola seemed to float across the intervening space as languorously as a bird in a dream, the spinning weights throwing off warm gleams. The splinter gun rose toward Ruiz, inexorably. Ruiz threw himself sideways and down; the floor was impossibly far away. He pointed the ancient handgun as he fell, but his first shot was an impotent click.

The splinter gun fired with a soft stuttering cough, just as the bola struck the cyborg. Splinters sleeted through the spot Ruiz had just vacated, ricocheting off the bulkhead in all directions, some embedding themselves in Ruiz's back.

The bola's chains snapped tight, pinning the splinter gun to the cyborg's torso at a momentarily useless angle.

Ruiz gasped, pulled the trigger again. The gun boomed, an ear-shattering sound in that enclosed space, and the slug knocked the cyborg against the port. Marmo bounced off the armorglass, apparently undamaged, but he had lost his grip on the splinter gun. The cyborg floated forward, ripping at the chains, but Ruiz was faster. He leaped across the deck, snatched up the splinter gun, threw himself onto the cyborg's back. He pressed the muzzle to the soft flesh under Marmo's chin.

"Be still," Ruiz said, "or I'll eat a hole right into you. You're mine, tin man."

Marmo turned his head, looked into Ruiz's eyes. "I see that. Be careful, please. I am more fragile than I appear."

Ruiz tugged the bola chains down, tucked the ends tightly. He fished the knife from his shoe, worked it into Marmo's shoulder until he had severed the hydraulic lines that powered Marmo's metal arm.

"Was that necessary?" Marmo seemed no more than mildly curious.

Ruiz made no reply.

Marmo's blank steel eyes flickered past Ruiz's shoulder for a moment. A wave of misgiving filled Ruiz as he whirled to look out the port. A small white shape ran toward the perimeter.

"Nisa," Ruiz whispered. He grabbed at the collar controller. Red and yellow buttons marched in rows. Color codes marked each pair of buttons, so he could locate Nisa's buttons, but he had no way to tell which button exploded the collar and which injected the anesthesia. Nisa was almost to the perimeter, and overhead Ruiz heard the whine of the ruptor turret coming to life. Ruiz looked about wildly. He could not identify the ruptor controls; there was probably no time to disarm it, even if he could find them.

Ruiz thrust the controller at Marmo. "Which kills, red or yellow?" he demanded.

"Yellow," Marmo said without perceptible hesitation.

Ruiz's finger quivered over the controller; then he stabbed the yellow button. Just for an instant, he closed his eyes and sagged against the cool glass of the port. But he heard no explosion, and when he opened his eyes he could see Nisa sprawled on the ground, just short of the perimeter. He whirled, just in time to dodge the cyborg's rush. Marmo thumped the glass with enough force to have crushed Ruiz; the impact seemed to disorient the cyborg for a moment. Ruiz jumped at him, crooked an elbow around Marmo's neck, and set his foot against the bottom of Marmo's floater chassis. Ruiz heaved, and the cyborg slowly tipped over, to fall with a crash on his side.

Marmo spoke in a gently reproachful voice. "This is a sad situation. I cannot raise myself from this position."

"You lied to me; I should cut your head off," Ruiz said. "But I'll wait a bit. Who knows, I might even let you live, if you can find a way to be useful to me."

Marmo sighed. "I trust that I can."

"Begin this way. Where is the key to our collars?"

"I fear Corean has the only one."

Ruiz knelt by the cyborg and smiled. He raised his stiletto and began to saw methodically at the tough fabric that underlay the segmented coupling between Marmo's head and torso.

"Uncivilized. You should use the gun; so much more efficient." Marmo's steel eyes rolled.

Ruiz laughed, bore down. The tip of the stiletto slipped between the segments, and a drop of bright blood welled up. The cyborg jerked, tried to twist away.

"Wait!" Marmo said. "I suddenly recall that a backup key is locked under the main console."

Ruiz flipped the stiletto shut. He went over to the console, looked beneath it. Set in the tangle of wires was a small black case. On it a red light flashed beside a small keyboard.

"How can I trust you to give me the code?" Ruiz asked.

"A problem," Marmo said mildly. "Let me think."

Ruiz glanced out the port. Nisa still lay by the perimeter, and he felt a sudden twinge of anxiety. "Think fast," he admonished the cyborg, and then he opened his stiletto again.

"Calmly, calmly. I have it. Roll me over to the lockbox, and I'll open it for you. If it's booby-trapped, I'll take the brunt of it."

Ruiz set his foot and rolled the cyborg over. Three turns later Marmo lay under the console.

"You'll have to loosen my arm," Marmo said.

"In a moment." Using the point of the stiletto, Ruiz teased open the access plate on the side of Marmo's torso.

Inside was the cyborg's main power cell. Ruiz got a good grip on the handle of the cell.

"What are you doing?" The cyborg's voice had a nervous edge to it.

"I'm a fast thinker, too," Ruiz said.

Marmo sighed, seemed to shrink a little. Ruiz freed Marmo's flesh arm from the bola chain; the cyborg reached up and tapped at the lockbox. The key, a strip of mnemonic plastic, dropped out.

Ruiz caught it. "Thank you," he said politely, and jerked the cyborg's power cell.

Marmo sagged, became still. Ruiz ran from the control blister, down the passageway, out through the hold into the night.

RUIZ REMOVED NISA'S collar before his own. He picked her up, carried her past the others, who stood by their tents wearing looks of sleepy astonishment.

As they passed Flomel, the mage stepped forward and caught at Ruiz's arm. "What's happening?" Flomel demanded. "What are you up to?"

Ruiz looked at Flomel, raised the splinter gun. Flomel went pale, and his hand dropped away. Ruiz carried Nisa up the ramp into the boat. Behind him, he heard the mage whispering in outraged tones, then Dolmaero's calm rumble.

He laid her on a couch. She seemed to be breathing without difficulty, her color was good, and when he laid his head against her breast, he could hear her heart beating strongly. He remained there for a moment, cheek pressed to her warmth. He caught a strand of her hair between his fingers, marveled at its silky texture. He buried his nose into her hair, breathed in her scent.

Ugly pictures rose in his mind, things that might have been—Nisa running, the flat crack of the ruptor, the splash of flesh and bone, the precious body opened up like a butchered animal's, nothing more than a decaying scrap, empty of Nisa. He pushed the pictures away; it had not happened. He could not understand why he was still shaking.

After a while, he went to Marmo and searched through the cyborg's numerous pockets and compartment and storage slots. Mostly he found a collection of hand-held games, which soon formed a little glittering mound next to the cyborg. But Ruiz found useful things as well. He found a small multifunction cyberprobe, which Marmo had no doubt used to monitor his mechanical health. He found three spare magazines for the splinter gun. He found a master key to the boat's other cabins. He found a credit chip, which he speculated was to be used at the end of their journey. He found a skinpopper made in the same style as the collar controller, which he decided must contain the antidote to the collar sedative. He found a crumpled piece of paper, on which was scribbled what seemed to be a call-in schedule, and at this discovery Ruiz's heart sank. The next call was due at midmorning.

When Ruiz had emptied every hiding place on Marmo's chassis and stowed the useful gear in his own pockets, he returned to Nisa's couch. She showed no sign of waking. He strapped her to the couch, to prevent her from injuring herself should she try to rise before her equilibrium returned.

RUIZ WALKED DOWN the ramp, carrying the splinter gun and Marmo's power cell. The other prisoners sat by their tents, eyes wide in the light that spilled from the boat. Ruiz smiled at Dolmaero, gave Flomel a hard look, nodded at Molnekh. Kroel made a whimpering sound and scurried into his tent.

"Things have changed," Ruiz said. He threw the power cell far out into the darkness.

Flomel got painfully to his feet. "How so?" he demanded. "What terrible thing have you done? I've heard all about you and your murderous ways. If you've harmed any of the Lady's employees, you'll regret it."

In spite of himself, Ruiz was astonished. "You *are* an idiot, Flomel. What did you imagine yourself to be? One of her 'employees'? You were her slave, a piece of property."

"You're a liar," Flomel snarled. "You'll suffer for this, oh *yes.*"

Ruiz saw that reason would be wasted on the mage. He sighed and raised the controller. Flomel's eyes bulged. He fell back, raised his hands defensively.

Dolmaero stood up. "Ruiz, wait," he said. "Master Flomel is a fool, but should he die for that? If we kill all the fools, who'd be left?"

Flomel shot a malevolent look at Dolmaero, and Ruiz thought, *Flomel won't thank him for that.*

Ruiz touched the yellow button by Flomel's color code, and the mage dropped unconscious. "He'll live, so I imagine," Ruiz said. "But I'll get some use out of him. I think I have the antidote to the collar anesthesia; I'll experiment with him before I try it on Nisa."

He went to Dolmaero, pressed the collar key to his neck. The collar dropped away. Dolmaero rubbed his throat thoughtfully. "How did you manage this? I'm impressed beyond words."

"Banessa's dead, and the half-man disabled. I'll tell you about it later." Ruiz looked at Molnekh. "Molnekh, I must ask you: Will you do as I tell you, if I release you?"

Molnekh smiled nervously. "I assume that my other choice is to remain here until the Lady arrives."

"No, I won't leave you here. Sook has an interesting variety of predators; without the ruptor, they'd soon have you for dinner. I won't even leave Flomel, but I'll have to lock him in the hold."

The thin mage blinked. "You're not so bloodthirsty as we've been told. In any case, I have no desire to meet the Lady again; she'll be put out by these events, I suspect. Lead on."

Ruiz released him from his collar. "Thank you," Molnekh said.

"You're welcome," Ruiz said. "But what about Kroel? Is he capable of acting rationally?"

Molnekh pursed his lips. "I'm unwilling to venture a guess. What do you think, Guildmaster? You're well known to be a good judge in such matters."

Dolmaero scratched his head. "I don't know. Master Kroel has an inflexible and brittle mind, and under these circumstances . . . I don't think I'd put much trust in him."

"Then for the time being, we'll leave the collar on him. What of Flomel? Can logic penetrate his skull?"

Dolmaero looked at the sprawled mage. "Flomel is an intelligent man, if not a very pleasant one. He may listen. By the way, where is the woman-man?"

"Dead, in my tent."

Dolmaero raised a quizzical eyebrow, but asked no more questions.

DOLMAERO AND MOLNEKH carried the slumbering Flomel into the hold, still collared. He snored vigorously.

"Do you think you can fetch Kroel?" Ruiz asked Molnekh.

"I'll try."

"Here's the leash key," Ruiz said, retrieving it from Nisa's tent. "We'll leave the collar for a bit."

Ruiz watched from the top of the ramp while the skinny mage squatted by the opening to Kroel's tent and talked to Kroel. After a few minutes, Kroel came forth, moving uncertainly, leaning on Molnekh's frail shoulder.

Molnekh helped Kroel into the hold, murmuring reassurances. Kroel sat heavily on the bench, staring at the floor.

"Master Kroel," Ruiz said. "Give me your attention, please." The mage nodded without raising his eyes. "Things have changed, it's true, but for the better. I promise you this."

Kroel nodded again, a childlike bobbing of the head, incongruous in such a burly man.

Dolmaero touched Ruiz's back, where blood from the splinter wounds soaked the cloth. "You're injured," he said.

Ruiz winced. "It's not bad. But if you'd be kind enough to pick the splinters out, I'd thank you."

Dolmaero smiled. "That much I can probably do." Ruiz located a med kit, let down the top of his overalls. Dolmaero doctored him quite gently. When he was finished, and Ruiz's wounds were covered with patches of pseudoskin, Dolmaero spoke with courteous curiosity. "I would have expected a man such as yourself to have more scars."

Ruiz smiled, clapped Dolmaero on the shoulder. "I keep my scars on the inside, where they belong."

Ruiz brought out the skinpopper, pressed it to Flomel's neck. The mage jerked when Ruiz triggered the popper, and then his eyes flew open. He struggled to rise, spluttered in impotent rage.

"Shut up," Ruiz said sharply. "Keep silent and listen, or I'll put you under again. You're no longer in charge."

Flomel's face froze, and his eyes burned. But he clamped his mouth shut.

Ruiz sighed. "All right. Listen, all of you. You've surely guessed that Corean is a slaver. Her plan was to make you perform for an audience of bidders. I'll tell you this: The phoenix troupes of Pharaoh bring a high price on the pangalac market—she'd have made a tidy sum from you."

Dolmaero spoke. "Why are *you* here, Ruiz? You're not of Pharaoh."

Ruiz lied automatically. "An accident. I was a tourist on Pharaoh; I was as surprised as any of you when we were snatched up."

Dolmaero rubbed his chin thoughtfully. "What of Master Flomel's story? That you jumped onto the stage just before we were taken?"

"Yes," Molnekh said. "I saw you, too."

Stop underestimating Dolmaero, Ruiz thought. He improvised. "I was just trying to get a good picture. With my camera—a picture-making machine all tourists carry. I tripped. But none of this is important now. Now we have to decide what we must do."

"What can we do?" Dolmaero asked.

"Sensible question. First, there is a large corpse to be removed from one of the cabins. Then I'll see to reviving Nisa. Then we'll examine the boat and see if we can control it."

THEY LEFT KROEL huddled in the hold, secured to the bench. Flomel followed a few paces behind, as if fearing to be associated with the others. At Banessa's door, Ruiz paused. "There's an ugly sight inside. But we've got to get her out; she'd make an intolerable stink after a few days, if we had to leave her in there."

He pushed open the door. The giantess lay on the bunk, face black, legs spraddled.

"It won't be easy," Dolmaero said. "She must weigh two hundred kilos. How did you manage to overcome her?"

Ruiz shook his head, unwilling to provide details. "Surprise. Now roll her out of the bunk, and we'll see if we can drag her."

Flomel stood at the head of the bunk. He touched the sensie helmet. "What's this?"

Ruiz lifted it away, dropped it, crushed it under his foot. "You don't want to know, Master Flomel."

While Dolmaero and Molnekh rocked the corpse until it spilled out onto the deck, Flomel wandered about the cabin, examining the things that lay there. He started to pick up a jeweled dagger, but Ruiz shook his head. Flomel shot him a look seething with hatred, but he drew back. He moved on, came upon the jar in which the giantess had kept her pickled penises. "What are these—" Flomel started to ask. He went pale.

"A good person, would you still say, Master Flomel?" Ruiz smiled at Flomel, and for once the mage had no response. Flomel stood musing, wearing a dourly pessimistic face.

Meanwhile the others had tied the corpse's wrists together with wire from the sensie unit and were ready to try to move her.

"Good thing we got here before she went stiff; we'd never have gotten her out," said Dolmaero.

The three of them were just able to move her, pulling in concert. Flomel trailed as before, thinking private thoughts. When they reached the hold, Kroel started up in terror, but Molnekh was able to calm him.

"I'm going to wake Nisa, now," Ruiz said. "Roll Banessa down the ramp. You help," he said, pointing at Flomel.

"I? I am no casteless mongrel, to touch dead things!"

Ruiz frowned. "I won't kill you for being a fool. But I don't have to feed you, and I can keep you chained in the hold, if you refuse to take direction."

For a moment Flomel looked as though he might fly at Ruiz. But after a long appraising moment he nodded sullen acceptance.

"Good," Ruiz said. He pressed the key to Flomel's collar, removed it, tossed it out. He climbed out of the hold.

NISA LAY QUIETLY on the couch. Ruiz sat beside her for a moment, admiring her. She was still beautiful, despite the bedraggling effect of the night's events. He pressed the popper to her neck and she gasped. When her eyes fluttered open, Ruiz was shocked by the dark look in them.

"No, no, it's all right, Nisa," he said, and gathered her up. After a moment her arms went around him, tight.

"I thought I was dead," she whispered. "And lucky to be so. I thought you were dead."

"We're both alive. With a little luck we'll stay that way." He touched her throat where the collar had clasped her. He kissed the line of her jaw.

Some time later, she pulled away slightly, looked around the dark control blister. She saw the tipped-over Marmo and trembled. "Dead?"

Ruiz followed her gaze. "No, not dead, I think, but powerless. And the giantess *is* dead. The others are throwing out her body."

"The others?"

"All safe."

"You should kill the conjurors, Ruiz. Or leave them here. They can't be trusted; they think they're better than anyone else."

"You mean . . . they're like princesses?"

She twitched between amusement and annoyance. "No, I'm serious, Ruiz. It would be safer. And you can kill without difficulty, true?"

"You think so?"

She seemed to see something unpleasant in his face; she drew away and wrapped her arms around herself. "Have you killed a great many, Ruiz?"

He stood and went to the port. "Some," he muttered.

"What?"

"I said—" He turned and looked at her. "Well. The worlds are wide, Nisa, and full of life. Out of all those trillions . . . some don't deserve life. Besides, didn't you just tell me to kill the conjurors? I assure you: Despite what they did to you, they're scarcely less innocent than you are. Why should they die?"

"All right. You're right; let them live. I'll watch them." He laughed. "Yes, a good solution."

NISA FELT THE first stirrings of hope, as she watched Ruiz explore the boat's control system. His strong hands seemed to know what they touched. They caressed the switches and lights and screens, slowly searching out the meaning of all those bewildering things. He was almost a god, he could destroy with a god's nonchalance; *perhaps,* she thought, *he could make miracles as easily.*

When the sun rose over the pink veldt, Ruiz asked her to pass out food packets to the former prisoners. Nisa went to the locker he indicated, fumbled with the unfamiliar latch that held it shut, finally got it open. "Be reassuring," Ruiz said. "Don't frighten Flomel; if he tries to hurt you, Dolmaero will stop him. Come back when you're finished."

She carried the packets down to the hold. Dolmaero and Molnekh took their share eagerly. Kroel looked at her dumbly, eyes vacant, and did not raise his hand. She set the packet by him on the bench.

When she approached Flomel, the senior mage stared at her, his face shifting between hate and fear. "Master Flomel," she said, holding out the food. "It's not poison. Ruiz Aw says I mustn't try to kill you again, so I won't."

He snatched the packet, lips clamped in a narrow line.

"You're welcome," she said.

When she passed the lock, she could see the giantess lying sprawled at the foot of the ramp. Already the corpse was attracting carrion bugs, great golden beetles with shimmering wings. When one flew inside and bit Molnekh on one of his lean cheekbones, Ruiz retracted the ramp and shut the lock.

"Come up to the control blister," Ruiz said. He turned

and spoke kindly to Kroel, still huddled on the bench.
"Master Kroel, will you wait for us? Above are dangerous
machines, and you'll be safer here."

IN THE CONTROL blister, Ruiz leaned against the main
board. "We have a problem."

Only Dolmaero laughed, though Molnekh smiled his
wide toothy smile.

"Yes, well . . ." Ruiz grinned at them. "But what I
mean is this: The boat is programmed for Corean's destination. I can't change it. So we must either ride the boat in
that direction or strike off on foot. It's my opinion that the
veldt is too dangerous. I don't know much about the wildlife
in this part of Sook, but Corean's people were afraid of
something."

Ruiz did not mention the stirrings of the mission-imperative in his mind, a voice that demanded he proceed with his
investigation. The mission-imperative was weakening, with
time and the slippage of the death net, but it was still strong
enough to make him very uncomfortable, and thus less effective.

Molnekh spoke up. "I'm afraid too. Hungry things live in
the grass; I'm sure of it. But whatever Corean had planned
for us has no appeal for me now."

"Nor me," said Ruiz. "But there's some good news. We
can ride the boat toward our destination, and if we see a
good spot to stop—a village where we can get transport to a
neutral launch ring, for example—the program will allow
me to land."

"This then is what we must do." Flomel spoke in an
assured tone.

Ruiz looked at the mage, surprised. "I'm pleased that
you agree with my assessment, Master Flomel."

The mage's face was a mask of affability, and Ruiz
thought Flomel had never looked more treacherous.
" 'When the Hellwind blows, even the strongest tree must
dance'; so it is said." Flomel smiled, a somehow ghastly
expression.

Ruiz glanced at Nisa, saw a look of loathing pass over

her face. She was watching Flomel intently; when her gaze flickered to Ruiz for a moment, he winked.

Dolmaero perched on the edge of the couch. He seemed troubled; his fingers twisted together, and he stared at the floor.

"What of you, Guildmaster?" Ruiz asked. "Give us your opinion."

Dolmaero looked up, clearly uncomfortable. "I think your plan is the only possible one. But . . . Ruiz Aw, I must ask you: What are your intentions toward us? Has our ownership passed to you? And can we hope to return to Pharaoh?"

Ruiz blinked. "No, no, I'm not your owner. You're free, as far as I'm concerned. Anyone who wishes may leave now and make their own way." He turned and looked at Nisa. "Though I would regret it. As to getting home to Pharaoh . . . I'm sorry, but I think it unlikely, at this point."

Nisa jerked her gaze away from Flomel and looked at Ruiz, shock written in her face. The others mirrored that emotion.

"Ahh . . ." said Dolmaero heavily. "This is a blow, Ruiz Aw. But not completely a surprise. Until you took the boat, I'd put such hopes away. Still, will you tell us why we couldn't somehow return?"

Ruiz was uneasy. How could he tell them that under pangalac law they were still the property of the Art League, that the only way they could ever return legally to Pharaoh was as brainwiped cargo? He temporized. "Travel between the stars is expensive, and few ships call at Pharaoh."

Dolmaero watched him sadly. "I fear that isn't the whole story."

Ruiz looked down. "No. It's a complicated matter. We'll talk of it later, if you wish, but now we need to be moving. I'm expecting a call from Corean; she'll be unhappy when none of her folk answer. I've checked as best I can for override circuits, and I don't believe she'll be able to take control from us. But I can't be sure; I'd like to make as much progress as we can before she calls."

Ruiz turned to the main panel, began to ready the boat for travel. Without turning, he said, "Everyone sit on the couches and fasten the restraint webbing; it's possible we'll have a rough trip."

When the engine began to whine, and the boat lifted into Sook's sky, he looked back at them. All sat stiffly in the webbing. Three wore identical frowns of uncertainty.

But Nisa smiled as she watched him, her eyes full of some sweet emotion that lifted his heart.

꧁꧁꧁꧁꧁꧁꧁꧁꧁꧁꧁꧁꧁꧁꧁꧁꧁꧁

HERE IS AN EXCERPT FROM
THE EMPEROR OF EVERYTHING
BOOK 2 IN THE EMANCIPATOR
SERIES

It's out of the frying pan and into—what? Ruiz Aw
and his fellow escapees from slavery face new and
puzzling dangers in *The Emperor of Everything* by
Ray Aldridge, the sequel to *The Pharaoh Contract.*
Coming in January 1992, *The Emperor of Everything* takes us across the face of the planet Sook and
finally below its surface at the bizarre city of Sea-
Stack, where Ruiz seeks the help of his old acquaintance, the monster-maker Publius. . . .

R UIZ WAS VERY close to the center of Publius's labyrinth now. He had taken a hundred turns, walked for kilometers. He had seen no other monsters, and now he no longer expected to encounter any; the monster-maker used his failures to patrol the outer passages of the maze, thus discouraging uninvited visitors. But he prohibited these creatures from returning to the laboratories where they'd been decanted, so as not to repulse the paying customers who came to see his marvels.

The lighting had improved; the moss was supplemented now by an occasional glow plate and the floors were cleaner and dryer. Ruiz was still cautious, but now he began to worry about his reception. Would Publius even agree to see him—or would he simply have Ruiz ejected or killed? He became so involved in this unhappy speculation that he was a little slow to notice the oncoming shuffle of many feet, until he almost collided with a party of merchants leaving the inner sanctum with their purchases.

He slipped into a dark side passage just an instant before

the point guard came around a curve. He stepped to the wall and became still.

They did not see him, and he was unimpressed with the party's vigilance—he could effortlessly have killed the half-dozen guards and taken their merchandise, which was carried in two large cloth-shrouded cages by eight sweating litter bearers. The three merchants were Grasicians in elaborate pink bell-suits, wearing fashionable jeweled masks and carrying pomanders against the stench of the corridors. Ruiz wondered what horrors they had bought from Publius.

When they were gone he resumed his walk, and shortly reached the high-ceilinged rotunda at the center of the labyrinth.

The lighting here was mercilessly bright, and a trio of Dirm bondguards waited at Publius's security lock, a monocrete and armor structure over the elevator that would carry Ruiz down into Publius's domain.

They instantly aimed heavy grasers at Ruiz's chest. He stopped, raised his arms, displayed his empty hands, then clasped his hands atop his head. "I'm here to see Publius," he called, and waited.

"Name?" demanded one Dirm.

"Ruiz Aw."

"Purpose of visit?"

"Business."

At the mention of business, the Dirms relaxed fractionally. The one who had spoken to Ruiz whispered into a lapel communicator.

After a moment, it raised its weapon and gestured for Ruiz to approach, but the others' aim never wavered.

The first Dirm slung its graser when Ruiz reached him and expertly patted him down, relieving Ruiz efficiently of most of his arsenal of personal weapons. Then it used an odor analyzer/detector to deprive him of the rest.

When it was satisfied that he was as innocuous as possible, it stepped back and said, "You may reclaim your possessions on your return."

Ruiz fervently hoped he would return—and that he

would return wearing the same shape that he now wore. But all he said was, "Thank you."

It nodded and pressed a switch on its controller armlet. The armored blast door slid aside, then the decorative grille of the elevator. Ruiz stepped inside and watched the grille slide shut. The gleaming palladium filigree suddenly resolved into a montage of howling faces, almost human faces, stretched into bizarre shapes by terror.

Ruiz shivered, and wondered if he had been wise to seek out Publius.

But it was too late, so he concentrated on refining his story as he dropped swiftly down into the roots of the stack. He seemed to fall forever, and he began to worry that Publius planned to dump him into the unexplored levels below Publius's laboratories.

The elevator decelerated violently enough to make Ruiz's knees buckle a little—probably a little joke. Publius had an eccentric but relentless sense of humor.

The doors slid aside, to reveal Publius standing in the foyer with arms spread in welcome. Or he thought it must be Publius, though the body Publius wore was unfamiliar—a tall lean body with a supercilious aristocratic face. Surely it was Publius; who else had that uniquely demented gleam in his eye?

"Ruiz," shouted Publius gladly. "Can it be? My old friend, come home to roost at long last?"

Ruiz stepped cautiously from the elevator. "Publius?"

"Who else?"

Ruiz allowed Publius to fling his arms around him and managed a brief embrace in return. Publius apparently didn't notice his lack of enthusiasm; he held Ruiz by the shoulders and examined him, eyebrows jiggling up and down with curiosity.

"Still beautiful, I see," he said to Ruiz approvingly. "You're wasted as a leg-breaker for the League. I always tell you this, I know, but I'll tell you again: find a way to become notorious, then sell your clones. You'd be a rich body-source in no time. I'd buy one myself, make a pretty snakeweasel of you, sell you to some wealthy old woman for a lap dog."

Ruiz swallowed his revulsion. "I'm not a League enforcer any more, Publius."

Publius laughed, a low-pitched sound oddly reminiscent of water draining into a sewer. "Oh sure. Don't worry. I'd never tell anyone you're League—though I don't blame you for being cautious—this *is* SeaStack, after all."

"No, truly," said Ruiz. "I'll never work for them again."

"Oh? I'm astonished—an adrenaline addict like you, swearing off murder and pillage and high wages? What in the world has happened? Are you dying? Have you fallen in love?"

"Don't be silly," said Ruiz, straining for conviction.

"You're right, you're right. What could I have been thinking of?" Publius laughed again. "You're the famous Ruiz Aw, a paragon of mindless self-sufficiency, never tempted by the softer things of life, ruthlessly devoted to your own intermittently flexible code of ethics." There was a sour undertone to Publius's voice now, and Ruiz feared that he was remembering their time on Line, when Ruiz had deserted the cadre of freelance emancipators commanded by Publius.

"Ah . . ." said Ruiz, grasping for a diversion. "How have you been?"

"Well might you ask," shouted Publius in a booming voice. "How long has it been, since the last time you came crawling to blackmail me into doing you yet another favor? Thirty years? Forty? Much has happened, my art has flowered, my fortunes have waxed, my power is substantially enhanced, though not enough, never enough." Publius had discarded his mask of good humor, and his ugly essence shone through the new flesh. "But what's that to you, eh? What do you want of me now, Ruiz Aw. Old friend."

"Nothing too elaborate, Publius," said Ruiz. He strove to show no fear or resentment, though he was terrified.

"No? I'm astonished. So, what is this 'nothing too elaborate'? And what can you pay for it?"

Ruiz took a deep breath. "I need transport up to the Shard platforms, for myself and three slaves. I can pay a fair price."

Publius made an airy gesture of dismissal. "Nothing more than that? The simplest thing! Are you mad? What makes you think I could do such a thing for you? The pirate lords are currently in the grip of a massive paranoiac hysteria; did you not know this? My customers fume in their hostelries, unable to leave, and their goods stink up the place until the customers are driven to try to return them. I've had to kill a baker's dozen of complainers in the last twomonth alone—can't have them tarnishing my reputation."

"I hadn't realized," said Ruiz dismally.

"Just got into town, eh? Well, how grand that you thought to visit me first. Come, come . . . we'll tour the labs and talk." Publius pasted a grotesquely sly look on his face and winked, apparently over his brief rant. "Things are never so bad as they might seem, eh?"

He put his arm around Ruiz's shoulders, and tugged him from the foyer, into a world of white-tiled floors, stainless steel vats, and horror.

Publius's laboratories were extensive, covering thousands of square meters, and always teeming with activity. The monster-makers creative passion was only matched by his lust for wealth; the two drives conspired to push the labs to their maximum output. It always astonished Ruiz that the pangalac worlds' appetite for monsters could keep pace with Publius's mania for production—it was another illustration of the ungraspable immensity of the universe and the countless folk who crowded it.

Publius led him past a railed-off pit arena, in the depths of which dozens of stocky ursine warriors hacked and stabbed at each other with long knives, snarling, white fangs gleaming, inhumanly quick. "Elimination trials," Publius said, by way of explanation. "We started with over two hundred experimental scions. In another day or so the best will emerge—though we'll run the trial a few more times, to eliminate the possibility of flukes. But they'll do well for some berserker prince on a rich Hardworld, won't they?" He beamed in a parody of fatherly pride. "They'll have to wear muzzles, perhaps, but nothing's perfect. On the other hand . . . you're good with a pigsticker, aren't you, Ruiz? You wouldn't last two seconds against the feeblest of these."

Technicians scurried past, shoulders hunched and eyes down, as if they feared their employer as much as Ruiz did.

Publius led him past a series of one-way windowed cubicles, each containing a different variety of joyperson. Some of them seemed to be no more than human men and women, their somatypes modified toward some animal standard. There was a slender languid lizard girl, who groomed her eyescales with a long forked tongue, a young boy with a face like a mastiff, muscular and bow-legged. They passed an armless woman with a bald shapeless head, her soft white skin glistening with mucus. An androgynous creature stroked feathery antennae; it had a segmented thorax and a tubular proboscis curled on its chest.

But others were much stranger. They appeared to partake of the characteristics of aliens for which no analogue existed on Old Earth—though Ruiz knew that their genetic material derived primarily from human DNA. Publius was a purist in that way. He averted his gaze from latticed tentacles, stony silicoid carapaces, pulsing masses of stringy yellow fiber. There was even a lumpy creature covered with Gench sensor tufts, gasping through trilateral mouth slits. The symmetry was maintained with three plump breasts, three vaginas.

The Genchlike creature made him shudder, and a wave of disorientation passed over him. He felt the death net stir . . . and then stabilize. He had avoided thinking about the Gencha since his arrival in SeaStack, apparently for good reason. He wondered how many more near misses he could stand, before either the net decayed, or he lost interest in survival.

"Samples. See anything you'd like to try?" Publius slapped him on the back, laughed his strange bubbling laugh. "No, no, I'm teasing you; I know you're a devoted prude."

They passed surgeries in which white-coated technicians operated lamarckers, carving cloned bodies into new shapes. Other spaces held DNA keyboards, where Publius's employees created new races of monsters for clients who were willing to pay extra for reproductive functionality. Banks of half-gestated clones floated in clear nutrient baths, autogurneys trundled back and forth, some carrying grotesque corpses, others bearing anesthetized monsters in various stages of completion.

And over all, thick enough to gag Ruiz, was the special stink he associated with Publius and his works; a miasma of organic stenches and chemical wafts, of riotous life and casual death, of creativity and dread.

Finally they reached the apartments Publius used when in residence at his laboratories, and they passed from frenetic activity into silent isolation.

Publius slid the lock shut, and turned to Ruiz, a look of weary contempt blooming on his face.

"So, will you threaten me again? Will you never grow tired of hanging over my head, a ruination waiting to strike me? You cannot live forever; have you no mercy?"

Ruiz adopted a humble tone of voice. "You gave me no choice, Publius. If I failed to take precautions, you would instantly destroy me. I regret as much as you do that you confided your origins to me—had you not, you wouldn't hate me so virulently, and I wouldn't be forced to threaten you."

Long ago, over a campfire on Linc, a badly wounded, delirious Publius had told Ruiz his greatest secret—that he had been born in a Dilvermoon Holding Ark and was not, as he had claimed, the bastard of a noble Jahworld family. Ruiz had never completely understood the intensity with which Publius defended his pretensions, but he had realized their importance to Publius when the monster-maker had tried to murder him, years later. In self-preservation, he had filed a posthumous memorandum, which would be broadcast over public datastreams in the event of his death or disappearance.

In late years, he had begun to worry that Publius had lived with the possibility of exposure for so long that it no longer gave Ruiz any leverage over him. "Truly, I wish you could convince me that my precautions are no longer necessary."

Publius grunted. He moved across the rug-covered floor of his public room and took glasses and a decanter from a cabinet. He poured, offered a snifter of pale lilac liquor to Ruiz. "Well, at least you can drink with me without fear of poisoning. Few can, eh?"

Ruiz nodded and sipped.

"I'm such a bad boy," said Publius, sitting on a deep-cushioned sofa and gesturing Ruiz to a nearby chair. "Now: escape. Where's your expensive little starboat? The *Vigia*, isn't it? My memory is a wonder!"

"Hidden on a faraway world. I arrived on Sook a stowaway."

"Somehow that seems appropriate," said Publius. His eyes had lost some of their customary fey brilliance; he seemed a more ordinary man, for the moment. "And what was your mission, if it's no great secret?"

Ruiz shrugged. "Not anymore. I was hired to sniff out a poacher on a League Hardworld."

"And did you succeed? No, a foolish question, eh? You never fail, do you?"

"I know who the poacher is," said Ruiz.

"You see, I was right." He took a mouthful of liquor and swilled it around noisily before swallowing. "So, let us suppose you get up to the Shard platforms—you then plan to take commercial transport?"

"Yes."

"Ah. Well, as I said, the pirate lords are hysterical, at the moment. They've apparently stumbled across a big secret. . . . They don't know what to do about it. Some argue for destroying it, others for exploiting it. Does it surprise you to learn that I know the secret too?"

Ruiz shook his head.

Publius laughed his odd laugh. "Nothing about me surprises you, does it? Perhaps that's why I don't squash you like the insignificant bug are; you help me to maintain a certain perspective. I'm going to exploit the secret, of course, if I can get my hands on it. Tell me, how does this sound: Emperor Publius, the Emperor of Everything?"

Ruiz hardly knew what to say. "What's the secret?" he asked, finally.

Publius giggled. "Why, it's a *secret*; didn't you hear me?"

"Oh."

Publius adopted a businesslike expression. "Now, I don't say it's impossible to leave SeaStack now, but it's exceedingly difficult. Expensive. Dangerous. I might be able to help you—but you must perform a service for me first. No, don't bother to wave your terrible revelation at me. I no longer care; I've outgrown my origins by so vast a margin that it no longer matters what they were." Publius smiled a rapacious smile. "Such a promising omen, that you should arrive after all these years, just as I need someone exactly like you."

Ruiz was suddenly weak-kneed with apprehension. "What," he croaked, "do you want me to do?"

"The simplest thing, for a slayer like you," Publius said. "I want you to kill a man."

IN THE MORNING, Corean took Lensh and Marmo into the SeaStack's major auction pit—the proctors refused to allow the Moc inside, so she left it outside the security lock.

Flomel was being kept in one of the small independent pens adjacent to the pit, so she went there first, satisfied the ident processor that she was Flomel's owner, and opened the door to Flomel's holding cell.

The conjuror was sitting on his narrow bunk, shoulders slumped in dejection, when the door moved aside. He glanced up, saw Corean.

A range of unexpected emotions slid across his face. She

had expected to see terror and abasement. Instead he appeared first astonished, then delighted.

"Noble Lady!" he said in glad tones. "I knew you would come."

Corean was a bit taken aback. Either Flomel was much cleverer than she had supposed, or he had absolutely no grasp of the situation. In either case, she was willing to play along. "Did you?"

"Oh yes. I knew you wouldn't abandon me. The others were corrupted by that snake-oil vagrant, but not Flomel. I know Ruiz Aw for what he is, a casteless slayer, a thief, a troublemaker. I knew my faith would be rewarded . . . and here you are."

Corean smiled. She was willing to accept his cooperation, though she had intended to punish Flomel—if not for any part he might have taken in the theft of her boat, then for his simple presence when the deed occurred. But she could be flexible, she could defer Flomel's punishment. She sat beside Flomel, patted his knee. "Tell me all about it," she said.

COREAN REQUIRED ALL her meager store of patience to listen to Flomel's account. The conjuror's recollections included constant references to the outrages perpetrated on his dignity. Several times Corean had to interrupt before Flomel entirely lost the thread of his narrative. He seemed unable to grasp that she was uninterested in his personal feelings, but she summoned all the forebearance she possessed, and continued to smile and nod sympathetically at appropriate points.

When Flomel told about the judging in Deepheart, her interest quickened.

"He flailed about, convulsing and drooling in a most vulgar manner," said Flomel. "There he revealed his low origins again. Perhaps he's dead; he was very still when they took him out, and his face was a bit blue."

"Wait," she said. "Try to remember—did they rush him out, or was it a leisurely process?"

Flomel frowned. "What a difference would that make?"

She ran out of tolerance. She shot out a hand and gripped Flomel by the throat, squeezed with the augmented muscles of her slender fingers. He tried to speak, could only wheeze. He half-raised his hands, as if to claw at her, and she clamped down a little tighter, so that his eyes bulged. "You," she said, "are my property. You do not ask me for explanations. Do you understand?"

He nodded painfully. She eased the pressure on his throat slightly. "So, tell," she said.

"Fast," he gasped. "They took him out quickly."

She released him, and stood. "Then he's probably still alive. I think I would feel it if he died—we're connected now, somehow. Perhaps it's my need for satisfaction. . . . What else, Flomel?"

He rubbed at his throat and coughed. "There's not much else to tell, Lady, They took me to my room, and in the morning brought me to this place. I didn't see the others again, and you're the first person I've seen here."

She turned away from him and spoke musingly to Marmo. "I wonder . . . is he still in Deepheart? What did you find out about them, Marmo?"

"I spent last night hooked into the datastream, but useful information is difficult to come by. They're a self-development corporation, chartered on Dilvermoon but entirely contained within their facility here. They espouse a cult of sexual diversity. . . ."

"I'm not interested in their philosophy, Marmo. What I want to know is: how well defended is their facility? How difficult to infiltrate?"

Marmo was silent for a moment. "Recall what I said about useful information. But I can infer a probability: They are well-defended. In the nearly two thousand standard years since the present facilities were completed, the datastream records no successful hostile incursions into Deepheart. This is somewhat surprising, since they are reputedly a very wealthy corporation; presumably they've attracted the avarice of the pirate lords."

"Discouraging," said Corean, thinking. She refused to accept that Ruiz had found a hiding place where she could not reach him. "But we must do what we can, eh, Marmo? Come, let us visit a friend."

She tossed a leash to Lensh. "Collar the mage and take him to a suitable holding pen; then meet us back at the hotel."

RUIZ LEANED BACK, set his goblet carefully aside. "I'm not an assassin," he said.

"Oh?" said Publius, bright-eyed. "Since when?"

"I've never been an assassin."

"Oh, of course not, of course not. But you were always willing to kill anything that got in the way of your job, whatever it might be. Tell me, how many corpses have you left behind this trip out?"

Ruiz had no answer.

Publius laughed in a jolly manner. "You see? What difference does one corpse more or less make? Eh? And I assure you, he's a very evil man, almost as evil as I am—he deserves killing almost as much as I do. Help me out, and I'll get you offplanet, no matter what it takes, money or time or blood. But if you won't do this little favor for me, I'll take you and chop you up and make toys out of your pieces. I'm tired of worrying about your foolish little blackmail; a man like you will eventually perish, probably sooner rather than later, so why not get it over with? In a hundred years, who will care? Not I."

Ruiz tensed his muscles and prepared to leap at Publius. The monster-maker had once been formidable, but perhaps his skills had deteriorated; perhaps Ruiz could subdue him, could hold him hostage until he had escaped the laboratories.

Publius raised his hand in an odd gesture, and stunner muzzles slid from the wall behind him, pointed at Ruiz. "Don't be silly, old friend—and please, don't make me wonder if you consider me so stupid as to sit and chat with you, protected by nothing but your famous good will. I must tell you, I'd be terribly insulted, if I ever imagined you thought such a thing. And you know what a temper I have."

Ruiz sagged back in his chair, defeated. A feeling of futility came over him; what had he expected? That he would walk in and Publius would help him, out of the nonexistent goodness of his monstrous heart? Foolish, foolish.

"Who is the man?" Ruiz said.

Publius stood gracefully and beckoned. "Come. I'll show him to you."

RUIZ STOOD WITH Publius, looking into an observation cell. He saw a man of medium height and build, dressed in a moderately fashionable unisuit. His face was unremarkable, even-featured, neither plump nor thin. His hair was an indeterminate color, neither brown nor blond, cut in a conventional style. He sat in a comfortable chair, face almost expressionless, except for a subtle quality of alertness. Ruiz wondered if he was a spy of some sort—he looked the part to perfection.

"Who is he?" Ruiz asked.

"His name is Alonzo Yubere."

Ruiz was puzzled. "Why would you require my assistance? There he sits; why not just kill him yourself?"

Publius smiled and malicious delight spread over his face. "Oh, it's not *this* Alonzo Yubere I want you to kill. No no. It's the other Alonzo Yubere, the one who controls the secret. You know, the secret that's so inflamed the pirates."

Ruiz assumed a look of blank curiosity. Publius would explain.

"You see, *this* Yubere is actually an old servant of mine, torn down and rebuilt in this undistinguished form. Alas, poor Hedrin—he served me well, but I had greater need of his body than he did. I long ago had Hedrin Genched, by the way. Everyone needs at least one henchman he can trust. So his loyalty, even in this new form, is absolute."

"Ah," said Ruiz noncommittally.

"Do you begin to understand? It's an old idea, of course —replace the key person with a duplicate who belongs to you. But you know how tediously exact ident procedures can be these days, so it isn't often tried anymore, and is less often successful. And Yubere is the most careful of men; his ident data was very difficult to come by. But," said Publius, holding out his hands and wiggling the fingers. "My virtuosity with flesh and spirit has become prodigious, more than adequate to the task, and Hedrin has become Yubere, in every aspect but his basic loyalties."

"I see. Still, why not simply buy an assassin in the market?"

Publius clapped him on the shoulder. "That was my plan, until you appeared on my doorstep as if by magic. And who am I to sneer at Fate's gifts? Besides, I have vast faith in your skills; if it's possible to get to Yubere, you're definitely the one who can do it."

Watch for The Emperor of Everything, coming in January 1992 from Bantam Spectra.

From two of science fiction's greatest storytellers
comes the stunning tale of a civilization
facing its greatest fears and its impending doom.

Isaac Asimov
& Robert Silverberg
NIGHTFALL

In 1941, Isaac Asimov published a short story about a
world whose six suns set simultaneously only once
every 2,049 years. When nightfall comes to the world of
Lagash, its people -- who have never seen the stars --
must deal with the madness that follows. The tale,
"Nightfall," named greatest science fiction story of all
time by the Science Fiction Writers of America, remains
a landmark of the genre.

Now, two of science fiction's greatest names join to tell
this story in all its immensity and splendor with a novel
that explores all the implications of a world facing
ultimate disaster. When academics at Saro University
determine that 12 hours of darkness are coming, a
group of religious fanatics called the Apostles of the
Flame begin to capitalize on the event, preying on the
fear of the general populace by "saving" converts and
damning non-believers. Both groups -- in conflict for
centuries -- know that the coming night will mean the
end of their civilization, for the people of Lagash have a
proven fear of the dark, and in the wake of unspeakable
horrors, must rally to save the fragile remnants of their
world.

Now available in Bantam Spectra paperback.

"Banks has given us one of the most dazzling and accomplished pieces of space adventure to appear in the last decade."--*Chicago Sun-Times*

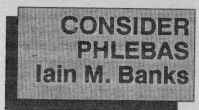

CONSIDER PHLEBAS
Iain M. Banks

"A splendid, rip-roaring adventure by an author who's clearly at home in the genre....Some books will keep you up half the night reading. **Consider Phlebas** is that rarer achievement worth reading again."--*Locus*

In the vast war between the Idrians and the Culture, one man is a free agent--his name is Horza. As a Changer, with the ability to transform himself at will, he works for the Idrians, and it's a fair exchange as far as he's concerned: his work is his most effective means to undermine the smug, sterile, highly advanced Culture that he despises.

Horza's latest assignment is to capture a renegade Culture mind--a form of artificial intelligence well beyond Idrian technology--hiding on a dead planet. Retrieving the mind is the easy part--it's the journey that's the challenge. He'll be facing cold-blooded mercenaries, a cannibalistic tyrant literally out for his blood, and a deadly game of Damage played out to the last minutes on a space habitat about to be blown to bits.

"Imaginative and gripping."--*Kirkus*

Consider Phlebas
On sale now wherever Bantam Spectra Books are sold.

AN328 -- 9/91

SLOW FREIGHT

A transporter system capable of transmitting matter
across space...and time...

SLOW FREIGHT

A faster-than-light stardrive that operates on
a whole new physical principle
and warps time...

SLOW FREIGHT

A first encounter with an alien race complicated by an
inadvertently violent crossing of paths...

And now, time is running out. Not just for the crew of
Earth's first starship, *Starfinder*. Not just for the crew of the
alien craft. But for all of Earth. The aliens power their ship
with huge amounts of matter, and damaged, failing and
limping through space-time, their nearest stop-off for fuel
are the planets orbiting Sol. More specifically, the home of
the creatures whose ship threatened their very existence:
Earth.

SLOW FREIGHT
by F.M. Busby

On sale now wherever Bantam Spectra Books are sold.

AN331 — 9/91